CELG

# A WINTER WEDDING

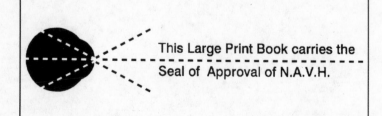

This Large Print Book carries the
Seal of Approval of N.A.V.H.

WHISKEY CREEK SERIES

# A WINTER WEDDING

## BRENDA NOVAK

**THORNDIKE PRESS**
*A part of Gale, Cengage Learning*

GALE
CENGAGE Learning·

Farmington Hills, Mich • San Francisco • New York • Waterville, Maine
Meriden, Conn • Mason, Ohio • Chicago

**GALE**
CENGAGE Learning·

**LIBRARY OF CONGRESS CATALOGING-IN-PUBLICATION DATA**

Names: Novak, Brenda, author.
Title: A winter wedding / Brenda Novak.
Description: Large print edition. | Waterville, Maine : Thorndike Press Large
   Print, 2016. | © 2015 | Series: Whiskey Creek ; 8 | Series: Thorndike Press
   large print romance
Identifiers: LCCN 2015042591| ISBN 9781410487230 (hardback) | ISBN
   1410487237 (hardcover)
Subjects: LCSH: Large type books. | Christmas stories. | BISAC: FICTION /
   Romance / Contemporary. | GSAFD: Love stories.
Classification: LCC PS3614.O926 W56 2016 | DDC 813/.6—dc23
LC record available at http://lccn.loc.gov/2015042591

Published in 2016 by arrangement with Harlequin Books S.A.

Printed in Mexico
1 2 3 4 5 6 7 20 19 18 17 16

To Novak's Notables, that
special group of women
who do so much to support me online.

Dear Reader,

It's always a joy for me to return to Whiskey Creek. Even though it's a fictional town, these days it feels like my second home. I love imagining the quaint bed-and-breakfasts, the Gas-N-Go, the ice-cream parlor, Just Like Mom's Diner, even the spooky old cemetery — and I'm especially excited about this book because I've had so many readers request Kyle's story. He first appeared in *When We Touch* (part of the *Together for Christmas* anthology, if you read print, and the digital prequel to the series, if you're an ebook reader), so those of you who've read Brandon and Olivia's story will know Kyle's made a few mistakes. If you've been following the rest of the series, you will also know he's paid for them and is a really kind, fabulous person who deserves his own happily-ever-after. But if you haven't visited Whiskey Creek before, don't worry. This book is written to stand on its own; you won't be missing out.

Not only am I writing books set in Whiskey Creek, I've been working on a new trilogy set on Fairham Island, a fictional place off the coast of North Carolina. The first book in that trilogy, *The Secret Sister,* is already out, with more coming. You can find information about these and my other works on my website at brendanovak.com. There, you can also enter to win my monthly drawings, sign up for my newsletter, contact me with comments or questions or join my fight to find a cure for diabetes. My youngest son suffers from this disease. Thanks to the support of many, many wonderful people, I've been able to raise $2.5 million for the cause so far.

Happy reading!

*Brenda Novak*

# WHISKEY CREEK
## CAST OF CHARACTERS

**Phoenix Fuller:** Recently released from prison. Mother of **Jacob Stinson**, who is being raised by his father, Riley.

**Riley Stinson:** Contractor, father of Jacob.

**Gail DeMarco:** Owns a public relations firm in LA. Married to movie star **Simon O'Neal**.

**Ted Dixon:** Bestselling thriller writer, married to **Sophia DeBussi**.

**Eve Harmon:** Manages Little Mary's B&B, which is owned by her family. Recently married to **Lincoln McCormick**, a newcomer.

**Kyle Houseman:** Owns a solar panel business. Formerly married to Noelle Arnold. Best friend of Riley Stinson.

**Baxter North:** Stockbroker in San Francisco who is moving back to Whiskey Creek.

**Noah Rackham:** Professional cyclist. Owns Crank It Up bike shop. Married to **Adelaide Davies**, chef and manager of Just

Like Mom's restaurant, owned by her grandmother.

**Callie Vanetta:** Photographer. Married to **Levi McCloud/Pendleton**, veteran of Afghanistan.

**Olivia Arnold:** Kyle Houseman's original true love but married to **Brandon Lucero**, Kyle's stepbrother.

**Dylan Amos:** Owns an auto-body shop with his brothers. Married to **Cheyenne Christensen**, and they have a baby boy.

# 1

"Your ex-wife is on the phone again."

Kyle Houseman squeezed his eyes shut and massaged his forehead. There were few people in the world he considered as difficult as Noelle.

Actually, he couldn't think of *one.*

"Did you hear me?" Morgan Thorpe, his assistant, stood at the entrance to his office wearing an impatient frown. Noelle (who still used his last name, which bothered him, since they'd been together for only a year) hadn't been able to reach him on his cell. She'd tried three times in the past fifteen minutes and he'd let it go to voice mail. So she'd called his business line, which he'd specifically asked her not to do. He didn't like the way she aired her complaints about him — and everything else — to anyone who'd listen.

His employees didn't like it, either.

"I heard," he replied.

"Are you going to take her call? Because if I have to talk to her again, I'm going to tell her exactly what I think of her."

He gave Morgan a look to make sure she understood that would be a mistake. At forty-five, she wasn't old enough to be his mother, but she often took a maternal approach with him, probably because she'd been working for him since he started First Step Solar. He'd hired her the same week she came out of the closet and moved in with her partner, who was as soft-spoken as Morgan was bold. "No, you're not."

"Why?" she cried. "Noelle's a terrible person! She deserves whatever she gets!"

"We were once married. We still live in the same small town. We can figure out some way to get along."

She rolled her eyes. "If it's that easy, why are you avoiding her?"

She had a point. Dodging Noelle's calls wouldn't do him any good, anyway. She'd just track him down at his house or even a restaurant, if she had to. She did that kind of thing all the time — to plead for an advance on his spousal maintenance, a "small loan" to prevent her utilities from being turned off or money to get her car repaired. Once, she'd even asked him for five hundred bucks to go toward fixing her

12

boob job (apparently, her body kept rejecting the implants, but instead of having them
removed, she kept trying to make them
work). It didn't seem to matter that none of
that was his responsibility anymore.

"Put her through," he said with a sigh.

"That woman is *insufferable.* I don't know
how you tolerate her," Morgan grumbled as
she left.

He didn't, either.

He glanced at the light blinking on his
desk phone. Surely Noelle would find someone else and get remarried. He wished that
would happen soon. It would save him
$2,500 a month, not to mention the relief
of not having to deal with her anymore. But
he'd been wishing that for the past five
years, ever since the divorce. He was beginning to suspect that as long as she had him
to pay a hefty chunk of her monthly bills,
she'd be unlikely to tie the knot with someone else. She wasn't the type to part with a
freebie. Besides, she saw his financial support as punishment for the fact that he'd
never been able to love her — and, truth be
told, he saw it in the same light. That was
why he'd agreed to that amount and why
he helped her out as often as he did. Guilt
demanded it.

"Someday," he muttered as he picked up.

"Someday what?" Noelle asked.

Someday he'd be rid of her. But he couldn't say that. "Nothing. What's going on? Why have you been blowing up my phone?"

"Why are you ignoring my calls?" she countered.

"Because I can't think of any reason you'd need to talk to me. We *are* divorced, remember? And with all the money I've given you over the past few years — in the past several months alone — I'm a good six months ahead in my payments. That pretty much leaves you with no excuse."

"It's my water heater," she said.

"Your *what*?"

"My water heater."

She'd found something new to complain about? "What's wrong with it?"

"It went out on me. I can't take a shower or do laundry or dishes. I don't have any hot water."

He rocked back in his chair. "Then . . . shouldn't you be looking up a plumber instead of bothering your ex-husband?"

"Why are you being rude? I'm calling because you happen to own a solar manufacturing plant. Can't you give me a deal on a solar system? So I can get my hot water bill down?"

"I manufacture *photovoltaic* panels, No-elle. They run air conditioners and other *electrical* appliances. Anything that requires gas is a whole separate thing." They'd been *married,* for God's sake, and she still didn't understand what he did for a living?

"You have connections for hot water systems, too. You put one in for Brandon and Olivia's neighbor."

*Why* had they told her he'd done that? "Mrs. Stein is nearly eighty and she lost her husband a year ago. I saw that she got a deal. That's all."

"You bought it from the manufacturer at wholesale and let her have it at cost. And your *photovoltaic* installers put it in for her."

"Because she could use the break. Brandon asked me to help her out. Occasionally, I do favors like that for my brother."

"Come on. You didn't do it for Brandon's sake."

Irritation clawed deeper, causing his eye to twitch. "Of course I did. We've been getting along great," he said, and that was true. He and Brandon had once been rivals. They hadn't met until they were in high school, when Brandon's mother married Kyle's father. Two large-and-in-charge boys so close in age would understandably have a difficult period of adjustment. But the dynamic was different these days. In spite of everything that'd happened back then, and with Noelle and Olivia since, Kyle cared about Brandon. He got the impression Brandon cared, too. At least, he heard from his stepbrother quite a bit. He also saw Brandon and Olivia every Friday at Black Gold Coffee. They'd joined the close-knit group of friends Kyle had grown up with.

"Quit lying to yourself," she spat. "You'd do anything for Olivia. The way you stare after her when she leaves a room — or you avoid looking at her if you're in the same room — makes it *so* obvious. They'd see it themselves, except they don't *want* to see it."

His blood pressure shot a little higher. "Fine," he said. "You want a solar hot water system? I'll offer you the same deal I gave Brandon and Olivia's neighbor."

She seemed startled that he'd capitulated so suddenly. But there wasn't any point in refusing. She'd never be able to afford it. Besides, he didn't want to talk about Olivia. What Noelle said was true. Olivia was her sister — which was a big part of the reason Noelle had gone after him in the first place — but Olivia had been, and still was, the one great love of his life. She'd been with him before she'd ever been with Brandon.

"That's better," Noelle said. "So . . . how much will it cost? I have nearly $250 in my account."

She stated that amount proudly. She wasn't good at saving money, so this did signify quite a feat. But, as usual, she was completely clueless — or, more likely, *calculatedly* clueless. "That's what I thought," he said.

"What?"

"You don't have enough to buy even a traditional water heater."

"I don't?" She sounded dismayed. "How much are they?"

"A decent one will run you eight hundred or more."

"And how much is solar?"

"Nearly three grand."

"You've got to be kidding me!" she cried. "How do you expect me to pay that?"

"*I* don't expect you to pay it. You need to drive over to the hardware store and see what's in your price range."

"In other words, you don't give a shit whether I'm in a bind."

His head was beginning to pound . . . "I'm sorry your water heater died, but it's not *my* problem."

"You can't help me?"

Morgan tapped the glass between her

workstation and his office and made a face at him.

He waved her away. "What do you expect me to do?"

"A solar hot water system can't cost *you* that much," she replied.

"It can and it does. Check the retail price and you'll see it's around six grand. Wholesale would be about half of that."

"Then maybe you can put one in and let me make payments."

"We're divorced! And you're only renting. Call your landlord."

"Harry won't do anything. He's letting me stay here for a lot less than he'd charge someone else. Why do you think he gave me such a good deal?"

"Because he's your cousin?"

"Because in order to get that deal, I have to take care of all maintenance and repairs."

"Then it's on you."

"If you can't get me solar, can you at least help me pay for a regular water heater? From what you just told me, I only need another $550. What're a few hundred bucks to you? You make so much more than I do!"

"That doesn't mean *I'm* obligated to pay for it. You got extra money out of me last month. *And* the month before."

"Because I needed a D&C, Kyle. I've been

18

having female trouble ever since I lost the baby. *Remember?*"

As usual, she'd chosen something he had to be careful not to question. That didn't stop him from wondering, however. Had she really needed a D&C? Or were the documents she'd shown him forged? It could be that he'd paid for another boob job, after all. He wasn't even sure she'd lost the baby that had supposedly created the need for a D&C. Had she even had a "miscarriage" five and a half years ago? Maybe she'd aborted it. He'd always suspected her of lying, suspected that after she got him to marry her, she'd purposely terminated the pregnancy. At that point, she wouldn't see any reason to risk damaging her figure, which she protected above all else.

"I remember," he said through gritted teeth. He didn't want to talk about that, either. It was easier to bury the doubt and the suspicion and try to forget the past.

"You don't care."

Maybe he would if he believed it was true. But with Noelle — who could say? Whenever she needed money, she came up with an excuse he'd be hard-pressed to decline — medical treatment, that she'd be evicted, that she wouldn't have electricity or food.

"Look, I paid for the procedure," he said. "That's all that matters. I hope you're feeling better. Now I've got to go. I have a lot to do here —"

"Wait! What about my water heater?"

"What about it?" he asked in exasperation.

"You seriously won't give me a small loan? Then will you let me stay in the farmhouse until I can get it fixed on my own?"

No way was she coming anywhere near his property. She would *never* live there. "Absolutely not. I've got the farmhouse cleaned up and ready to lease."

"But it's been ready to lease for two months, and it's sat empty that whole time. Why not let me move in until I'm back on my feet? You're not likely to get someone now."

What was she talking about? "Why not?"

"The holidays. People are busy with shopping and wrapping and decorating."

"Not everyone. Matter of fact, I have someone coming to see it tonight. He's ninety percent sure he wants it. He just has to see it in person to confirm. Then he'll sign."

"Who is it?" she asked.

Kyle checked the information he'd jotted on his desk calendar. "Guy by the name of

20

Meade."

"Never heard of him . . ."

"He's from Nashville. Only needs it for a few months, but he asked me to furnish it, so —"

"Furnish it with what?" she broke in. "It's not like you have a furniture warehouse."

"There are companies that rent furniture. I called a place in Sacramento, chose some items from their website, and they brought it all out. The place is move-in ready now. Looks great."

"You went to that much trouble for someone who's only staying for a few months? I thought you wanted a year's lease. That's what you told me when *I* asked about it."

"He's paying a premium — for the furniture, my time and trouble in acquiring it *and* the short term. Even if he decides he hates the house and I have to send the furniture back, he's covering all of that. In any case, you didn't lose out, because I wouldn't let you move in, no matter what." The past few months, she'd been trying her best to get back with him. The last thing he needed was to allow her to be that close — not to mention he'd never see a dime of rent.

"Even though I'd be willing to sign for a year?"

"Even if you'd be willing to sign for ten."

"You can be so mean," she said.

*Mean?* He thought he was being incredibly nice — considering that merely talking to her made him want to punch himself in the face. "We've talked about this before. I'll take Meade's deal, if I can get it, and try to find another tenant next summer, when school's out."

"That's great for you, but what about me? Can't I use it until he moves in?"

The childlike whine that entered her voice made his eye-twitch worse. *Patience,* he reminded himself. *Breathe deeply and speak kindly.* "He hasn't said when that'll be. But since he's coming all the way from Tennessee to look at it, I'm guessing he could move in tonight."

"In the middle of the storm that's coming in?"

"Why not? He'll just carry in his luggage. How hard can that be, whether there's a storm or not?"

"So you're going to leave me in the lurch — the woman who would've been the mother of your child if that child had survived?"

Before he could respond, Morgan knocked briskly and opened the door. "Don't tell me you're still on with *her.*"

He sent her a frown that told her to mind her own business, but she didn't leave.

"I have a call from LA," she said. "Some guy wants a special deal on a 10-megawatt order."

Which was such a big order, no one at his company could provide the pricing but him. He changed the phone to his other ear. "Noelle, I've got to go."

"I can't believe you're doing this!"

"What else am I supposed to do?"

"You have the contacts. You could get me a water heater and let me make payments, if you weren't so stingy."

"Kyle?" Morgan prompted, reminding him — as if he needed her to — of the far more important caller on the other line.

He almost told Noelle to go down to the hardware store and have the checker call him for his credit card information. He wanted to get rid of her, and they'd done that kind of remote purchase before, when someone threw a rock through her window (likely the girlfriend of someone she'd flirted with at Sexy Sadie's). But the more he gave her, the more she'd keep coming back to him. He had to break the cycle . . .

Fortunately, he thought of a solution that should've been obvious to him from the start. "I've got a water heater here," he said.

"It's the one I took out of Brandon's neighbor's house. If you'll have someone pick it up and install it, I'll give it to you."

"You're sure it works?"

Morgan propped her hands on her hips and scowled at him, refusing to leave until he took that business call.

"It did when my guys removed it. No reason that should've changed. She wanted solar mainly to be responsible to the environment." He'd been planning to donate the water heater to a poor family who could use it. But Noelle fit the bill. She didn't have much money, despite juggling two jobs. Working in retail part-time, and then as a barmaid nights and weekends, she didn't make a whole lot. What she did earn, she spent on clothes and beauty aids.

"Okay. Thanks." Noelle lowered her voice. "I'm happy to oblige if you'd like . . . *something* in return."

"I don't need anything," he said.

"You sure about that?"

Where was she going with this? *"Excuse me?"*

"I remember the kinds of things you like . . ."

The suggestion in her voice made him uncomfortable. "I hope you're not referring to —"

24

"It's not like you're getting laid anywhere else," she interrupted. "A visit here and there could be our little secret, a temporary solution, so you don't have to go without. I mean, what's the big deal? It's not like we haven't slept together before."

"I'm going to pretend I didn't hear any of that," he said and hung up.

Morgan, who'd changed her position to stand with her arms folded, fingers drumming her biceps, raised her eyebrows. "What's she after now?"

"Nothing."

"You look thoroughly disgusted," she said and laughed at him when he growled at her to get out and shut the door.

Kyle was wrapping up his conversation with the client from Los Angeles when Morgan came in again. This time she sat in the chair across from his desk while waiting for him to finish.

"Don't tell me Noelle's already here," he said when he'd disconnected.

"No. I'm hoping to be gone by then. This is *good* news."

He sat up taller. After having his ex-wife, of all people, make an issue of his dismal love life, he could use some good news. "What is it?"

"I received a call from that dude who

wants to rent the farmhouse."

"I hope he's not canceling," Kyle said. "Noelle keeps asking if she can move in. I'll be relieved when it's occupied and she can't bug me about it anymore."

"Can't she just move out of town instead?" Morgan responded. "No one would miss her."

Yet another reason Kyle forced himself to be decent to her. Despite all the terrible things she'd done — especially to him — he felt sorry for her. She couldn't seem to avoid screwing up her own life. "She's trying to launch a modeling career. Maybe she'll be discovered and relocate to New York or LA."

"She's delusional if she thinks anyone's going to pay her to model! She —"

"What's your news?"

She scowled in apparent frustration. She was all revved up, and he'd removed her target. "Fine," she said, shifting gears. "Meade's no longer coming, but —" she held up a hand so he wouldn't react too soon "— he wasn't looking at the house for himself, anyway."

"Who's it for?"

"A client he manages." She grinned. "Are you ready for this?"

"You have my full attention," he said drily. He liked his assistant, but she got on his nerves occasionally. After dealing with Noelle, he preferred to be left alone right now so he could get some work done. He didn't want to stay late tonight. He didn't live far, but he'd rather not get caught in the storm they were expecting. It was supposed to be the worst they'd had in twenty years.

"Lourdes Bennett," she announced.

The way she'd said the name sounded like *ta-da!*

"Bennett? Is she related to our police chief?"

"No! There's no connection. You don't recognize the name Lourdes Bennett?"

"Should I?"

"She's a country-western singer!"

"Am I supposed to be familiar with every country-western singer?"

"Not necessarily, but she has several hit songs — and she was born and raised less than an hour away."

Now that she'd jogged his memory, Kyle realized he *had* heard of Lourdes. He just hadn't expected the person who might be renting his farmhouse to be someone truly famous. "In Angel's Camp, right? This is the Lourdes Bennett who sings 'Stone Cold Lover'?"

"That's the one."

"Why would *she* have any interest in coming here?" he asked.

"I have no clue," Morgan replied. "But you're about to find out. She flew into Sacramento Airport this morning and rented a car. She's on her way, should be here any minute."

"Is she coming by herself?"

"Sounded like it."

Kyle scratched his head. "That seems odd."

"What seems odd?"

"The whole thing. If she's from Angel's Camp, why isn't she going there? Why would she want to spend the holidays in Whiskey Creek?"

"You'll have to ask her," Morgan said. "Unless you want *me* to show the house. I'd be happy to take over for you."

He glanced at the clock on the wall. "Sorry, you have a couple of hours before quitting time, which you'll spend here. I'll take care of meeting Ms. Bennett."

She huffed. "Great. I'll be the one to get tortured by your ex-wife."

"Just point her to the back corner of the warehouse, where I put that used water heater."

"I'd like to point her somewhere, but it isn't to the back of the warehouse."

28

He chuckled. "Be careful crossing her. She can be vengeful."

"You're too nice to her. She doesn't deserve a guy like you, even as an ex." She mimed zipping her lips. "But that's it. That's all I'm going to say."

"Thank you."

She straightened the cowl of her sweater. "I hope Lourdes Bennett wants the house. Wouldn't it be exciting to have her in town — on *your* property?"

He wasn't so sure. Thanks to Noelle, he'd had about all he could take of difficult women. "Unless she's a diva. But if she *is* a diva, I can't imagine why she'd rent my house. A diva would want something fancier — in Bel Air or the Bay Area."

"Whiskey Creek may not be as famous as San Francisco or LA, but it's beautiful here in the foothills. And she'll love the house. After what you've done to the place, who wouldn't?"

Built in the thirties, it had once been a farmhouse, which was why they still referred to it as *the farmhouse*. When he'd purchased the land so he could expand his plant, he'd decided to update the house that was there and turn it into another rental. He already had a couple of places he rented out, so it made sense. "The house is only about a thousand square feet." He'd opened up the kitchen and living room areas and expanded the office, but there were only two bedrooms and two baths. That wouldn't be conducive to hosting a large group, so if she planned to bring her whole entourage for a Christmas party or something, it wouldn't work.

"One person can't need any more space than that," Morgan said.

"If it is just one person." Kyle was tempted to search Google for Lourdes's name. He sometimes listened to country-western music, enough to be familiar with her song "Stone Cold Lover" as well as one other that he couldn't remember the title of. But he didn't know anything about her background, family, age or marital status, and now he was curious. From the pictures he'd seen, she didn't look much older than twenty-five or twenty-six, but who knew how current those photos were? She could've played the bars and honky-tonks for years before getting any serious attention.

He would've taken a few minutes to read up on her if he hadn't been afraid Noelle would arrive before he could leave. That made him decide to use his smartphone instead of his computer, since he could do it off the premises.

Grabbing his coat, he told Morgan he'd see her in the morning and drove over to the rental.

# 2

This was what all the fame and fortune she'd earned so far boiled down to?

Lourdes Bennett frowned as she pulled up beside the truck that was parked at the address she'd been given and removed her sunglasses so she could get a better look at the place. The countryside she'd passed through felt familiar — little wonder, since she'd grown up in a similar town not far from Whiskey Creek. And the house, an old-fashioned, wooden A-frame, was charming. A swing hung on the front porch, further enhancing its homey appeal. But Whiskey Creek wasn't where she'd be if all was well in her life. So far, her exile was self-imposed, but if she couldn't get back on top of her career, there'd be no point in returning to Nashville for professional reasons.

A man appeared in the doorway. Had to be the landlord. He must've heard her drive up.

Quickly sliding her sunglasses back on —
as a shield against his recognition of her
more than anything else, since that could be
awkward — Lourdes opened her door and
stepped out. It was starting to get dark, but
she could still see.

"You found it okay, huh?" the man said as
he came toward her.

The wind had kicked up and tossed her
hair, and she held it back. "Just followed
my GPS."

"I'm glad it didn't lead you astray. GPS
can be kind of squirrelly in some places.
With all the hills in Gold Country, you can't
always get a signal." When he drew close, he
stuck out his hand. "Kyle Houseman."

Fairly tall, maybe six-one, her landlord
looked a great deal like Dierks Bentley, only
with darker hair. She'd played several gigs
with Dierks over the years, so she could easily compare them. Not only did they have
similar facial features, they also were both
fit, both in their midthirties, and they both
had million-dollar smiles.

"I'm Lourdes." She didn't mention her
last name. She preferred not to make a big
splash. That was why she'd asked Derrick
to handle the negotiations, and why she'd
chosen Whiskey Creek instead of Angel's
Camp. Whiskey Creek was as close to home

as she could get while keeping a low profile.

"I'm familiar with some of your songs," Kyle said. "Congratulations on your success."

Her first album had received quite a bit of radio play, which was more than most aspiring artists obtained. The success had been fun while it lasted, but after the decade it had taken to land a major label, it hadn't lasted nearly long enough. "I hope you don't mind, but I'm not looking for that sort of attention — for *any* attention, really. I just need a quiet place to get away for a few months." And to try to reclaim what she'd destroyed when she attempted to make it in an even bigger market and switched over to pop music. "You know, without anyone noticing."

"No problem. Not on my end, anyway. But . . ." He studied her for several seconds. "You grew up in a small town."

"Yes."

"Then you know what they're like, how people talk."

"Of course. I don't plan to be seen much. And this house seems to be off the beaten path. Surely no one would approach me in my home . . . er, *your* home." She couldn't say the same for Angel's Camp. After her father died of bladder cancer, her mother

34

had followed her to Nashville. She'd always wanted to be there, since she'd once had dreams of a music career of her own. So, shortly after Lourdes's two younger sisters, Mindy and Lindy, identical twins, had graduated from high school, Renate bought a nice three-bedroom, two-bath condo not far from Lourdes's own place. And once Mindy and Lindy had finished college, they'd settled in Tennessee, too. They were currently sharing an apartment. Although her family had never expected Lourdes to help them financially, everyone wanted to be part of the exciting things that were happening to her, to experience something new. Lourdes would've liked to go back to Angel's Camp. She missed it. But her old friends — and her family's friends — knew her well enough that they wouldn't even attempt to respect her privacy.

"I can't imagine they would," he agreed.

She looked beyond him at the front porch. "Then I like the place so far."

"It's small," he said, as if that would be a drawback for her.

"I don't need a lot of room. I'll just be writing some new songs." *Just.* That was the understatement of the year. She had to come up with billboard gold . . .

"You're planning a new album?"

"I am." Did he know how badly *Hot City Lights* had tanked? That would depend on how well acquainted he was with the music world. Although the critics had liked the album, it hadn't sold. Everyone who really counted understood that she was losing everything she'd established. She needed to win back her fans and prove to Derrick that he hadn't bet on the wrong girl. And she didn't have a lot of time. The further she went between releases, the harder her comeback would be. Timing might be even more critical to her relationship with Derrick. He'd recently acquired a new client, an up-and-coming artist named Crystal Holtree, whom the media had dubbed "Crystal Hottie." Lourdes had seen the way he looked at Crystal, couldn't help remembering when he'd looked at her that way —

"Something wrong?" Kyle asked.

Hitching her purse higher on one shoulder, Lourdes returned her attention to her prospective landlord. "No. I apologize. I was daydreaming. Shall we take a look at the inside?"

The house was every bit as wonderful as the photographs she'd seen online. It was old where old was preferable, with tall ceilings, hardwood floors, heavy framed windows and moldings, plus the original doors, complete with fancy hardware. And it was new where new was preferable, featuring an expansive kitchen, two large bedrooms, each with a walk-in closet, and completely updated bathrooms. Best of all, there was a beautiful set of French doors leading to an office, which she'd use as her music room.

Although he might have had help, her landlord had even done a halfway decent job of furnishing the place. There weren't any window coverings, but the location was secluded enough that they weren't necessary.

Derrick had been right; it was perfect.

So why had he decided, at the last minute, not to come with her?

Because he preferred to be with Crystal. As much as he denied that, Lourdes could feel it in her soul . . .

She was on her own for the first time in years, without the man she loved, who was also the manager who'd promised to take her back to number one, and without real hope that she'd be able to reclaim the momentum she'd lost in both her personal and professional lives.

Still, she had her guitar. That was all she'd started with when she moved to Nashville at eighteen, wasn't it? If she could come up with a handful of songs that were special —

no, *groundbreaking* — maybe it wouldn't be too late to turn her luck around. And this place, isolated and yet familiar enough for her to feel comfortable, would offer just the refuge she needed.

"I'm ready to sign the rental agreement," she said.

Lourdes Bennett had arrived at Kyle's farmhouse only a few minutes after he did, so he hadn't had time to read about her. He'd barely pulled her up on Wikipedia when he'd heard the sound of her car and shoved his phone in his pocket. But now that he was home and could surf the internet at his leisure, he'd spent over an hour visiting her website as well as exploring several other links that contained less official information.

He hadn't been nervous about approaching a woman in a long time, but when she'd gotten out of the car, and he'd caught his first glimpse of her, he'd suddenly — and against all expectation — gone a little weak in the knees. He didn't care about her fame. His best friend had married a major movie star, so he knew someone far more famous. It was that she was *so* attractive. Usually the pictures people posted looked a lot better than the real thing. That wasn't the case with Lourdes Bennett. Her blond hair had fallen about her shoulders in a thick, wavy mass. Her skin was pale, but she also had the smoothest, creamiest complexion he'd ever seen. And her eyes! They reminded him of the azure color of the Caribbean Sea.

"Of course she has a boyfriend," he muttered when he found a picture of her at the Country Music Association Awards posing with none other than a man identified in the caption as Derrick Meade, her manager. Apparently, her relationship with Meade went beyond business. The same caption indicated that after Derrick had helped America "discover" her, the two had started dating, and they'd been a couple for six months, even though he had to be at least twelve to fifteen years older.

That picture had been taken two years ago, before her last album came out. Kyle couldn't find as many public appearances after the release of *Hot City Lights,* and nothing more about her and Derrick. But he guessed they were still seeing each other. It was Derrick who'd called to line up the farmhouse, wasn't it? That meant he'd probably be joining her periodically — maybe on weekends — and certainly for Christmas . . .

Disappointed in spite of all the reasons he

shouldn't have gotten his hopes up, he went into the kitchen to crack open a beer. Then he jumped. Someone was at his window, peering in at him!

A second later he realized who it was. Noelle.

With a curse, he put down his beer.

"What are you doing here?" he asked as he swung open the door.

She threaded her way through his shrubbery to reach the porch. "My, aren't you in a good mood."

"What did you expect? You were peeping at me!"

"Oh, don't flatter yourself. Your truck's in the drive, so I was trying to see where *you* were. I knocked but you didn't answer."

"Because I didn't hear anything." He must've been too absorbed in researching Lourdes Bennett. "What do you need?"

"I couldn't get someone to help me with the water heater until after your office closed. A.J. and I have been trying to get in, but —"

"A.J.?" That wasn't a name he'd heard around Whiskey Creek.

"Yeah. He works with me at Sexy Sadie's. He took Fisk's place when Fisk moved to Vegas and a job opened up at the bar."

Once upon a time, Kyle would've known

40

all the bartenders at the local pub. He'd
hung out there quite a lot over the years.
There weren't many other places to go for
fun in a town of only two thousand. But
now that nearly all his friends were married, he spent most of his weekends working.

"I was hoping you'd lend me the key,"
Noelle said. "We'll bring it back after we
grab the water heater."

No way would he ever trust her with access to his office. "I'll drive over and let you
in," he said. "But . . . why didn't you just
call me? I could've met you there."

"Check your phone," she said. "You didn't
pick up."

His phone hadn't rung; it hadn't even
buzzed. But when he pulled it from his
pocket, he could see why. He'd inadvertently
turned on the "do not disturb" feature.

Or maybe he'd done it subconsciously. He
really didn't want to be interrupted tonight,
especially by her.

"Give me a minute. I'll be right out."

He went to his bedroom to retrieve his
coat before scooping his keys off the counter.

It took longer to load the water heater in
A.J.'s truck than Kyle had thought it would.
A.J. needed to clarify the instructions on

how to install it — again and again. Kyle almost offered to do it himself. Obviously, A.J. wasn't mechanically inclined and wouldn't be much help to Noelle. But then Kyle got a text from a number he didn't recognize that said:

This is Lourdes. I can't get the furnace to come on, and it's freezing in this house.

"What is it?" Noelle asked.

He lowered his phone so she wouldn't be able to read the message. "There's a problem with my new renter. I've got to go."

"So that Meade guy took the place? The farmhouse has been leased?"

He hesitated at her assumption. His tenant wasn't the man he'd mentioned to her earlier. But Lourdes didn't want to be bothered while she was in Whiskey Creek. And if he told Noelle they had a famous country singer in their midst, she'd spread the word all over town. She might even show up at the farmhouse, claiming she was his ex and therefore had some right to the property.

He couldn't allow that to happen. "Yeah. It's a done deal," he said.

"That was fast!"

"He was serious. He had me furnish it,

remember?"

She didn't seem to mind that A.J. was tying down the water heater without her help. "I remember," she said. "But what does someone from Nashville want with a house on a remote piece of land outside Whiskey Creek? This isn't exactly Tahoe. If it was, maybe I'd have a shot at being discovered," she added wryly.

If only she *would* move to Lake Tahoe or LA. Or New York. The farther, the better. But her lack of resources precluded it.

"He's looking for some solitude," he said. "An escape from the demands of his usual life."

"How long's he staying?"

"For a few months, like I told you."

"That sucks. You should've rented to me."

Kyle felt his eye-twitch coming back. "The duplex you're living in is fine. What's wrong with it?"

"It's a dump compared to the farmhouse."

"Maybe you can find something you're happier with after Christmas," he said, but for once, placating her didn't seem to be necessary. He could tell by her expression that she'd already switched gears.

"How old is he?" she asked.

"About our age."

"Is he handsome?"

Apparently, she and A.J. didn't have anything going on romantically, or she wouldn't be asking such obvious questions with her helper in hearing distance. "I couldn't tell you," Kyle said. "I'm not used to judging other guys in that way. But it doesn't matter. He's with someone."

"He's married?" she asked.

"It might not be that official, but he's been with the same woman for a few years. So enough with the nosy questions. My renter isn't an option for you."

"You've gotten ornery," she complained.

"What are you talking about? I just solved your hot water problem." *And* he was standing outside, freezing his ass off because of her when it was about to snow.

"You comin'?" A.J. called as he jumped to the ground and circled around to the driver's side.

"Yeah, I'm comin'," Noelle said. Then she surprised Kyle with a hug. "You look good, you know that? You look real good. God, I miss you."

Before he could react, she released him and turned away. But as she got in with A.J., she called over her shoulder, "Think about what I said before. You've got to be lonely. Now even Riley's getting married. Who will you hang out with when he's as pussy

44

whipped as your other friends?"

"Baxter's moving home," he said. He'd been consoling himself with that news for several weeks . . .

"Baxter's gay, Kyle."

"You think I'm not aware of that?"

"You're not being realistic. I doubt he'll be interested in going places where you can meet girls."

He frowned as he gazed at the wind-tossed branches of the trees. "Don't worry about it."

"I'm just saying I'd be happy to be your buddy if you want me to." With a wink, she shut the door.

He could never be that desperate. If only he hadn't been stupid enough to get involved with her in the first place, *he'd* be married to Olivia. Instead, Olivia was married to Brandon.

He waited until Noelle and her bartender friend drove off before taking out his phone to respond to Lourdes's message.

I'm on my way, he wrote back.

Lourdes was wearing a holey Budweiser T-shirt she'd inherited from a member of her stage crew, a pair of Victoria's Secret sweat bottoms and a belted, big-collared sweater her mother had given her a year ago for Christmas. None of it matched, including her fuzzy socks. She'd bought those for their softness alone. Too bad they weren't as warm as they looked. She'd forgotten her sheepskin slippers at her estate in Tennessee, which was a mistake. The weather outside was reminding her that even parts of California could get cold.

Since she was waiting for her landlord, she considered changing. Not only was she wearing frumpy, shapeless clothes, she'd removed her makeup and piled her hair on top of her head. But she was too depressed to care. So what if Kyle Houseman was handsome? He was probably married. Even if he wasn't, *she* was in a relationship.

A knock alerted her to his arrival. She went to answer the door but paused after peeking through the peephole. Was she really going to let him see her like this? It wasn't just that he was so good-looking; she'd grown accustomed to maintaining her image. Being famous meant that people had certain expectations of her, and those expectations weren't always realistic.

But this was exactly the type of pressure she'd come to Whiskey Creek to avoid. For her own sanity, she had to escape the need she felt to compete — in the music world *and* in her personal life with the incomparable, and much younger, Crystal. She needed to be a regular person for a while. Needed to take a step back and root out the panic and neuroticism that was taking hold and turning her into someone she no longer recognized.

After tightening the belt of her sweater, she opened the door. "I'm sorry I had to bother you," she said, stepping aside to let him in.

"Sounds to me as if you had every right. I'm sorry you couldn't get the furnace to work. It's a brand-new unit, so I can't believe there's anything terribly wrong. I'll try to figure out what's going on."

He had a tool chest in one hand, which he put on the floor while he fiddled with the thermostat.

Instinctively, she folded her arms across her chest. She was wearing so many layers he'd never be able to tell she hadn't put on a bra. But there was something about him that made her more aware of him than she should be. "So you handle your own repairs?"

"Only the easy ones."

She wasn't sure why she was feeling self-conscious; he'd hardly looked at her.

"To be honest, I'm no handyman," he added. "But it's after five, so I'm all we've got for today."

He had a nice skin tone. She also liked his dark five-o'clock shadow, which contrasted with his kind eyes and the laugh lines around them. It made him look a little uncivilized. "Then what do you do for a living? Besides own rental property?"

"I'm a solar manufacturer. You can't see the plant from here, because of the trees and the rolling hills in between, but if you drive east about half a mile, you'll reach my factory."

"No wonder you got here so quickly."

"I happened to be at the plant taking care of something when you texted me, but my house is even closer." He frowned as he adjusted the thermostat. It was digital, with an abundance of programs and cycles. Lourdes didn't understand why a device that could've been so simple — and used to be — had been made so complex. Maybe the furnace didn't work because she'd been messing with the various buttons and screwed something up . . . .

She perched on the arm of the leather sofa in the living room. "Solar must be a thriving business, what with everyone talking about carbon footprint."

"As time goes by and the price of solar modules comes down, more and more people are making the switch."

"Then you're poised for growth."

"Thanks to various government incentives, it's been a good field — and it's getting better."

If she couldn't create the kind of album she needed, maybe *she* could learn enough to open a solar plant. Except she'd be miserable. All she'd ever wanted to do was sing.

She picked up her guitar and ran through a few chords. She used it so much and had used it for so long that it almost felt like a part of her. It was comforting just to have it in her hands. "Does this house have solar? Is that why we have no heat? Because there's been no sun?"

He chuckled.

"What?" she said.

"Nothing. I had to explain to someone else that — Never mind. Anyway, yes, this place has solar, but it also has a gas furnace. The solar system delivers the electricity. So the air-conditioning, most of the appliances, the sprinkler system and the lights all run off the solar. I could've installed a special heating unit, too. But it didn't seem cost-effective for a rental."

"Tenants usually pay their own utilities."

"That's a consideration for some landlords, yes." He frowned as he turned to her.

"There's nothing wrong with this thermo-stat — not that I can tell. I'll check the unit itself."

After reclaiming his tools, he went out back while she set her guitar aside and stood at the kitchen window, watching his flash-light bob as he walked. He looked good in those jeans, she thought — then stopped herself. She had no business admiring his backside.

He returned about fifteen minutes later but said he couldn't find anything wrong with the unit itself, either. He suggested it might not be getting power and tried throw-ing the circuit breaker.

When that didn't work, he came back in and, muttering something she couldn't hear, tried the thermostat again. Only then did he reluctantly admit that he couldn't fix it. "I'm sorry," he said. "I'm not an HVAC guy, but I can get one out here first thing in the morning. The bad news is that this place won't get any warmer tonight. So I'll pay for you to stay at one of the two bed-and-breakfasts in town. They're both comfort-able, and you can have breakfast in bed, which is more than you'll get if you stay here."

He was trying to make it as appealing as possible. She was tempted to accept his solution, especially when he gave her a crooked grin that revealed how uncomfortable he felt at having to ask. But she wasn't interested in staying anywhere else. "I can't go into town," she said. "I'd rather not be seen, don't want to deal with . . . all that celebrity stuff. I told you before, I'm here to lie low."

His eyes widened slightly. "I wish I had a better solution, but I don't. You can't stay here. It's too cold, and it's going to get colder. Maybe you haven't heard, but we have a huge storm moving in. It's already snowing."

Once again, she tightened the belt on her sweater. "I've noticed."

"So, please, will you allow me to put you up somewhere? One of the B and Bs in town? Little Mary's belongs to a good friend of mine. I'll call her. If she hasn't left for the day, she'll let you in the back way."

Lourdes really didn't want to deal with any strangers. She felt bruised and battered by all the setbacks she'd experienced in the past few months. She just wanted to hide out. That was why she'd come here to begin with. She could've gone to a motel or a B and B anywhere.

"I'd rather not."

He seemed at a complete loss. "So . . .

51

what are you going to do?"

"I'll be fine here. I'll . . . wear my coat and pile on the blankets, get through the night somehow."

"Are you serious?" he said.

"Yes. I'm serious. I'll survive."

A scowl descended. "There's a real possibility you won't. In any case, I can't take that risk. I'd be too worried. And think of all the people who'd be devastated if something happened to you."

She wondered if that would include Derrick, or if he'd be, on some level at least, relieved that he could pursue Crystal without having to worry about her anymore.

Then she felt guilty for even thinking that. Derrick would never cheat. He said he loved her. They'd been talking about getting married.

But that was before Crystal had come into his life six months ago. Since then, he'd been saying things like, "There's no need to rush into anything."

Was that merely a coincidence?

"Would you rather stay closer to where you grew up?" Kyle asked. "I could try to find someplace in Angel's Camp."

That *definitely* wasn't a solution. Although she longed for the place where she'd been raised, she needed anonymity more. "Absolutely not."

"You have to go somewhere," he said.

She shook her head. "No, I don't."

His scowl darkened. "Yes, you do!"

They stared at each other in a silent contest of wills, until he sighed and jabbed a hand through his hair. "Come on, Ms. Bennett. Help me out. I'm just trying to keep you safe and warm."

"Fine, *Mr.* Houseman." It felt odd to be addressing a contemporary so formally. But he'd set the precedent. "If that's what you want, I'll go home with you."

His mouth fell open. "What'd you say?"

"You told me you live close by. We'll just . . . go over to your place until morning. As long as your wife won't mind letting me sleep on the couch —"

"I don't have a wife," he said.

"That makes it even simpler."

"But . . . you don't know me."

"I hardly think my staying under your roof will provide you with any new opportunities."

"What does that mean?"

"We're alone right now, aren't we? Besides, I'm sure you have a key to this place other than the one you gave me, so you could come back at any time."

"I have a key," he admitted. "But only in

case you lose yours or get locked out or something. I'm not going to *hurt* you."

The appalled look on his face lent those words plenty of credibility. "My point exactly. I'll grab my bag."

He spoke before she could leave the room. "Staying with me — *that's* the solution you'll accept?"

"If it means I don't have to see or speak to anyone else, yes."

"I live alone. I don't even have a dog because I work so much."

"See? This will be perfect — well, as perfect as we're going to get under the circumstances. We don't have far to go, and your refrigerator's probably stocked."

"You're hungry?"

"I am. And as far as I'm concerned, you owe me dinner for this. So your place sounds like the best solution all around."

"Okay," he said, but he looked so stunned she almost laughed as she hurried into the bedroom.

"I'm sorry for the inconvenience," he called after her. "Practically everything in this house is new. I had the renovation done when the weather was good, so I've never tried to turn on the heat. And now I'm convinced the person who installed the furnace didn't check it thoroughly."

"I realize this wasn't your intention." She closed her suitcase and dragged it out, grateful that she hadn't completely unpacked.

She found him leaning against one wall with his tools at his feet and his hands jammed in the pockets of his coat. "If you'd feel more comfortable, I could ask one of my female friends to put you up for the night," he said. "I didn't offer because . . . well, I never thought you'd prefer staying in my home to a B and B. But Callie's married and pregnant and also lives out of town. I bet you'd like her farm."

"I'm not willing to meet anyone else, so your place will be fine." She grabbed her guitar; no way would she ever leave that behind. "Let's go. It's getting colder by the second. And it might take you some time to work out what you're going to feed me."

# 3

Kyle's cupboards weren't filled with the ingredients he felt he needed to make a meal for Lourdes Bennett — or any other woman he would've liked to impress. He hadn't been to the grocery store in over a week, which meant he was down to some condiments, some frozen meat, a few eggs and half a loaf of bread.

As he stared into his refrigerator, trying to figure out what he could make, his unexpected houseguest wandered around his living room. At least the teenage girl he paid to clean his house and offices had come yesterday. He'd never been happier that he'd let Molly Tringette talk him into giving her a part-time job so she could save up for college.

"You must like old houses," Lourdes said.

Giving up on the fridge, he moved to the pantry. "I do. But it's not as if I set out to buy any. This place happened to be on the land where I built my plant. Made sense for me to live here."

"Looks like it's been recently updated."

"Yes. I used to live in a smaller house even closer to the plant — for fifteen years, ever since I graduated from college. I rented this one out for quite a while."

"That's when you opened your business? Fifteen years ago?"

"I was set on manufacturing solar modules from the beginning."

"You must have rich parents to start such an expensive business right out of college."

"No. Not at all."

"Then how'd you get into it?"

Canned goods. Crackers. Oatmeal . . . Nothing jumped out at him. But he supposed he wasn't going to find a Caesar salad, bacon and cheddar-topped potatoes and filet mignon in the pantry. He'd have to make whatever they ate, and he didn't have a lot to work with. "Somehow I convinced the president of our local bank to give me a loan. What with all the new regulations, I doubt the same scenario could happen these days. He lent me that money based solely on his confidence in me."

"I can only imagine what you must've been like — so young and full of ambition."

"I was certainly driven. But solar was a

gamble back then. When I think about it, I'm still surprised he did it." Giving up on the pantry, he returned to the fridge — as if he might see something different when he looked in it a second time.

"Why was solar such a gamble? Most people see it as the wave of the future."

"That long ago, the 'wave of the future' was too expensive for all but the richest people. That made it hard to sell."

"*I* would've bet on you, too. In a heartbeat."

He turned to look at her. "To what do I owe such a compliment? My trustworthy face?"

"I'd credit it more to your inherent confidence. You believe you can do . . . whatever, so the people around you believe it, too."

How had she come up with that? They knew virtually nothing about each other. "I had no idea I was so confident that complete strangers could tell."

"I'm good at reading people." She gestured around her. "So . . . you fulfilled your obligation to the bank, and then you remodeled?"

He wondered whether she'd mind if he ran to town to get dinner. He almost suggested it. But she'd said she was hungry, and he guessed she'd prefer not to wait. "I wasn't in a hurry to put any money into the house. The business has always been my top priority. But last year when I bought the property with the house you're renting and decided to clean it up, I figured I might as well update this one, too, and move into it."

That he'd finally gone ahead and made so many improvements drove Noelle nuts, since she'd been dying to fix up one of his houses while they were married. Actually, she'd started out begging him to buy her a big house in town — something that would show wealth and status, and where she could be at the center of activity. He'd refused, and his refusal had caused so many arguments between them that he'd stone-walled her when she eventually gave up and asked for a remodel of one of his current homes instead.

Now he felt like a stubborn ass. He could've allowed her to enjoy the process — as well as the finished product. But he'd been so irritated with how shallow she was, and was so miserable being married to her, he'd dug in his heels.

In retrospect, he understood that making her live in an old house he could've remodeled but wouldn't was his revenge for knowing she'd trapped him to begin with.

"You must've used the same contractor,"

Lourdes mused.

"Yes. One of my best friends, Riley Stinson."

"He does quality work."

"Come spring, he's planning to renovate the house next door, which I'm currently renting to one of my employees, and the one closer to the plant, which is currently empty. They'll look a lot different when he's done."

She stared out at the snow falling into his backyard, which wasn't a yard so much as a large field. "How many employees do you have?"

"Fourteen, at the moment."

"That must make you the biggest employer in Whiskey Creek."

He chuckled as he moved the ketchup and pickles to see if there was anything behind them.

He found . . . butter. *Great.*

"Possibly," he responded. "But that isn't saying much."

"Were you born here?"

"I was." What if he made eggs and toast? It wasn't a fancy meal, but he had a whole shelf of homemade jelly he'd bought from Morgan's partner, who canned every spring and then foisted off on him whatever she couldn't sell elsewhere. Along with some

60

good coffee, fried eggs could be enjoy-
able . . .

"Have you ever considered leaving?" she
asked.

He straightened. "Whiskey Creek? No, not
really. Why would I want to do that?"

"Don't you ever feel it's too . . . confining?"

He thought of Noelle. *She* found it too
confining. But he wasn't like that. He loved
it here, couldn't imagine going anywhere
else. Noelle was the only thing that ever
made him want to leave. "No. My parents
are in town, and they're getting older. With
my sister and her kids living in Pennsylvania,
I need to help look after Mom and Dad. I
don't want to leave it all to my stepbrother,
Brandon. Besides, I like the people here,
the land, the freedom. Being in a big city,
with the traffic and the noise and the pollu-
tion . . . that's not me."

"I see. You're a cowboy at heart."

"Not a cowboy. I don't rope or ride. Don't
own a pair of cowboy boots or a Western
buckle. But I'm definitely a small-town kind
of guy." He lifted the carton of eggs. "Any
chance you'd be interested in breakfast for
dinner?"

She turned away from the window. "I
could eat almost anything."

"Why didn't you stop and get something after you landed?" Except for the fact that he didn't have much to choose from, he didn't mind feeding her. But with her determination to avoid public places, what would she have eaten if she'd stayed at his rental tonight? There was nothing in those cupboards, other than some coffee he'd taken over as an afterthought. He'd been asked to provide furnishings, not food.

"I should have," she admitted. "I was in a hurry. Since I'd never seen your house in person, I wasn't convinced it would work for my retreat, and I wasn't sure where I'd go if it didn't. I felt I needed to reserve time for plan B, just in case."

"Makes sense, I guess." He found a spatula, but then he began to wonder if he should give her other options. Not everyone cared for dairy foods. "Would you rather have canned soup? I've got tomato or vegetable."

"No. I'll take the eggs."

He pulled out a frying pan. "Good choice."

The eggs popped and sizzled as he stood at the stove. While he waited to flip them, she moved over to his mantel to examine the framed pictures he had there. "Don't tell me this is Simon O'Neal!"

He could understand why that might surprise her. Simon was one of the biggest movie stars in America. "Actually, it is," he said. "A few years ago, Gail, one of my best friends, opened a PR agency in LA. She took Simon on as a client, and long story short, they fell in love. They're married now and have three kids."

"And you hang out with them?"

"They're in LA most of the time, or on location, but we get together whenever they come to visit."

She moved on to the other photographs. "All the rest of these people are . . ."

"Those are my parents, on the left. The kids you see are my niece and nephew."

"Your sister's children, the one who lives in Pennsylvania?"

"Since she remarried and moved there a few years ago, yes. For a while, she was living in one of my rentals."

"And these other people?"

He glanced over. "My friends."

"You have a lot of friends," she said.

"I'm guessing you do, too."

"New friends aren't the same as old friends."

Was she referring to the paradox of being famous and yet lonely? "Are you missing home?" He supposed that would explain why she'd come to the Sierra Nevada Foothills.

"I'm missing *something,*" she said.

He flipped the eggs. "And that is . . ."

She turned away from his pictures and came back to the table. "Nothing. Never mind."

Lourdes enjoyed dinner. Kyle — they were now comfortably on a first-name basis — was down-to-earth and didn't seem too affected by her celebrity. He wasn't overly solicitous, just real. Somehow that put her at ease, made her feel at home when she'd been on edge for so long. Maybe, since he was used to socializing with someone far more famous than she was, he didn't consider her to be any big deal.

Or maybe it was just that Kyle was so comfortable in his own skin. Had she ever met a man more self-assured? She'd seen plenty of *arrogance* in her line of work. And vanity. The vanity was worse than the arrogance. But Kyle was different. He seemed to be at peace with who and what he was, and she admired his quiet strength, even though she didn't know him very well.

He was the calm at the center of the storm, she thought and felt a spark of creative excitement. That was it! Her first idea! She'd write a song about how one person could provide a safe harbor for others in the middle of life's chaos and confusion.

The fact that she felt like writing *anything* lifted her spirits. This was the first time she'd experienced that desire since her last album . . .

"What are you smiling at?" Kyle asked.

She sobered. "Nothing. It just feels good to be full. And warm."

"You can turn the thermostat up higher, if you like." He raised one eyebrow. "But I might have to go sleep in the garage if you do."

She laughed as she handed him her plate, since he was standing at the sink, and went back to finish clearing the table. "You're safe. The temperature's perfect in here."

"Glad to hear it."

"So . . . you're single," she said as she brought him their cups.

He seemed startled by the comment. "Yes."

"An entrenched bachelor?"

"Not quite. I'm divorced."

She hesitated before going back to get their orange juice glasses. "Do you have kids?"

"No. And considering what my ex-wife is

like, that's a blessing."

She wanted to ask him more — how long ago he was married, how he met his wife, whether or not she still lived in town. Lourdes also wondered, but wouldn't ask, why they hadn't had children. But then her phone buzzed on the counter, where she'd put it earlier. She'd left Derrick several messages while she was at the airport and then when she'd arrived in Whiskey Creek, and he was getting back to her.

*Finally . . .*

"Excuse me," she said, taking her phone into the spare room where Kyle had put her bag.

Kyle tried to ignore Lourdes's voice. She was whispering, so she wouldn't be overheard, but her whisper was so loud it actually drew *more* attention to her conversation.

He was about to turn on the television. Whatever she had to say to Derrick Meade — there was no doubt it was him, since she'd said his name a number of times — was none of his business. But then he heard tears in her voice and couldn't help pausing to listen.

"You must've been with her . . . Then where were you all day? You had to know I was trying to reach you . . . You always have your phone with you. You'd have it surgically implanted into your ear if you could . . . That's what you constantly tell me, but that's not what I'm feeling . . . Then why continue to put off the wedding? Before you met Crystal, you were in such a hurry . . . So it's what's happened to my career that's made you back off? If I'm not the hottest singer in Nashville, you're no longer interested? . . . I get that, but what else am I supposed to think? . . . So are you coming here or not? . . . Never mind. Go ahead and do whatever you have to do for Crystal . . . No, I'm not! You're the one who's acting weird . . . Forget it. I've got a lot to do, too. I'm fine here without you."

The sudden silence led Kyle to believe she'd hung up. He also guessed she was crying. It sounded like it.

Should he knock on the door and attempt to console her? He'd always been someone who tried to fix whatever was broken, and that included the people in his life. But he couldn't imagine something that intrusive going over very well for either one of them. They'd barely met.

Assuming she'd prefer her privacy, he put on Thursday night football. Hopefully, that would distract him and give her enough background noise to hide her sniffles.

But it was only fifteen minutes later that the door slammed against the inside wall and she charged out of the bedroom. "Kyle?"

He lowered the volume and looked over at her. Her red, swollen eyes left little doubt that there'd been tears. "Are you okay?" he asked.

She wiped her cheeks. "Not really, but I haven't been okay in a while."

"What's the matter?"

"It's my problem, and I'll take care of it, but I was wondering if you'd do me a favor."

He took his feet off the coffee table and sat up. "What kind of favor?"

"It's sort of an odd request."

This made him leery. Noelle always approached him with one odd request or another. "I'm listening."

"I was hoping you'd call my manager and ask for Crystal Holtree."

"Who's Crystal Holtree?"

"If you don't know yet, you will within the next year. She's another singer — Nashville's new darling. Derrick manages her career, too."

"And you want to see if he's managing a bit more than that."

68

Her chest rose as she took a deep breath. "Yes."

"Are you sure you should check up on him like this?"

"My heart is telling me he'd never be unfaithful, but my head is telling me something else. I'm going crazy, becoming so insecure. I have to know if it's him — or me."

He rubbed his chin as he thought about her request.

"It's just one phone call," she said.

"But he knows who I am."

"Okay, it's one phone call and you'll have to claim to be someone else."

"Like . . ."

She spread out her hands. "Robin Graham."

"Who's Robin Graham?"

"No one. I made up the name. You could say you're Robin Graham with *Country Weekly* or CMT and you'd like to interview Crystal. That's all you'd have to do. He wouldn't want her to miss *that* call. If she's with him, he'll hand over the phone, and if he hands over the phone, he's been lying to me."

"But he has my cell number in his contacts. I put it in the rental ad."

"You don't have another phone?"

"Not here at home. I guess I could block my number . . ."

She nibbled uncertainly on her lower lip. "No, a blocked number wouldn't be believable."

"Then we'd have to go over to the office. I have an extra line that wouldn't give the name of my company on caller ID."

She appeared more hopeful. "Would you mind?"

It wasn't really his place to get involved. Also, it was snowing pretty hard. He could hear the wind railing against the house. But he had a four-wheel drive, they wouldn't have far to go and the storm didn't seem to be nearly as bad as forecasted, certainly no worse than several they'd had in recent years.

Besides, he could feel her uncertainty. Maybe Derrick Meade wasn't cheating. Maybe they could relieve her anxiety so she could focus on writing those songs she'd mentioned. She seemed to be down on her luck, but not in the same way Noelle always was. Lourdes had seen a lot of success. She might be someone for whom a little help would make a big difference. "I wouldn't mind, but —" he checked his watch "— it's nearly nine in Nashville. Won't it seem strange to get a business call that late?"

"Not from a harried reporter trying to hit a deadline."

"Okay," he said. "Come on."

# 4

After Kyle waved her into the seat across from his desk and picked up the phone, Lourdes could only wring her hands. Was she about to find out if all the anxiety and concern she'd been feeling had a basis in reality?

"What's his number?" he asked.

He could look it up on his cell, but there was no need when she knew it by heart.

She rattled off the digits as she shook snow off her coat. Then she held her breath as he dialed. On the drive over, she'd educated him so he'd sound like a believable country magazine reporter, but she had no idea how he'd handle himself once he had Derrick on the phone.

"Hello?"

Derrick must've answered! Lourdes felt her stomach twist into knots.

Clearing his throat, Kyle stood. "Mr. Meade? This is Graham . . . Gibb with

*Country Weekly.*" He threw her a quizzical look that told her he'd gapped on the name she'd given him and had to improvise. Fortunately, he'd remembered the magazine correctly. That would've been a lot tougher to fake, since Derrick knew all the magazines that mattered in their industry. "I understand you manage Crystal Holtree . . . Yes, I've heard that song. It's amazing. I apologize for calling so late, but I'm up against a deadline and was wondering if she might be available for a quick interview . . . Mmm-hmm . . . Right. What I'd originally planned for this issue fell apart, so I thought I'd change it up and write a piece on an emerging artist . . . Okay . . . Sure."

He covered the phone. "He's giving me her number," he mouthed. "What should I do?"

"Hang up," she whispered.

"Won't he get suspicious?"

"He won't guess it's me. I've never done anything like this before." She'd never felt she had to, not until Crystal entered their lives . . .

Flicking his wet hair out of his face, he removed his hand from the receiver. "Sorry for the interruption. My wife's telling me that my editor's been trying to reach me. She's already backfilled the interview with someone else, so I apologize for the false alarm. I'll keep Ms. Holtree in mind for future articles, though . . . Yes, I agree. She's talented. I'll see what I can do in the next few months."

He hung up. Then he sank into his chair. "I'm not sure that was completely believable."

Lourdes couldn't be sure, either. She'd been straining the bounds of credulity when she'd had Kyle call so late. Crystal was generating sufficient interest that it wasn't inconceivable, but it was Lourdes's emotions that were driving her these days — not logic. That was why she'd had to pull away from Nashville. She needed to get her priorities straight, put recent setbacks in perspective. "You handled it well."

"But we didn't learn anything. Maybe she was there, and he's just too smart to give himself away."

"Did he even *try* to suggest me for the interview? Or for another one later?"

"No. He might've if we'd talked longer."

"He would've a year ago, no matter what."

Kyle drummed his fingers on the desk. "Maybe he couldn't."

"You think she's there?"

"I didn't say that."

"You sensed a hesitancy or something that

makes you wonder."

He grimaced as if he didn't want to admit that, but she could tell it was true.

She dropped her head in her hand. "Shit."

Before he could respond, the office phone rang.

He glanced over at her. "It's the Ooma line I just used, and I shouldn't be getting any calls this time of night."

Her heart began to pound. "What happens if you don't answer?"

"It rolls over to the regular lines and eventually goes to voice mail for First Step Solar."

"Grab it," she cried, but he must've come to the same conclusion, because he was already reaching for the handset.

"Graham Gibb."

Lourdes held her breath. If Kyle's caller happened to be looking for solar panels, he or she would be quite confused. But, in the next second, it became apparent that Derrick was calling back, just as they'd feared.

"Great," Kyle said. "That's convenient . . ." He squeezed his forehead with one hand as if he regretted getting mixed up in her little ruse — or was worried about the fallout. "Of course I'd like to speak to her . . . Sure . . . Put her on . . ."

Derrick must've transferred the phone to

Crystal, because, for the next several minutes, Lourdes had to sit there and listen to Kyle feign interest in Crystal's burgeoning music career. When he could do so without seeming too dismissive, he cut in to say he had to go if he was going to finish his article tonight, that it had been a pleasure speaking to her and he'd get back to her if he ever had the opportunity to give her some press.

When he hung up, he rubbed a hand over his mouth. "So what do you make of that?"

"She called back awfully fast."

"Derrick said she just stopped by to drop something off after we hung up."

Lourdes felt sick to her stomach. She wished she could believe it was the coincidence Derrick claimed, but her intuition wouldn't allow it. "What could Crystal need to drop off that she couldn't email?"

Kyle shook his head.

"What did *she* say?" Lourdes asked.

"That she wanted to reach out and let me know she'd be happy to speak to me whenever. We could even have lunch. That sort of thing."

"Was it convincing?"

He didn't seem too keen on committing himself.

"Kyle? Did you get the impression Derrick was pretending she'd suddenly shown up?"

"That's a tough question," he hedged.

She blew on her hands, which hadn't warmed up since their journey through the storm. "Because you think they're having an affair."

"Because I don't really know!"

"God, I hate this," she said. "I hate feeling as if I'm being taken for a fool. And I hate feeling I can't trust the man I love."

"Has he ever cheated on you before?"

"Not that I know of. But he's never been so preoccupied and distant, either. Never been so swept away with someone else." He also had a history that included an extra-marital affair with an intern, well before he met her, but Lourdes didn't volunteer that information. She'd chosen to believe he'd just messed up, that he regretted it — but she understood that others might not give him the benefit of the doubt. Maybe he was merely enamored with Crystal's potential, as he claimed. "It doesn't help that she's younger, prettier and more talented than I am," she grumbled.

Kyle looked shocked. "She might be younger, and I'm no judge of singing talent, so I can't weigh in there. But she *couldn't* be any more beautiful."

It was a nice compliment. One that sounded sincere.

Maybe if Lourdes hadn't been so distraught, she could've appreciated it.

Kyle stared at the ceiling for at least an hour after he went to bed. He felt bad for Lourdes. Clearly, she was stumbling through that unique hell reserved for partners of the unfaithful. *Can he change? Will he change? Should I give him the opportunity to change? Does he really love me — or does he love her?* Kyle had discussed those questions with her at great length over the past three hours. While the snow continued to fall outside, they'd shared a bottle of pinot noir and Lourdes had told him that even though coming to Whiskey Creek had been her idea — she'd seen it as a way to withdraw from public life so she could "reset" — Derrick had promised to come with her. He'd said they'd use whatever time she didn't spend writing to rebuild their relationship, since they'd been having so much difficulty getting along. So even if Derrick hadn't been lying about Crystal tonight, he'd put Lourdes off and that led Kyle to believe he probably *was* too caught up with his new client. Hearing from Crystal so soon after calling Derrick was certainly suspect, despite Derrick's explanation — since that explanation was flimsy at best.

Lourdes seemed like a nice person who didn't deserve the turmoil she was going through. But whether or not Derrick was cheating wasn't the only thing on Kyle's mind. Discussing her problems had forced him to face that his own life needed an overhaul. The woman he loved — had always loved — was married to his step-brother, which created an awkward challenge whenever he saw them (and he saw them often). To make matters worse, he had an ex-wife who wouldn't let go, who claimed she still loved him, even though, from what he remembered, she'd hated being married as much as he had. And almost all his friends were not only in committed relationships but having children, too. They'd moved on and he hadn't. He felt lonely and shiftless whenever he wasn't completely immersed in his work. So he worked longer and longer hours, which made it even harder to meet someone.

He was approaching forty. If he was going to marry and have kids, he needed to do it soon. But he hadn't met a woman who could replace Olivia — and he was beginning to fear he never would.

His phone buzzed. Leaning up on one

elbow, he squinted to see who'd texted him. It was Riley Stinson, the most recent of his close friends to find a mate.

You still up?

Kyle had missed a call from Riley earlier. He hadn't gotten back to him, so although he was exhausted, he shoved himself into a sitting position.

I am. Sorry I missed your call today. Got a tenant for the farmhouse. Been handling that. What's up?

Kyle wasn't sure why he'd asked what was up. He *knew* what was up with Riley. After months spent trying to atone for their difficult history, Riley had finally talked Phoenix Fuller into marrying him. They'd set the date for December 30 and were planning a big wedding. It was all Riley could talk about. And, if Kyle was being honest, that made him a lot less eager to take Riley's calls. Now that Riley was settling down, Kyle would be the only single member of their group, except for Baxter — and, as Noelle had pointed out, his relationship with Baxter wouldn't be very conducive to meeting women.

Instead of texting back, Riley called. "Hey,

you rented the farmhouse, huh?"

Kyle could hear the wind buffeting the trees against the house, but the worst of the storm seemed to be over. "I did," he said as he dropped onto his pillows.

"To who?"

The words "Someone from Nashville" were on the tip of his tongue. That was what he planned to tell most people. But Riley was one of his best friends. He could trust Riley with his life. "Lourdes Bennett."

"Lourdes who?"

"Bennett. She's a country-western singer — sings 'Heartbreak' and 'Stone Cold Lover.' "

"*That* Lourdes Bennett? Are you kidding me?"

"No, but don't tell anyone she's in town. She's trying to keep a low profile."

"I won't tell a soul. But if Lourdes wanted to move here, why wouldn't she buy her own place? She's got to have the money."

"This is just a short-term thing, until she finishes writing the songs for her next album."

"Don't most major artists buy songs from songwriters?"

"I'm sure some do, but I guess she prefers to come up with her own material." He heard the toilet flush down the hall. Lourdes was still up — which didn't surprise him. Derrick had called as they poured the last of that bottle of wine. She'd probably just finished talking to him. "Did you need something when you tried to reach me earlier?" he asked Riley.

"Mostly I wanted to check in, see what you've been up to. Seems like we've both been so busy with work we hardly talk anymore."

It wasn't because of work. It was because Riley's private life was doing what it should and Kyle's wasn't. But he didn't comment on that. No one enjoyed hearing other people complain about something they couldn't have. "We'll see each other tomorrow morning at Black Gold, won't we?"

"Yeah, I'll be there. So will Phoenix. But besides checking in, I was hoping to talk to you about the wedding."

The wedding. Of course. Olivia was planning it, so Kyle heard about it even from her. "You're down to what . . . four weeks? That's crazy."

"It's coming up fast, which is why I'm in sort of a hurry."

"To . . ."

"I was wondering if you'd marry us."

Kyle nearly dropped his phone. Riley's teenage son would be best man. He hadn't

82

expected to do anything other than standing in Riley's line, along with the rest of the guys in their group of friends. "You mean . . . *perform the ceremony?*"

"That's exactly what I mean."

"Doesn't that require a preacher?"

"Apparently not. I was remodeling a kitchen the other day when the guy who hired me said he'd performed his daughter's wedding. He told me all he had to do was sign up online."

*"Where?"*

"I'm sure it'll come up if you look for it on Google. If you can't find it, give me a call and I'll ask him."

"And Phoenix . . . she's okay with having me play that role?"

"You know how Phoenix feels about you. She was thrilled when I suggested it."

"But your parents will expect you to use their minister, won't they?"

"This isn't their wedding. I plan to make sure it's everything Phoenix wants."

Kyle smiled even though Riley couldn't see it. "You really love that girl," he said, and he could understand why. He'd taken a special liking to Phoenix, too — wished he'd written to her while she was in prison so he could've offered some emotional support. What she'd been through was terrible — to be convicted of something she didn't do. Yet she'd stood tall and weathered those tough years completely on her own.

"She's the one for me," Riley said. "I can't explain why she's different from all the other women I've dated, but she is."

"I'm happy for you." He seemed to be saying that a lot lately. He was happy for Brandon and Olivia and their perfect marriage. He was happy for Riley and Phoenix, happy that they were finally getting together — something that would've happened years ago if life was fair. He was happy for Callie and Levi, too, who were expecting their first baby, and Eve and Lincoln, who'd had their first child a few months ago. Everyone had something to celebrate.

If Noelle could find another love interest, maybe *he'd* have something to celebrate . . .

"So you'll do it?" Riley asked.

He tried to imagine standing at the altar with Riley and Phoenix and felt ill equipped, but how could he say no to one of his best friends? "I can honestly say that performing a marriage is something I never pictured myself doing. But sure. Thanks for asking me."

"Glad you're willing. And you have my promise that I'll do anything you ask me to when you get married."

"Are you expecting that to happen soon?" he joked.

"You never know, man. You could be married right now if you weren't so damn picky."

His father told him basically the same thing. But in his mind, he wasn't being picky, he was being careful. He'd rather be a confirmed bachelor for the rest of his life than make *another* mistake. The last one had been a pain in his ass for six years.

He thought of Noelle calling about her water heater, and the money for her boob job and for her utility bill. She was still a pain in his ass. He should never have married her — but he had the sneaking suspicion that if he hadn't, she would've gone ahead and had the baby, forging an even stronger bond. His mistake had been letting her seduce him in the first place. It all went back to one drunken, foolish night when she'd claimed to be on the pill . . .

"I'm fine the way I am," he insisted.

"Noelle put the fear of God into you. And I can see why. She's freakin' psycho. We knew she was trouble before you married her, and if she hadn't been pregnant, you wouldn't have done it. Nothing like that will happen again."

Anything could happen. That was why he

was being more vigilant. "I was an idiot to let her trap me."

"She's an extreme example. Forget about her."

If only he could. If only she'd allow it . . .

"What about the girl you brought to Ted's Halloween party this year — Danni Decker?" Riley asked. "She seemed cool."

"For one thing, she lives in the Bay Area. For another, she has a high-powered investment job."

"You say that like it's a bad thing."

"We're too similar. She'd never give up her job to move here. And I wouldn't move there. So why would I pursue a relationship with her, when it's bound to end with both of us miserable? Besides, she doesn't want children, and that's a deal breaker for me."

"You're looking for a homemaker?"

"Not necessarily a homemaker — but a woman who's willing to be a mother. Most of all, I want someone who's satisfied with who I am, what I do and where I live." No way was he ever going to be happy with a wife who constantly nagged him to leave Whiskey Creek. He'd already been down that road.

"I guess that's not asking too much, but . . . you've got to get over Olivia first, Kyle."

This was the second time in a day that someone had called him on his true feelings for Olivia. But Noelle taunted him whenever she could. Ironically, she claimed it was his feelings for Olivia that had broken up their marriage, but she'd known he had feelings for Olivia when she approached him at the bar. He'd dated Olivia for two years before she put their relationship on pause and moved to Sacramento to pursue her wedding planning business.

"I've been over Olivia for ages," he said, but he'd been claiming that ever since she'd married Brandon.

Riley didn't respond.

"You still there?" Kyle asked.

"I am. I'm just . . . Never mind."

Riley was skeptical. He knew nothing had changed, but Kyle couldn't admit that, not without doing his brother a disservice. He *wanted* to be over Olivia; he just wished he could get his damn heart to cooperate. "Don't worry about me," he said. "I don't need a woman."

"I still wish you could find someone. Marriage doesn't have to be what you had with Noelle."

Problem was . . . he had yet to meet any viable alternatives. Most of the women his age were already in relationships, like Olivia and even Lourdes. Or they were entrenched in a career somewhere else. Or there wasn't any spark.

"Who would've thought Phoenix and I would wind up together?" Riley said. "You'll find someone — the person you're meant to be with."

Not as long as the woman he was meant to be with was married to his stepbrother. "Like I said, it's fine even if I don't."

"I'm exhausted. I've got to go. I'll tell Phoenix and Olivia you'll perform the ceremony. They'll both be glad to hear it."

"I'll do the research tomorrow, right after coffee at Black Gold."

"Sounds good. I appreciate it."

Kyle started to hang up, but Riley stopped him. "Kyle?"

"Yeah?"

"Before I go, can I ask you something?"

He sighed. "Does it have to do with Olivia? Because I'm pretty much done with that subject."

"I just want to know why you invited her and Brandon to join us for coffee. I've always wondered. I think everyone has."

"What can I say? He's my brother." There was no escape. And it was *his* fault things were the way they were. Why shouldn't

Brandon be included? He'd done nothing wrong.

"It can't be easy to see them so often."

"Noelle's the one who makes my life hard," he joked, hoping to lighten up the conversation.

"Is she still pushing to get back together?"

Kyle thought of her offer to provide him with sex and grimaced. "She still calls me far too often."

"Maybe she'll move. She's been talking about going to New York or some other big city for years."

"Sometimes I'm tempted to give her the money so we can both be happy. I'm thinking London would be nice."

Riley chuckled. "Except she'd only come back as soon as her pockets were empty."

"That's why I don't actually do it," he said. "Have a great night."

"See you in the morning."

Kyle disconnected, plugged his phone in to charge and tried, once again, to get some sleep. But he could hear muffled sounds that led him to believe Lourdes was in another heated conversation with Derrick. He didn't envy her the upset or the arguments — or the doubt and suspicion that were eating her up.

Obviously, love didn't work for everyone.
Maybe he really was better off alone . . .

# 5

"Oh, my gosh! *You have Lourdes Bennett staying at the farmhouse?*"

Kyle blinked in surprise. He'd just walked into Black Gold Coffee to meet his friends, twelve of whom were crowded around their usual tables in the back corner, when he was confronted by this question. It'd come from Callie Vanetta-Pendleton, the woman he'd suggested Lourdes stay with, but he didn't look at Callie. He shifted his gaze to Riley. "You *told* them? What happened to 'don't tell anyone — she's trying to keep a low profile'? And 'this is Riley, the friend I can trust with my life'?"

Riley flinched. "I don't recall that bit about trusting me with your life."

Dylan and Cheyenne were there with their one-year-old. So were Addy and Noah and their little girl, Emily, who was slightly older than Dylan and Chey's boy. Eve had shown up without her husband and baby, since she ran the B and B her parents owned in town, even though they now lived in Placerville. Ted and Sophia, Callie's husband, Levi, Riley and his fiancée, Phoenix, rounded out the group — along with Brandon and Olivia, of course. As always, Kyle was hyperaware of their presence, as well as whether or not he'd be sitting close to them. He figured, since he couldn't put Olivia behind him, he'd be conscious of details like that forever. "Maybe not, but that's what I was thinking."

A sheepish expression appeared on Riley's face. "Sorry 'bout that. But if it'd been something important, something more than an interesting development that didn't affect you much either way, I wouldn't have breathed a word. And these guys are the only ones I've told. You can trust them as much as you can trust me, right?"

"Now I'm hoping I can trust them more!" Taking great care not to focus on Olivia, Kyle pulled out a chair and slid it to the left so that once he sat down, their knees wouldn't touch.

Callie had gone silent the moment she realized she'd gotten Riley in trouble. But at this, she leaned forward. "Your secret is safe with me, with all of us. I'm just excited. I'm a huge fan of Lourdes Bennett's. Do you suppose she'll ever come into town? Maybe I can arrange to bump into her."

"I'm sure she'll have to buy groceries at some point," he told her. "But she really wants to go unnoticed, Callie, so be careful about approaching her."

"Why is she here?"

It was Olivia who'd asked this question, so he had to look at her, but he did his best to seem impassive. With her wide blue eyes and honey-blond hair, he still found her one of the prettiest women he'd ever seen. "She's sort of having a difficult time. I don't think she'd want me to say much more than that."

"Wow. Sounds like she's already told you what's going on — and you're protective of her," Brandon said.

Kyle scowled. "I'm just trying to give her the space and privacy she requested."

"Is she here by herself?" Callie asked.

Grateful for the distraction, he moved his attention away from Brandon and Olivia as he nodded.

"Oh, no!" she exclaimed. "Don't tell me she and Derrick have broken up."

"You know her boyfriend's name?" Kyle said. "You really are a fan."

Callie pressed a hand to her swollen stomach. He got the impression her baby was moving, but she didn't say so. She was too caught up in *his* news. "Anyone who follows her on Twitter knows Derrick's name. For a while there, they were talking about getting married. She even posted a few pictures of various engagement rings she liked. But he hasn't given her one yet — not that she's revealed, anyway. What's going on?"

Kyle shrugged. "Every relationship has its ups and downs."

Eve frowned at him. "Really? That's all you're going to say?"

"I'm trying to be discreet."

"With *us*?" Callie acted wounded.

He sighed. "They're having some problems, okay? Just like you've guessed."

"Is that why she came here?" Callie asked. "To get away from him?"

Shit. He'd already said too much. "No. She's here on business, to write her next album. She needs peace and quiet. So . . . let's all keep our mouths shut."

Callie shifted again. She was obviously at the uncomfortable stage of pregnancy. "Is this a country album?"

"Of course," he replied. "Why wouldn't it be?"

"Because her last one wasn't, and it didn't do very well." Cheyenne lifted her chubby baby from his carrier. "As far as I'm concerned, it was too much of a departure from what made her famous."

"I haven't heard it," Kyle said, and several others, mostly the guys, said the same.

"It was more . . . pop," Cheyenne explained as Dylan helped her ready a bottle.

"I didn't like it as much as her other work, either," Addy agreed. "And I *love* pop music. Lourdes Bennett is just more . . . authentic as a country artist, if that makes sense."

"You listen to her, too?" Kyle asked.

"Don't you?" she replied.

"I've heard a few of her songs on the radio, but it's not like I've ever downloaded them onto my iPod."

Addy wadded up a napkin and dropped it on her empty side plate. "Is she as pretty in person as she is in her pictures?"

"I think so." That was the truth, but Kyle said it nonchalantly so he wouldn't give away how strong his feelings actually were on that subject. Then, eager to avoid all the attention he was receiving, he checked the order line at the register. It had been winding out the door when he arrived. He still needed to get his coffee and a muffin but had been trying to outwait the rush.

"She must really be something." The tone

95

of Addy's voice said she wasn't fooled. "And she's staying at the farmhouse? That's *very* close to your place."

"I suggest you see if she needs dinner out occasionally," Noah chimed in, catching on to the implication.

"Or, better yet, you might want to bring dinner *in,*" Dylan joked.

The line hadn't shortened. If anything, it'd gotten longer, and Kyle wasn't willing to wait, not when he could have Morgan bring him a cup of coffee once he started work. "Why hold off until dinner? She's at *my* house right now, not the farmhouse. I could bring her breakfast." He knew better than to get them excited but couldn't resist having a little fun.

Eve put her coffee down so fast it sloshed over the side. "So she *did* break up with her boyfriend."

"No."

"Then what's she doing at *your* house?" Riley asked.

"She was sleeping when I left," he replied, pushing the joke a bit further.

"Holy shit!" Brandon exclaimed. *"You spent the night with Lourdes Bennett?"*

"Kyle, you should be more careful!" Eve warned. "You don't want an angry boyfriend to come calling."

Having provoked the reaction he'd been looking for, Kyle lifted a hand. "I'm just messing with you guys."

Brandon did a double take. "So she's *not* at your house?"

"She is, but strictly for practical reasons. We couldn't get the heat to come on in the farmhouse yesterday, and I didn't want her to freeze to death. So I let her stay in one of my spare bedrooms."

"She agreed to that?" Noah asked. *"She went home with you?"*

He shrugged. "I offered to get her a room at Eve's B and B but she wouldn't hear of it."

"What's wrong with my B and B?" Eve demanded. "It's the best in town — no matter what A Room With A View has done to steal my business."

"It had nothing to do with your B and B," Kyle said. "She wouldn't go to A Room With A View, either. She doesn't want to be seen in public, needs a break from all that, like I told you."

Brandon clapped him on the back. "Lucky you. She's rich *and* famous. I say you help her forget this Derrick dude. Sweep her off her feet."

Of course Brandon would say that. He had to be tired of trying to ignore the fact that his brother was in love with his wife.

Ted Dixon, a bestselling novelist who took a more measured approach to everything, moved the sugar packets closer to Levi. "Do you like her?"

"I do. Surprisingly, she's as nice as she is pretty." Kyle couldn't help wondering if Olivia cared that he was admiring another woman. He was ashamed for even having that thought; it was the kind of thing that had made him start avoiding family events. He'd once believed that, with time, he'd get over her, and all the weirdness would go away. But after six years, the feelings themselves hadn't gone anywhere. He just felt worse for having them.

Dylan dusted the crumbs of his muffin from his hands. "Then I'd say she's fair game."

Kyle waved them off. "She's only staying in town for a few months. And I'm sure she'll stick with Derrick in the end. He's perfect for her."

"In what way?" Eve asked. "You haven't met him, too, have you?"

"No, but he works with her, understands the music business, supports her career, doesn't mind the travel. I want . . . something else." He stretched out his legs and crossed them at the ankles, hoping he'd said enough to put an end to the subject. "Don't we have some things to go over for the wedding?" He grinned at Riley. "Like who'll be performing the ceremony?"

"Riley said *you're* doing it," Brandon replied, and, fortunately, the conversation moved on from there. They discussed other aspects of the wedding, how to make the most of the "winter wonderland" theme, how they'd all help set up and when they should schedule the bachelor and bachelorette parties. Once they'd hammered out those details, Noah said he'd heard that Baxter would be moving back before Christmas for sure, so they used Noah's phone to call him and put him on speaker. He told them his last day of work was supposed to be the fifteenth, but even if he didn't get moved right away, he could easily make the bachelor party on the twenty-third — good news.

Fortunately, no one mentioned to Baxter that Lourdes Bennett was in town, so Kyle didn't have to swear yet another person to secrecy.

As soon as they hung up, he stood.

"You getting your muffin?" Brandon jerked his head toward the cash register to signify that the line was shorter.

"Yeah," Kyle said, "but I'm getting it to

go. I've got a lot to do."

Brandon's eyebrows shot up. "You're leaving already?"

"Busy day ahead. I have to get the guy who installed the HVAC system in the farmhouse to fix it before the weekend."

"Why rush to have it repaired?" Riley gave him a meaningful grin. "If you like having Lourdes Bennett at your place, you could always have the HVAC guy come on Monday."

Kyle rolled his eyes. "She's not my type."

"What do you mean, she's not your type?" Ted asked. "You said you like her."

"She's probably only twenty-eight or twenty-nine, so I've got a few years on her. And I wouldn't want her kind of life," he explained.

"Maybe she'll retire," Eve said.

Kyle scowled at her. "Are you kidding? She's had a good taste of fame. It's in her blood."

"I can understand why you'd hesitate," Dylan said. "I wouldn't want to be with someone who's in the public eye. Gail and Simon handle it well, but I'm too private. I like being in my own space and not having to travel all the time. And I'd hate it if Cheyenne was always gone."

"I wouldn't like it if Phoenix was gone a

100

lot, either," Riley admitted.

Eve pushed her coffee cup away. "It takes a special kind of person to handle the challenges that come with having your spouse in such demand. You have to be able to share him or her."

"Not an easy thing," Sophia said.

"Then I'm glad we all agree." But whether they agreed or not, after Noelle, Kyle understood his limitations.

He checked his watch. "Great to see everyone. I'd better roll."

"Thanks for giving Noelle that water heater." Olivia spoke before he could walk away. "That was *really* nice of you."

What Noelle had done to get him to marry her had driven a wedge between her and Olivia for years. But last Christmas they'd made inroads toward rebuilding their relationship, and although it must have taken a great deal of patience, understanding and forgiveness on Olivia's part (that was the case with anyone who had to put up with Noelle), they were acting more like sisters now than ever. Kyle was relieved there'd been progress in that area, at least.

"It was nothing," he said, shrugging off her thanks. Although she claimed she'd forgiven him, and he'd been the one left hurting the longest, she had to be thinking he got what he deserved — having to put up with Noelle's shit all the time.

"If you decide to have a Christmas party so we can all come over and meet Lourdes, let us know," Callie joked.

"I don't even have a tree," he said.

Eve beamed up at him. "You've seen my B and B at Christmastime. I can fix that."

"We'll see if the opportunity arises." He loved getting together with his friends on Friday. But ever since Brandon and Olivia had started joining them, that weekly ritual had become a form of torture. So the moment he stepped outside, he took a deep breath, as relieved to get on with his day as he'd been eager to come.

Lourdes was just getting out of the shower when Kyle returned. She hadn't been able to fit everything she'd wanted to bring to California in her suitcase and didn't have a robe with her, so he caught her in nothing but a towel as she walked down the hall to her room. His eyes swept over her, obviously taking note of her near nudity, but he didn't make her feel threatened in any way, or even particularly self-conscious. He acted as if it wasn't any big deal — as if they were roommates and seeing her like this was a common occurrence.

Lourdes didn't know whether to be re-lieved that he respected appropriate bound-aries, or disappointed that he didn't seem compelled to push beyond them. It was a strange reaction on her part — evidence of the state of her self-esteem. Now that she was losing her grip on everything she'd once had, she wanted to be reassured that she still had the ability to attract a handsome man — especially one who didn't care about her fame. There was something stimulating about that alone.

Or maybe she just didn't want to admit that she was attracted to Kyle. She wasn't sure how that could be possible when she was in love with someone else . . .

"Brought you some breakfast." He held up a sack with a logo that said *Black Gold Coffee.* "I'll put it on the counter for when you're dressed."

"That was nice of you." Her eyes were red and swollen again. But she made no excuses, and he pretended not to notice. He under-stood what she was going through. He hadn't told her much about his life when they were talking last night, but he had said he was in love with a woman he'd dated for two years — who was now married to his stepbrother. That had to involve some pain.

"No problem," he said. "I have some bad

news, though. So . . . when you're ready, why don't you come out and we can talk about it."

"Just a sec." She hurried into her room and pulled on the sweats she'd been wearing yesterday. She would've liked to dry her hair; it was dripping down her back. But she was too eager to hear Kyle's bad news so that she could determine if she had a new crisis to worry about. These days she wouldn't be surprised if someone had gone to repair the HVAC in her rental and discovered black mold, which would mean she'd have to find some other safe haven — *without* Derrick's help.

She would've had time to make herself presentable, however. When she found Kyle in the kitchen, he was on a business call.

Instead of going back to dry her hair, she sat down. Besides coping with a great deal of anger, she was so busy vacillating between determination to overcome Derrick's defection and the most debilitating discouragement she'd ever experienced that she didn't have enough energy to obsess over her hair and clothes.

"What's going on?" she asked as soon as he hung up.

He pushed the sack he'd brought home closer to her. "I bought the HVAC unit for the farmhouse from Owen's Heating & Air. I called them not long after they opened this morning, but Owen was already on a big job in Stockton."

"Stockton's what . . . an hour away?"

"That's about right. But he doubts he'll get back before late this evening, and he's taking his wife to Lake Tahoe for the weekend to celebrate her birthday."

Relieved that this was only about getting the furnace fixed and not the house itself, she removed a cardboard cup of coffee from the bag, along with a cheese Danish, a bagel and a blueberry muffin. "Is this all for me?"

"Yeah. I wasn't sure which one you'd like."

"Unfortunately, I like them all." She was sad enough to eat them all, too. If she wasn't careful, she'd gain so much weight while she was here that she wouldn't fit into any of the clothes she wore when she performed.

A little something extra to worry about . . .

"Did you hear what I said about Owen's Heating & Air?" he asked.

"I did. You're telling me I won't have heat until Monday."

"I'm sorry. I could call a few other companies, but even those places will probably tell me it'll be the first of the week before they can get a tech out here. I figure if that's the case, we might as well wait for Owen. He

105

should guarantee his work." He bent his head to peer into her face. "I hope you're not too upset . . ."

She'd probably lost the man she'd expected to spend the rest of her life with and, unless she could come up with a Hail Mary pass, she was looking at the demise of her career. Waiting a couple of days to have heat in her rental seemed like a fairly minor problem by comparison. "I'm not." She felt him watching her while she tried the coffee. "This is good."

"Glad you like it. No one has better coffee than Black Gold. So . . . what do you want to do? Again, I'm happy to pay for a bed-and-breakfast. But you're perfectly welcome to stay here until I get the furnace working."

She didn't care to go anywhere else, wasn't convinced — in her current state — that she'd be able to summon a brave smile for the strangers she might encounter. Besides, the prospect of hanging out at Kyle's place a bit longer didn't sound unpleasant. He had a clean, comfortable house with plenty of room. And, considering her situation with Derrick, it might actually be helpful to have the right kind of company. She didn't want to break down and call Derrick. Last night, during their final conversation, she'd told him not to contact her again unless he passed Crystal on to some other manager. She was afraid she'd be more prone to give in if she was staying on her own. "It's only for the weekend," she said. "As long as you can put up with me, I should be fine."

He seemed surprised. "You'd rather stay here?"

She nodded. "Having someone to talk to last night . . . That helped," she said. "But don't worry. I won't keep crying on your shoulder."

"Did you have the chance to work things out with Derrick?"

"No. But I did what I felt I had to do."

He didn't ask, although she could tell he was wondering, so she said, "I've put everything on hold for now, until he decides how he feels about Crystal."

"He admitted being involved with her?"

"No. He'd *never* admit that. I didn't want to tell you earlier, but . . . he cheated on his wife when he was married. With an intern who works at one of the major record labels."

"He was married?"

"Yes, but it didn't last long." She'd believed him when he'd told her how demanding his wife had been, how he'd been so

107

frustrated and unhappy and how things had unintentionally gotten out of control when that intern had started flirting with him. Now she felt like an idiot. Was it a onetime mistake, as he'd said? Or was he a serial cheater, more to blame for his divorce than he'd ever taken responsibility for?

Kyle had indicated that his marriage hadn't lasted long, either, but he made no mention of that now. "Was it the cheating that broke them up?"

"Who can really say what goes on in a marriage? I only have his side. I can tell you that his ex is still bitter about it, though."

"So you know he's had at least one extramarital affair."

"Yes, and I don't care how many times he swears he's a changed man, *something* is going on. I can feel the difference in him. So unless he's willing to let go of Crystal completely, I can't stay with him."

"I admire you for taking a stand."

"If I was the one he wanted, he'd make it plain. There wouldn't be all this suspicion and angst and heartbreak, right?"

Obviously recognizing the doubt that had crept into her voice, he gave her a kind smile. "I'm sorry."

She felt a familiar lump rise in her throat but fought the tears that went with it. "You understand how it feels, don't you? That it hurts like hell?"

"I do."

"Great. We have heartbreak in common." She laughed humorlessly. "Any chance you could bring home another bottle of wine when you get off work tonight?"

"I can manage that. But will you be okay here alone?"

Did he think she might hurt herself? She hoped not, but she could see why he'd wonder. He didn't know her well enough to determine how she might react to what she was going through. "Of course. I've never been suicidal, if that's what you're worried about."

"Good. Because you have a lot to live for. Remember your new album? It's going to shoot you into the stratosphere. So maybe you should get started on it."

She frowned, implying that she wasn't too sure she could tackle such a big challenge at the moment.

"Working might take your mind off . . . things. Provide an outlet," he went on.

Her feelings were too raw to be able to concentrate. She'd checked her phone before getting in the shower. Derrick hadn't tried to reach her. She'd thought, after the way they'd ended their conversation last night, he'd call first thing this morning to say he'd told Crystal she'd have to find another manager. It was two hours later in Nashville, almost eleven. He had to be up. And yet he hadn't even texted her.

Were they really over? After three years and the hope that they'd soon be *married*?

It was almost inconceivable that so much could change so fast. How could he do this to her, on top of the huge helping of disappointment she'd been served in the past year? He knew what she was dealing with, and yet he didn't seem to care. All he could talk about — when she overheard him talking to others — was how talented Crystal was. It felt as if the whole music industry had turned its attention to Crystal and forgotten about her.

"I'll try," she said, but as soon as Kyle left, she barely cast her guitar a glance before crawling back into bed.

# 6

After a brief hello to Morgan, who updated him on how production was going in the plant, Kyle went straight to his office, closed the door and searched the internet for HVAC companies in the area. Lourdes seemed to be okay with staying at his place for a few more days. He could drop the matter, just wait for Owen to show up next week. But he suspected that wasn't the best or smartest decision. Feeling that the man she loved was passing her over for another woman left Lourdes in a vulnerable position — and considering how his body had reacted when he saw her in that towel, he was in a vulnerable position, too. He didn't want what had started out as a promising friendship to take a wrong turn. But there was always the threat. He'd gone without sex long enough that he was thinking about it too often and at inappropriate times and places. That wouldn't help him maintain much discretion about who he got involved with.

His search engine pulled up quite a few heating and air-conditioning companies. Most were in Stockton, Modesto, Sacramento or the Bay Area. But he called several, despite the distance. By offering a bonus to compensate for the short notice, he figured he *might* convince someone to handle the job right away. The storm had already passed, so it wasn't as if they'd have particularly bad weather to contend with.

After several tries, he reached a woman who said she'd send out a repairman. Feeling encouraged that his life would soon be back to normal, he clicked away from the list of HVAC companies and began to search various websites for information on how to legally perform a wedding in Amador County. He hadn't even finished learning all he needed to know, however, when the receptionist for A Better HVAC Company called back to say she couldn't arrange for a tech to drive over to Whiskey Creek, after all.

So he'd simply leave Lourdes on her own at night, he decided as he ended the call. There was no need to get any closer to her. She'd come to Whiskey Creek to be alone and to concentrate on her work. Besides, it'd been ages since he'd gone out for a drink.

But where would he go? Noelle worked at the only bar in town, so he couldn't go there — not if he planned on enjoying himself. And if he went elsewhere, he wouldn't know anyone.

The vision of Lourdes in that towel popped into his mind again. So he grabbed the phone on his desk and called Riley, who answered on the first ring. "Hey, man, what's going on?"

"I've submitted my application to be ordained an American Marriage Minister," Kyle announced.

"You have to become a *minister*? That isn't what I understood."

"It's in name only. Says on the website that I don't need any prior education or experience, and I can be of any belief or background. I don't even have to register with the state. There seems to be one hard-and-fast rule — I have to be over eighteen."

"It's been a while since either of us has seen eighteen, so we're good there," he said wryly. "How much will it cost?"

"Nothing, and it never expires. They only charge for extra documents. There was a link that showed how to fill out a marriage license, so it can be recorded afterward. Easy."

"That's a relief. You won't be nervous?"

"Why would I be nervous?" he said. He didn't see any point in causing Riley to worry, but of course he'd be nervous. He'd never performed a marriage ceremony before and wouldn't want to screw up Riley and Phoenix's wedding, especially since it had taken them both so long to find happiness. Their son was a senior in high school, and they were only now getting together.

His mind reverted to Lourdes and his current dilemma. "What are you doing tonight?" he asked.

"Phoenix and I are taking her mother out to see the Christmas lights."

"Lizzie Fuller is leaving her trailer?" That was guaranteed to be an epic event. Phoenix's mom was a severely obese woman who'd refused to be seen in public for years and years.

"She's not too happy about it, but with Phoenix cooking for her, she's lost some weight. And we've hired a limo, which should be big enough to fit her. She has to get out of that damn trailer once in a while or she won't be able to handle the wedding. And despite all her bluster, she doesn't want to miss seeing her daughter say I do, even if it is to me."

Kyle chuckled. It wasn't just Riley that Lizzie didn't like. She didn't like anyone, including herself. "Sounds like an important evening. Good thing the weather's cleared."

"That storm was kind of a joke, anyway. And they had us all so worried — 'worst storm in twenty years' and all that."

"It's been plenty cold."

"True, but even if it starts to snow again, we'll probably still try to get Lizzie out. If we're hoping to help her feel safe in public so she'll come to the wedding, we don't have a lot of time left."

And here he'd just wanted to go out for a drink — trivial by comparison. "Will Phoenix's brothers be at the wedding?"

"Yes. I have to pay their travel expenses. But don't tell Phoenix. I'm afraid it might tarnish her excitement about the fact that they agreed to come."

"I won't say a word."

"What are your plans tonight? You could join us."

He'd clued in to the primary reason Kyle had called. They used to go out on weekends all the time — before Phoenix came back into Riley's life. "That's okay. I just wanted to let you know I've got my ministerial duties under control. You can check that off your list."

"I appreciate it. With her family being so dysfunctional, we've got our hands full."

"I'm sure."

"Thanks for being part of everything."

"Happy to do it."

Kyle sighed as he hung up. He supposed he could go over to his parents' house — or Ted and Sophia's, Cheyenne and Dylan's or any of his other friends. But his parents wouldn't be up to much, and most of his friends had children or were pregnant. Callie had had a liver transplant before she married Levi, so her pregnancy was high-risk. She had to be careful to take her meds and get plenty of rest.

Bottom line, he didn't want to spend his Friday night watching TV for a few hours and then go to bed early. That wouldn't do much to distract him from the beautiful woman staying at his house.

His cell phone rang. He hoped it wasn't Noelle, calling to thank him for the water heater. That would be like her. She used any excuse to contact him, even though he didn't need her thanks. He needed some space. From her.

It wasn't Noelle, thank God. But it was Brandon. Kyle wasn't sure that was any better. Since Lourdes had arrived, the whole issue of Olivia had been pushed into the forefront of his brain — and suddenly he wasn't dealing with it as effectively as he had for the past several years.

It felt so damn fresh . . .

But it wasn't, he reminded himself. And this was his stepbrother, someone he loved. So he answered. " 'Lo?"

"Hey, glad I caught you."

"What's going on?"

"I was wondering if you might have a few minutes this afternoon. I'd like to talk to you. I could swing by your office."

Kyle sat up straighter. Talk to him about what? They'd seen each other at Black Gold this morning. Brandon could've mentioned anything he had to say then. Unless it was private. But what did he need to convey that he couldn't bring up in front of their friends?

Was he finally going to confront Kyle about Olivia?

Closing his eyes, Kyle rested his head on the back of his chair. If that was Brandon's intent, he supposed he had it coming. But what could he do? He wasn't holding on to those old feelings on purpose. "Sure. I'll be here all afternoon. Feel free to swing by whenever it's convenient."

"Will do," he said. Then Kyle began

watching the clock, wondering how, exactly, Brandon would approach The Olivia Issue — and what he'd suggest they do about it.

Someone was in the house; Kyle must be home.

Lourdes hadn't intended to sleep all day, but when she heard the noise in the kitchen, she opened her eyes to discover that it was dark outside. Apparently, she'd been out for a number of hours — so why did she still feel so utterly *drained*?

"Buck up," she muttered to motivate herself. But the brief flutter of strength those two words gave her was crushed beneath the thought of Derrick.

Had he tried to call?

She reached for her phone to check.

There were no texts from him. No calls, either.

Her heart sank. He'd given her up that easily? He'd chosen Crystal?

Wincing at the pain that slammed into her, she curled into a ball. Rejection happened. Heartbreak happened. Setbacks happened. She wasn't alone, and she had the same choices as anyone else. She had to overcome her challenges, despite how daunting they seemed.

She could start by getting out of bed.

*In a minute,* she told herself and burrowed back under the covers — until the smell drifting into her room encouraged her to sit up. Kyle must've brought dinner. It was turning out to be a really good thing that she'd had to stay with him. If she'd been in the rental, she'd be going without, because she sure as heck didn't feel like driving into town. If she couldn't even make herself comb her hair or put on makeup, she wasn't likely to do much else.

With the promise of food as motivation, she dragged herself out of bed. She had to stand still for a few seconds to regain her equilibrium, then shoved a hand through her hair to straighten out some of the tangles. "Smells delicious out here. What'd you bring?" she asked with a yawn as she shuffled down the hall.

She reached the kitchen a second later only to discover that it wasn't Kyle at all. Some woman, who seemed to be about her age, was in front of the stove. She'd been putting various dishes in the oven, but now she just stood there, gaping at Lourdes. "Who are *you?*"

Lourdes didn't have to answer that question very often. These days, most people recognized her. But she knew that at the moment, she didn't look much like her pictures. "I'm . . . I'm Kyle's tenant," she said, hoping to avoid full disclosure and all the exclamations that would go with it. "Who are you?"

"I'm his ex-wife."

Kyle had led Lourdes to believe things were over between him and his ex. So what was she doing bringing him dinner? Especially a dinner for which she'd obviously gone to a lot of work?

The woman's eyes narrowed as if she wasn't too keen on finding a possible "rival" in Kyle's house. "Did you just roll out of bed?"

"I did."

"But . . . if you're renting the farmhouse, what are you doing here?"

"The furnace is broken over there."

Seemingly mollified, she put another dish in the oven and closed the door. "Oh. So . . . where's your husband? You must be married to the guy who came from Nashville, right?"

Lourdes didn't intend to explain what'd happened to that *guy*. "No, I'm the only one who came."

She scowled. "Kyle didn't tell me he rented to a woman. I wonder why —" Her words fell off the instant recognition dawned. The mention of Nashville had obviously sparked a — albeit delayed — connection.

"Oh, my God! You're Lourdes Bennett, the country star! I hear your songs all the time where I work. At Sexy Sadie's." She added the name as though Lourdes should recognize the place.

"I take it that's a honky-tonk of some sort?"

"Yes, the only bar in town."

That explained what she was wearing. With a low-cut top and a short skirt, it was a server's uniform of the more risqué variety. "You must be on your way there now."

"I am. And I can't be late, or I'll be fired. My manager is such a douche."

For expecting her to show up on time? Lourdes didn't bother to comment. "So you don't have a date with Kyle . . ."

"No, not tonight," she said. "I've got to work, or . . . or we'd probably do something."

*Really?* Kyle hadn't acted as if he had any plans with his ex — or second thoughts about her. "Does Kyle know you're here?"

"No. I wanted to surprise him. And instead . . . look at you! I'm the one who's surprised. Wait until I tell everyone at work that we have another celebrity in Whiskey Creek, and that you're staying for a few *months.* Simon O'Neal comes here at least three times a year, but he never stays long. Why would he, when he has half a dozen dream homes all over the world? If that was me, I'd *never* come here."

Lourdes raised one hand. "You said you were going to tell everyone at the bar about me. But please don't. I . . . I'm here to work."

"Are you putting on a show? *Where?*"

"No, I mean I'm going to be writing songs for my next album and I'd rather not be disturbed."

"Oh." She didn't seem nearly as excited about that idea.

"What did you say your name was?" Lourdes asked.

"Noelle. Noelle Houseman."

"I'm sure Kyle will appreciate the food, Noelle."

Kyle's ex eyed what she'd created with satisfaction. "It's all his favorites."

"That's . . . nice of you."

"Thanks." Intent on making everything perfect, she went back to her preparations. "I have to go," she said a few minutes later. "But I'm leaving the lemon chicken and the baked beans with pineapple in the oven on warm, so remind him to take those out when he gets home. The heat won't hurt the beans, but I'd hate for the chicken to dry out."

"Will do," Lourdes said.

After taking a final look, Noelle hurried to the door, where she turned back at the last second. "Oh, and if he asks, will you say you let me in?"

Lourdes felt her eyebrows go up. She'd assumed the door had been unlocked. "Um . . . since I'm here, he probably won't ask."

"Good point." She hesitated again. "I can't believe Lourdes Bennett is renting the farmhouse," she said. "Wow. I'm going to kill Kyle for not telling me! Wait until I get a hold of him!"

"It's my fault he didn't tell you. I asked him not to."

"Oh. Gotcha. Well, when I come back, can I get a picture with you?"

Hadn't Noelle been listening to what she'd just said? "Are you coming *tonight*?"

"No, I work late. But how about tomorrow?"

Lourdes hoped she wouldn't come back *ever.* "Sure. Provided I'm . . . prepared for company, of course."

Noelle's gaze ranged over her. "What's wrong? You sick?"

"Sort of." Breathing a sigh of relief when

the door closed, she walked over to the note Noelle had propped against the bottle of wine she'd placed in the center of the table.

Lourdes knew she had no business reading it. It was for Kyle. But there was something about Noelle's visit that didn't feel right, and that made Lourdes curious. Was Kyle still seeing her or not?

She slid the small card out of its envelope. *Thanks for helping me yesterday. It's marvelous to have hot water again. I owe you — and I'd be happy to pay up. XOXO*

Her phone, which she'd left in the bedroom, rang, and Lourdes stuffed the card back in its envelope so she could go answer. She thought maybe she was finally hearing from Derrick. But it wasn't him. Her mother was trying to reach her — no doubt to make certain that Lourdes had arrived safely in California.

Lourdes sank onto the bed as she held her phone and stared at the incoming call. Her mother wasn't pleased that she'd decided to leave Tennessee right before Christmas. "You'll be back for the holidays, won't you?" She'd asked that at least half a dozen times before they got to the airport.

Lourdes didn't want to go back for Christmas. She didn't even want to *have* Christmas. She was pretty sure this was going to be the worst holiday of her life.

The call transferred to her voice mail — and Lourdes couldn't make herself call back.

Brandon showed up as Kyle was getting ready to leave for the day. With Lourdes at his place, probably needing a meal, since he hadn't bought any more groceries yet, he felt he couldn't stay late.

"*There* you are," he said when Brandon rapped on the open door before strolling into his office. "I thought you'd changed your mind about coming over."

His stepbrother closed the door. "No, I didn't want to interrupt your work, and I figured you'd be winding things up about now."

"I am. Your timing's excellent." Except that he'd had to spend the whole day wondering what the hell Brandon planned to talk to him about. "Want to sit down?"

"Sure." He collapsed into one of the two chairs across from Kyle's desk.

"Everything okay?" Kyle asked.

His stepbrother crossed one leg over the other, then switched them. "This is going to be an awkward conversation, but I care enough about you that I want to have it."

That lead-in did nothing to put Kyle at

ease. "Go on . . ."

"We haven't always gotten along, but . . . I've come to look up to you. No matter what happened or didn't happen in the past, I know in my heart that you're a good man."

Kyle might've been flattered. Brandon didn't talk this way very often. They'd just moved on without addressing the past, since there wasn't a whole lot anyone could say that would change the situation or make it any better. But *I've come to look up to you* felt like a setup. "I'm almost afraid to thank you, because I can tell something else is coming."

"As you've probably guessed, this is about Olivia."

Kyle's stomach tensed. "What about her?"

"Frankly, I feel bad being with the woman you want. And that's gotten harder and harder the more I care about you. The weird thing is . . . I thought we were getting past it."

"We were," Kyle said. "I mean, we *are*."

"No." Brandon shook his head. "Lately, things seemed to have reversed. I get the feeling the past is coming between us again, and I'd like to stop it."

"The past *isn't* coming between us. Nothing can come between us. And just so you know, I'm being honest when I say that I would never hope for you and Olivia to break up. It's not as if I'm sitting over here, greedily rubbing my hands and hoping that someday I'll have another chance with her. I've always wanted to tell you that. I'm glad you're happy together. You deserve each other. For the record, I'd do anything I could to keep either one of you from ever getting hurt."

Brandon pursed his lips as he formed a steeple with his fingers. "That's just it. I don't doubt that. I believe you'd rather see me happy, even if it means you live without. And that only makes the situation harder."

"You're overthinking it," Kyle said. "Stop worrying."

Brandon got to his feet. "I can't help it. You got a bum deal with everything that happened. I'm still shocked that you stepped up and married Noelle. I told you at the time it was foolish, but . . . it was also noble. That's the part I never mentioned until now. I've secretly admired you for it."

Kyle stood, too. "Don't feel sorry for me, Bran. That just makes it worse. I brought what happened on myself, as you well know."

"You made a mistake, one that's somewhat understandable. You and Olivia weren't even together at the time, not technically."

"Doesn't matter. I slept with her sister."

"You were angry with Olivia. And her sister purposely seduced you when you were drunk. Those two things together did you in."

"Maybe. But there are consequences to actions, and I'm prepared to live with mine."

Brandon grimaced as if he wasn't willing to settle for that response. "But your 'punishment,' if you want to call it that, should've ended with the divorce. Being married to Noelle was bad enough."

Kyle smiled. If only he knew how bad it really was. "She's definitely a trial. But I'm fine."

"You're sure?" He shoved his hands in his pockets. "Because Mom tells me you're struggling. She says that every time she invites you over for dinner, you ask if Olivia and I will be there, and if the answer is yes, you come up with some lame excuse."

Had he been so obvious? "Your mother told you that?"

"For the record, she considers herself *your* mother, too."

"Then why would she try to cause trouble between us?"

"That wasn't her intent. She's worried. Wants me to do something to stop what's happening."

So here he was . . .

"Is it true?" Brandon demanded.

Kyle rubbed his neck. "I'm trying to figure out where I want my life to go from here, that's all."

"That's what I was afraid of."

"Look, it's not *your* problem. I don't want it to affect you. Or Olivia."

"It can't help but affect us! Especially because what I have to tell you won't make your situation any easier."

"And that is . . ."

He leaned forward, resting his knuckles on the other side of the desk. "Kyle, you remember how hard it was on Olivia when she miscarried last February."

"Of course."

"She was afraid to get pregnant again for fear the same thing would happen. But I wanted you to be the first to know that . . . we're expecting."

Kyle forced what he hoped was a believable smile, just as he'd been doing since Brandon and Olivia's wedding. "That's wonderful. I'm thrilled for both of you."

*"Really?"*

Resisting the jealousy he'd been battling for so long, Kyle came around to slap his stepbrother on the back. "Yes, really. And I hope the pregnancy goes well this time."

"I'm sorry I was such a competitive asshole when we were younger, Kyle. I don't think I've ever told you that."

"I wasn't any nicer to you."

"True," Brandon teased, and Kyle chuckled.

"Thanks for dropping by," Kyle said. "I appreciate it."

"I'm glad we had this talk."

"So am I."

Brandon pulled his keys from his pocket. "So are you coming this Sunday?"

"Where?"

"To Mom and Dad's. Don't play dumb. Mom invited you, too."

"Oh, right," he said. "I remember now." He was about to offer his regrets. He hadn't planned on going, not in his current frame of mind. But that would only add fuel to what Brandon was already feeling, and Kyle didn't want to drift apart now that they'd finally found each other as brothers. "That's *this* Sunday?"

"Day after tomorrow," Brandon replied. "We're family, Olivia and I. Don't try to avoid us."

Kyle swallowed a sigh. "I'm not trying to avoid you," he said. "I'll be there."

# 7

When Kyle first saw that dinner was on the table, he thought Lourdes must've picked up groceries in her rental car and cooked. That was a pleasant surprise, far more than he'd expected. But when she came out of her bedroom, he could tell she hadn't even combed her hair today, so he doubted she was responsible for the meal.

Then he saw the note on the table. He'd just set down the wine he'd brought home and was reaching for it when she said, "Your ex stopped by."

"My ex?" he said. *Why?*

Lourdes shrugged. "According to what she wrote on that note, she feels she owes you something."

He turned to face her. "You read what she wrote?"

She looked at him with a sheepish expression. "She's an interesting person. Definitely aroused my curiosity."

131

"She's obsessive. I can't escape her."

"You're saying you have a small-town stalker?"

"It's beginning to feel that way."

"Then you might want to get your house key from her."

Kyle frowned. "What are you talking about? She doesn't have a key to my house."

"She let herself in somehow," Lourdes said. "I was in my bedroom when I heard her out here, arranging all this stuff."

Anger shot through him like a bullet. "Are you kidding me?"

"No. She asked me to say that *I* let her in, but I owe you more loyalty than I do her."

"Where could she have gotten a key?" He said this more to himself than he did her. He was searching his memory for any time he might've given Noelle one, but he couldn't recall even speaking with her about it.

"She lived here when you were married, didn't she?" Lourdes said. "You gave me that impression when we were talking the other night."

"It was a different house, but . . . I kept all the spare keys in a drawer."

"She must've helped herself."

"I should've had the locks changed on everything. But her uncle's the locksmith in town. I didn't want her family to think I was suggesting she was dangerous. She was already upset that I'd made her sign a prenup before we got married, and she didn't get half my assets. I was trying to keep the breakup as amicable as I could. So I just insisted she return the key for the house we lived in together."

"She probably had a copy made of that one, too."

He wouldn't put it past her. And yet he'd thought she was as eager to get rid of him as he was her. They'd fought so much during their short marriage; she'd called him names he wouldn't have called his worst enemy. But considering how she'd behaved since, as if she was hoping to reconcile, maybe she *had* hung on to various keys.

How many times had she let herself into his house and gone through his things?

He hated to contemplate the answer to that question. "I'm changing the locks."

"That should solve the problem." She frowned at the dinner table. "Thank goodness there'll be no more meals appearing out of nowhere!"

He could tell she was being facetious. But when he looked more closely, he noticed the blush on her cheeks and the glassiness of her eyes and decided she was also a little drunk. "Did you break into the wine?"

"I didn't think you'd mind, since you promised to bring more. It helps to focus on something other than my own misery."

"Like alcohol? What happened after I left? Did you hear from Derrick?"

Tears filled her eyes as she shook her head.

"It's his loss, Lourdes."

She blinked quickly. "Right. That's what I'm supposed to tell myself."

"In this case, I'm convinced it's true. You seem like a really nice person."

"So do you. You obviously *are* a nice person — taking me in."

"Don't give me too much credit. I was supposed to have that rental ready for occupancy, wasn't I?"

She cleared her throat, somehow managing to avert her tears. "You tried. But . . . tell me this. Do you wish I wasn't here?"

He remembered how hard he'd searched for a contractor to get the heating unit fixed so she could leave. But it wasn't because she was *bothering* him. "Not at all," he said.

"You're sure?"

"Positive." He rested his hands on the back of a kitchen chair. "Did Noelle recognize you when she saw you?"

"Not at first. Eventually."

"I bet she flipped out."

"She said she couldn't wait to tell everyone at work. I guess she's a server at some
honky-tonk where they play my music?"

"Sexy Sadie's."

"I asked her not to mention my being in
town to anyone."

"That won't change anything. I hate to
say this, but you should brace yourself.
She'll spread the news all over town."

Lourdes covered her face, rubbed her eyes
and then dropped her hands. "Just what I
need. Everyone wants to be gawked at when
they're at their most vulnerable."

"I won't let that happen," he said. "You'll
be fine as long as you're here."

"And when I move back to the farmhouse?"

There wasn't much he'd be able to do
then. He'd be her neighbor, but he wouldn't
be next door. "We'll figure something out."

Lourdes jerked her head toward the note
he'd tossed aside. "What'd you do to help
Noelle?"

"Gave her a used water heater."

"That's romantic."

He grinned at her sarcasm. "It wasn't
meant to be."

"So she believes what she wants to believe."

"She looks for any reason to bug me. And

135

this has been going on since the divorce. She'll make a concerted effort, I won't respond, and she'll give up. Until she decides to try again. Sometimes I'll catch a break when she starts seeing someone else. But when the relationship fails — and they always do — she gets lonely, and the next thing I know, she's set her sights on me all over again."

"Because there's no one else in *your* life," Lourdes pointed out. "She doesn't see why it can't be her, especially since it was before."

He shrugged. "There's not much I can do about that."

"Maybe not. But you could quit giving her things, even water heaters, if you really want her to leave you alone."

"Trust me, I've tried. She drives me so crazy, I finally give in just to get rid of her."

"This isn't an accusation — and I'm not digging for information — but . . . if you're still sleeping with her, you may never get rid of her."

He stood up straight. "I'm not sleeping with her!"

"Well, she's offering." She gestured at the food. "That's what this means."

"I'm not interested."

"How long has it been?"

"Since we slept together?"

She nodded.

"Before the divorce."

"Has there been anyone since — for you?"

He nearly laughed. "Are you asking me the last time I've had sex?"

She waved a hand. "Sorry. You don't have to answer that. My curiosity's getting the better of me again."

Curiosity and too much alcohol. But Lourdes didn't live in Whiskey Creek and wouldn't be staying long — certainly not long enough to encounter many people in town. So he didn't have to be guarded with her. "A little over three years," he said.

She rubbed her palms on her sweats. "Wow. It's only been a month for me, and even *that* feels like forever."

"You haven't been with Derrick in a month?"

"We've been having problems. What's your excuse?"

"I live in a small town. That doesn't present a lot of sexual options, if you know what I mean. Out here, a relationship has to be serious before it gets . . . serious."

"And there's that old flame who's standing in the way. What's her name?"

He wished he'd never mentioned Olivia. Maybe if he stopped acknowledging how he felt about her — even to himself — he'd stop missing her, wanting her. "There's no one else."

"I'm talking about the one who's married to your stepbrother," she said.

"I know. Let's forget about her."

"Sure. No problem. And I understand what you're saying about options. I come from a small town, too, remember? Angel's Camp isn't all that different from Whiskey Creek. But three years . . ." She whistled. "Go to a bigger place every once in a while, why don't you?"

"Maybe if I were in my twenties, I would. At thirty-eight? Don't you think going out just to get laid would be a little . . . shallow?"

"Yeah. Don't listen to me," she said. "I'm drunk."

"Precisely why I'm not taking anything you say to heart. Besides, it's not only because of Olivia that I don't do more about that area of my life. I don't like putting myself in uncomfortable situations."

She wrinkled her nose. "Sex makes you uncomfortable? I wouldn't have guessed that."

He rolled his eyes. "No. It's *expectations* that make me uncomfortable, and nothing creates expectations like sex. The last girl I was with — in that way —"

"Three years ago," she broke in.

"Yes. We've established that."

She shook her head. "It's just hard to believe."

He ignored that. "Anyway, this woman tattooed my name on her arm after we'd been seeing each other for only two weeks."

"You must be *good,*" she said with a laugh.

"She couldn't have been all there."

Lourdes made a clicking sound with her tongue. "You seem to bring out the crazy in a woman."

"Fortunately there's no danger of bringing out the crazy in you."

"True." She grimaced. "Derrick's already done that."

Although he wasn't pleased that Noelle had gone inside his house when he wasn't home, he *was* hungry, and the food smelled good . . .

"There's lemon chicken in the oven," Lourdes said when she noticed that his attention had shifted to the food.

"I love lemon chicken."

"She made all your favorites."

That softened the blow of knowing she had access to his house, as it was probably intended to do, since Noelle hadn't gone to any great pains to hide it. How would she have explained being able to get the food inside had Lourdes not been staying with him?

She'd say he'd forgotten to lock the door, which he occasionally did, since he worked close by and there was so little crime in the area. "I should package this up and drop it off at her place," he said. "Eating it will only encourage her to do this again."

"But it saves you from cooking, doesn't it? And maybe she'll just think you're even. You helped her, and she repaid you."

"That's a positive way to look at it."

"We shouldn't let this go to waste."

She was hungry — and so was he. "You have a point," he said. "I rarely get any home cooking these days." And he got even less now that he was avoiding Sunday dinners with his family. "Should we dive in?"

She rounded the table and pulled out a chair. "I was afraid you'd never ask."

He chuckled. "You read a private note and nearly polished off the wine, but you didn't feel you could eat without me?"

"I didn't want to go too far," she said with an impish grin.

She was cute in spite of her dishevelment. Derrick had to be a fool, Kyle thought as he got the lemon chicken out of the oven. Lourdes had said Derrick was forty. What could twenty-three-year-old Crystal possibly have to say that he'd find interesting?

"Do you have any plans tonight?" she asked.

He'd hoped to go out and do something, even if he had to do it alone. He hesitated to spend too much time with Lourdes. But she didn't seem to be in the best shape . . .

"No, I'll stay here and drink with you."

"Great," she said. "Pour me another glass."

By ten, they were *both* drunk. And laughing. Kyle wasn't sure why everything seemed to be so funny, but he hadn't let go like this in ages. They challenged each other to card games like Speed and War. They played beer pong. They even competed in feats of strength, including arm wrestling, which she'd insisted, for some strange reason, that she could win, which was laughable, since she couldn't even put up much of a fight. Kyle couldn't remember when, exactly, they'd put on a movie, but when he woke up, it was almost three in the morning, they were lying on the floor with a pillow and a blanket — and Lourdes was asleep on his shoulder.

He felt a jolt of panic when he found her in his arms — until he realized they were still dressed.

"Hey," Kyle said, waking her. "It's late. We'd better get to bed."

When she looked up at him, he felt an unexpected tenderness. For someone so famous, she wasn't remotely arrogant. And, even though her hair was a mess and he hadn't seen her in anything more stylish than her baggy sweats, he found her no less attractive than when she'd gotten out of her rental car that first day.

"What'd you say?" she murmured, still half-asleep.

"I said we'd better get into our beds."

She lifted her head to look at the TV, which was playing an infomercial on some diet drug. "Did Derrick call?"

"I don't know," Kyle replied. "I don't think you've checked your phone."

"Well, that's saying something," she said. "I can probably make it through the next few months — when our breakup hits the tabloids and pictures of him and Crystal begin to show up — if I continue to soak my brain in alcohol."

He assumed she was joking. "I doubt that's the direction you want to go."

"What are the drawbacks again?"

Now he *knew* she was joking, but he answered as though she'd asked a serious question. "You're planning to write an album. Being drunk would interfere with that. Besides, there'd be no sweeter revenge than reclaiming your success — without him."

This elicited a thoughtful expression. "True. I'd love nothing more. But losing him will make my comeback that much harder. I'll have to find a new manager, and it's easier to find a new manager when you're on the rise. No one who's any good will be excited about taking me on at this point."

"Never assume rejection. Anyway, it's the weekend. Use the next two days to get back on your feet, then make some calls on Monday."

She pulled her phone from her pocket and squinted at it. "He hasn't tried to contact me. I can't believe it."

*Kyle* couldn't believe she hadn't moved out of reach. They were cuddled up as if . . . as if they knew each other a lot better than they did. "Maybe he's taking some time to make a decision."

"If he has to think that hard about whether or not he wants me, I don't want him."

He smoothed her hair off her face. "You don't need him."

She didn't respond. He almost said they

143

should turn in for the night, but he'd made that suggestion once, and she hadn't acted on it. He got the feeling she needed to be held.

"Why couldn't I have fallen for a nice guy like you?" she asked.

He felt his groin tighten. The way she was staring at him, it was almost as though she was asking him to kiss her. But he had to be wrong about that. Even if he *was* right, he knew it would make their situation awkward tomorrow. "Because you'd never be happy in a small town like this," he replied. "You're meant for bigger things."

"The next year will be lonely . . ."

Was she hoping he could change that? He could feel the sudden tension between them, knew what it meant. And the skin on her neck tempted him. "But your heart will heal eventually," he said. "And you'll meet someone else."

"You mean I'll get over him like you've gotten over Olivia?"

She had him there.

"Are you even dating?" she asked.

"I go out every now and then."

"You can't be dating often if you haven't slept with anyone in three years."

"I haven't met the right woman."

"Maybe you need to *look* for her." She

grinned. "Have you ever thought of that?"

At the moment he couldn't think of anything except the attraction he felt to *her.* "I've been busy."

"That's an excuse. Not a reason."

He couldn't fault her logic. So he said nothing, and they continued to stare at each other, almost as if they were held in suspended animation.

"Never mind," she said at length, turning away. "I don't want to give you a hard time. It's wonderful to have found a friend here. I thought I wanted to be alone to work, but now I realize just how terrible being alone would be at this stage of my life. So thank you."

A *friend* here . . . Was she trying to tell him something? That what her body wanted and what her head wanted were two different things? He didn't plan to take advantage of the conflict, would hate to make her situation any worse. "It's not as if you're hard to put up with."

She pulled far enough away to lean on one elbow. "I'm going to do you a favor," she announced.

His hands now free, he covered a yawn. "What's that?"

"Before I leave, I'm going to find you the perfect woman. I'll make sure you forget about Olivia."

Since nothing he'd tried had worked, he wasn't convinced it was possible. "Knock yourself out," he said. But he had no idea where that simple exchange would lead — until the following morning.

# 8

"Can I get a good picture of you?"

Kyle was surprised to find Lourdes already up and in the kitchen. They hadn't gotten much sleep, and it was barely ten. He could've understood why she might not have been able to sleep if she'd been crying again. But he saw no evidence of that. She looked . . . better. She'd even showered and was wearing a pale blue sweat suit that fit far more snugly than the less-appealing sweats of before.

"Why do you need a picture of me?" He opened his empty refrigerator and gazed in. He was hoping that, somehow, miraculously, a jug of orange juice had appeared — maybe when Noelle had come over to drop off dinner. Orange juice was a favorite of his, too, wasn't it?

"We don't have any groceries to speak of," Lourdes said. "I checked. Unless you want to eat leftover lemon chicken and rice pilaf for breakfast, you're going to have to go to the store."

He should've done that last night and would have, if Noelle hadn't surprised him with dinner. He'd brought the wine from work — a gift one of his vendors had sent him for Christmas — and stopped by to see what Lourdes wanted to eat. But with food on the table, going out again hadn't been necessary. "For both of us?"

"I'll contribute to the cost. The shopping is on you. I don't want to be seen, remember?"

He winced against the hangover that had asserted itself the moment he opened his eyes. "Don't worry about paying for groceries. It's the least I can do to compensate you for the inconvenience of having to move in here. But how can you talk so loudly? Isn't your head killing you?"

"Fortunately, I had some ibuprofen in my purse, because there doesn't seem to be any painkiller in your cupboards."

"I doubt I've ever bought any. I can't remember the last time I needed it."

"Well, I can tell you need it now. And, after last night, I guessed you might wake up feeling a bit off, so I set a glass and two tablets on the counter for you right there." She indicated the spot before going back to whatever she was doing on her computer.

It was thoughtful of her to anticipate his need . . .

"So . . . is this a good sign?" he asked after he'd swallowed them. "Is this you getting back to work?"

"No, this is me fulfilling my promise to *you*. Since we only have three months, I thought I'd better get started. Plus, it gave me a reason to get out of bed this morning."

"There's always that album you have to write."

"Stop reminding me," she grumbled. "You're only adding to the pressure."

He definitely didn't want to do that . . . "I take it you haven't heard from Derrick."

"Actually, I have. He texted me at six this morning to say I'm being unreasonable."

Which brought up the question — what was Derrick doing last night? Lourdes didn't volunteer that she had any concerns on the subject, so he didn't mention it. Kyle did wonder, however, if that brief message from Derrick would be enough to change the situation. Maybe she wouldn't stay. Maybe she'd go back to Nashville to fight for her man. "And you responded . . . how?"

"I haven't. I figure if he can let me stew for a day, I should have the same privilege."

He smiled at her. "You're talking tough this morning."

She pinched her bottom lip with her fingers as she studied something on her screen. "I'm distracting myself from the pain."

"By doing *me* a favor."

"No one can write a more appealing solicitation for a dating site than I can."

He slammed his water glass down on the counter and hurried around to the table. "Oh, no," he said. "You're not . . ."

She seemed taken aback by his displeasure. "What's wrong? There won't be a woman on Single Central who wouldn't want to respond to *this* ad."

"I don't do online dating."

"Obviously — because you're not doing *any* dating. We established that last night."

He read through what she'd written so far. "I look like Dierks Bentley? No, I don't. Come on, don't put that up."

She scowled at him. "How are you ever going to get over Olivia if you won't even try?"

"It's not that I won't date. It's just that online dating seems so . . . desperate. Especially once you reach my age."

"It's not desperate, it's practical. Especially for someone with such a limited dating pool."

"Lourdes, no."

"Don't resist the very thing you need!" she argued. "You never know who you might meet. And don't worry. I'll help you vet the women who respond. I'll make it easy."

"If you think it's so easy, why don't you create a profile for yourself, too?" He figured that would put a quick end to it.

"I can't," she said. "And you know why. Besides the reaction it would cause in the media, and the gold diggers who'd step forward, I'm in love with someone else. That makes me emotionally unavailable."

He opened his mouth, but she spoke before he could.

"The person you love has been married to your brother for nearly five years. You have to release her. It's time."

"But I can't afford to get together with another woman like Noelle — someone who might be completely narcissistic and obsessive!"

She tapped her fingernails on the table as she considered this latest objection. "Granted, there're a few horror stories connected to online dating. But there are also a lot of people who meet this way and end up living happily-ever-after. We'll be able to spot the undesirables and weed them out."

"It's not that simple. If undesirables were that obvious, they wouldn't continually screw up the lives of innocent bystanders."

"If you look for the right qualities, it isn't hard," she told him. "You can't let yourself be blinded by a pretty face, or a nice set of . . . well, you know."

"You think I'm that easily distracted?"

"You're a guy, aren't you?"

"That's a stereotype if ever I heard one."

"Stereotypes are stereotypes for a reason. I saw the way you were nearly salivating when I was in that towel."

*"Salivating?"*

"Okay, it was only a glimmer in your eye, but it was enough to tell me that it's been too long since you were with a woman. And that leads me to believe you might be susceptible to getting caught up in the physical." She seemed to rethink her words. "Now that I mention it, maybe we should work on getting you laid first. Bringing your drought to an end would remind you of what you're missing and make you more eager to find someone — so eager that you'll reach beyond your usual prejudices and boundaries."

"Those aren't prejudices and boundaries. They're standards, for your information.

You're going to have to think of some way to forget your problems other than by solving mine."

"Why?" she asked. "I feel we're friends. I'd like you to be happier for having met me."

"I am. I have a lot to be grateful for. I'm satisfied with my life."

She tucked her hair behind her ears. "But you can't be *completely* satisfied, not without Olivia."

"Olivia's with my stepbrother now. He just told me that they're expecting their first child. I would never want anything to hurt their family."

"Which is why you have to give up on her." Twisting around in her seat, she rested an arm on the back of her chair while he searched for his keys. "Can you tell me why?"

He found them under some mail he had yet to sort through. "Why what?"

"What made you do it? What made you crawl into bed with Olivia's sister?"

His friends had asked him the same thing a hundred times. There wasn't a good explanation. He'd probably never have an adequate answer. It was almost as if he'd purposely driven into a brick wall. "I told you. Olivia and I were on a break. And I was drunk when Noelle approached me."

"You were drunk last night, too, and yet you behaved like the perfect gentleman."

In spite of what he'd been feeling. So she recognized that. But he was older and wiser these days, more aware of the consequences. "It's hard to explain. I was ready to marry Olivia when she moved to Sacramento to establish her business. The fact that she left in spite of my proposal told me I didn't mean nearly as much to her as she meant to me."

Lourdes toyed with the zipper on her sweatshirt. "Maybe she wasn't ready to settle down."

"To my mind, she should've been ready. It wasn't as if we were just out of college. In retrospect, I can see that I should've backed away and given her some time. She'd been born and raised here, wanted to experience something other than small-town life before starting a family. But I'd never expected her to call a halt, even a temporary one, and it threw me. I was afraid she might meet someone else and never come home. I felt maybe she was out there, looking."

"That's reasonable. You were hurt and angry, so you screwed up."

"I was more than hurt and angry. After she left, I was so lonely I didn't know what

154

to do with myself. It felt more like a divorce, since we'd been so close. I was used to seeing her almost every night. I was used to eating with her. Sleeping with her. When she moved away instead of moving in like I expected — like *everyone* expected — it left me sort of stunned and reeling."

Lourdes flinched. "So you filled in with her *sister*? Couldn't you have chosen someone else?"

"I'm getting there. I was listless and bored and sexually frustrated. And I was constantly reminded of her defection. Everyone else was as shocked as I was. Almost daily, I had to hear someone say, 'But I thought you two would get married,' as if even he or she believed Olivia had moved on without me. Anyway, I tried to fill the hours I usually spent with her at work but often wound up at Sexy Sadie's when I couldn't sleep at night."

"Drinking."

He put on his coat. "I did more of it then than I ever have, before or since."

"And Noelle worked there."

"Not at the time," he clarified. "Like me, she came in as a patron that night."

"And when she arrived . . ."

He pictured her wearing the tight red dress that revealed so much — and those high heels, which made the most of her legs. "She came over and . . ." He let his words fall off as he remembered how she'd rubbed her lower body against his while they danced. How she'd whispered in his ear that she often touched herself, pretending it was him.

"Hello?" she prompted.

He wished he could block those memories from his mind. He was mortified that he'd let her turn him into such a chump. "And she soon made it clear what she wanted," he finished.

"She wanted *you.*"

"Basically. I mean, she'd flirted with me before, and I'd never had any difficulty resisting her. But that night it was more blatant than usual. And since I was convinced I'd already lost Olivia, there didn't seem to be any reason to refuse her. Maybe I was even looking for a little revenge, since she seemed to move on so easily."

"Did you tell Olivia what you'd done after it was over?"

He rubbed his face. "Didn't need to. The news that I'd gone home with Noelle spread all over town, and I'm betting she had a hand in that. She wanted people to know — was quite proud of herself for finally being able to . . . divert my attention," he said, choosing a euphemism instead of the more vulgar expression that came to mind and probably described the situation better.

"That must've been horrible."

"It was the worst year of my life."

"So did you apologize to Olivia?"

"Not at first. Once I'd slept with Noelle, I figured I'd ruined any chance I ever had with Olivia. I knew she'd never get beyond it. So, for one desperate weekend, I tried to keep an open mind where Noelle was concerned, tried to convince myself I'd slept with her because I was attracted to her and hadn't destroyed my life."

"I can guess how well that worked out."

He'd soon disliked Noelle so much he could hardly stand to be around her. *That* was how well it'd worked out. "After only a couple of days, I realized I wasn't interested. So I tried to extricate myself from the relationship."

"How'd that go?"

"The whole situation was pathetic," he admitted. "It was weird how fast my perspective changed. Olivia needed a year or so to experience life somewhere else and build her business, and suddenly that didn't seem so bad. I realized I was an absolute idiot to have sacrificed my best chance at happiness."

"You weren't alone in what you did. Why would Olivia's *sister* ever get involved with her boyfriend?"

"You'd have to know her to understand. She's always been jealous of Olivia, always wanted whatever Olivia had and constantly tried to outdo her. That's partly why I felt so bad. I'd let her use me as the greatest weapon she could ever hope to find."

"She finally had a big stick she could use to hit her sister."

"Exactly. Only she tried to make herself look as innocent as possible by telling her family I'd been secretly coming on to her for years. That she'd been drunk, and I'd caught her at a vulnerable moment."

"She turned the tables on you!"

"Yes."

"But surely they didn't believe her."

"It was easier for them to believe her lies than to face the truth — that she'd purposely acted to destroy her sister's happiness. I got the impression her father didn't completely buy it. But her mother? Probably."

"You didn't set the record straight?"

"I couldn't see any point in arguing over it. I shouldn't have gone home with her. Besides, of the two of us, I was the only one Olivia could feasibly cut out of her life.

Family is family. They're forever. An old boyfriend on the other hand . . ."

"She held you more responsible than her own sister?"

"She expected more from me. What Noelle did wasn't a surprise to her."

"I'm thinking that knowing her sister the way she must've known her, with time, Olivia might've been able to get beyond it."

"Except just when I began to hope that might be the case, Noelle called to tell me she was pregnant."

"No!"

"Yes."

Lourdes got up and came over to where he stood. "Was it even your child?"

"I had to assume it was — at least until the baby was born and we could get a paternity test."

"You said you don't have any kids. Don't tell me, after you married her, it turned out the baby belonged to someone else . . ."

"Who can say? She miscarried at about five months and we separated shortly after." If she'd *really* miscarried. He knew there'd been a baby; he'd made her show him the results of her pregnancy test. But what had actually happened to their child remained a mystery to him. Noelle had walked out of the bathroom one day, crying and claiming she was bleeding.

"And now she's coming around, hoping to get back together?"

"She knows Olivia's happily married, that I'll never be with her, so like you said before, until there's someone else in my life, she'll probably continue to see me as a possibility."

"She has tenacity. I'll give her that."

"She's very thick-skinned."

"Obviously. But what she doesn't see coming . . . is me."

*"You?"*

"Yes. I'm going to hold your hand through this process, help you find someone who's everything you want. Someone you'll fall madly in love with, so madly in love it'll be as if Olivia never existed."

Her enthusiasm tempted him to believe it might be possible. "And you think online dating is the way to go."

"You've met everyone who lives in town, haven't you?"

"Everyone who's single and anywhere close to my age."

"Then it's time to introduce you to new prospects."

He was still reluctant. "I'd be meeting people who live out of the area."

"So?"

"So I like it here. I won't move."

"I'm sure we can get someone who doesn't live too far."

"Even then, I can't expect her to move if I'm not willing to."

"Quit being so fair. People relocate to be closer to a love interest all the time. Maybe you'll find some woman who's looking for a change."

"At my age?"

"How old are you?"

"Thirty-eight."

"You're talking like that's ancient."

"It's old enough that most people have established lives. And if they don't, it could be a major warning sign that there's something wrong with them."

"Then we go a bit younger."

He eyed her disdainfully. "How young?"

"Twenty-eight, twenty-nine."

"No. That's a whole decade."

"What's wrong with ten years?"

"It was partially Noelle's immaturity that grated on me. I thought she'd never grow up. Anyway, marriage is hard even *without* that much of an age difference."

"Plenty of people marry older spouses and never have a problem with the age difference."

"My odds of success will be better if I

meet a woman my own age. Twenty-nine is too young."

She seemed to take umbrage. "Whoa, *I'm* twenty-nine. You like me, don't you?"

"You're not a possibility," he said and hid a smile when that only offended her more.

"Why? You're bored or . . . or irritated by me?"

"Of course not. But I wouldn't date you if you were one of the women who responded to my online profile, because you're too young."

She propped her hands on her hips.

"What?" He could tell she didn't like being counted out, and yet she couldn't argue that he should consider her. Not only was she in the middle of a nasty breakup with a man she still loved, she didn't live in the area.

"You realize you're making my job more difficult," she said, but he knew that wasn't the only thing that bothered her. It was just the safer response.

"Taking charge of my love life was your idea," he pointed out.

"And it's a good one! So will you go and get me a picture? Or here . . . I'll take one with my phone."

"No. Forget it," he said. "I'm going out to buy us some breakfast."

He was halfway through the door when she called his name. As soon as he turned, she snapped the picture.

"Hang on," she said as she examined it. "Okay. You can go."

He almost demanded she show it to him. He couldn't imagine she'd gotten a shot that made him look very appealing. But he thought her efforts were doomed from the outset, so he decided not to say anything. How could someone else find him the right woman?

"I'll put that you're searching for a mate who's between thirty-five and forty," she said. "But, in my opinion, you're blocking out a huge sector of very viable candidates. You should really go twenty-five and up."

"No way!"

"How about thirty? Any older, and you're looking at the secondary market."

"The secondary market?" he echoed, holding the door. "Did you really just use that term?"

"Yes. I'm talking about people who've already been married, have kids, exes to cope with, et cetera."

"You mean like *me*."

"Not exactly like you, no. You don't have kids. And Noelle was just a goof up. Not a true marriage."

"It felt real at the time. And in case I forget how real it was, she's still using my last name."

"She's proud to have been associated with you."

He cringed. "It's a constant reminder of my own stupidity."

"You let a conniving woman get her hooks into you — and now, with my help, you're going to escape her and the damage she caused."

He narrowed his eyes. "I'm not sure I want you to get involved."

"Come on, have some faith. You rescued me. Let me rescue you."

"How'd I rescue you?"

"By taking care of me. I'm lucky the furnace went out in the rental. Otherwise, you wouldn't have come into my life when you did."

Was it only friendship she was looking for? After last night, the situation with Lourdes was a little confusing. The attraction they'd felt didn't seem to have disappeared with sobriety — not that he was going to let an attraction to the wrong woman, or anything else, trip him up again. "I'm sure you have other friends who would've supported you."

"It wouldn't be the same. I've been too busy, too insulated by my work to socialize very much. And they would all have had an opinion. You don't push me to break up with Derrick *or* give him another chance. You're neutral yet supportive. Perfect."

Did she really believe that? Because he was far from neutral, and that concerned him. "I don't know Derrick. Otherwise, I'd probably be giving you more advice. So please don't feel you have to do anything for me in return. I've been set up on dates before. Many times. It never works."

"It'll work this time. You'll see. Go thirty. You'll thank me in the end."

She seemed so convinced. He could tell he wasn't going to talk her out of it. He wasn't all that motivated to resist, anyway. He liked having her interested in his love life, even if it was ostensibly to find him someone else. So he decided to let her have her fun. He'd just shoot down anyone who didn't look promising. He could do that until Lourdes lost interest, couldn't he? It wouldn't be long before she was back in Nashville, trying to restore her career instead of finding him a wife. He doubted she'd be able to spare a thought for him then.

With a roll of his eyes, he said, "Fine, go thirty," and left.

# 9

Noelle called while Kyle was at the grocery store.

"I can't believe you have Lourdes Bennett at your house," she said as soon as he answered.

He'd taken her call only because he felt he should thank her for the meal — and so he could tell her he'd drop off her dishes. He didn't want to give her any excuse to come back to his place. If he timed it well, he could leave the dishes on her doorstep while she was at work. "She's begging for privacy, Noelle. You'll let her have it, won't you?"

"Of course! I won't tell a soul."

He was willing to bet she'd already told *many* souls. It was probably all she could talk about at work. "I mean it."

"Stop being so grumpy. If word gets out, it won't be *my* fault."

"Yes, it will," he insisted. "You're the only

one who knows she's here."

"I'm *not* the only one!"

Instead of grabbing a cart and entering the store, he moved off to one side, away from the automatic doors. "If you know that, you've talked to *someone* about her."

"Just Olivia. My sister. You trust *her,* don't you? You must, since you told her yourself."

He sighed as he dragged a hand through his hair. "All I'm saying is that . . . Lourdes doesn't want to be bothered, okay?"

"Then maybe *you* should quit telling people she's here!"

"I just told the people I trust." Noelle must've brought it up to Olivia, because Olivia wouldn't have mentioned it otherwise.

"Me, too!"

That tic in his eye started up again. "Fine. Whatever," he said. "I don't want to argue about it. All I'm asking for is your discretion. Anyway, thanks for the meal last night."

"You liked it?" She seemed so delighted to hear this, she let him change the subject without complaint.

"I did. It was great. Really."

"See? I know how to please you. I remember every detail."

He wrestled with the revulsion that welled

up. He couldn't pinpoint exactly why he was feeling so negative toward her when she'd done him a good deed. Except that he suspected she had an ulterior motive. Ignoring the part about knowing *how to please* him, since he could easily guess that she was hinting at his sexual preferences and not his food preferences, he moved on. "I'll drop the dishes by later. Do you work tonight?"

If so, he'd take them once she left . . .

"I was supposed to, but I've been putting in so many hours that I got someone else to cover my shift. I thought maybe we could take Lourdes to San Francisco and show her around."

No way did she just say that. "Are you *kidding*?"

"Why would I do that?"

"Lourdes doesn't want to go to San Francisco, Noelle."

"How can you be so sure? Have you asked her?"

"Because I know why she's here — to write her next album *uninterrupted.*"

"Well, she can't work *all* day and *all* night. We could leave late — like eight or nine. Most of the good clubs don't get busy until after ten, anyway."

He choked back the diatribe that was going through his mind — which began with the reminder that they were exes and not friends. She'd just say he was being mean.

Taking a deep breath to bolster his patience, he opted for a simple "No."

"No, what?"

"We're not going out with you."

There was a long moment of silence. "So are you going *without* me?"

He pressed his palm to his forehead. The painkiller Lourdes had provided was no longer doing its job. "Lourdes has a boyfriend. We're not going out at all. I'm her *landlord.* I'm letting her stay at my place only because the furnace at the farmhouse isn't working. The moment that's fixed, she'll be moving in there."

"You aren't attracted to her?"

He wasn't admitting to *anything.* "She's too famous for me. I wouldn't enjoy the attention."

"And no one can replace Olivia." Her voice had turned sour. "Believe me, I can guess what you're thinking."

Clutching his hair, he squeezed his eyes closed — until someone came up and touched his arm. "Kyle, are you okay?"

He opened his eyes to see Mrs. Higgins, an older widow who lived in town, looking at him curiously.

Curving his lips in a reassuring smile, he nodded. "Yes. Of course. I'm fine. How are *you* today?"

"Creaky. But I'm creaky most days. Comes with age," she teased and left him to finish his phone conversation.

"Where are you?" Noelle asked.

"Picking up a few groceries."

"Why don't you stop over? We should talk. I feel as if the nicer I am, the meaner you get."

Her words did nothing to help him relax but he worked a little harder to master his irritation. "I apologize," he said curtly. "It isn't intentional."

"That's better. So are you coming over?"

"No."

"Because . . ."

"Because we don't have anything to talk about! I gave you a water heater. You thanked me with a meal. And now I'm arranging a time to return your dishes. That's a polite exchange, isn't it?"

"*Polite?* It doesn't matter to you that we were once married? You're never going to get Olivia, Kyle. You might as well settle for me."

He'd *never* be that desperate. "We're divorced, Noelle. Divorced people do not continue to see each other."

"That's not true! A lot of them do. And some of them get back together."

"I'm sorry, but we won't be reconciling. Ever."

"*Why?* You married me before. I must have something you like."

Was she forgetting about the baby? Which she'd used to force his hand?

"I've changed," she went on. "If you'd give me a chance, I could prove it to you. But you're too busy holding grudges."

"I'm not holding any grudges. I'm being as nice as I can."

"You're fighting what you feel because you don't want to get hurt again. But I won't hurt you. I'll be a better wife this time around. I promise."

Kyle dropped his head back, appealing to the sky. Was this really happening? At what point had he given her *any* hope? "I'm sorry. I'm not interested."

"You won't even consider it? Wait until you see what I'm wearing." Her voice turned sultry. "You won't be able to resist me."

"Noelle —"

"I'll let you tie me to the bed. That would be fun, wouldn't it? I'll be your sex slave for the whole weekend, let you do things you never dreamed you could do with a woman."

"Stop it!" he shouted. "We tried to get along. It didn't work."

"We're not the same people these days. Why grow old alone when we could make each other's lives more fun and more . . . comfortable? I'm working so hard, but I can barely make ends meet. You're making plenty, but you must be tired of living without a woman in your bed. We each have what the other needs."

"Quit dangling the promise of sex. It —" He searched for a kinder way to say what first came to mind. "It's not an option, okay? I'm fine the way I am."

The tone of her voice hardened almost instantly. "You don't want me as your enemy, Kyle."

What the hell did she mean by that? It sounded like a threat. "Excuse me?"

"You heard what I said," she replied and disconnected, leaving Kyle scratching his head and staring at his phone.

Kyle was quiet when he got back. He'd bought a lot of groceries, but he didn't seem to be in a very good mood. Lourdes wondered if it was the prospect of online dating that had him out of sorts, his hangover from last night or simply the hassle of grocery shopping.

"Are you okay?" she asked, frying the sausages so he could make the French toast.

"Of course, why?"

"You seem upset."

He continued to whip the eggs in a big red bowl and didn't answer right away.

"Kyle?"

"I'm not upset," he said. "Just bugged. My ex-wife is annoying the hell out of me."

"Did you talk to her this morning?"

"I answered her call because I wanted to return her dishes without having her come to the house."

"I appreciate that. But . . . I assume she didn't appreciate the offer?"

He looked a little bemused. "She keeps trying to get me back in bed with her. I might be an idiot for admitting this, but I'd rather go without — *for the rest of my life.*"

Lourdes nudged him. "You won't have to go without much longer."

He surprised her by laughing out loud. "And you know this . . . how?"

"There are some very interesting women on that dating site. Pretty, too. After breakfast, we can go over the ones I've marked as the most promising, if you like."

Although his smile faded, he seemed encouraged. "What the hell. I guess it's

173

worth a shot."

When her mother called a couple of seconds later, he offered to take over at the stove, but she jerked her head to indicate that he should continue with the French toast.

"Hey, Mom. Sorry I didn't get back to you yesterday." She held the phone with one hand while turning sausages with the other. "I was really busy." Busy breaking up with Derrick. She wondered how her mother would respond to that news. She was curious — and yet hesitant to mention it. Her mother was so excited about the wedding. She didn't see the need to heap her family's disappointment on top of her own. Why not give herself some time to recover first? It wasn't as if they'd set a date and someone was booking the venue or making other financial commitments.

"I just wanted to be sure you'd arrived safely and that the house was what you hoped," her mother said.

"The house is perfect. I love it."

"That's a relief. Derrick takes such good care of you."

"He does?" He'd hardly done a great job over the past six months.

"Isn't he the one who lined up that place?"

"Oh. Yeah." At her request . . .

"Will he be joining you soon?"

She stepped back as Kyle reached for the cooking spray, which was in the cupboard by her head. "That was the original plan, but . . ."

"Something's changed?" her mother asked.

"Derrick's busy. I'm not sure he'll be able to make it."

"Wait . . . he's going to leave you there alone?"

"It's better if he doesn't come," she replied. "I need to concentrate on what I'm doing."

"But won't you be lonely? You don't know a soul in Whiskey Creek. Or are you planning to visit Angel's Camp?"

"I'd like to go home, see the old house, maybe visit a few of our friends. But not until I have my album written." She hoped she'd be feeling more in control of things then, more capable of handling the myriad questions she'd get about how her career was going and what was coming next.

"How long will that take?"

"Who knows? This album has to be the best I've ever produced. I'm not going to rush it." She needed to feel stronger, more confident, before she could start writing. And just now, she felt as if she'd been hit

175

by a bus and left on the side of the road. Only her new friendship with Kyle made her feel halfway human.

"I don't understand why you can't write it here," her mother said. "It can't be fun being out there all alone, especially with the holidays coming up."

Kyle elbowed her, pretending she was crowding him, and she smiled. Fortunately, she wasn't as alone as she'd thought she'd be. "I'm in a good place."

"You're still coming home for Christmas, though, aren't you?"

The sausage popped and sizzled as she turned them. "I haven't decided yet."

"You might stay *there*?"

"Like I said, the album has to be my first priority. So I'll stay if I need to."

That didn't leave her mother much room to complain. She understood that Lourdes's entire future hinged on this next project. And she was supportive of her efforts. No one understood Lourdes's aspirations quite like her mother, who'd given up her own dream of a music career to live in a small town and raise a family. "Should we come there, then? We will, if you'd like us to."

Her mother's kindness made her eyes water. "No, I don't have room for everyone. But I appreciate the offer."

"You sound funny. Are you sure you're okay? What's going on? Why isn't Derrick going there to join you like he planned?"

Lourdes almost told her they'd broken up, but couldn't when she imagined her mother's response — shock, outrage, anger, disappointment. It was too much in addition to what she was already feeling. She couldn't tolerate the sympathy. "I told you, he's busy. And so am I."

They talked about her sisters and the tree her mother had put up. Then Lourdes said she had to go. The sausages were done, and Kyle had set a piece of French toast on a plate beside the stove.

"Your mom doesn't like you being gone for Christmas, huh?" he said when she placed her phone on the counter.

"This will be the first Christmas our family won't be together."

"You could go back for a few days."

"No. That'll only make what I'm going through harder. Derrick will be in the area. So will Crystal. There'd be no way to keep the truth from my family, which means that Christmas would end up being more of a pity party. I'd rather not do that to them — or myself." January would be soon enough to deal with all that. It wasn't as if there was any chance that her mom and Derrick would talk while she was away. Derrick had always been too invested in his work to build much of a relationship with her family. They didn't even have his cell number.

"Then you can join *my* family," Kyle said.

She met his gaze. "You mean Brandon and Olivia?"

"And his mother and my father."

Somehow, joining Kyle and his family actually sounded appealing. "Maybe I will."

# 10

Lourdes felt great about the women she'd chosen for Kyle. There were several matches on Single Central he found interesting and attractive. Fortunately, he agreed with her opinion on who was the most appealing.

"What about this one?" she asked. "I marked her as a maybe."

The picture showed a well-toned woman wearing workout clothes. She looked good.

"Why would there be any question?" he joked.

Lourdes frowned. "I don't care for what she wrote in her profile. There's something superficial about it. She goes on and on about bodybuilding and focuses too heavily on meeting someone who's as 'active' as she is, which I interpret as a euphemism for saying she expects whoever she dates to be completely dedicated to the gym."

She waited for Kyle to read the profile himself.

"I don't frequent a gym, but I run most days," he said. "And I lift three times a week. You don't think that'll be enough for her?"

"It's more your approach." She'd seen the weights in the extra room. She could tell he used them. But he didn't seem obsessed with his body. "You're more practical about fitness than she seems to be. I'm guessing you work out to live a healthier life."

His expression indicated that he found her statement odd. "Is there any other reason?"

"Yes. Working out *is* her life. That body is a badge of honor."

"You never know," he said. "She might be okay. Most people want to look good, especially if they're single and their photos are going up on a site like this."

"That's generous, but I'm guessing she comes with all kinds of dietary restrictions. A woman doesn't get as muscular as a man without making some sacrifices — or taking steroids."

"That's more of a city thing," he mused. "I haven't seen a lot of women who are into weight lifting out here."

"I've seen plenty of it in my line of work. It gets old."

"Do you lift? Or do any other kind of exercise?"

180

"When I'm at home, I go to the gym every day. I have to, if I want to keep up with the competition." Crystal was gorgeous. "But I resent the pressure to achieve physical perfection."

"Who's keeping track? I mean, are you sure you're not the one putting yourself under pressure?"

"The tabloids are keeping track, for starters. You must've seen what they've said about people like Kirstie Alley, Wynonna Judd, Garth Brooks and Kelly Clarkson." Derrick threw those names up to her all the time — whenever she ate something she shouldn't, or when she hadn't made it to the gym. He told her if she wasn't careful she'd wind up the next pathetic fat girl on the cover of *National Enquirer* and she'd be eclipsed in popularity, since so much of a female singer's success depended on her beauty. "Name one artist who's fat and ugly," he'd say whenever she'd try to suggest that her fame was based on her talent. And she couldn't — unless that artist had started years and years ago, when she looked better. Lourdes could come up with plenty of male singers who weren't in top physical form, but there seemed to be more forgiveness in the industry for men.

Still, Derrick's reminders were irritating,

especially since he didn't work out himself. "I'm not in the public eye," he'd say.

"It's all part of show business," she told Kyle. "Anyway, I say we pass on this Barbie. We're talking about finding you a mate — not a woman who's primarily interested in the way she looks."

He shrugged. "I'm fine with seeing how it goes with these other women first. We can always come back to her later."

Lourdes liked that he seemed to understand what she was saying. "Do you have a picture of Olivia?" she asked.

He glanced up from her computer screen, where he'd been reading about another candidate named Mandy Suffolk.

"Why do you want to see her?"

"I'm curious."

After a slight pause, he pulled his phone from his pocket and showed her a wedding photo.

"*What?* You were in your stepbrother's line when he married the woman you love?" she said.

"Olivia was in Noelle's line when Noelle married me, too. That was probably worse, since what I'd done was so fresh."

"What you and Noelle *both* did," she corrected, but he ignored it.

"I still can't believe that Olivia's mother

asked her to plan the wedding," he murmured.

Lourdes sat up taller. "*Olivia* planned your wedding?"

"She doesn't do much of that these days. Brandon used to be a professional skier and has all the money they need. But she plans a few events here and there — for instance, she's doing another friend's wedding right now."

"Still. Planning her sister's wedding, when her sister stole her boyfriend? Talk about adding insult to injury."

"It saved their folks a lot of money. It was practical. And, as I've learned since, family is family."

"Not always. There are plenty of families with estranged members."

"In a small town it's harder to have that sort of thing going on. Besides, dividing the sisters would only penalize her parents, who've done nothing wrong."

"I guess that's true." Lourdes studied the bride. No question Olivia was attractive — quite a bit more attractive than Noelle. Maybe that was where Noelle's jealousy came in. Maybe she'd been constantly passed over for Olivia and was determined to have her turn, for a change.

Brandon wasn't bad-looking, either,

Lourdes decided. Not that she planned to volunteer her opinion to Kyle. "So you like blondes?"

"I don't have a preference," he replied.

"I'm glad to hear that, since all the women I've chosen for you happen to be brunette."

"I notice that some of them have children, too." He took over at the mouse and clicked through the various profiles. "I thought you were opposed to that 'secondary market' stuff."

"I'm not *opposed* to it. It just makes for a more difficult relationship, because of the variables involved." She reached for the mouse and clicked on the mail icon for a woman named Ruby Meyers. "Let's send these ladies a message, shall we?"

*"Let's?"* he repeated. "No way. I can handle that part myself. Later." He got up and grabbed his coat. "It's December 3 — three weeks before Christmas. I say we go get a tree."

"You want me to go with you?" she asked. "To leave the house?"

"Why not? No one will see you. We'll go out in the woods and cut our own."

Despite everything, she felt a spark of excitement. The past few years she'd been so busy with her career she hadn't paid much attention to the various holidays, and

Christmas was no different. This reminded her of Christmases past, when she was a little girl and would go out with her family to get a tree. "Is that a tradition of yours?"

"No. My assistant puts up a fake one at work. I usually let it go at that, since that's where I spend most of my time. But . . . I think you could use a tree."

*"Me?"*

He grinned at her. "*I'm* not the one who's been crying."

"How will a Christmas tree fix what's wrong with me?"

"It won't, but it can't hurt to remind you of other things that matter."

He had a point. "Okay," she said. "Let's go."


Kyle had just chopped down the tree Lourdes had chosen. It was so large, he doubted it would even fit in his house, but she was so adamant that it would be perfect, she'd bet him $50.

"I feel like an icicle," she said, rubbing her hands and jumping from one foot to the other. "We need some hot chocolate."

Kyle couldn't understand why she was cold. She hadn't brought any snow gear, so she was wearing his heavy coat, hat and gloves. Then again . . . he'd done all the work. He'd been too afraid the tree would fall on top of her if he let her chop away — although it was far more likely she would've just wasted her time and effort hacking ineffectively. She'd obviously never handled an ax.

"We can go by the grocery store and buy some to make at home," he said. "Or we can grab a cup at the Gas-N-Go. Your choice."

"I say the Gas-N-Go. I want whipped cream on top."

Breathing heavily from the exertion, he straightened to give himself a rest. "You're not acting too depressed."

"I feel strangely . . . happy," she admitted. "As long as I don't think of Derrick."

As far as he could tell, she hadn't checked her phone since they'd left, which made him believe she hadn't yet answered Derrick's earlier text. "Yeah. Watching me chop down a tree is pretty exciting."

She chuckled. "I do have you to thank. You keep distracting me from my misery."

He gave her a wry smile. "You like playing matchmaker, like talking about those women you found."

She cocked her head. "Whom you don't seem in any hurry to contact."

"I'll get around to it. In the meantime, my

profile is up."

"Meaning what?"

"They can write me if they want to."

"So you *are* arrogant."

"And if I said the opposite, I'd be sexist," he teased.

When she took out her phone, he thought maybe she was finally checking to see if she'd heard from Derrick again. "Can you get a signal out here?" he asked.

"I don't need a signal. I'm taking a picture." She raised her cell phone. "Smile!"

"Another photo for my profile?" he asked. "Now we're going to portray me as a guy who's full of Christmas cheer?"

"This is actually for me. I think it's funny watching you single-handedly wrestle that giant tree into your truck."

He got a better hold on the trunk and lifted it cleanly. "Here you go. Now everyone on Single Central will see that I don't need a gym," he joked.

Her breath misted as she laughed. "Show-off!"

After another ten minutes spent tugging and dragging and maneuvering, he finally managed to get the darn tree into the bed of his truck and securely tied down. "I won't be pleased when I can't get this through the front door," he warned as he examined his work. "Even if I will be fifty bucks richer."

She stamped the snow from her boots, which were too big, since they were his. "Did we ever shake on that?"

"Did we have to?"

She glanced at him skeptically. "I don't want to bet anymore. It looks *a lot* bigger now that it's been cut down."

He gave her the evil eye. "Don't you dare say that. I tried to warn you, but you wouldn't listen."

"I might've been wrong," she said with a sheepish grin. "But . . . we can always cut off more. Make it work."

Exhausted, he climbed into the cab of the truck while she did the same. "It'll take a second for the heater to get going," he said. He turned it on full blast, but he didn't think she needed that much warm air. She was practically buried under his winter gear. "Look at you," he said, reaching over to pull the hat farther out of her eyes, since her own hands were encumbered by the oversize gloves.

"You sure know how to show a girl a good time," she teased.

He shifted into Reverse. "*I* did the chopping. *You* get to do the decorating."

"Fine," she said. "Do you have any ornaments?"

"Come to think of it, I don't," he replied. "But I'm sure my mother has some she'll let us use."

"*Your* mother? Or Brandon's?"

"Brandon's. My stepmom."

"What happened to your own mom?"

"She died of an amniotic fluid embolism when I was five."

"I've never heard of that . . ."

Kyle couldn't decide whether or not to explain it. He didn't want to frighten her away from the idea of having children at some point. "It doesn't happen very often." He hoped she'd leave it at that, but she didn't.

"So what is it?"

"Like I said, it's rare. It's a complication of childbirth."

"She was having a baby? Did the baby make it?"

" 'Fraid not. For whatever reason, she went into labor early. They were struggling to save what would've been my younger sister and then, without warning, my mother went into cardiac arrest. We lost them both."

"That's terrible! I'm so sorry."

"I wish it'd never happened. But it was a long time ago, so don't feel bad."

His phone rang as he was about to pull off the narrow dirt pathways onto the main road they'd taken to get to this remote place. It almost transferred to voice mail before he could get the darn thing out of his pocket — and then he wasn't sure whether to answer.

"It's Derrick." He stayed where he was, letting the engine idle as he showed her his caller ID, which indicated a Tennessee area code.

Lourdes bit her lip. "Why would he be contacting you?"

"No idea. Maybe he figured out *I'm* the country magazine reporter who called him up and he's pissed off."

"Don't answer it," she said, but he brought a finger to his lips to ask for silence, since he'd already pressed the button.

"Hello?"

"Kyle?"

"Yes?"

"This is Derrick Meade. Lourdes's manager."

"I guessed as much when I saw your number. What can I do for you, Derrick?"

"I haven't been able to reach Lourdes today. I was wondering if . . . if you could swing by and check on her."

Kyle glanced over at the woman in question. "Sure. But is there any reason I should be concerned? Have you tried her cell?"

"I've tried to call her — and I've texted her several times — but I haven't received a response."

"I see. I'll drop by and take a peek."

"I'd appreciate it."

"No problem."

After Kyle hit the end button, he dropped his cell between the seats.

"What'd he want?" Lourdes asked.

"Said he hasn't heard from you. Wants me to go by and make sure you're okay."

"Why didn't you tell him I'm sitting right here in the truck beside you?"

"I thought it might make him realize that call we made was bogus and we were in on it together — since you're supposed to be in seclusion and writing your next album."

She pulled off his gloves and hat. "I'll text him," she said, but she didn't volunteer what she was going to say.

# 11

Kyle stopped at the Gas-N-Go to get Lourdes some hot chocolate. Then he swung by his parents' house, hoping to borrow their extra Christmas decorations. But when he pulled up, both his father and Brandon were outside, hanging lights — and they immediately turned at the sound of his vehicle, so it wasn't as if he could drive on past.

"Shit," he muttered as his father waved, confirming that he'd been instantly recognized.

"Oh, my gosh! That's Brandon, isn't it?" Lourdes's eyes skipped over his father to his stepbrother.

"Yeah. I'm sorry. I never dreamed anyone would be outside." At the Gas-N-Go, he'd said he would just run inside and grab what they needed while she waited in the truck.

"It's okay," she said. "Unless they listen to country-western music, they probably won't recognize me." She turned the rearview mirror. "Yikes! They might not recognize me, anyway. I have hat hair and no makeup. Plus, I'm wearing your coat, and I'm drowning in it."

Maybe his father wouldn't realize who she was, but Brandon would. Kyle had told him and their friends at Black Gold that she was in town, so Brandon would guess who she was without having to recognize her. "You can still stay in the truck. I'll tell them you're my renter, and that I'm helping you get a tree. My folks will be fine with that."

Lourdes seemed reluctant to accept the out he offered her. "I don't want them to think I'm rude . . ."

"They won't."

"Of course they will."

"What does it matter?"

"I don't want *anyone* to think badly of me."

"I'll say we were in a hurry. No big deal."

She gazed out at the home in which he'd been raised. "Will Olivia be here, too?"

Kyle hadn't been expecting the change in subject. "Probably. She's usually with Brandon if he's not at work."

"Then I'm going in."

He caught her arm as she reached for the door handle. "Why?"

"Because I'd like to meet her — to see what my Single Central candidates are up against."

"That isn't a good idea," he said with a scowl. "The fewer people who see you, the better, right?"

"We don't have to explain what I do for a living. If they figure it out on their own . . . we'll deal with it. We're talking four people — your family. It's not like I'll be walking into a crowded room filled with strangers."

He opened his mouth to warn her that he'd already mentioned her to Brandon, but she hopped out before he could say anything.

He met up with her as she came around the front of his vehicle.

"Hey, look who's here!" His father had descended the ladder he'd been using and was walking toward them. "We weren't expecting to see you until tomorrow," he said to Kyle. "What's wrong? Why aren't you working?"

"It's Saturday," Kyle said.

"That makes a difference to you? Because it hasn't for the past several months." He adjusted the bill of his cap so he could get a better look at Lourdes. "Who's this?"

Just in case Brandon hadn't shared the fact that they had a country-western star in town, Kyle scrambled to come up with a response that wouldn't give her identity away. "Uh, my new tenant."

But Lourdes suddenly piped up, providing her real name as she stuck out her hand. "Nice to meet you."

His father grinned and kept his eyes fastened to her face while addressing him. "Where'd you find this gal?"

"Through a place on the internet that lists rentals all over the country."

"I guessed she was an out-of-towner. We would've noticed someone this pretty long before now."

"She's from Nashville." His father, Bob, didn't show any sign of recognition, which led Kyle to believe that Brandon hadn't mentioned her.

"You should've put an ad on the internet long before now," he said with a laugh.

"I didn't have an available rental," Kyle pointed out.

Brandon climbed down from his ladder, too. "Good to see you, brother."

Kyle wondered if Brandon would indicate that he knew who Lourdes was, but he didn't. He merely smiled, introduced himself and shook Lourdes's hand.

"Looks like Dad's put you to work." Kyle gestured toward the string of lights dangling from the last hook.

"It was Mom who asked us to come over," Brandon explained. "She wanted Olivia's help baking cookies for the church Christmas party this evening."

"Did you say cookies?" Kyle echoed. "Are they done yet?"

Brandon chuckled. "I hope so. I'm ready for one — or half a dozen."

After removing his cap, their father rested his forearms on the back end of Kyle's truck and studied his cargo. "You're putting up a tree this year?"

"It's Christmas, isn't it?"

"That's my point. Most years no one would know it, going by your house."

Kyle rubbed his hands. He'd washed them at the Gas-N-Go, but tree sap was one of the most difficult substances to get off. "What goes up must come down. I admit it can all seem a bit pointless to me."

"Scrooge," Lourdes muttered.

"I do believe this was my idea." He gestured at the tree he'd gone to so much trouble to hack down and was rewarded with a saucy grin.

"Come on in." His father beckoned them toward the house. "Your mother will be excited you're here."

"We don't need to bother the bakers,"

Kyle said. "We were just hoping to borrow some tree trimmings from the garage, if you have extra."

"Of course we have extra. Paige has so many Christmas decorations she doesn't know what to do with them all. But you can't take that stuff and go, not without saying hello to her."

"Then we'd better go inside and say hello." Lourdes said that so sweetly Kyle was probably the only one who understood her motivation. She was reminding him that she wanted to meet Olivia. But he wasn't keen on that. He'd admitted to Lourdes what he hadn't admitted to anyone in the past six years — because he hadn't expected the two women to ever meet.

Problem was . . . he couldn't get out of going inside, not without hurting his mother's feelings. "Fine. Just a quick hello. We only have a second," he said, but once they were inside, it was clear that he wasn't going to get Lourdes out anytime soon. His stepmother recognized her — whether Olivia had anything to do with that or not, he couldn't tell. Paige was almost beside herself with excitement even before his father could boom out her name.

"I *love* your voice. You're *so* talented," she said.

Lourdes allowed a hug, but that much enthusiasm made Kyle uncomfortable. Surely Lourdes got tired of people wanting to touch her.

She did nothing to imply that, however. "Thank you," she said. "You have a lovely place."

"It's nothing fancy, but we like it."

Lourdes focused on Olivia. "And you are . . ."

Kyle stifled a smile — because it was obvious to him that Lourdes was far more interested than she was letting on. "This is Brandon's wife."

"Olivia." Brandon, who'd followed them in, along with his father, added her name.

"Good to meet you," Olivia said.

"Likewise," Lourdes responded. "So . . . do you live close by?"

"Not far," Brandon replied. "Maybe five minutes."

Once again, Lourdes attempted to draw Olivia into conversation. "I believe I've met your sister."

Olivia glanced at Kyle. No doubt she was wondering how much Lourdes knew about their situation.

"Noelle dropped dinner off to thank me for the water heater," he explained.

"Oh." Olivia sighed. "I'm sorry. I keep

198

telling her to quit bothering Kyle, but . . ."

"It was delicious," Lourdes said.

Kyle thought of the odd comments Noelle had made when they were on the phone this morning but chose not to mention them. He figured it was just more of Noelle doing what Noelle did. Her emotions carried her in all kinds of different directions. She was in love with him one minute; she hated him the next.

"Would you like a piece of fudge?" Paige asked. "It's homemade."

"How can I refuse anything that's home-made?" Lourdes said and let Paige talk her into sitting at the kitchen table and sampling one of everything.

Lourdes seemed more comfortable as time passed, but her gaze kept drifting to Olivia, who seemed to be at least as curious about her. Whenever their eyes met, they'd both smile and shift awkwardly, and Kyle would make a renewed effort to get Lourdes out of the house. But Paige thwarted his every attempt by pressing some new treat on Lourdes. So then he'd have to wait a few minutes longer.

Finally, he stood. "Why don't you make a little plate for us to take home?" he suggested. "I'm afraid Lourdes is going to be sick if she eats any more right now."

"Great idea!" Paige exclaimed.

While his mother bustled about the kitchen, Olivia walked over and sat next to Lourdes. "How long will you be in town?"

"I'm not sure, to be honest. I've got a lot of work to do. When I finish it, I'll go back."

"It's lonely being away from home, especially during the holidays. I know I speak for Kyle's parents when I say that we'd love to have you come over for Christmas dinner."

This kindness seemed to take Lourdes by surprise. Kyle had made the same offer, but that was different. This was coming from Olivia. "Thank you. I'll definitely consider it."

"I hope you'll come," Olivia said, and then, at last, Paige was done.

Armed with a mountain of fudge and cookies and directions on where to find the extra Christmas decorations in the garage, Kyle motioned Lourdes ahead of him.

"Aren't you sorry you went in now?" he murmured once they had the ornaments and garland and were in the privacy of his truck.

Lourdes looked a bit baffled. "No. Not at all. I just wish I hadn't liked her so much."

"Olivia?"

She made a face at him. "Who else? It

would be impossible not to like your mother."

He started the engine. "Don't tell me my little matchmaker is feeling discouraged."

"A bit overwhelmed by the challenge ahead of me," she said. "But I've managed difficult feats before."

He pulled away from the curb. "Exactly. And you'll do it again."

When she smiled, he knew she understood that he wasn't referring to the challenges in *his* life.

"It's gone."

Kyle had just wrestled the tree through the door. He'd had to cut off another two feet at the base, and the top was crammed against the ceiling, which made it look like just the midsection of a tree. But at least he'd salvaged their efforts by finally getting it into the tree stand. For the first hour, he'd thought they'd have to scrap what he'd cut down and start all over. "What's gone?" he asked absently, brushing the pine needles from his clothes.

"All the dishes," Lourdes said. "Even the food."

Now she had his full attention, because he had no clue what she was talking about. "What dishes? What food?"

"The meal your ex-wife brought. I planned to warm up the leftovers so we could eat before we decorate, but . . . there's nothing left."

His eyes darted to the kitchen table, where he'd begun to stack the empty containers. They were gone, just as she'd said. "She brought four chicken breasts, and we only ate two."

Lourdes froze as she noticed something else. "Oh, boy . . ."

Thanks to the change in her voice, Kyle was fairly certain that *oh, boy* wasn't related to his accounting of the leftovers. "What is it?"

She moved the gloves and hat she'd dropped onto the counter out of the way and handed him what she'd spotted — a note.

"Fuck you!" it read. There was no signature.

"That's got to be from Noelle, doesn't it?" she asked.

He didn't know anyone else who was pissed off at him. And she had a key. "Has to be," he agreed.

"Wow. What set her off? She was so friendly when I spoke to her."

Kyle continued to stare at those two ugly words and at the deep indentations of the pen that showed how angry Noelle had been when she'd written them. "I couldn't tell you. I didn't do anything that would warrant *this.*"

"Is she angry that I'm here — staying with you? Does she think there might be something going on between us?"

At odd moments — last night, and then while they were getting the tree, and even when they were at his folks' house — it *did* feel as if there was something going on. But he couldn't say that. If Lourdes felt the same thing, she was in denial about it. Every time they accidentally touched, or their eyes lingered on each other a second too long, she'd bring up those women she'd found on Single Central.

"No," he said. "She knows we've just met." He remembered Noelle's many attempts to hang out with him lately, the incessant calls, the suggestions that he drop by Sexy Sadie's while she was at work — and then the more blatant offers that had come later. "She isn't getting what she wants, so she's throwing a tantrum." He'd seen her do that before, plenty of times, hadn't he? But they'd been married then. Or going through the divorce. This shouldn't be happening *now.*

"And what does she want?" Lourdes asked.

"To get back together."

"She came out and told you that?"

"She didn't need to. I knew it. But yes, this morning she mentioned something about there being no need for us to grow old alone when we could have each other."

Lourdes looked more closely at him. "Are you *sure* you're not still sleeping with her? I can't imagine a woman doing this unless —"

"Because you've never met anyone like Noelle," he interrupted. "I haven't touched her — despite her many offers. She asked me to come over today. I refused. That's it. I've tried to let her down gently, but she makes that impossible. She pushes you until you have no choice except to be blunt."

"Should you be worried?"

*You don't want me as your enemy, Kyle . . .* He knew she had a temper, and not much of a conscience, but it was difficult to conceive of her doing anything that might seriously harm someone. He wouldn't put it past her to do other things, pettier things. "No, not really." He glanced around the house, wondering what else she might've touched. This was an obvious display of power, a way to show him he wasn't as out

204

of reach as he thought. "But it's well past time to get those locks changed."

"Will changing the locks even do any good? You told me her uncle's a locksmith."

"He's trustworthy." Shit, weren't situations like this supposed to get easier with time? It'd been more than *five years* since they were divorced.

But Noelle hadn't found someone else in all that time. That was why she wouldn't move on and forget about him. And she perceived him as having money, which she was convinced would solve all her problems.

"She certainly knows how to kill the Christmas spirit," Lourdes said.

Kyle crumpled the note and threw it away. "This is nothing. Don't let it upset you."

She didn't seem capable of forgetting it, though. "Maybe we should go over to the farmhouse to sleep tonight. She doesn't have a key to that, does she?"

"No."

"Good. I wouldn't want to become the subject of some *Dateline* episode."

He was fairly certain she was joking, but Noelle's sudden rage did make him uncomfortable — because it was so unprovoked, and there was nothing he could do to placate her. He wasn't going back to her no matter what. "It's too cold at the farmhouse, remember? We'll be fine here."

Although she'd taken off his coat, and it was warm in the room, she rubbed her arms. "Spurned lovers can do some crazy things."

"We divorced more than five years ago. That's got to make a difference. She can't be as into me as she thinks she is."

"Maybe you're not as easy to get over as *you* think you are."

Their eyes met in one of those moments when neither seemed capable of looking away, even though that shouldn't be happening. "Olivia got over me without any trouble," he said, to break it.

She frowned at him. "She still cares about you. Most people can't say anything nice about their past partners, but Olivia genuinely admires you and wants you to be happy. At least, I got that impression."

"Well, we *are* sort of related these days."

"I'm guessing she'd feel that way regardless."

Determined to conceal whatever sizzle he felt when he was with Lourdes, he crossed the kitchen to stare into the fridge. "I should've waited to piss Noelle off until we'd finished the food. The water heater should've been worth that much."

"You got a lot of groceries this morning,"

she said. "I'll throw a meal together."

He turned. "You can cook?"

"Believe it or not."

"What are you making?"

"How about you go ahead and put the lights on the tree and I'll surprise you."

Although he felt more like calling Noelle and having it out, he agreed. Coming into his house when he wasn't home — even if it was to get her dishes — underlined how delusional she was. It didn't matter that they'd been married. She didn't have, and shouldn't have, the same kind of access to his house and belongings as she once did. What was there about "divorced" that she didn't understand?

"She's *so* maddening," he muttered. But Lourdes had used her smartphone to put on some Christmas music, and he could smell delicious scents wafting out of the kitchen. He didn't see any reason he should let Noelle ruin the good time he could have with Lourdes.

So he put his ex, and her nasty note, out of his mind.

Derrick kept texting her.

Why aren't you responding? What's going on with you? Have you lost your mind? Do you know how much money I'd be out if I passed Crystal on to someone else?

He said plenty of other things, too, but he didn't agree to forgo being Crystal's manager. He was so adamant that Lourdes was being unreasonable, she was beginning to second-guess herself. Was she overreacting to the excitement a manager would naturally feel toward a promising new client? Was she letting jealousy, and her fear of failure after soaring so high, ruin the one great thing she had left — her relationship with the man she loved? Derrick often talked about how quickly some of his more successful clients turned into "divas." He held that kind of behavior in contempt and often threw it up to her when he felt she was overstepping the bounds.

But what she was feeling had nothing to do with being a diva. No woman would enjoy having her fiancé pay too much attention to a rival. "Whatever you do, don't act like Miriam," he'd say, referring to one of the worst of his early clients, one he'd frequently complained about.

"You almost done?"

When Kyle came into the kitchen, Lourdes shoved her phone across the counter so she couldn't be tempted to keep looking at it and stirred the pasta sauce simmering on the stove. "Just about. You finished with the tree?"

"I am. Come and see. It looks really good."

She laughed at his boyish eagerness. "I will. But first . . . can you grab an oven mitt and take the garlic bread out? It'll burn if we don't do it soon."

"Where'd you get garlic bread?" he asked as he nudged her aside to open the oven door.

"I used the rest of that loaf you bought for French toast this morning and added butter and garlic."

"Making do, huh? I wouldn't have expected such resourcefulness from a pampered celebrity like you."

He was joking. She saw the twinkle in his eye. But after what she'd just been thinking, she couldn't help taking those words halfway seriously. *Was* she acting pampered, or spoiled and temperamental, with Derrick? Or, since her career had taken a turn for the worse, was she trying to make him suffer along with her? (This was one of his most recent allegations. At first, she'd found it preposterous, but she had to admit that his excitement over Crystal stung all the more because of her own situation.)

"What is it?" Apparently, Kyle had been able to tell that his words hadn't been interpreted the way they'd been intended.

"Derrick says I'm allowing my insecurities to ruin our relationship."

"Because he knows he's losing you and he's feelin   )anicked. That doesn't mean what he sa   is true."

"Do you  nink that's it? Or could what we're goin   through be more my fault than I realize? I'm not in a position of strength right now. I feel hurt. It seems to me that he's part of the problem, not someone I'm taking out my hurt and anger on. But perhaps I'm not the best judge."

Kyle studied her for several seconds. "It might be time to hire someone."

"Hire someone?" she echoed.

"A private investigator."

She brought a hand to her chest. "You're suggesting I have someone *spy* on him?"

"Your doubts are driving you nuts. Maybe a private investigator will be able to put your fears to rest so you can move ahead with confidence — get married, like you planned."

And maybe a private investigator would do the exact opposite.

But wouldn't it be better to know, once and for all? To stop second-guessing?

Her heart began to race. "Checking up on him feels creepy. I don't want to be the type of partner who'd resort to that."

"He's acting so shady I'm not sure you have any choice. You told me he'd never admit that he was cheating."

He wouldn't. Not unless he planned to leave her for Crystal and, at this point, she doubted he'd be confident enough of someone that young. He wouldn't want to end up without either one of them. Derrick had to have a love interest at all times; he hated being alone. "If he prefers her, he'll have to tell me eventually."

"He *has* to know what he has in you. If he's cheating, he's not looking for someone new. He's having a little fun on the side."

She could imagine Derrick justifying sex with Crystal by telling himself it didn't mean anything on an emotional level, and that made Lourdes sick. "Having his cake and eating it, too, as the cliché goes."

Kyle shrugged. "I'm not trying to lead you to any particular conclusion. We don't know for sure."

"But we could find out, if I hire someone."

"It's a possibility, if the person you hire is any good."

Suddenly a bit shaky, she steadied herself by gripping the counter. "I'll think about it."

They carried the food to the table. But before they sat down to eat, she insisted on seeing the tree, since he'd been so excited about showing it to her. "It's beautiful. You did a great job."

Obviously proud of his efforts, he rested his hands loosely on his hips. "Thanks. It's all ready for you to finish," he joked.

"Sure, I'll finish — as long as it goes with me when I move to the farmhouse," she said.

He gave her a mock scowl. "Don't tell me we're going to have a custody battle over our tree!"

She smiled. Not only was he handsome, he was charming, too. Her own father must've been like Kyle when her mother met him — committed to the small town where he'd grown up, assured of what he wanted in life, happier away from the limelight. Otherwise, why would Renate have let him derail *her* dreams? "We're not going to have a battle unless you fight me for it."

"I wouldn't do that," he said. "Not when it means more to you. But —" he made a clicking sound with his tongue "— I'm not looking forward to moving it. I'm hoping you'll change your mind."

"Good point. On second thought, I don't think I'm *that* dedicated to taking it with me."

"I love a reasonable woman." With a wink, he started back to the kitchen, but she caught his arm.

"I want to go ahead and . . ." She swallowed when he turned to look at her. She had such a visceral reaction to being this close to him, and it always caught her off guard. How could she feel such a strong awareness of another man when she was so upset about what was going on with Derrick?

"And . . ." he prompted.

"Hire a private investigator."

His eyebrows drew together. "It might

cost a couple grand. You should be warned about the price up front."

She nodded to acknowledge that she understood. "It'll be worth it. I have to find out if the doubts I'm feeling have any basis in truth."

Callie went into labor that night. Kyle got the call as they finished dinner and he and Lourdes were deciding which movie they wanted to watch. After the hangovers they'd had this morning, they definitely didn't plan to do any more drinking.

"But . . . isn't it too soon?" he said to Levi, who was calling him on Bluetooth as he rushed his wife to the hospital.

Lourdes stopped clearing away the dishes.

"She's thirty-six weeks," Levi told him. "That's . . . not as bad as it could be."

*Not as bad as it could be* wasn't exactly the reassurance Kyle had been hoping for. The anxiety in Levi's voice made his own anxiety worse. "Right. Thirty-six weeks is . . . good," he said, even though he'd heard Callie mention that a full-term pregnancy lasted forty. One month. How much difference could one month make?

When it came to creating a baby, surely four weeks could mean a lot . . .

"Can you call everyone else?" Levi asked.

"I need to concentrate on . . . on her."

And battle his fear . . . "Right. Of course. I've got it. You just get her to the hospital and we'll be there soon."

"What is it?" Lourdes asked as he pressed the end button on his phone.

He remembered Callie as he'd seen her at Black Gold, trying to get comfortable in her chair. "One of my closest friends is having her baby."

"Everything should be okay," Lourdes said, obviously reading the expression on his face for the concern that it was. "Granted, a baby who comes four weeks early isn't in an *ideal* situation, but has an excellent chance of surviving."

He experienced such an upwelling of emotion it almost brought tears to his eyes. His mother had died in childbirth, and she'd gone into the delivery room with no known health problems. "I'm not worried about the baby," he said. "At least . . . not as worried as I am about the mother."

"You said yourself that . . . embolism thing doesn't happen often."

"It doesn't. But Callie nearly died when her liver failed a few years ago," he explained. "At the last minute, they were able to find her a donor and do a transplant, and she's been doing well since. But she's on a lot of immunosuppressant drugs, which makes her more susceptible to infection and illness. Having a baby when her health is already so precarious is . . . tempting fate, in my opinion. If she was my wife, I never would've agreed to it."

Lourdes moved the last of the dishes to the sink. "I'm sorry she's had it so rough. What caused her liver to fail?"

"She had nonalcoholic fatty liver disease. And don't ask me what causes that, because no one seems to know."

"Was the pregnancy an accident, then? Unexpected?"

"No. Her doctor told her that a planned pregnancy for someone in her situation was relatively common. There are added risks, of course, but she was willing to take those risks so she and Levi could start a family." He found his coat.

She moved her guitar and sat down on the couch. She hadn't played it since she'd come to his house, but he noticed that she always kept it close. "There's always adoption."

"He says he was open to that. She wanted at least one natural child."

"So maybe he had to go along with it, to keep her happy. I could see a guy doing that for a woman who's been through so much."

The memory of when he'd been at the hospital, waiting to learn if Callie would survive the transplant, was indelibly etched on Kyle's mind as one of the longest, most nerve-racking days of his life. "But he could lose her. We all could."

She pulled her guitar into her lap and rested her arm over it. "I hope it doesn't go that way."

"So do I." Kyle searched for his keys and discovered them on the counter. "I've got to go to the hospital. Will you be okay here alone?" She'd been planning to stay alone while she was in Whiskey Creek anyway, but it still felt odd to be rushing off and leaving her behind, in *his* house, when they'd been about to spend the evening together.

"Of course."

He was already dialing Dylan and Cheyenne, to begin the process of alerting everyone else in their group, when she caught him at the door.

"Will you text me?" she asked. "Let me know how it's going? That may seem like an odd request, since Callie's a total stranger to me, but I can't help being concerned."

Dylan had answered Kyle's call by then, so Kyle merely nodded and hurried out.

Hour after hour dragged by. The updates

Lourdes received from Kyle were few and far between, since he had to step outside the hospital to get his message to go through. But he didn't have much to report, anyway. Lourdes knew Callie wasn't having a Cesarean. The doctors felt she'd have a better chance delivering naturally. But that was the extent of her information.

She tried to distract herself from the temptation to call Derrick by researching the complications Kyle's friend might face. According to one site on the internet, 40 percent of infants born to women who'd had a liver or kidney transplant were premature, so it was probably fortunate that Callie's pregnancy had lasted as long as it did. Four weeks wasn't as early as it could've been.

Callie was still looking at a whole list of dangers, however — high blood pressure, kidney infection, preeclampsia and cholestasis, to name a few. The baby faced its fair share of peril, too — stunted growth, hepatitis B, hepatitis C, various infections and immune deficiencies, even birth defects. To make the situation even less certain, there hadn't been sufficient testing to determine the effects that some of the newer antirejection drugs might have on an infant. Lourdes couldn't even guess what Callie had been taking, of course. It could be corticosteroids, cyclosporine, azathioprine, tacrolimus or a whole host of others she saw listed on various websites. But Callie was likely on several. Everything Lourdes read suggested someone in Callie's situation would have to be, and Kyle had said as much, too.

Lourdes could understand why he was worried. She was worried for Callie, too. But reading about childbirth was making her uncomfortable for other reasons. She was fairly certain *she* wanted to be a mother someday, but she couldn't really see that happening if she stayed on her current course. Derrick didn't seem particularly interested in raising kids. He never talked about it and put her off if she brought it up. She felt that at forty he should be more interested if he was *ever* going to be interested. They were both too involved in the constant challenges of the music business. Chasing success was like an all-consuming drug, so all-consuming that when she was in Nashville, it was easy to feel nothing else mattered.

Here in Whiskey Creek, however, she had to ask herself if chasing her dream meant she'd miss out on another important aspect of life.

*Stop,* she told herself. Even if she and

Derrick could get past their current problems, she couldn't have a child anytime soon. Her career would be completely dead if she had to pull away for even a few extra months — and trying to resuscitate it afterward would be almost as hard as starting over. How would she juggle those long days and late nights with a new baby?

She went to the couch and strummed her guitar, but she couldn't shake the idea that she was standing on the verge of taking one of two very different paths. That reminded her of Robert Frost's poem "The Road Not Taken." She could still recite some of it. "Two roads diverged in a yellow wood . . ."

Could the downturn in her career be a wake-up call? she wondered. A chance to stand back and reassess, to decide whether she really wanted to exchange fame and fortune for *everything* else?

Her phone rang. Once she reclaimed it from the dining table, she saw that it was Derrick — and silenced it. But when he called back again and again, she finally slid the answer button to the right.

"What do you want?" she snapped. Her uncertainty about him — about so many aspects of her life — left her unprepared to talk to him.

"Don't be mad. Come on. I miss you,

babe. You can't be serious about Crystal. She has nothing on you."

He'd been drinking. She could hear it in the way he slurred his words. "*Mad?* That's what you think? That I'm mad, and when I calm down it'll all go away?"

"That's what I'm hoping. You must be on the rag to be so bitchy."

She almost couldn't believe her ears. "Could you be any more dismissive of my feelings and concerns? Any more disrespectful to women in general?"

"I wouldn't suggest it if it wasn't true. You get like this when it's that time of the month."

"No, I don't," she argued, getting up to pace. "I'm having a legitimate problem with the attention you're devoting to Crystal, and I've had that problem for months. How dare you blame it on my hormones!"

"It's jealousy, plain and simple!"

"In addition to feeling as if I'm being misled!"

"Women!" he cried. "You're all the same. Do you have to be so damn insecure?"

Lourdes gripped the phone tighter. She'd had enough of their arguing, but the cavalier way he was acting now incensed her again. "If you're saying that your ex-wife behaved in the same way, she had good reason, remember? You cheated on her — and I'm guessing more than the one time you admitted to me."

"Because she didn't make me happy."

"Then you should've left her!"

"I should never have told you what happened," he said. "I *knew* you'd throw it up to me one day."

"Was that the only time?"

"There were a couple of others, but that was after our marriage fell apart. There was no saving it. I didn't even want to."

"So, yes, you cheated multiple times." She pivoted at the far end of the room. "Don't you dare act as if *I'm* the one in the wrong!"

"I shared something I wouldn't tell just anyone. I'm asking you to cut me a break, that's all."

Was she being insensitive and unreasonable? A shrew for raising the past?

Resisting the urge to continue the fight, she curled her fingernails into her palms. "I just want the truth, Derrick," she said calmly, evenly, as she paused at the dining table. "If we're going to continue, there has to be honesty between us."

"I'm not in love with Crystal!"

Again, Lourdes forced back the emotion that came rushing to the forefront of her mind — and her mouth. "That's not necessarily the issue. I'm asking if you've ever had sex with her. A simple yes or no will do."

The silence that followed lasted a long time — and the longer it stretched out, the more chilled Lourdes became. He had *something* to say.

"Derrick?" she said, her voice a plea. "Tell me the truth. *Please.* Have you *ever* been with her?"

"Damn it, Lourdes. Why do you have to keep pushing? *Yes,* we were together once, okay? Are you happy now? It didn't mean anything! We were working late one night and . . . and we got carried away. I would've told you, but I knew you'd make a much bigger deal out of it than it has to be."

Lourdes's whole body had gone weak at *yes.* She hardly had the strength to remain on her feet and keep the phone to her ear. She could hear Derrick talking — pleading and cajoling and apologizing. There was at least one "I love *you*" in there. He kept pausing, obviously expecting her to react, but she couldn't drag a single word to her lips. A loud voice sounded in her head, over and over, like a blaring horn. *He just admitted it! He just admitted it! You were right all along!*

"Lourdes? You still there? You gotta believe

me, babe. It was stupid and . . . and me-chanical. It meant nothing. I swear."

Light-headed, Lourdes lurched back to the couch, leaning on all the furniture in between for support. Then she sank down and put her head between her knees.

"Aren't you going to say *anything*?" he asked. "Go ahead. Yell. I deserve it. Just know that . . . that it wasn't your fault. And it has no bearing on how I feel about you."

She squeezed her eyes shut. *Breathe.*

"Honey? Don't take it too hard. Please! I wanted to tell you from the beginning. You have to believe me on that. But you've been so touchy about Crystal. And you've been dealing with . . . such terrible setbacks in your career. I didn't want to *add* to that."

Then why had he? Apparently, she'd been trying to cope with those setbacks while he'd been off banging his new client.

"I always planned to tell you — later. I didn't think this was a good time," he was saying when she tuned in again.

"When would be a better time?" she asked breathlessly. "*After* we were married?"

"There was no rush. We haven't even set a date."

"Because of this."

He went silent.

As Lourdes sat up, her dinner threatened

to come up, too. She barely managed to hold everything down. But some masochistic need to ferret out all the details took over. "How many times?"

"Once. Just once."

Like he'd first claimed with his wife? "When?"

"A month ago. And it hasn't happened since."

The tears burning in her eyes began to roll down her cheeks. She sniffed, trying to hold them back.

"Don't cry," he said. "I hate myself for this."

She dashed a hand across her cheek. "So why won't you ask her to find another manager?"

"Because, like I said, it was one stupid night — a mistake. There's no need to let that ruin everything. My career depends on selling artists. And you need me to maintain good contacts in this industry. That's the only way I'll be able to help *you* get back on top."

Ah, here was the spin. He was keeping Crystal as a client *for her,* even though she'd pleaded with him to do the opposite. "I have to go," she said.

"What do you mean? We were just starting to talk about this. You said you wanted me to be honest, so I stepped up. Don't cut me off when I only did what you asked."

That was wrong on so many levels, Lourdes didn't know where to begin to explain that she owed him nothing for his confession. "Or what?" she said. "Next time you won't tell me?"

"No . . ." He seemed to flounder with that for a few seconds before coming up with an acceptable answer. "It's not going to happen again. I promise."

But she knew how much his promises meant. He'd already promised her, after cheating on his wife, he'd never cheat again.

Suddenly, she began to realize that it didn't matter if he had Crystal find a different manager. *Crystal* wasn't the problem. *He* was. "I'd stay on the phone," Lourdes said, "but there's no need to continue the conversation."

*"Why?"*

"Because whatever we had is over," she said sadly and hung up.

# 13

When Kyle returned, it was three in the morning, so he was surprised to find Lourdes awake. Her guitar was in her lap, but she wasn't playing it. She was watching TV.

"What happened? You quit texting me," she said, setting her guitar aside and coming to meet him as soon as he walked in.

"Sorry about that. When it started getting late, I assumed you'd go to bed. I didn't want to keep you up by constantly making your phone buzz."

"I wouldn't have minded. I've been worried."

She'd also been crying. He could tell from the puffiness around her eyes. "You okay?" he asked.

"Fine." She lifted her chin as if she couldn't imagine why he'd ask. "How's Callie? That's what's important."

He managed a tired smile. "Turns out we

had nothing to worry about."

"She made it through without any complications?"

"The doctors are still keeping a close eye on her, but . . . yeah."

"That's wonderful!"

The aftereffects of the adrenaline that had saturated his system during Callie's labor and delivery had hit him hard on the long drive from UC Davis Medical Center in Sacramento. He could hardly keep his eyes open. "She's *so* happy."

"That must mean the baby's healthy, too."

"Yes. Little Aiden is underweight — only five pounds — but otherwise he seems to be in fine shape. From what the doctors were saying, the lungs are the last organs to form, so they're watching him for pneumothoraces, which are caused when holes in the lung tissue allow air to escape. If he gets one or more of those, they'll do some sort of oxygen treatment, and if that doesn't work, they'll insert a tube in his chest until the holes heal. For some reason, it's more common in boys who are born early than girls."

She moved her guitar to a more secure spot. "Still, a great report. Levi must be relieved that his family came through it so well."

Kyle was surprised she remembered Levi's name. "He is. I've never seen him quite as emotional as he was tonight." He chuckled as he remembered the tears in his friend's eyes. "He's always been a tough guy, a man of few words. We'll give him shit about it later."

"If he's that tough, he can take it."

"He does his share of teasing in our group." He tossed his keys on the counter. "So you ready for bed?"

She nodded.

He wanted to ask about Derrick, if something had happened while he was gone, but he hesitated to upset her, especially just before they finally got some sleep. "I'm glad tomorrow's Sunday," he muttered. All he had to worry about was dinner at his parents' . . .

"Since I came here, one day isn't very different from the next for me," she said.

"They will be once you're working."

"Right." There didn't seem to be much conviction in that word. But she didn't argue with him. While he got a drink of water, she turned off the TV and started down the hall.

"Good night," he called.

"Good night," she called back. "I'm really

glad your friend's okay — and her baby, too."

"Thanks." By the time he put his glass in the sink and walked down the hall himself, her door was closed. But as he came nearer, she opened it.

"By the way, there won't be any need to hire a private investigator to spy on Derrick, so don't feel you have to find me one."

Shoving his hands in his pockets, he leaned against the opposite wall. "So what does that mean? He's managed to convince you?"

"No." She offered him a sad smile. "He admitted to the affair."

Shocked, Kyle straightened. "I thought you said he'd *never* admit it."

"I never dreamed he would."

How had she gotten it out of him? He opened his mouth to ask, but she didn't give him the chance. Slipping back into her room, she closed the door softly.

The following morning Kyle didn't see Lourdes until it was almost time to leave for his parents' house. And then she stumbled out, gripping her head as if she had a hangover, even though he didn't think she'd been drinking last night. They were out of wine. The only alcohol in the house was some hard liquor pushed to the back of his cupboards; it hadn't been used since Halloween, when he'd hosted the party he and his friends always had.

"You have a headache?" he guessed, muting his football game as she reached the kitchen.

She found her purse on the counter and began digging through it. "I think it's a migraine."

"Do you normally get migraines?"

"No. But it feels like my head's about to explode, so it's worse than the usual headache." After swallowing some pills, she shuffled back down the hall.

He got up to go after her and knocked on the door she'd closed. "Can I make you some breakfast?" he called through the panel. "Maybe if you eat, you'll feel better."

"No, thanks," she said. "I just need to sleep."

He wondered if he should push her a little harder. Eating some healthy food would probably help. "You shouldn't take pain-killer on an empty stomach."

When she didn't respond, he went to the kitchen, scrambled some eggs and brought them, along with a piece of toast, to her door. "Lourdes?" he said as he knocked again.

Nothing.

"I'm coming in. Be prepared."

She didn't say he couldn't, so he opened the door to find the room dark and smelling slightly of her perfume. She had the blinds down to keep out the sun, and all of her, except a bit of her hair, was buried beneath the blankets.

He carried the plate to her bedside. "Will you eat this?" he asked.

"Don't try to help me," she replied dully. "And don't expect me to be too friendly. I need a couple of days to feel sorry for myself."

"Feel sorry for yourself all you want. But do you have to starve while you do it? How's deprivation going to improve things?"

Her phone started to buzz. He looked down at where it was lying on the nightstand, but she didn't even stir. The caller was identified as "Asshole."

"That must be Derrick," he said.

"I don't want to talk to him."

After several more buzzes, the call transferred to voice mail.

"I have to go," Kyle said. "I've got that dinner at my parents', remember?"

"Have fun."

He pushed her phone to one side so he could put the plate down, and sat on the edge of her bed. "Listen, I'm sorry about Derrick."

"Better to find out now than later," she said. At least, that was what he thought she said. Her response was muffled by the blankets.

"There you go. Fortunately, you haven't married him yet — and you don't have any kids."

"Don't say that," she muttered. "Don't mention kids."

He'd meant to encourage her, without minimizing the situation. "Maybe that's being too practical, but it's true."

Suddenly, she threw back the covers and looked at him. "What am I going to do?"

"You're going to get up and dust yourself off," he said.

"How?"

"You could start by eating." He slid her breakfast closer. "What do you say? As far as first steps go, it's not a hard one, is it?"

Glumly, she took the fork and stuck a bite of egg in her mouth. "Two years ago I was in Paris for Christmas. Derrick had four dozen long-stem red roses delivered to our penthouse suite and a box of the best chocolates I've ever tasted."

Kyle grinned. "I can bring home some flowers and chocolates, if that's all it'll take to cheer you up."

She huffed as she dropped her fork. "I'm not hinting for flowers and chocolates. The point is . . . I was riding high. I was hitting the top of the country music charts. Do you understand how few people — how few women — get that far? I won CMA's Best New Artist Award that year. I was the only female nominated."

"That's incredible."

"And this is how it ends? I come tumbling from my lofty perch to land on my ass — without even my manager to give me a hand up?"

"What went wrong with your career?"

"I insisted on releasing a pop album, and I left my label to do it — over Derrick's objections, by the way, which of course makes it worse. He wanted me to play it safe, while I insisted it was time to take a risk. And, bottom line, that risk didn't pan out. Most people in the music industry thought the album was good, but it wasn't embraced by my fans. I saw how quickly the people who claimed to love me and my work could turn into my toughest critics."

He could tell that had taken a heavy toll. "Did it cause problems between you and Derrick?"

"A few. We certainly had arguments over it."

"But you still have the songs that were so popular before. No one can take that away from you. Go back to what your core fans like about your earlier work and rebuild."

"That was my plan. But now my confidence is so badly shaken, and my personal life is in such turmoil, I'm not sure I can pull it off. Like I said, I don't even have Derrick."

"He's been calling and texting. You could forgive him and take him back."

She handed him the plate and drew up her knees so she could rest her chin on them. "Yes, I could, but it wouldn't change anything."

"Because . . ."

"This isn't about forgiveness. It's about character. He had a chance to reform, and he didn't respect it. He hasn't changed at all from when he cheated on his wife. And now he's abused my trust, too." She dropped her head lightly against the headboard to stare up at the ceiling. "On top of everything else, I feel like the biggest fool in the world."

"For giving someone a second chance?"

"For turning a blind eye."

Kyle frowned at the barely touched eggs.

"Why don't you come to my folks' place for dinner? Derrick and your problems with him have gone around in your head enough. I'm not convinced that analyzing your relationship over and over will do you any good."

"You mean I should forget my troubles and move on."

"If you're not going to take him back, what other choice do you have?"

She picked up the plate and shoveled another forkful of scrambled egg into her mouth. But the mechanical way she chewed suggested she wasn't enjoying it, wasn't even tasting it. "No, thanks. I'll eat this. I can't face going out today."

"A change of scenery might help."

"That'll mean putting on a happy face. I just can't. But I'll get back on my feet soon. I promise."

He hoped so, because — whether it had heat or not — he couldn't take her back to the farmhouse and leave her there alone if she was feeling as bad as she was now.

"Okay." He stood. "I've got to go do my familial duty."

"Good luck with that." She took one more bite before setting the plate aside and ducking back beneath the covers.

■ ■ ■ ■

Kyle had hoped to beat Brandon and Olivia to his parents' house, to be seated in the living room, comfortably watching football with his father, when they walked in. But, after making those eggs for Lourdes and coaxing her to eat them, he wound up being slightly late. As soon as he arrived, his father ushered him into the kitchen, where everyone was taking orders from Paige so they could get the food on the table.

"Smells good in here," he said.

They all offered him a friendly hello, and Paige stopped yelling out commands and mashing potatoes to welcome him with a hug. "Thanks for coming, honey. Dinner isn't the same when you're not here."

He almost said he came whenever he could, but these days that wasn't strictly true, and he feared someone might call him on it. So he said, "Good to see you, too."

"We're having one of your favorites. Pot roast."

Her babying him somehow made everything worse. "Is there anything I can do to help?"

"Hold that pan of potatoes for me so I can scrape them into a bowl."

He did as she asked. Then she stuck a serving spoon in the potatoes and asked him to carry them to the table.

"I was hoping you'd bring Lourdes," his father said, following Kyle with the pot roast.

"I invited her, but she's not feeling that great."

"What'd you say?" Paige called.

Kyle raised his voice. "I said I would've brought Lourdes, but she wasn't feeling well."

His father motioned with his head for Kyle to move some water glasses so he could put down the roast. "What's wrong with her?"

Olivia and Brandon, who were bringing in the asparagus and the gravy, set their dishes on the table, then waited to hear his answer, but he didn't want to go into what had happened with Derrick. He didn't see anything to be gained by revealing personal information Lourdes deserved the right to keep private. "Nothing huge," he said. "A headache. I'm sure she'll be fine tomorrow."

"So you left her at your place?" Brandon asked.

"Yeah. She's taking a nap."

Paige carried in three beers. She didn't drink, and now that Olivia was pregnant, she wouldn't be having a beer, either. "Do you have the HVAC guy coming to the farmhouse tomorrow?"

Kyle moved out of her way. "I do."

His father took a seat at the head of the table, while his mother went back to the kitchen for whatever was left. "Has it been difficult having a complete stranger staying with you?"

"Not at all. We get along really well."

"You don't think you two would ever start dating, do you?" his mother asked, bustling in with the homemade rolls.

"No," Kyle replied.

"Because . . ."

"Lots of reasons."

She frowned to show her disappointment. "Oh."

Olivia sat across from him. Brandon sat next to her. After his mother perched on her own chair, the one remaining empty seat was beside Kyle. The fact that he was the only single person in the family hadn't really bothered him before, but it was bothering him now — especially since he seemed to be the only single person in whatever group he associated with.

"What happened between you and Noelle?" Olivia asked.

Kyle forgot about his discomfort. He even

239

forgot about the tempting array of food his mother had made. "What do you mean?"

"She had to take a shower at my house today."

"Why? The water heater I gave her isn't working?"

Olivia peered more closely at him. "She had some guy friend tear it out and throw it in her yard. Said she wouldn't take anything from you."

She'd never refused one of his spousal maintenance checks. But Kyle didn't say that. "You know what she's like."

Olivia raised her eyebrows. "That's all you're going to say?"

He scowled at her. "Do you really want to hear the latest?"

"*I* do," Brandon said. "What's going on?"

"Basically, she wants to get back together. I guess she's tired of trying to find someone else to marry and would like some financial support."

A crease formed on Olivia's normally smooth forehead. "That's not what she says."

Irritated that Olivia would question him — since no one understood what Noelle was like more clearly than she did — Kyle shifted in his seat. "What did *she* say?"

"That you keep hitting her up for —" she

glanced at Paige "— you know. That she's tired of putting out for you when you won't date her legitimately."

Kyle dropped the fork he'd just picked up, causing a loud clang as it hit his plate. "You've got to be fucking kidding me!"

"Kyle!" his mother cried. "We're at Sunday dinner! Please, watch your language . . ."

What he'd said had exploded out of his mouth — the result of years of pent-up frustration where Noelle was concerned. It wasn't as if he'd put any thought into it. "Sorry, Mom, but . . ." At a complete loss, he shook his head. "Who's she telling this to?"

When Olivia flushed, he got the impression she'd initially bought into her sister's lies, at least to some extent. "My parents. Noelle said you expected something in exchange for that water heater, and she refused."

He pressed his fingers to his temples. "Don't tell me they believed her."

Olivia's expression turned to one of sympathy and concern. "I'm afraid they might have. She acted so convincing. They said they were proud she had some 'moral fiber.' That she didn't need you because *they'd* buy her a water heater."

Kyle hit the table as he surged to his feet, rocking the glasses and nearly tipping them over. "That's bullshit!"

"Kyle!" Paige said again, but no one was paying attention to her complaints about his language.

"Why would she say something so terrible?" Bob asked, obviously disgusted.

"Because she's sick in the head." Brandon gestured that Kyle should return to his seat. "Relax, bro. We know she's lying. She lies about everything."

Olivia shot her husband a wounded look, as if her loyalties were torn, and that was all Kyle could take. He was glad the two sisters had formed some type of peaceful relationship, but it was beyond belief that Olivia, who'd once known him so well and been the victim of so much of Noelle's unkindness over the years, had bought into the crap she was saying about him.

"There's something *seriously* wrong with her," he said and stormed out.

# 14

Kyle drove past Noelle's house on the way home. Sure enough, the water heater was right there, dented on one side and lying on the grass for everyone to see. That meant the story Noelle was telling would be familiar to more than Olivia and her family. No doubt the neighbors had heard he was trying to get back in Noelle's pants, and God only knew the number of people they'd told.

Too bad Noelle didn't have whoever helped her remove the damn heater drop it in *his* yard. Then he could've disposed of it. But she wanted to make a statement, pile on the drama.

*Typical . . .*

"Damn you." He parked at the end of the street and sat there glaring at her beat-up Honda, which was in the drive. Who did she think she was? Did she really believe she had the right to malign his reputation? He'd done enough to damage his own reputation when he'd gotten involved with her six years ago.

She destroyed every life she touched. Instead of being angry, he should be thanking God he didn't have a child with her, he decided.

Putting the transmission back in Drive, he rolled closer to her house. He wanted nothing more than to go and knock on her front door and tell her exactly what he thought of her. His assistant was right. He'd been far too nice. There'd been *so* many times he'd bitten his tongue when he'd simply wanted to tell her to get the hell out of his life. He was dying to say that now.

But any interaction would make things worse. She was *trying* to engage him. So, resisting actual contact, he pulled to the curb only long enough to put the water heater in the bed of his truck. Then he waved at Prinley Pendergast, who'd come to her door across the street holding one of her children.

When she didn't respond, just peered out at him as if he might inflict bodily harm on her neighbor, he hopped in his truck and drove off.

He was almost home when he got a text from Noelle. He glanced at it while he was waiting at a stop sign.

*What the hell? Did you take my water heater?*

His fingers itched to reply. But he kept driving, and when he eventually reached home and parked next to Lourdes's rental car, he was immediately distracted by the sight of her sitting on his porch all bundled up in the snow gear he'd let her use when they cut down the tree.

Dropping his phone in his pocket without responding to Noelle, he turned off the engine and opened his door. "Isn't it a little cold to be sitting out on the porch?"

"It's California," she said. "I'm making it work."

With all that down in his jacket, and his hat and gloves, he figured she wasn't in any real danger.

"Good to see you out of bed," he told her, "even if it is to sit outside in the cold for no particular reason."

"I'm trying to reset."

"And that means . . ."

"I'm starting over. Embracing the future."

"I see."

"You don't have any Christmas lights up," she said, studying his eaves. "There aren't any decorations in the yard, either."

"There won't be decorations in my yard

until I have kids," he said. "No point in doing that sort of thing just for myself. I wouldn't pay any attention to them."

She zipped his coat up a bit higher. "Does the same go for lights?"

"I don't feel as strongly about lights. If they're important to you, we can put them up at the farmhouse." Anything to make her feel better . . .

Folding her arms, she sank back, all but disappearing into his coat. "I'm not convinced I want to go to the farmhouse."

He froze for a second, then locked his truck. Now that he knew Noelle had a key to his house, and she was acting vindictive, he wasn't going to create an opportunity for her to vandalize his vehicle. He'd get the locksmith out tomorrow, as soon as he finished up with the HVAC guy over at the rental. "What does that mean?" he asked. "Have you decided to go back to Nashville?"

"No. *Definitely* not."

He experienced more relief than he should have, which bothered him almost as much as the anger he was feeling toward Noelle. "So you're going to Angel's Camp? Or somewhere else?"

"Actually, I was hoping you'd consider taking me on as a roommate."

He nearly dropped his keys. "You want to

stay *here*?"

She met him halfway down the walk. "Why not? I'll continue paying on the lease, of course. And if we start to feel crowded or irritated with each other, or I'm not getting enough work done, I'll move."

She no longer wanted to be alone.

He was flattered that she felt she could recover with his support. But he wasn't sure she was as safe with him as she assumed. Olivia or no Olivia, he couldn't forget the jolt of awareness that'd hit him when Lourdes first stepped out of that rental car. And there'd been other instances when he'd felt the same attraction — like that night he'd had her in his arms.

"Um . . ."

"You could do the shopping and I could prepare our meals," she said, trying to entice him. "I'm not much of a cook, but I'd make you a hot dinner to come home to every evening."

A hot dinner after a day at work sounded nice. It was a luxury he hadn't enjoyed since he was married. Even then, Noelle hadn't inconvenienced herself to cook very often.

Besides, the arrangement was temporary, Kyle told himself. For all Lourdes's talk about being done with Derrick, she could reconcile with him at any time, and that would change her plans completely.

So what was he afraid of? He couldn't get too caught up with a woman who wouldn't be around long enough for a relationship to happen . . .

"Now you're speaking my language," he said. "Why not? Sounds like fun."

Her pretty but troubled eyes searched his. "Are you positive?"

His hesitation had spooked her, made her suspect he might not be too eager to have her around. "Of course," he said. "I was just worried that you wouldn't get the privacy you came here to find, but —"

"I feel comfortable with you," she assured him. "I like it here."

Having someone to buy her groceries protected her from the curious stares and whispers she'd encounter otherwise. If news of her breakup with Derrick hit the tabloids, she'd have additional reason to avoid the public eye. He wanted to shield her from that kind of attention. But he could always do her shopping if she was living in the farmhouse . . .

Or . . . maybe not. If they weren't under the same roof, it was entirely possible that she wouldn't feel comfortable calling him up to ask for the little things she needed.

"Let's give it December and see how it

goes," he said. The least he could do was get her through Christmas . . .

She slipped under his arm and put her own around his waist as they headed to the door. "Thank you."

Releasing a sigh, he curved his hand around her shoulder. She felt good tucked up against him. *Too* good. He should send her back to the farmhouse, because he was no friend. Even now he felt a heightened sexual awareness.

But she needed him, and he couldn't let her down. "What are friends for?"

Noelle sat on the floor of her bedroom, painting her toenails with friend and fellow server Genevieve Salter. Noelle loved the bright red polish she'd bought. She planned to freehand some white snowflakes on top. Her red-and-white toenails would be perfect for the holidays, but it was tough to feel excited about Christmas or anything else when she was so angry with Kyle. According-ing to her neighbor across the street, who'd called a few minutes earlier, he'd picked up the water heater she'd tossed in the yard and yet he hadn't bothered to come to her door.

How dare he ignore her! Didn't he care that she was upset? Wasn't he going to do anything about it?

"*I* think he believes he can get Lourdes Bennett," she told Genevieve. "Isn't that the biggest joke you've ever heard? *A country music star?* I mean, Kyle's good-looking and has a nice build and all that. But let's be realistic. Lourdes can get a man with *real* money. A star like herself. Why would she settle for some small-time solar panel manufacturer who won't leave this shit town even though there are so many better places to live?"

Forehead puckered in concentration, Genevieve kept her head bowed over her knees so she wouldn't make a mistake. "I like it here in Whiskey Creek."

Noelle rolled her eyes. "Because you just moved here last year, so it's new — and you have *more* freedom now that your mother's helping you raise Tommy." He was at Genevieve's mother's house right now, thank God. Only two, he got into everything or threw a tantrum if he was refused. Noelle couldn't stand the little monster.

"A town can't get any cuter than this one. As soon as my mother moved here, I knew I wanted to come, too." She added a slight shrug. "But you grew up in this area. I guess you can't fully appreciate it."

"What's to appreciate?" Noelle wiped a

red smear from the side of her big toe. "That I'll never get my lucky break living with all these backwoods rednecks?"

"We're in California. There aren't many rednecks," she said with a laugh that only irritated Noelle further. "Unless you're talking about timber country farther north. Anyway, you should go to the Midwest if you want to see a *real* redneck. You're just mad at Kyle."

"Of course I'm mad at Kyle! He thinks he can screw me over whenever he wants."

The smell of acrylic intensified as Genevieve opened a bottle of topcoat. "*Screw you over?* That's a bit harsh, don't you think? What's he done? He's been making his payments. I know *that,* because it was his money we used to go to San Francisco last month." She sent Noelle a conspirator's smile. "You told him you were about to have your utilities turned off, remember?"

"I *was* about to have my utilities turned off. I just told him I needed more than I did. I deserve to get out and have some fun every once in a while, don't I? *He* does."

"At least he helped you out. And he gave you a water heater when yours broke, didn't he?"

Genevieve had stopped by while they were installing the water heater or she wouldn't

251

have known about it. That was sort of inconvenient, because it made Kyle look nicer than he really was.

"This isn't about money," Noelle said.

"Okay . . . but from what I can tell, he can't be *all* bad. You should see what *my* ex-boyfriend was like." She pointed to a jagged scar on her temple. "That's where he hit me with the claw side of a hammer. If I hadn't been stepping away from him at that exact moment, who knows what kind of damage he would've done?"

Noelle scowled at her. "Why do you have to bring everything back to *your* ex? We weren't talking about Doug."

"Fine. Jeez. What's gotten into you? We can talk about Kyle, if that's what you want. But he doesn't seem so bad, and I thought you agreed. You were grateful for that water heater when you were installing it. You said it would've cost nearly a thousand bucks to buy a new one."

"That just goes to show how easily I let him buy me off."

Genevieve put the lid on the bottle of topcoat and stretched out to let her toes dry. "Does this have something to do with that meal you made him? Didn't he like it or wouldn't he eat it or —"

"Yeah, he ate it," she said, but that meal

was just more proof of how hard she'd tried. She was tired of being overlooked and taken for granted, tired of feeling she wasn't good enough for him. Even when they were married, he'd treated her as if she had some communicable disease, as if he'd rather not get too close. Whenever they made love, she had to initiate it, and then he'd make sure she got what she wanted, but he didn't seem to enjoy it much himself.

He'd never loved her, never given her a chance the way he should have. Now that she thought of all the pain and anguish he'd put her through, she couldn't believe she'd ever had a kind word for him.

"Do I have to keep guessing?" Genevieve asked. "Why don't you tell me what he's done and get it over with?"

"I'd rather not go into it. Everyone thinks he's *so* great. But they don't know him like I do."

"Come on," Genevieve said. "Quit being so mysterious. What'd he do to piss you off?"

Besides making her feel like shit for the past six years? Wasn't that enough? She remembered the day she went in to end her pregnancy. They'd had such a terrible argument a few nights before. She'd wanted him to suffer some backlash, to lose something *he'd* cared about. So she'd aborted the baby. She'd thought, when she told him she'd had a miscarriage, that he'd regret being so harsh with her, that he'd show her a little of the love and concern she craved. But even the comfort he'd tried to offer had been strangely devoid of true feeling. And he'd looked at her with that doubt in his eyes, as if he *knew* she hadn't miscarried in spite of what she'd said. Worse, he would no longer touch her, not to achieve any pleasure of his own. He'd use his hands, his mouth, even a vibrator to get her off — anything to avoid the risk of another pregnancy.

He'd never given her a fair chance, Noelle decided. He could've made her happy if he'd wanted to. But he refused to see anything except the worst in her, and now she was going to make sure he understood what feeling that shitty was like.

"Noelle?" Genevieve prompted.

Noelle dragged herself out of the hell of her own thoughts. "I don't want to talk about it. Anyway, it's too complicated."

"So you hate him now?"

Shouldn't she hate him? All she'd ever wanted was to feel the way he'd made her feel that first weekend. She'd never experienced anything so heady or exciting in her life. But whatever had made him want her had faded fast. After the first couple of days, he'd acted as if it was a chore just to put up with her.

Unwilling to feel what those memories evoked, she turned her attention to the revenge she'd achieved instead. "I told my family that he's been trying to get me to sleep with him again." She'd known how much it would incense her parents to think Kyle was trying to use her. They were so adamant that she attend church, straighten out her life and have some self-respect that they'd immediately flown to her defense.

Whether Olivia had believed her, however, Noelle couldn't tell. Although her sister tried to be supportive these days, Brandon still wouldn't give her the time of day.

Genevieve's eyebrows had drawn together. "Is it true?" When Noelle shrugged, Genevieve smiled broadly. "Because if *that's* your only problem, send him over to my place. I'd be happy to have him in *my* bed —"

"Shut up!" Noelle snapped. "Do you have to be such a stupid whore?"

Stung, Genevieve sobered instantly. "Wow. I'm sorry. I didn't mean to . . . to upset you. I was just making a joke."

"Well, it wasn't funny."

"I've heard you joke like that yourself," she said.

The sullen note in Genevieve's response made Noelle angrier. "I don't care what you've heard. Get out."

"You want me to leave?" she asked, blinking in astonishment.

"Yes, and if you can't have more sympathy for me than that, don't ever come back."

"But —"

"Get out of my house!" Noelle shouted, and once they reached the door, she gave her friend a shove.

"Have you had dinner?" Kyle asked as he dragged various ingredients out of the refrigerator. "Would you like a sandwich?"

Lourdes had come into the house with him, but then she'd gone to the couch to strum her guitar. "Don't tell me you're hungry," she said. "You barely got home from dinner."

He gave her a grim smile. "Yeah, well, that didn't go as planned."

She thought he'd returned awfully fast . . .

Setting her guitar aside, she walked over to the counter. "You were only gone an hour or so, but I assumed you'd eaten."

" 'Fraid not — although I probably should've stayed. Now I'll have to go back later and apologize to my mom."

Once she could smell the food, Lourdes

realized she *was* hungry and pulled some slices of bread from the loaf he'd gotten out. "What happened? Don't tell me you got into an argument with your brother or his wife."

"No. Noelle's causing trouble again."

"Trouble? That's vague."

He slathered a piece of wheat bread with mayonnaise. "Trust me, you don't want to hear any more about it."

"Actually, I do," she said. "Maybe it'll take my mind off my own screwed-up life. What's going on?"

"Basically, she's unhappy that I'm not more receptive to her advances."

Once he was finished with it, Lourdes took the knife. "More of the same? Why would that ruin dinner?"

"Because she seems to have turned a corner. She's figured out that we're never getting back together — and now she's angry."

"Good thing I've committed to do the cooking from now on."

He added several slices of turkey to his sandwich before handing over the meat. "Are you sure you're up to it?"

"Of course. Don't let my tear-streaked face fool you."

His smile slipped away, replaced by a rueful expression. "I just hope she leaves it at what she's done already."

"Which is . . ." She piled on some more turkey but skipped the cheese. She didn't want the extra calories.

"She's been telling lies, spreading rumors, trying to make me look bad."

Lourdes dabbed mustard on her sandwich. "You can't be worried that anyone will believe her. Everyone around here knows you — and her. Don't they?"

"For the most part, but we each have our own circles. Thanks to what she's been telling her parents, they hate me. *And* I'm getting the feeling that Olivia is torn. She wants to believe her sister and fall in line with her family for a change, even though she's well aware that Noelle is hardly reliable."

"How could she want to side with the same sister who purposely stole you away from her?"

"Now that she's happily married, I guess it's easier to forget the past. Anyway, bottom line, I don't need all the shit Noelle brings into my life, and I'm getting tired of it."

Lourdes placed a slice of tomato on her turkey. "So *that's* what has you bugged."

He put the top on his sandwich and grabbed it with both hands. "*Bugged* is too mild a word for what I'm feeling. I've put up with her for years. I've even tried to be good to her. I keep telling myself there's no reason exes have to be nasty to each other. But *nothing* seems to get her out of my life."

"She sounds like a very troubled person."

"She's not deep enough to be troubled. I'd leave it at difficult."

"So what are you going to do?"

"Ignore her. What else can I do? With any luck she'll get bored and go in search of someone who's more interesting to torment."

"And if it doesn't happen that way?"

"We'll see what she does and take it from there," he said, but no sooner were those words out of his mouth than his phone began to buzz — and when he looked down he frowned as if he didn't like what he saw.

"What is it?" she asked.

"I can't believe this."

"Tell me what's wrong."

"It's Ed Hamilton, the editor of the local paper."

A cold chill ran down her spine. "Do you have any idea why someone from the paper would want to get hold of you?"

"No."

"You think he's calling about me."

When he gave her a sympathetic look, she

understood she'd lost her temporary safe haven.

# 15

Kyle paced back and forth while he spoke to Ed. As he'd thought when he first saw Ed's number, Noelle had struck again. She'd alerted the editor, who also served as the paper's only staff reporter, to the fact that they had a celebrity in town. She'd even told him about the furnace in the farmhouse not working and that Lourdes was currently staying with him. Now Ed was following up to see if he could get an interview.

The privacy that Lourdes needed would be much harder to get after this . . .

"It's not every day we have a country music star in our midst," Ed said. "Especially one who's hit the top of the charts, like Lourdes Bennett."

Kyle pivoted at the fireplace. "But we do have a famous movie star who stays in Whiskey Creek from time to time, and Simon has given you plenty of interviews."

"That may be true, but he's not coming

back for Christmas this year," Ed argued. "At least not that I've heard."

"What does *that* have to do with anything?" Kyle asked.

"I'm looking for good content. A paper needs new content in every issue. What was published three or four months ago isn't relevant anymore. So what Simon's done in the past is great, but I need to find more things like that. Folks here are familiar with him. It's time they learned more about Lourdes."

"Why? She's not interested in doing media interviews. She's looking for some quiet during the holidays. You can understand that, can't you?"

"What I don't understand is why you're so hot under the collar," he said. "*I* won't bother her. I just want to talk to her for a few minutes."

He didn't seem to understand that talking to her *was* bothering her. But Kyle had to continue to live here after she left, and he liked Ed. Lowering his voice, he said, "That may be true. One interview wouldn't be a big deal. But after you print that she's in town, everyone else will want to talk to her, too. So I'm sorry, she's not willing to do an interview."

"Wait! You haven't even asked her."

Kyle stabbed a hand through his hair. Damn Noelle. He'd wanted to throttle her for a long time, but never more than now. She didn't give a shit about Ed or the paper. He doubted she'd ever read more than a handful of issues. She'd done this simply because she knew he wouldn't want her to — that it would cause problems.

She was probably hoping he'd lose his tenant . . .

"I'll tell Lourdes you called, and she can contact you if she's interested," he said. "How's that?"

"It's not what I'd hoped for," he admitted. "If she's staying with you, why can't I just stop over? I won't be there long . . ."

"Have you been listening to me, Ed? *Do not come over.*"

"Jeez, calm down, Kyle. I'm only doing my job."

"And I'm only protecting my friend!"

"From what? I'm not going to hurt her! Oh, forget it. I'll wait until the heat's back on at the farmhouse and swing by when she's moved in and I can catch her alone. You won't be able to run interference then," he said and hung up.

Incensed that Ed wasn't willing to drop the matter, Kyle called him right back. But Ed wouldn't answer. "*Don't.* Bother. Her," he said when Ed's voice mail came on.

Lourdes looked a little pale as she sat on the couch. He could tell she was as upset as he was, but his argument with Ed seemed to be affecting her differently. She sat frozen in one spot while he couldn't stop moving.

"See what I mean?" he said as he tossed his phone on the couch. "See what she's like?"

Lourdes clasped her hands in her lap. "Maybe I should do the interview. Get it over with. It never works to make an enemy of the media."

He shook his head. "You should have the choice of taking some time off. It's Christmas, for God's sake."

"But I don't have a choice! Not really. I can't afford *any* negative press right now."

"If you do the interview, everyone in town will be out to catch a glimpse of you. You'll probably have a parade of well-wishers coming by. They'll be carrying plates of Christmas cookies, because this is Whiskey Creek and they're nice folks, but they'll be interrupting your solitude all the same." And if she didn't want that, he'd rather not subject her to it.

"He could write that I'm here whether I give him permission or not, Kyle. He could even put in a snippet about me renting your farmhouse, and then everyone in town will know where to find me."

"Good thing you'll be here with me instead of at the farmhouse," he said. "I'll turn them away at the door."

"You'll be at work most of the time. Besides, I can't continue to stay with you now that word's getting out. What do you think the tabloids will make of it? I've had a steady and very public boyfriend for years. They'll describe us — you and me — as lovers, because that's the most salacious slant they can take, which will mean *I'll* bear the blame for the breakup with Derrick. And you'll be scrutinized along with me."

"I can't believe she went after you. What's her problem?" he muttered, talking about Noelle.

"She's out to punish you for rejecting her. Maybe she's seriously dangerous."

"What do you mean?"

"Just what I said. You don't think she'd ever show up with a gun and shoot you or . . . or something."

"No . . ."

"I wouldn't discount the possibility out of hand. Stranger things have happened."

He had a hard time seeing someone he'd known for so many years as a threat to his life. But there was no question that Noelle

265

could be vengeful and narcissistic in the extreme. "I doubt she'd ever go so far as to bring a weapon here, but that aside, maybe you should move to another town," he said. "Somewhere like Placerville, where you'd have a shot at maintaining some anonymity."

"And what guarantee do I have that it won't happen there, too? That people won't figure out where I am?"

"Placerville's not that far away. I could bring you groceries and whatever else you need. You wouldn't have to leave the house."

"That would be too much trouble for you."

"So what do *you* think you should do? Go home?" He was strangely reluctant to suggest that, but he thought it might be what she'd wind up doing — and maybe it was even best for her.

"I won't go back where Derrick is. I'm not ready yet."

"Then what?"

"I'll do the interview. Suck it up and act as if I don't mind, as if I'm just here to experience Christmas in Gold Country. The more I act as if I *don't* want press, the more of it I'll get. We need to rethink this, sell it right."

"And if some of your old friends from

Angel's Camp see the paper and turn up at the door?"

"They won't know how to find your farmhouse, like folks here do. It's a bit of a drive, which will deter them, too. So they'll call, and when they do, I'll tell them I'm coming to visit after Christmas, once I have my next album done."

"You'll put them off."

"Yes."

Finally, he sat down. "I'm sorry about this."

"It's not your fault," she said.

Suddenly determined to overcome whatever Noelle threw his way, he draped a lap blanket over Lourdes's shoulders and held it together under her chin. "Don't worry," he said. "You do the damn interview, and I'll take care of everything else."

"How?" she asked, gazing up at him.

"I'll turn them all away, like I said — make sure no one bothers you."

"So you think I should still room with you? Despite the furor that might cause in the tabloids when they find out?"

"Let them print whatever they want. Can't be any worse than having them report the truth about Derrick."

"True," she muttered. "It's hurtful and embarrassing enough that he'd cheat — but with my biggest competitor? That'll ensure it's gossiped about much longer than it would've been otherwise."

"You might as well get your story out first. Besides, I love the fact that knowing you're sleeping down the hall from me will drive Noelle mad."

If only having Lourdes so close wouldn't drive *him* mad at the same time. As she slipped her hand in his to confirm that they'd stick together, he had the sudden urge to pull her closer so he could kiss her, and had to stand up and move away.

Lourdes looked spectacular, every bit the beautiful music icon he'd seen in the media before he met her. She'd done her hair and makeup and gotten out of the sweats she'd been wearing since she moved in with him. And nothing about her smile suggested she was ill at ease. Ed Hamilton had to believe she didn't have a care in the world.

She was putting on a brave front, and Kyle couldn't have been prouder of her.

"How did you come to know Kyle?" Ed asked.

Kyle tried not to be annoyed with Ed's overly solicitous manner. He owned a newspaper, so of course he'd pursue interesting stories to go in it. Times were difficult for his industry, what with most people getting their news online or via television. But, bottom line, Kyle felt more protective of his guest than sympathetic to his fellow townsman.

"I met him online a few months ago," she replied. "On my Facebook page."

Kyle was surprised by the implication that their relationship had started sooner than it had. He was pretty sure Noelle and everyone else would be surprised by it, too, but he didn't care. It *could* be true. No one knew what he did on his computer except him.

"So you came out to see him."

"I rented the farmhouse, thinking it might give us a chance to get to know each other better."

"And then the furnace wouldn't work."

"Right, and it was too cold to stay."

"So you came here, but . . . you could've gone to a B and B. There are two in town."

"Derrick and I've been having some . . . disagreements. I didn't feel like being out in public. And there wasn't any need, since Kyle was kind enough to take me in."

"But just until he can get the heat back on, *right?*"

That was a leading statement if Kyle had ever heard one.

"Actually, I'm not sure I'll move back." She flashed him a smile. "Kyle and I have been having too much fun."

Ed straightened in his chair. "You might *continue* to live here? *With Kyle?*"

"Why not?" She shrugged. "He's easy to get along with."

When Ed's gaze landed on him, Kyle could feel the man's shock, but he didn't look directly back at him. He couldn't jump in to elaborate, because he wasn't sure where Lourdes was going with this.

Ed cleared his throat. "Then . . . you're friends?" he asked, trying to press her into a definitive answer on their relationship.

Kyle expected Lourdes to say they were, that although they'd only recently met in person, it felt as if they'd known each other their whole lives or something similar that would be ambiguous as to whether their connection included any romantic elements. So his jaw dropped when she said, "I wouldn't limit it to friendship, no."

As Ed scribbled on his notepad, Kyle raised his eyebrows at Lourdes, and she winked. Apparently, if she had to do this interview, she was going to use it to exact a little revenge on Derrick.

It would make Noelle squirm, too, but she'd asked for it. Why not let her assume his sex life had suddenly improved? There were worse things than to have people think he was Lourdes Bennett's new lover. Maybe folks around Whiskey Creek would finally believe he'd gotten over Olivia, which should stop the pitying looks and whispered comments that seemed to follow him more and more as time went on and he didn't get married.

Problem was . . . implying to other people that they were sleeping together also made *him* think the kinds of thoughts he'd been trying to avoid.

"So how would you say it went?" Lourdes had gone in and put on her sweats again. Now she was sitting cross-legged on the couch facing Kyle so they could discuss the meeting.

"You gave him one hell of an interview," Kyle replied. "Ed was so excited to get home and write his darn article, he was nearly tripping over his own feet as he rushed out of here."

She studied him more closely. "Do you mind?"

"That you *strongly* hinted we were having sex?" He chuckled. "No."

"I figured it'd be smarter not to leave Ed, or the next reporter, anywhere to go. There's no point in accusing people of something they freely admit. Takes all the fun out of it."

"That's ironic."

"What?"

"That you feel you have to admit to things you didn't do just to get some peace . . ."

She'd learned a few tricks over the course of her career. "The life of a celebrity. It's great on the way up. But coming down? That's a bumpy ride."

"You'll be back on top again someday. Someday soon."

She liked how he encouraged her. She got the impression he really believed it was true, and that helped.

"So you think the press will leave us alone now?" he asked.

"I'm hoping. Since I basically told him we're romantically involved, there's no big secret to reveal, no reason to keep badgering me or digging for dirt."

"Smart."

"But you'll have to play along while I'm here — to make it believable."

"No problem."

"Okay, thanks. I'm sorry I didn't have the chance to discuss it with you beforehand. I didn't go into the interview planning to say what I did. I thought of it when he started asking questions and went with it because I decided it might be as good for Olivia to read as Derrick."

He propped his hands behind his head. "Olivia doesn't care who I sleep with."

Lourdes wasn't so sure. Kyle had made some mistakes, but he was still special. No one could miss seeing that. "It's always hard when an ex-lover moves on," she argued. "There's nostalgia attached to it, if nothing else. Anyway, even if Olivia doesn't care, Brandon will be happy. Your folks, too. Now maybe the past can stay in the past, and she can view you as her brother-in-law and not her ex-lover."

"It'll make Sunday dinners easier to tolerate — although my folks will certainly wonder when you don't show up with me."

"Maybe I'll go." She imagined holding his hand and gazing up at him as if she was in love and didn't think that would be very difficult to feign. "We could put on quite a show."

When he smiled, she sensed that he found their deception amusing but wasn't taking it seriously. "Thanks for pretending to be my girlfriend," he said.

She grinned. "I owe you one. And since you can't seem to get a girlfriend on your own . . ."

"Whoa! I haven't even emailed those women you chose on Single Central."

"True. So when are you going to do it?"

"Soon. Anyway, I'm still surprised by what you told Ed. I thought *I* was supposed to be protecting *you.*"

"You've never dealt with the press."

He stared off at the tree they'd decorated. "How will Derrick react to our involvement when he hears? Because he *will* hear."

"Of course. We can count on it. But I'm not sure how he'll take the news. I've always been so loyal, so dedicated to him. It'll come as a shock to think I've already moved on."

"Will he believe it? I mean . . . you were with him last week."

"I *saw* him last week, but I haven't slept with him in over a month, as you know. He'll assume you're the reason, I guess."

"I never called him back the other night when I was supposed to go by and check on you."

"That'll only make this more convincing."

"He might tell Crystal to take a hike and come after you."

"I suppose anything's possible."

Kyle leaned forward. "Is that what you're hoping for?"

"No. I can't go back to him now." She

lifted a hand so he wouldn't interrupt. "It's not just that he had sex with another woman, although that's bad enough. It's that he slept with my *competition.* We've had other problems — when I did the pop album, the way he looks at women sometimes, that sort of thing — but I feel we could've overcome those. No relationship is perfect. It's that he let me down when I was at my most vulnerable. That tells me I can't count on him when I need him, which leaves me no choice. I have to get over him. There's no going back."

"So we're in the same boat."

"Yes. You have to get over Olivia, and I have to get over Derrick."

"I can't wait until Noelle reads that article," he said. "Normally, I don't react to all the shit she does — not these days. It took me a while to learn that I was falling right into her trap when I let her lure me into an argument. I'd walk away feeling terrible about the whole thing, and she'd accuse me of being 'just as bad' as she is. But this . . . I have to admit, it feels good."

"She asked for it."

He got up. "I say we celebrate. Would you like a glass of wine?"

"No. One hangover a week is enough for me, thanks."

"You won't have even one glass?"

She picked up her guitar to keep her hands busy. "Not tonight." She didn't want anything to erode her self-control. Now that she was officially on the rebound, she needed to focus. With every day that passed, being with a man like Kyle looked more and more appealing.

# 16

Noelle probably wouldn't have seen the paper if she hadn't specifically asked to see it. And she did that only because, when she showed up at Sexy Sadie's on Wednesday night to work her shift, everyone was talking about a particular article.

The bartender on duty wasn't A.J. At least she was catching a break there. He'd been calling her quite often since he'd helped her put in and then take out the water heater, wanting to see her. She could tell he was interested in her, but with three different baby mamas and a rap sheet that included domestic violence, he didn't have much to recommend him. If she was going to get with someone who lived in Whiskey Creek, it was going to be someone who was well respected, someone who could offer her more than she already had, not less. A.J. could barely cover his own rent. And he wasn't particularly good-looking. Not nearly as good-looking as Kyle.

She'd been stupid to let Kyle get away. She'd been *married* to him — and she'd blown it. Yes, he'd made her sign that damn prenup. But even so, not many guys would've stepped up the way he did. Most of the men she'd dated since certainly wouldn't have cared whether or not she was pregnant. The best she could've hoped for from any of them was a ride to the closest abortion clinic.

The fact that she'd taken that trip of her own accord five and a half years ago made her sick. If she'd handled the situation differently, she and Kyle might still be together. At the very least, she'd have his child, and that was something he never would've been able to change.

"Why do you want the paper?" the bartender who was on duty asked. She wasn't sure what his first name was. No one ever used it. Everyone just called him Pope.

"Because I'd like to see it, that's why!" she said.

He was busy wiping down the bar. "You never ask to see the paper. Can you even read?" he teased.

He'd lost a tooth in a fight that'd broken out in the bar a few weeks ago. Sexy Sadie's didn't have bouncers, so he'd gotten involved to break it up and taken an elbow to the mouth. But he *was* sort of cute. Too bad he was married and, more to the point, loyal to his wife. He often said things to Noelle that would've made her fighting mad had they come from anyone else. He had a way of softening everything with that crooked smile of his. He didn't mean any harm. She'd come to view him like a brother.

"Hand it over before you lose another tooth," she snapped. She liked to joke around with him. But at the moment, she wasn't feeling too playful. As soon as she'd walked into the bar, Genevieve had taken great pleasure in saying something that had upset her. She was desperately hoping it wasn't true, that Genevieve was just trying to get back at her because they'd had that little spat on Sunday.

Pope made a disbelieving sound. "Talking tough tonight, are we?"

"I mean it. I'm not in the mood."

"I guess you've already heard that your ex has a new woman."

"She's not his *new woman.* She's a country music star. She won't stay here. And he'll never leave. No one knows that better than I do."

Pope slapped the paper he kept behind

the bar down in front of her. "I wouldn't be too sure about that, if I were you. *She's* the one who gave the interview, not him."

Noelle sank onto a bar stool as she read the title. *Lourdes Bennett Finds Love in Whiskey Creek* . . . "This is bullshit," she said, scowling at Pope, who'd stopped washing the counter to observe her reaction.

"Don't freak out too soon. That's plain old sensationalism. The article doesn't go nearly as far as the headline does. She only got here last week, so she can't be *too* in love, and she doesn't actually say she is. She's just staying with him while she writes her next album."

"*What?* I thought she was moving back to the farmhouse once the furnace was fixed. And what happened to her boyfriend? Weren't they supposed to get married?"

"They've broken up. She does say that." He pointed at a paragraph farther down the page.

Noelle hadn't gotten there yet. And now she didn't want to continue reading. She'd never dreamed someone *famous* would swoop in and take the man she'd always assumed *she* could fall back on. Kyle was hers, the person who could give her the most in Whiskey Creek.

This wouldn't be happening if they were

married, she told herself. And they'd still be married if she hadn't made that one fateful error. It didn't seem fair that one bad decision could destroy her entire future.

Why did she keep screwing up? And how was it that her perfect sister never made any mistakes? Olivia had seemed so hurt when Kyle defected — and yet she'd rallied almost immediately and married his stepbrother, only to end up happier than ever!

Olivia always got what she wanted. It was hard not to hate her for that. Although their parents tried to hide it, even they were partial to Olivia . . .

"I need a drink," she muttered as the words *I wouldn't limit it to friendship* jumped out at her.

Pope tilted his head. "You can't be serious."

"I'm totally serious. Pour me one."

"You'll get fired if I let you drink."

"One sip won't do anything."

"You'll have alcohol on your breath. Do you really want to risk your job? How will that help?"

It wouldn't, but she didn't care. Her last best option in life was Kyle, and now he was sleeping with Lourdes Bennett. *Lourdes Freaking Bennett!* How could Noelle ever compete with a country music star if she couldn't even compete with her own sister?

"What's wrong with me, Pope?" she asked as the old bitterness welled up. "Why can't I find a guy who'll love *me*?"

"There are men out there who'd be happy to be with you." He tapped the bar for emphasis. "But you only want the ones you can't have."

She reared back. "Why should I settle? I should be able to get someone as good as my sister has."

"Your values aren't exactly what they should be," he said and walked away.

Because she was spoiling for a fight, she almost called after him. But her manager appeared from the back office, so she closed her mouth and tossed the paper at Pope instead. When it fluttered harmlessly to the floor, he barely cast her a sideways glance before stacking the glasses that'd been washed last night.

What did *he* know about values?

"What'd I tell you?"

Genevieve had come up behind her while she was glaring at Pope's back and keeping an eye on her manager at the same time. There were hardly any patrons in the bar this early, but old Crabtree wouldn't like the fact that she was "lounging around" while she was supposed to be working. He

282

said there was always something she could do to make herself useful — as if it was *her* job to help clean the place.

"Shut up," she growled to Genevieve.

"You're all talk," Genevieve goaded, "telling me how you were going to get Kyle back. He doesn't want you. I bet he *never* wanted you. Who would?"

"You'd better shut up and leave me alone," Noelle warned.

"Or what?"

"You heard me."

"There's nothing you can do, and I think it's high time you accept the truth — Kyle is *way* out of your league."

"He married me, didn't he? It's not like he'd ever touch a fat pig like you."

"Because you trapped him!" she yelled. "And then you were too stupid to see that the baby was the only reason he stayed with you and you aborted it!"

"No, I didn't! I've never said that!"

"You've made jokes about it. I've heard you!"

"Liar!" Noelle's anger flared so hot it wasn't until she'd charged Genevieve and knocked her to the floor, and Pope had pulled her off, that she realized she'd hurt her hands punching Genevieve anywhere she could land a blow.

"She attacked me!" Genevieve cried as blood ran from her nose. "She's crazy!"

"You asked for it," Noelle said.

But that wasn't how Crabtree saw it. He stalked over, took one look at Genevieve holding her hands over her face and scowled at Noelle. "You're fired," he said. "Get out right now! And I don't ever want to see you in here again."

"You can't fire me!" she yelled. "You have to give me my two weeks."

"Would you rather I called Chief Bennett to report this assault?"

"Yes," Genevieve cried, her voice so nasal she was difficult to understand. "Call the cops. She should be thrown in jail."

She meant it. Noelle could see that in Genevieve's hateful glare. Noelle recognized something almost as hostile in her manager's expression. Even Pope was shaking his head as if she filled him with disgust.

"I don't care about you," she snarled at her former friend. *"I don't care about any of you!"* she screamed to the room at large. Then she ripped the name badge from her chest, threw it at her ex-boss and stomped out.

On Thursday morning, when Morgan came to find him in the warehouse to tell him he had a visitor waiting in his office, Kyle was more than a little surprised to learn it was Olivia. He had no idea why she was there. Was it because of the newspaper article that'd come out yesterday? Did she have something to say about that?

If so, she wouldn't be the only one he'd heard from. So many people had called him or brought it up if they happened to see him. He'd never been slapped on the back so many times. "Lucky son of a bitch," Old Man Murphy had muttered and jabbed him in the ribs while he was waiting in line to buy a pack of gum at the Gas-N-Go this morning. He'd never gotten *that* kind of reaction from Old Man Murphy.

And no one had been more excited about his supposed new love interest than Morgan. She'd been positively pumping him for information. *Lourdes is living with you? She's not going back to the farmhouse? But it has heat . . . I paid the delivery charge for the part like you asked me to . . . Is that why you had the locks changed at your place on Monday? To protect her privacy against She Who Won't Be Named? . . . So you're finally moving on. That's hard to believe. Can I meet Lourdes sometime? . . . I could drop some papers by your house. I wouldn't make it obvious . . .*

It'd taken him over an hour to get Morgan to give up on devising a way to see her.

Afraid he'd only get his assistant talking again, he kept his mouth shut and didn't ask if she knew what Olivia wanted. Maybe it didn't have anything to do with the article. Maybe Brandon hadn't mentioned that he'd already told Kyle about the pregnancy and she'd come to tell him herself.

Or maybe she'd come to apologize. He still couldn't believe she'd bought into Noelle's claims that he was demanding sex as payment for the favors he did her. Yes, he'd allowed Noelle to seduce him the weekend that'd started everything, but that was years ago. He would've thought he'd managed to rebuild *some* of his credibility by now.

"Your life is getting interesting," Morgan said.

He didn't respond. He was too busy wondering when news of that article would reach Derrick — and what Derrick might do when he learned that Lourdes wasn't alone in some remote farmhouse, crying over their breakup. Would he try to contact her again? Attempt another reconciliation?

Kyle hoped not. It'd been only a few days, but already Lourdes seemed to be getting over him. At times, Kyle got the feeling she was as relieved about being out of that relationship as she was about being out of the spotlight. She'd told him that leaving Nashville had been necessary for her to feel human and real again. He believed separating from Derrick was part of that. One less burden to carry. He felt she'd been trying to make something work that'd been doomed from the outset. What she and Derrick had in common was a love of music and similar professional goals, and that was it.

Last night, he'd convinced her they should sneak into a hot tub. After thirty minutes or so, they got caught and had to run for it. They were laughing so hard by the time they reached his truck, which he'd parked well down the street, they could hardly climb in. He didn't tell her that the people who owned the hot tub were some of his best friends and wouldn't mind in the least. He didn't want to make her feel she had to be polite and meet them. Besides, the daring nature of slipping in and out of Ted Dixon's backyard was half the fun.

"There you are," Olivia said.

Kyle waited until Morgan started back to her own desk. The way his assistant was dragging her feet, he knew she was hoping to catch part of their conversation. He motioned to suggest she should move a little faster. Then, when she was far enough away not to hear, he closed the door. "What can I do for you?" he asked.

Obviously realizing that his smile wasn't entirely sincere, Olivia stiffened. "You can get over our tiff at Sunday dinner, for one," she said.

"I am over it." He shrugged. "In case Mom didn't tell you, I apologized to her. And now I'm apologizing to you. I'm sorry for causing a scene."

She stared at him as if she wasn't sure whether his apology was any more sincere than his greeting.

"Now it's your turn," he said.

"*My* turn?"

"To apologize."

"For . . ."

"Believing that shit your sister told you."

"It wouldn't be the first time exes have . . . remained intimate."

"The sex in exchange for money or favors element — that's what really bothered me, and you know it. For one thing, I'm not so desperate that I need some sort of leverage to get a woman in my bed. For another, she's the last person I'm interested in."

"I admit it didn't sound like you," she said. "But she's my sister. And sometimes she's so insistent." She shook her head.

288

"Anyway, what's gotten into you lately?"

*"What's gotten into me?"* Normally, he wouldn't grumble about Noelle to her. He felt it was his fault Noelle was in his life, and he had to stand up and carry that cross without complaining, especially to Olivia, the person he'd wronged by getting involved with Noelle in the first place.

But perhaps it was time for Olivia to understand the situation from his perspective. "Your sister is driving me nuts, that's what," he said. "We've been divorced for five years, and she *still* won't leave me alone. She calls me for money constantly. Asks me over to fix something when it's not really broken — or she broke it on purpose. Shows up uninvited at my place, sometimes at odd hours, like when she's getting off work late at night. Stops if she sees my truck in town so I can't visit a restaurant in peace. Calls to tell me a certain show is on. Hints that I should take her to romantic places — or just to dinner. Offers me sex, even though I don't want to be with her in that way and haven't been since before the divorce. Tell me, what does a guy have to do to get rid of her?"

She sat down. "Have you ever loved her?"

"That's your response?"

"It's a fair question."

Maybe it was a fair question, but it struck at the heart of his guilt. "What do *you* think?"

She gave him a pleading look. "Can't we have an honest discussion, Kyle? Please? So much between us has gone unsaid. We were both involved in the same emotional . . . wreck, for lack of a better word. There was a lot of painful drama. And now there are scars. Maybe it's time to . . . to finally address it all."

"Does Brandon know you're here?"

"Of course. He agreed I should come."

"Fine." He thought they might both live to regret the next few minutes but sank into the chair behind his desk. "What do you want to address? I never loved Noelle. You already know that." And she knew why, although he wasn't willing to state the reason. "I tried, but it was a losing battle from the start."

Her lips slanted down. "Don't you see how tragic that is?"

So this was going to be a pity party for *Noelle*? Kyle wasn't feeling it. "Of course I can see it. Or can't *you* see that her inability to function in life is what shackles me to her?"

When she studied him without speaking, he nearly stood as a signal that she should take her leave. What else could the two of them have to discuss? It didn't matter what residual feelings he might or might not have; nothing would change the fact that she was married to Brandon.

"I'm sorry if I hurt you," she said.

He rubbed his face. "That's something you definitely don't need to apologize for, Olivia. We all know that the whole thing was my fault."

"I didn't fall in love with Brandon to get back at you. I'd like you to know that."

"I understand. He's irresistible."

"Really? Sarcasm? That's how you're going to respond?"

He cleared his throat. "Sorry. Look, like I told him last week, I'm glad you're both happy. That's God's honest truth."

"Yes, that's why we've been able to have such a good relationship with you. Not many people would be capable of putting what happened behind them, no matter whose fault it was. And trust me, I have no illusions that Noelle wasn't as much or more to blame than you were." When she gave him the small, rueful smile that followed those words, he realized it was the first time since she'd arrived that he'd felt that little hitch in his chest — the one he normally experienced on first sight. "I want

291

to make sure the relationship we've built — as a family this time — isn't getting destroyed."

Brandon had said the same thing, so they'd clearly discussed it. "Every relationship goes through transitions. We'll be fine."

"I hope you're right." Her smile grew more relaxed. "So you're with Lourdes Bennett now, huh? A country music star? Ted said the two of you were in his hot tub last night."

"We're having some fun together. It isn't serious, though." That was what he and Lourdes had decided to tell everyone. Kyle was happy to do that — and yet there were moments when it didn't feel totally fake. Moments when he was beginning to feel certain things he'd only ever felt for Olivia.

Lourdes didn't know that, of course. He'd be a fool to take any of it seriously. He knew he wouldn't end up with her; they had no chance.

"I see."

He got the impression that Olivia had hoped he'd be more forthcoming on that subject. He wasn't going to add any more, but he had a question he'd always wanted to ask her. Had it really been as easy as it seemed for her to get over him? If so, she couldn't have loved him very deeply. Her

292

ability to bounce back so quickly had left one of those scars she'd mentioned. It was by far the worst he'd ever sustained.

"I knew you'd end up with someone special," she said.

Biting back The Question, he got to his feet. "Thanks. I'm glad you stopped by."

She got up, too, then hesitated. "I have something else to say."

It concerned him that she suddenly wouldn't meet his eyes. "And that is . . ."

"Noelle came over today."

"Don't you see her quite often?"

"I do, but . . . I guess you haven't heard."

"Heard what?"

"She was fired from Sexy Sadie's last night."

He moved around his desk. "What happened?"

She slid her purse strap higher on her shoulder. "She got into a fight with another server."

Somehow, this didn't surprise him. "Is the other girl okay?"

"Yeah. Noelle is, too. *You're* the one I'm worried about."

Kyle's discomfort grew. "Why would you say that?"

"It doesn't make a lot of sense, but . . . she seems to blame you."

293

Stunned, he stood taller. "How could I have anything to do with her losing her job?"

"She claims you set her up. That you made certain . . . promises, led her to believe you two were getting back together. And now you're with someone else. She told me she's tired of being cast aside whenever you decide you don't need her."

"That's crazy!"

"I know. But I felt I should warn you. The things she's saying are . . . harsh and . . . I wouldn't put it past her to . . . to try to punish you."

*He* wouldn't put it past her, either. She'd already gone to the *Gold Country Gazette* with news of Lourdes's presence in town, thinking that would land a blow.

Apparently, she didn't like the way her plan had backfired. "How?"

"I couldn't even venture a guess. When she was talking to me I just got a funny feeling that she was far angrier than she had any right to be. She was almost delusional in the way she ranted on and on about you. As if you *had* been sleeping with her and making promises of reconciliation. She seemed completely convinced you've been using her."

Kyle didn't have words for what went through his mind. All he could get out was

"I've never led her to believe I have *any* interest!"

"She builds up every little thing you do in her mind, tells herself you *must* care about her if you're willing to pay so she won't lose the use of her car or whatever. And I've known for a long time that she wishes she'd never lost you. She won't face the fact that it's truly over and prefers to think there's nothing standing in the way of getting you back."

"Only now there is something — or rather some*one* — in the way."

"Yes. Lourdes."

Kyle narrowed his eyes. "She'd never do anything to *hurt* Lourdes . . ." He'd told Lourdes she wouldn't, but the things Olivia was saying about her sister . . . He wasn't sure anymore.

Olivia's troubled eyes finally met his. "I doubt it would be anything *too* serious. But I wouldn't put it past her to target Lourdes in some way."

"Like . . ."

She spread out her palms. "Write her a hateful letter. Challenge her in public. Post unflattering reviews of her music. Spread gossip and lies — here and on the internet. The usual petty stuff."

He could easily see Noelle acting so spiteful. "I don't want anything to ruin Lourdes's stay here."

Flashing him another smile, Olivia reached out to squeeze his arm. "You really like her, don't you?"

Fortunately, Olivia went on before he had to admit or deny how he felt.

"I want what's best for you, so I'm going to be just as glad to see you happy as you are to see me happy with Brandon. I hope you believe that."

"I do." Impulsively, he gave her a hug to make up for some of his surliness, which had very little to do with her and far more to do with her sister, and was reassured when it felt . . . normal. Not sleazy, as if he was using it as an excuse to get close to her. Or stiff and awkward like the occasional brief hug convention had foisted upon them at various family holidays. It simply felt sincere and respectful, as an embrace between a brother- and sister-in-law should, not encumbered with the residue of all they'd once been to each other, which had been so hard to escape.

"We may outdistance the past yet, you and I," she murmured as she looked up at him.

Except that his relationship with Lourdes was a sham. And now, thanks to Noelle and her vengeful soul, Lourdes might have to pay for even the pretense of happiness.

# 17

"It's about time I wrote some of these women, don't you think?" That evening, Kyle sat at the breakfast bar, with his laptop open. "Or at least acknowledge the ones who've tried to contact me?"

Lourdes was moving around the kitchen across from him, baking a chocolate cake. She said she'd made up the recipe, and he was going to love it.

The house certainly smelled good. He was enjoying the hominess of having her around. More and more he looked forward to getting off work at night. But he was trying hard not to get *too* caught up in spending time with her. He was beginning to notice things he didn't notice about his other female friends — the way her eyes lit up when she liked something, the infectious sound of her laugh, the warmth of her body when she leaned close to show him a picture on her phone. He could still smell her perfume from an hour earlier, when she'd put his plate down at dinner, for crying out loud. They were all classic signs of infatuation; he recognized that. So he was going to do his damnedest to make sure he didn't get himself into another bad situation.

"You're on Single Central?"

She sounded slightly startled, and he could see why. Neither of them had mentioned the online dating site since shortly after she created his profile. He'd wondered about that, since she'd been so gung ho at the start. "I thought I should follow up."

After a slight pause, she said, "Why the sudden interest?"

"I figure there's no need to waste the time you spent getting me on here."

"On a site where you didn't want to be in the first place?"

Feigning greater interest in Debbie Mayo's profile than he actually felt, he said, "Maybe I was being too closed-minded." He had to do *something*, didn't he? After more than six *years* of carrying a torch for Olivia, and feeling guilty about it because of Brandon, he was grateful that those feelings were finally dissipating. But he couldn't let another woman — a woman with whom he had no better chance — replace her. To avoid that, he'd been thinking he should make more of an effort on the dating front, try to meet someone else, someone who might be a real possibility.

Lourdes came over to see what he was looking at. "I can't say she's not attractive . . ."

The scent of her perfume reached him again. It smelled so good he almost closed his eyes and breathed deeply. Fortunately, that was a temptation he resisted. "But?"

"Is there any rush?"

There hadn't been — until today. He'd thought he had his undying devotion to Olivia to keep him safe from the attraction he felt for Lourdes. But that shield seemed to be wearing thin. And with Lourdes so present and accessible, it suddenly seemed critical that he find another love interest.

"Not really," he lied. "Why?"

"It's just that . . . you know what I told Ed at the *Gold Country Gazette*. What he printed yesterday."

"He hinted that we're romantically involved."

"Yes. And I led him to that conclusion, since I'm staying in your house and people naturally assume that, anyway. You said yourself everyone's bought into it."

"They have." He indicated the profile of the woman he'd been considering. "But she isn't from Whiskey Creek. No one in town needs to know I'm dating anyone."

"I was thinking we should take down your profile, not use it yet. Single Central is a big site. No telling who might see it. And when the other papers pick up the story, the news that I've replaced Derrick with someone else — with *you* — will be everywhere."

So *that* was why she'd backed off the online dating idea. It'd been for strictly practical reasons. He'd been tempted to hope there was something else at play, that maybe she was starting to feel some of the attraction he was. The way she looked at him sometimes suggested it.

Or maybe he was making things up . . .

"I could've been wrong when I assumed word would spread that far," Kyle argued. He'd been wrong about the people of Whiskey Creek, hadn't he? Plenty of his fellow citizens had approached him when he was out and about, but no one had come banging on his door the way he'd feared. "It's possible Ed's article will go completely unnoticed, except by the people here. Who cares what's printed in the *Gold Country Gazette*?"

"Interest may seem localized at the moment. But there are services that scour the smaller papers for anything that might be of interest to the bigger papers and gossip rags. They'll find this." She wiped some flour from her cheek. "I'm sorry, but I didn't consider that when I was so flip with Ed. I thought I was doing us both a favor, since a 'relationship' with you allows me to save face, and you to get out from under the stigma of being hopelessly in love with your brother's wife."

"I'm still good with that plan." He just hoped it wouldn't make matters worse . . .

"Are you sure?"

"Of course." He gestured at his profile. "Go ahead and pull this down. You can help me put it up again when you're ready to leave."

She slid the computer over. "It's done," she said a few seconds later. "Thank you. The last thing I need is for someone to recognize you and notify the media that you might be as much of a cheater as Derrick. They'd say that I couldn't keep a man or something similar." She made a face. "The gossip rags love that type of thing."

"The Jennifer Aniston treatment."

"Yes."

He couldn't leave her exposed to more scandal. Lourdes was just beginning to relax and feel safe here. He wanted to give her the time she needed to heal. "So when's this cake going to be done? I'm ready to have a slice."

She got up and gave him a hug. "Soon."

Cursing the sudden awareness that flooded through him, he moved into the kitchen the moment she let him go. If he couldn't date — couldn't even distract himself by searching for someone he found attractive — he could be looking at the longest three months of his life. "I haven't told you what I heard today."

"What'd you hear?"

"Noelle got into a fight at work and was fired last night. I've been told it was because she was so upset about that article."

"She asked for that article! She's the one who told Ed I was in town!"

"True, but calling Ed is nothing compared to what she *could* do. Maybe I should go over there, see if I can defuse the situation." Noelle was the last person he cared to see, but if it would stop her from doing something spiteful to Lourdes . . .

"Please don't. I'm beginning to think she's the kind of person who'd hurt herself and say you hit her. The more I learn about her, the less I trust her."

"It's not *me* I'm worried about," he said. "I'm not a public figure, so I'm far less vulnerable than you are."

"Don't do it for me," she said. "She has no reason to go after me."

"Jealousy is . . . jealousy. It isn't rational."

"True, but there are no guarantees that going over there will help — especially since you can't give her what she wants. I say we go on as if she doesn't exist." She gestured toward the living room, with the Christmas tree lit up in one corner. "It's the holidays. Let's forget anything and everything that's upsetting and just enjoy the next few weeks."

"What about that album you need to write?" he asked.

She gave him a hopeful smile. "I've started my first song, although progress is slow. I've lost so much confidence that nothing seems to be any good. But I'm hoping the process will get easier with time."

"You just have to keep at it."

"Exactly."

He rested his hands on his hips. Maybe he'd be doing Noelle as much of a favor as he'd be doing himself if he quit trying to set a new standard for amicable exes and shut off all communication. Except that monthly check, of course, which he'd agreed to pay.

Actually, considering how much she'd borrowed, he didn't owe her a check, not for six months or more. But if she'd mind her own business and leave him alone, he'd be happy to send it. Now that she'd lost one of her jobs, she was going to need that money more than ever —

Suddenly, he realized that he *did* have some leverage with Noelle.

"Don't worry," he told Lourdes. "Everything'll be okay."

It was after midnight when Kyle called Noelle. It had taken that long for Lourdes to go to bed. He didn't want her overhearing the conversation, but he also didn't want to let another night pass without trying to head off any future trouble. As much as Lourdes felt he shouldn't do anything, Noelle wasn't the type to back off on her own — not when she was as fixated as she'd been of late. Lourdes just happened to come to town at a bad time, during one of the many periods when Noelle wasn't preoccupied with any other relationship and was making another run at him. She felt displaced and rejected, and Kyle guessed she'd make their lives miserable if she could.

As he paced on the back patio, waiting for her to pick up the phone, some of their worst arguments paraded through his mind. She'd often lost her temper and thrown things, broken things or come at him as if she was going to strike him. That was part of the reason he'd refused to buy her the big house and expensive jewelry, trips and clothes she'd demanded. He wasn't going to be that foolish with his money. Just because business was good didn't mean it would *always* be good. He had to prepare for the worst. But he also wasn't interested in rewarding her behavior.

Fortunately, she'd never caught him at enough of a disadvantage that she'd seriously hurt him. Although there'd been times when he should've called the police, he'd had too much pride. He didn't want his parents and friends — the whole town — to hear how terrible his marriage had turned out to be. So when she got confrontational, he'd hold her down, making it impossible for her to hit, kick or scratch. Or, more often, he'd leave. He'd spent many a night at his office, which Morgan knew; that was, no doubt, partly why she hated Noelle. Morgan was the one who'd arrive the next morning and find him on the air mattress he stored in the closet of his office. She'd probably told other people he wasn't happy with Noelle, so it wasn't as if he'd been able to keep his difficulties a secret. But at least no one knew his situation was quite as bad as it had been.

Noelle didn't answer. So he called again. She always had her phone close by, and if she was asleep, he meant to wake her.

Noelle seemed to be worse now than when he was married to her, he mused as the ringing started again. More reckless. More spiteful. Willing to go even further than before. And he'd been shocked by her behavior *then.* That was what had him so concerned. It was the reason he intended to make it *very* clear that she'd better not do anything to destroy Lourdes's image or hurt her in any other way. Because he would not let that slide.

"*Now* you call me?" Noelle snapped when she picked up.

She didn't sound as though she'd been sleeping. Not only was her voice strident, she acted as if he owed it to her to keep in touch, and she'd won some sort of victory in finally getting a call from him.

"I have no idea what you're talking about," he said.

"You caused me to lose my job. That's what I'm talking about!"

After speaking to Olivia earlier, he'd been somewhat prepared for this accusation. He knew Noelle tied that incident to him, although it made sense only in her own mind. "That's ridiculous. Surely even you can see I had nothing to do with it. I'm sorry it happened, but from what I hear, you have no one to blame but yourself. You started the fight, didn't you?"

"No, I didn't *start* it! She provoked me!"

He was too focused on making his point to ask who "she" was. "But I'm guessing you're the one who got physical."

"I wouldn't have gone after her if I hadn't been so upset by how shitty you've been treating me."

*There* was the connection, presented with her classic, twisted logic. But this time Kyle's curiosity about the identity of her victim overcame the need to direct the blame where it belonged. "Who's *she*?"

"Genevieve Salter."

"Your *friend*? You like her! I've seen you with her on several occasions."

"She *was* my friend. She's not anymore."

"Because . . ."

"Because she . . ." There was a pause as she tried to come up with an answer, but she must not have been able to devise one she liked. "Oh, never mind. You won't believe me, anyway. I know how you are."

"I'm honest, Noelle, while you'd rather lie to yourself."

"Shut up! What happened doesn't matter. Genevieve's not worth feeling bad about."

"And your job?"

"I didn't want to work at Sexy Sadie's anymore, anyway. That place is a dump. I deserve better."

"You were already struggling to get by." From her own admission, she had only $250 in savings — the money she'd told him she could put toward a new water heater — which, come to think of it, she still needed, since she'd foolishly torn out the one he'd given her. But, according to Olivia, Noelle had manipulated their parents into helping her, so maybe she still had a small financial cushion.

"I'm a good server," she said. "I'll get on somewhere else."

He doubted it would be in Whiskey Creek. There weren't a lot of jobs, and her reputation would precede her. Which meant driving to a different town or maybe the Indian casino that wasn't too far away . . .

But why get into that? What she did was *her* problem. "In the meantime, my spousal maintenance is going to be pretty important . . ."

There was another pause, this one longer than the last. When she finally responded, he heard a heavy dose of suspicion in her voice. "What's that supposed to mean?"

"It means you'll need money to get by, no

matter what you do. And you'll be relying on me to provide it."

"You make it sound like you're doing me a favor, as if you have some choice in the matter," she said. "You *have* to pay me. It's court-mandated. They'll take it out of your bank account if you don't."

"Except that I'm thousands of dollars ahead, and I can prove it." He hadn't added up the exact amount. Until now, he'd had no desire to see it. But he'd kept good records. "Considering the money I've given you, it would be six months or so before I'm required to make another payment."

"Six *months*!" she cried. "There's no way you've given me that much!"

"Think about it. For the past five years you've been treating me like an ATM. I paid over $2,000 to fix your car. I covered your rent several months when you ran short. I've paid cell phone and utility bills. And not too long ago, I paid your insurance deductible so you could get your operation. That alone was $3,500."

"You're holding my operation against me? My God! What kind of man are you? That was caused by the death of *our* baby."

"From the *miscarriage,* yes. Almost six years ago. We could look more deeply into that, if you feel it's necessary to bring up

310

the baby. In any case, I doubt the courts would see me as the responsible party if this ever turned into a legal battle."

"You bastard!"

He could hear the shock in her voice. He'd never played hardball with her; she wasn't used to it. But he was finished letting her get away with so much. Finished punishing himself for the hurt pride and stupidity that had led him to get involved with her. "I can also prove that I've bent over backward to be helpful."

Surprisingly, she seemed to make an effort to rein in her temper. "And I've been grateful. I . . . I brought you dinner the other night, didn't I?"

To her, that somehow made their contributions equal? "You did. That was a nice gesture." Even though she'd only done it hoping he'd get back in bed with her . . . "So I'll be generous and take a hundred bucks off the total I've paid."

Silence. Now he'd really thrown her. "What are you getting at, Kyle? *Are you saying you're not going to pay me from now on?*"

In the moonlight, Kyle could see the glimmer of snow clinging to the ground in small patches. He turned up the collar of his coat, but he could scarcely feel the cold. "No. That's not what I'm saying. I wouldn't want you to have to move back in with your parents." He knew she'd do *anything* to avoid that. Then they'd learn exactly how she was living — staying out all night, drinking and partying to excess, sleeping around, buying stuff she didn't need and then asking to borrow money.

"So why are you mentioning it?" she asked.

She could tell *something* was up. "Because I think it's time you and I came to an understanding."

"You're piling on, making things worse," she accused him.

"That isn't true."

"It is! You're so full of yourself now that you have someone else. But you should realize Lourdes won't be staying forever, Kyle. You won't be able to have a serious relationship with her. She won't even remember your name once she goes back to Nashville."

Noelle had stated that in her typical mean-spirited fashion, but Kyle believed it was true. "What happens between me and Lourdes is none of your business, Noelle. So don't give me any advice. All I want is for you to stay out of it."

"I'm just saying you might not want to be *too* nasty to me. Once she leaves, you may need me again."

What was she saying *now*?

"No, I won't, Noelle. I will never need you, and I haven't needed you in —" he almost said forever but figured there was no reason to be needlessly cruel "— a long time. And for the record, no matter what *you* seem to remember, we haven't had sex since before we separated. There were even three or four months at the end of our marriage when we slept in separate rooms." Once she'd told him she'd lost the baby, he hadn't been willing to risk another pregnancy. He hadn't trusted her. Nor had he desired her. And he had no idea why she felt that would change, except that, as usual, she was inventing things.

"Because you've always had a boner for my sister, even though she's with your own brother!" she screamed.

She'd hurled that accusation at him so many times. It used to bother him — because it was true. But tonight, when he could easily answer with "whatever" and mean it, he knew he was truly over the past. Finally!

"You'll be sorry for what you've done to me," she said. "You've ruined my life!"

His indifference had only made her angrier. "Don't hang up." He could tell she was about to. "You need to hear the rest."

"Go ahead and say it," she cried. "You're not going to pay me anymore. Isn't that what you're driving at?"

"Whether I pay will depend on *you.*"

*"How?"* This response sounded more sulky than angry.

He pivoted at the corner of the patio but kept his head down so his voice wouldn't carry inside the house. "You have to stay *completely* away from me and Lourdes. No more calls, no more pleas for help, no more seeing my truck and stopping when I'm trying to eat or shop or grab a cup of coffee —"

"Oh, get over yourself," she broke in. "You make it sound like I'm *stalking* you."

Sometimes it felt that way, but he went on as if she hadn't spoken. "And you'd better not do anything malicious to Lourdes. If I hear that you've been saying slanderous things, posting gossip on the internet or doing anything else that could damage her career — or hurt her in any way — you won't get another dime out of me."

"You can't refuse to pay me forever," she said, slightly less defiant than she'd been before.

"That may be true. But I can hold off until I owe you money. Then I can make you try to force me. And just before you

314

manage *that,* I can take you back to court and whittle down the amount I owe per month. I promise you, if it goes that way, you'll have to pay a lot more of your own bills than you're paying now."

"You've already had the amount lowered once! The judge won't let you do it again."

He didn't think she was totally convinced of that, despite her words. And neither was he. He'd been so eager for the divorce he'd agreed to pay far too much, so he'd gone back to court to have the amount adjusted. But the judge had simply consented to what he'd offered in lieu of the first amount, which was still more than he should have to pay, considering they'd been together for such a short time and didn't have any children. He'd been largely supporting her for the past five years. That was plenty of time for a childless partner to take over responsibility for her own finances.

"Are you willing to take that chance?" he asked. "Are you willing to risk getting much less? Or even zero?"

Nothing. No response.

"At least tell me you understand my terms," he said. "Otherwise, I'll assume you refuse to comply, and I won't send January's check."

"You're serious! I just lost my job, probably won't even be able to *eat,* and you'd do this?"

She always had her parents. He wasn't too worried about her eating. "I absolutely would," he said.

"You're not being fair —"

"Tell me you understand," he repeated. "That's all I want to hear."

After several seconds, she gave him a grudging, "I understand." Then she added, "But I'll never forgive you for this," and disconnected.

Kyle didn't feel the elation he'd hoped to feel after that call. Noelle's parting words left him uneasy. To keep the peace in Whiskey Creek, to prevent the past from tainting Olivia and Brandon's happiness, and to atone for his own mistakes, he'd always chosen to avoid direct confrontation. He'd stalled Noelle, cajoled her, ignored her when he could and compromised with her when he couldn't. His go-to solution had been to give her money, because that satisfied her the quickest. He'd never decisively kicked her out of his life — not until now — and wasn't entirely sure how she'd react.

But he meant what he'd said. He wouldn't hand her another dime if she did *anything* she shouldn't.

He was finished with letting what he'd felt

for Olivia control him. There was no question he was finished putting up with Noelle. Although he'd been shackled to both women, for different reasons, he was breaking free . . .

Taking a deep breath, he smiled. Maybe he *did* feel a little elated.

# 18

As soon as she got off the phone with Kyle, Noelle called Olivia, but Olivia didn't pick up. It took three attempts before she did.

"Hello?"

At last. When Olivia answered, Noelle could tell by the thickness of her voice that she'd been sleeping.

"Noelle? Is that you?" she said when Noelle didn't immediately respond.

Drawing out her sister's wait for dramatic effect, Noelle fiddled with the faucet on her kitchen sink. It'd started leaking about five minutes ago, and nothing she'd tried had fixed the problem. She needed a plumber — for this and to install a new water heater. As a matter of fact, she needed a lot of things, and she'd be much less likely to get them now that she'd lost her job. She wasn't sure why she'd been working at Sexy Sadie's, anyway. She shouldn't have to work two jobs, not when everyone around her had it so much easier. Olivia was planning Riley's wedding — as if *that* was hard.

"Noelle?" Olivia repeated, this time with the appropriate concern. "Are you okay?"

"No. I'm *not* okay," she said, faking tears. "Kyle just called me."

There was some rustling at the other end. "This late?"

"I told you. He isn't the considerate guy you think he is."

Olivia made no reply, but Noelle could hear Brandon in the background. "Who is it, babe? What's going on?"

"It's my sister," Olivia murmured. "Go back to sleep. I'll talk to her in the living room."

"Hang on," Olivia said into the phone and didn't speak again for several seconds — until she wouldn't disturb her beloved husband. The same beloved husband who wouldn't give Noelle the time of day. He was a prick, she thought, just as bad as his stepbrother.

"Okay . . . *what's* going on? *Why* did Kyle call you? And please don't suggest it was a booty call. He told me you two haven't been seeing each other in that way."

"Of course he'd say that. Now he's banging the great Lourdes Bennett, he has no use for me. He was calling to tell me he's not going to pay my spousal maintenance anymore. Can you believe that?"

"But Kyle knows he can't stop. When you divorced, he agreed to a certain amount every month. I remember that amount went down not too long ago, but he's been paying, hasn't he?"

"Apparently, he's planning to take me back to court and have it reduced to nothing." She sniffed. "I have no idea how I'll get by."

"Don't panic yet. I'm not sure the judge will allow —"

"Kyle's got the money to hire the kind of high-powered lawyers who can do it, Olivia," she broke in.

"Still, that doesn't sound like Kyle. He's tried really hard to be generous with you."

"You only say that because you don't want to believe he could be such an asshole. You'd rather believe *I'm* the cause of all the problems between us. Everything's *my* fault. It's always *me.*"

"Noelle, stop. I'm not pointing any fingers. I'm trying to figure out why he'd suddenly change course. He's been great about paying you. He's even gone above and beyond on occasion, probably more than I know."

"He hasn't gone *above and beyond.* He's been keeping track of every dime he's ever given me, and now he's charging me for it."

"Anyone would do that, Noelle. He doesn't owe you extra money, so even a loan is nice. All he owes is the amount specified by the court, which he pays — usually early, since you're so desperate for it."

"You want me to give him credit for that? Why would I? It's nothing, a pittance! If we were still married, I'd be living as well as he does."

"But you're *not* married, and you haven't been for five years."

"That doesn't matter. He doesn't have to count every dollar, especially when he has so much more than I do."

Olivia made a sound of irritation. "Sometimes the way you think — Never mind. Anyway, he just gave you a water heater. That was nice, wasn't it?"

"He gave me an *old* water heater."

"He didn't have to. And I'm sure he's not charging you for it."

"Because he wanted to get it out of his warehouse and didn't have anything better to do with it!"

After a brief pause, Olivia sighed audibly. Then she said, "I'm sorry. It must be upsetting for you. After losing your job, any new problems would seem overwhelming."

That was a dodge. As usual, her sister was

just paying her lip service. Olivia wouldn't truly take her side, not when it came to Kyle. She respected him too much and didn't have that same respect for Noelle. But who was Olivia to feel superior? She acted as if she'd done a great thing by forgiving Noelle for getting together with Kyle, but she and Kyle weren't even a couple when Noelle ran into him that night at Sexy Sadie's. Olivia had moved away to Sacramento, put her business ahead of her supposed "love." Then she'd played the martyr when Noelle stepped in to take what she'd left behind.

She always had to make Noelle look bad, even though Olivia had married Brandon, a man just as good-looking and successful as Kyle. Olivia had everything her spoiled heart could desire.

How was that fair? How was any of this fair?

"That's *all* you're going to say?" Noelle said. "I'm sitting over here in this piece of shit condo of Cousin Harry's, trying to keep it in some kind of decent shape, with Christmas coming up, no job and an ex-husband who's trying to pound the last nail in my coffin. And all you can say is you're *sorry*?"

"I don't know what else you expect."

322

"Why don't you do something to help me for a change?" she screamed. "Put some action behind all that sisterly love you're pretending to feel?"

"Noelle, have you been drinking? That's the only time you get so belligerent."

Slamming the faucet wide-open, Noelle let the water pour. "I've had a bit to drink. Wouldn't you, if you'd just lost your job and everyone was turning against you at the same time? Even my own sister won't help."

"In what way?"

"You have so much. You could get me through this rough spot if you really wanted to."

"Noelle, we've gone over this before. Brandon and I make our decisions together, and we've agreed that we won't give you any money."

"Because both of you are too stingy!"

"That's not true!" Olivia said. "You can call me stingy if you want, but Brandon is one of the most generous people I know. The problem is, you've manipulated people in the past. That makes it difficult to trust you."

"What a bullshit excuse. But if you won't lend me any money, even though you're my freaking *sister,* at least put in a good word for me with Kyle. He worships the ground you walk on. All you'd have to do is hint that you won't put up with him treating me badly, and he'd change his tune right away. He'd do *anything* for you — Lourdes Bennett or no Lourdes Bennett."

"I'm not convinced of that," Olivia said. "Not anymore."

"Oh, quit it. Kyle and I would still be together if it wasn't for how badly he wants you. *You're* the reason my marriage fell apart, and yet you think *you* have reason to be bitter."

"You leave me almost speechless when you say stuff like that. You knew Kyle wasn't in love with you when you married him, so you can't blame me as the reason it didn't work out. No matter how you twist things — that Kyle pursued you and you gave in during a weak moment, or however you've attempted to explain it to me in the past — you slept with the man your sister was in love with. The man your sister had been sleeping with for two years, and you did it practically the minute I left town. Even worse, you got pregnant by him —"

"As if I had any control over that! And I lost my baby! Don't you think I've suffered enough?"

There was a brief silence, after which Olivia spoke in a more measured tone.

"Noelle, let's stop this before . . . before we ruin the progress we've made. I can't get involved. I love you as my sister, but whatever happens with you and Kyle . . . that's between the two of you."

"Great. Thanks for nothing," she said and hit the end button. But she wasn't going to leave it there. Olivia, Kyle and Brandon and all their popular, stuck-up friends had everything. They'd *always* had everything, and they'd never been willing to spare even a few kind words for her.

She was going to get back at them if it was the last thing she did.

The article in the *Gold Country Gazette* hit the national media six days later, on Thursday. Lourdes had been about to start dinner when she received several texts from Derrick.

What the hell? You're seeing someone else? Already? When were you going to tell me?

And:

No response? What we had for three years doesn't warrant even a short explanation?

He'd tried to call her several times, too, but she'd let those calls transfer to voice mail. If he cared about her, if he was planning to save their relationship, he wouldn't have left things as they were since her ultimatum about Crystal.

Besides, she felt she should see what was circulating in the media before she took him on in any kind of argument.

Rubbing her arms against a sudden chill, she sat at the kitchen table with her laptop and put her name into a search engine.

Sure enough, there were quite a few Tweets, Facebook postings and blog mentions on the internet. Her love life wasn't exactly front-page news, but it was receiving a fair amount of attention in the world of celebrity gossip. Nearly an hour later, she was still sifting through posts and articles.

*Country Star Lourdes Bennett Bails Out on Love?*

*After more than three years, Lourdes Bennett is no longer romantically involved with her manager, Derrick Meade. According to an interview given to the* Gold Country Gazette, *a small paper in the town of Whiskey Creek, California, where she's taking a sabbatical from the music business, she's dating a new man . . .*

Lourdes didn't mind that article so much.

It was fairly factual. Many others were also based mostly on what she'd said. But some weren't.

*Has Crystal "Hottie" Holtree stolen Lourdes Bennett's man?*

*For several months rumors have been floating around the country music industry that chart topper Lourdes Bennett's highly anticipated wedding to her manager and longtime beau, Derrick Meade, might be on hold — or canceled altogether. It seems that interloper Crystal Holtree has not only upstaged Lourdes in her professional life but in her private life, as well. Word from an anonymous friend tells* I Heart Country *that the embattled Lourdes has abandoned Nashville for the safer climes of Northern California where she grew up . . .*

Which friend had spoken to the media? Lourdes wondered. Probably no one very close to her. Her real friends wouldn't betray her like that. For all she knew, it was one of the assistants or interns at her old label. Maybe someone there had seen her arguing with Derrick — out in the parking lot, perhaps? Because she'd never been stupid enough to reveal her displeasure in public.

For that matter, it could've been someone on her stage crew who overheard them arguing in her trailer . . .

Refusing to read the rest of that particular article, she skipped to the next link.

*Business or Pleasure?*

*You decide. What's going on in this tête-à-tête between country music's latest darling, Crystal Holtree, and her manager, Derrick Meade?*

The picture posted with that headline and blurb certainly didn't make Derrick appear very upset to have lost the woman he'd planned to marry. Judging by all the shopping bags, he and Crystal had been out buying Christmas gifts and were finishing up with an intimate lunch.

"Definitely *not* business," she muttered, and it was obvious from the comments that everyone who'd read the article agreed with her. Below the picture, the journalist had included three facetious multiple-choice answers.

*Crystal takes Lourdes's place on more than just the music charts.*

That one stung — and brought back the panic she'd been feeling when she first arrived in Whiskey Creek. Everything she'd built was ruined, gone. She was twenty-nine and it felt as if her life was over.

*Don't freak out. You've been doing so much better,* she reminded herself. Kyle had such a calming influence on her. She thought of him briefly and told herself he'd be home soon. But she couldn't turn off her computer before reading the rest of those multiple-choice answers.

*Quit assuming the worst! Crystal isn't leaning close to intentionally show Derrick all that cleavage. She's merely discussing the possibility of creating a baby . . . er . . . Christmas album with him.*

*Baby.* "Good luck with that," Lourdes muttered. She was fairly certain Derrick didn't want children and that he wouldn't be a very devoted father if he had any.

The last choice was:

*No judgments here. Give the guy a cigar. Any man who's slept with both Lourdes Bennett and Crystal Holtree is hands down the luckiest man on earth.*

Lourdes grimaced, disgusted that anyone would applaud his infidelity.

There was a noise at the door — the key in the lock. Instantly relieved, she looked up as Kyle came in.

"Hey, how was your day?" he asked when he saw her.

As usual, he'd left for work before she got up. That was becoming their routine. He'd head off at the break of day, she'd get up an hour or two later, do some yoga and then write until it was time to cook dinner.

Fortunately, she hadn't seen a soul since Noelle had dropped off that meal. Even Noelle hadn't been back for that photograph she'd requested.

"My day was good until I got on the computer," she admitted.

He tossed his keys on the counter. "Word's out?"

"Yeah. The vultures are circling, looking for any opportunity to pick my bones. You should see what these people have written . . ."

When he walked over, she thought he was going to read what she'd found. Instead, he closed her laptop. "Don't look at that stuff."

"You've seen it?"

"No, and I don't want to."

"It's just like I said it would be — crazy."

"I believe you. But who cares what they say? Let them say what they want. You'll show them when you put out your next album and it goes platinum within a few weeks."

She drew her legs up and wrapped her arms around them. "You really think I can do it?"

"I have no doubt."

That helped. The past couple of nights she'd sung him snippets of what she'd been working on during the day. She didn't have a lot done — a couple of melodies with partial lyrics. But they were seeds, good seeds, and she was grateful to have at least *started* her next album. When she'd arrived in Whiskey Creek, she hadn't been able to come up with a single new idea. She'd been too anxious, too preoccupied with all the wreckage in her life.

Until she'd met Kyle.

"Derrick's betting against me." She rested her chin on her knees as she gazed up at him. "He doesn't believe I can stage a comeback."

Kyle pulled out the closest chair and sat down. "How do you know?"

"He thinks Crystal has a greater chance of succeeding. Otherwise, he wouldn't be sticking with her."

"Then Derrick's a fool." His lips curved into the crooked grin she liked so much and, in spite of everything, she felt an answering smile tug at her own lips. When Kyle was around, her career and even her relationship with Derrick didn't seem as important as when she was alone.

He gestured at her computer. "I hope you didn't spend your entire day on the internet."

"No."

Angling his chin, he said, "Prove it."

She felt her eyebrows go up. "How?"

"Get your guitar and show me what you've accomplished."

She hadn't accomplished dinner. That was one thing she'd let go, and she felt bad about it. He bought the groceries; she did the cooking. They had a deal. But ever since those texts from Derrick, she'd been consumed by the same fear that had made it so hard for her to function in Nashville. "I added a bit more to that anthem you like."

"Good. The sooner you're done with it, the better. That's a kick-ass song."

She favored songs about women overcoming challenges or beating the odds, which was why Martina McBride and Kelly Clarkson had always been two of her favorite artists.

"What about the ballad?" he asked.

"I fiddled with the melody, changed the key to make it more interesting, but . . . nothing more."

"So let's hear it."

Normally, they had a companionable dinner. Then they'd have a glass of wine, which they'd take into the living room, and she'd test various lyrics or melodies on him. He seemed to enjoy listening to her. He claimed he didn't possess any musical or writing talent, but she'd tweaked several things because of his feedback. She'd also come up with a name and a few bars for one song she hadn't told him about — "Refuge," the song she'd thought of that first day when she'd moved into his house and felt so inspired by how safe she felt here. She wanted to finish that before she mentioned it. She doubted he had any concept of how much their friendship had helped her, coming as it did at such a critical time. She'd been prepared for the worst Christmas ever, one full of heartbreak and confusion and loss. Instead, she was finding a completely unexpected sense of steadiness and calm.

"After I get you something for dinner." She stood up, but he caught her hand as she walked by.

"Let's go out. You've been in this house for over a week. You must be claustrophobic by now. I think it would be good to get a break. It might even help your writing."

She *had* been feeling a little confined. But she didn't want to run into anyone who might recognize her, especially now that there was so much gossip going around the internet.

"We could drive over to Jackson," he said before she could refuse. "You could wear a hat and glasses, if you like. Other than our server, there really wouldn't be anyone to make a fuss. If anything like that starts to develop, I'll put a quick stop to it and get you out of there, I promise."

Had she trusted him any less, she might not have agreed to go. But she knew he'd do his best to look out for her.

"We can drive around and see the Christmas lights afterward," he said.

The thought of putting on some makeup and heading into the cool December air was invigorating. Going out allowed her to escape her computer, which seemed ominous sitting there on the table. Maybe she could just be a woman having dinner with a nice man and not the has-been artist, dumped-for-someone-else girlfriend of her fickle manager. "Okay. Where will we eat?"

"There's a dimly lit steak house with excellent food that I like. I suggest we go there."

She started down the hall. "I'll be ready in twenty minutes."

# 19

Kyle hadn't heard from Noelle since he'd put her on notice that he wouldn't pay her anymore if she continued to insert herself in his life — and he was feeling like a new man. He wished he'd insisted years ago that she not contact him. He hadn't even realized how smothered he'd felt until he no longer had to worry about her. In fact, he'd decided that once Lourdes left for Nashville, he wasn't going to feel any regret about remaining single. He planned to embrace his bachelorhood, make the most of it. Ever since he was young, he'd wanted a family, but people didn't always get what they wanted. And now that he was escaping those old feelings for Olivia, and the long reach of his ex-wife, he figured there were other ways to be happy.

The freedom he felt right now was making him happy, wasn't it?

So maybe searching for a partner wasn't

worth the risk, not when being with the wrong person could ruin his life. Think of the potential arguments and heartbreak he could avoid, he told himself. Sure, his friends were satisfied with their marriages. But he had no guarantee that the next woman he dated would be any better than Noelle — and that was a terrifying thought.

Anyway, he could think about marriage and children later, if he changed his mind. Maybe in five years or so he'd be willing to try again.

"You seem to be in a good mood," Lourdes said, appraising him from the passenger seat.

They were stopped at one of only two lights in town, so he didn't have to keep his eye on the road. But he barely glanced over at her. He didn't want to acknowledge how attractive she was. She hadn't worn the sunglasses and hat he'd suggested to camouflage her appearance. She'd put on a little black dress and come out of the bathroom looking as beautiful as if she was ready to step onstage.

But it wasn't just her appearance he found pleasing. He enjoyed her company. Each day he left work a few minutes earlier.

Still, his excitement at being able to relegate Olivia and Noelle to the past was tempered by a fair bit of caution. If he wasn't careful, he could end up in a situation that wasn't any more fulfilling than the one he'd gotten out of.

He had to guard against that, and he knew it. "How can you tell?"

"You were smiling a second ago."

"I was thinking about something."

"What?"

"I haven't heard from Noelle. I wish I'd threatened to turn off the money before. I could've saved myself a lot of grief."

"I'm surprised."

"That I'd be so relieved?" he said drily.

"No. That she'd back off. When you told me you'd called her, I was worried. You're clearly the best thing she's ever had. I was afraid she wouldn't let you go that easily."

"What can she do? Nothing, if she wants my money."

"Your money may not be as important to her as *you* are."

That idea brought a sense of claustrophobia. "Don't say that. She sleeps with other guys and she's had various relationships. It's not as if she truly cares about me."

"What if all those relationships have only showed her how good she had it with you? They might be what keeps bringing her back."

"But we weren't happy together. Even she has to acknowledge that."

"Not necessarily. Some people believe what they want to believe — and she might believe that her life would be perfect if she could get you back. Anyway, you'll still run into her here and there. You'd have to move away to avoid seeing her entirely."

"I don't mind the occasional random sighting. As long as it's from a distance and she doesn't try to approach me."

"She can't even talk to you?" she said with a laugh.

"No. I'm done. I've hit my limit. I don't know how I've put up with her for so long."

Lourdes adjusted her seat belt. "So this is a celebration. You've finally managed to rid yourself of your stalker."

"With all the crap you were reading about yourself on the internet, I realize it's not a celebration for you. But you're going to be fine. I have no doubt, because there's no questioning your talent." He'd heard what she could do, had become a real fan listening to her albums as well as the partial songs she played for him every night. "You'll find a good manager, a new label that'll really get behind you, and you'll soon be back on top."

"I hope you're right," she said.

"I am." He lowered the volume on the radio. "So are you feeling comfortable being out of the house?"

"Absolutely. You were right. I needed the change of scenery. There's nothing like Gold Country at Christmas. It could be the inspiration for all those idealized scenes on Christmas cards."

He wished he could show her Eve's B and B, which was always decorated to the hilt for the holidays, but he didn't want to push her. He was glad he'd talked her into going out to dinner. "You haven't had much of a chance to enjoy the season."

"That's why this is so nice."

Now that he'd convinced her to come out, Kyle was determined to make sure nothing ruined the evening. So once they arrived in Jackson, he had her wait in his truck while he went into the restaurant to speak to the manager. Then he took her in through the back, where a short, stout man by the name of Mr. Hines led them up a narrow staircase to a private room.

"What'd you tell him?" she whispered as the echo of their host's footsteps dimmed on the stairs when he went back down.

After being relieved of their coats, they'd been given a wine list and a menu. "That we'd prefer to eat alone, if possible."

She gazed around the small, garret-like room, which could seat sixteen people at most. "This is wonderful. And the manager was so respectful. I could tell he recognized me, but he wasn't obvious about it."

Kyle winked at her. "Don't worry. You're going to have a good dinner — one you didn't have to cook — and there won't be anything unpleasant to ruin it."

"But how'd you know this room existed? Have you brought other women here?"

"No. This is where we come whenever Simon's in town. It can get a bit crowded if we all come, but we squeeze in and make it work."

She smoothed the napkin Mr. Hines had placed in her lap. "Oh, makes sense. I forgot he's married to your friend. He probably can't go *anywhere* without attracting a crowd. I hope you don't think I'm pretending to be in his league."

"I know you're not pretending anything. Mr. Hines is good about giving Simon the chance to eat without public attention, so I thought it'd be worth asking if he'd do the same for you. That's all."

"It's very nice of him to accommodate us — and it was nice of you to think of it."

He leaned across the table and dropped his voice. "Before you thank me, I should tell you, in the spirit of full disclosure, that I did promise I'd try to persuade you to let me snap a picture while you're here so he can hang it downstairs."

"Of course. That's no problem."

"It'll be right next to Simon's photograph," he said as he sat back. "So you'll be in good company."

She opened her menu, lowered it, then lifted it again.

Kyle could tell she wanted to say something. "What is it?"

"Since *I've* been so reclusive and haven't been willing to meet any strangers, I probably shouldn't ask, but . . ."

"But?" he prodded.

"Could you introduce me to Simon someday?"

"Sure. If you're still here the next time he visits."

"Won't he be coming for your friend's wedding after Christmas?"

"Gail will be here. And she's bringing the kids to see her family. But Simon has to be in England, on the set of his latest project. He tried to get around it, but the delay would cost the production company some exorbitant amount."

"So he'll miss seeing you perform the wedding service."

Kyle rolled his eyes. "I still can't believe Riley and Phoenix asked *me* to do that."

"Why?"

"Because I have no idea what to say! My own marriage lasted less than a year. I'm about the only person left in our group who's single — and I'm considering staying that way for the rest of my life. I'm no one to offer the type of advice most people look for at their weddings."

"Maybe he's not looking for your advice. Maybe he just wants someone who means a lot to him to perform the service."

"That's flattering," he said. "But most people hope their wedding service will be memorable. I'm afraid this one will be memorable for all the wrong reasons."

"Speak from the heart and you'll be fine."

"If I did that, I'd say, 'Good luck. You may need it.' "

She frowned but waited to respond until Mr. Hines had delivered their water glasses and promised to return shortly for their drink order. "Not all marriages are as hard as the relationships you and I have had," she said when they were alone.

"I guess not. But I wouldn't expect you to speak up for marriage. What if you'd married Derrick and he'd met Crystal *after* the wedding?"

"I'm lucky that didn't happen."

Deciding that he didn't want to make this dinner about their failed love lives, Kyle grinned. "So maybe you should be celebrating tonight, too."

"Maybe so," she agreed, giving him a grudging smile in return. "Anyway, if you'd like, I'll help you write something to say at the wedding."

"You will?"

"Sure. I'm feeling bitter at the moment, too, but I'm fairly certain I can do better than 'Good luck.' "

Since he'd tried several times to come up with something profound and had nothing to show for those efforts, he felt a great measure of relief. He'd been mentally ticking off the days, watching the wedding march closer without feeling any more prepared. "Hallelujah! I consider myself saved."

"I'm not sure I'd say you're *saved*," she told him. "But there should be some overlap between writing songs and writing a few lines on love and commitment for a wedding. So we'll see what I can come up with. Or we can write it together."

When she looked up, he was reminded of another moment that had crackled with the same sort of energy. Last night, they'd turned off the TV and were saying good-night. But as they'd walked toward the hall, neither of them had seemed very eager to go to bed, despite how late it was. So they'd lingered outside her door, talking some more, and then she'd stood on tiptoe to give him a brief hug and thank him for letting her stay. Only it wasn't the natural kind of embrace he received so often from his other friends. As soon as she came up against him, he'd felt the strong desire to slide his hands down her back. And he got the impression she'd felt something she hadn't expected, too, because she quickly backed away.

After that, they couldn't escape into their rooms fast enough.

It'd been awkward. But it wasn't the awkwardness that had kept him awake most of the night. He'd been too aware of the fact that she was just down the hall. He'd stared at his ceiling for hours, listening for any sound of her movements while trying to keep the fantasy of removing her clothes out of his head.

Under the pretext of focusing on the menu, he pulled his gaze away. "I'll contribute what I can."

She studied her menu. "So what are you hungry for?"

He was hungry for *her*. Being with

344

Lourdes like this — out, as though they were on some sort of date — seemed to be messing with his mind. And there was something else that occurred to him. It probably wasn't a coincidence that he could only get over Olivia after Lourdes had entered his life . . .

"Damn it."

"What'd you say?" she asked in confusion.

He cleared his throat. "Nothing. Disregard that. I'm having the cowboy steak." He looked up. "Would you like a glass of wine?"

"No, thanks. But feel free to have a drink or two yourself. I could drive, if necessary."

"I don't need any alcohol tonight." He figured he shouldn't drink for the next three months — until Lourdes was gone and he was no longer face-to-face with the temptation to wreck his life just when he was regaining control of it.

Lourdes had salmon with capers and dill sauce, which was delicious. So was the chocolate soufflé they shared for dessert.

When the bill arrived, she grabbed her purse. She felt she should pay, since Kyle had been covering the cost of groceries. But he wouldn't hear of it. He picked up the tab, took that picture he'd promised the manager, even lifted her into his truck so her feet wouldn't get wet.

As they drove back, the wind whipped at the truck and the nearby trees, causing icy crystals of snow to click against the windshield almost like hail. Lourdes enjoyed watching the flakes fly at them or tumble to the ground in the beam of their headlights. She wasn't dressed for bad weather, but she was plenty warm inside the cab.

By the time they reached Whiskey Creek, it was only ten, but on a weekday that was late enough that they could go through the center of town without feeling conspicuous. Kyle braked here and there to point out his friend's photography studio, his other friend's auto shop, his favorite restaurant — a diner called Just Like Mom's. Little Mary's, the bed-and-breakfast he'd recommended to her, could've been the subject of a Thomas Kinkade painting. Evergreen garland adorned the porch and the black wrought-iron fence that surrounded the property. A battery-powered candle flickered in every window, and a giant, ornate wreath hung on the door. Even the cemetery next door looked festive, thanks to the lacy branches of the leafless trees and the church beyond the sentry-like grave markers.

"I can see why you wouldn't want to leave this place," she commented as they rounded the park at the far end of town so he could show her the giant Christmas tree. "It's something special."

"It's home," he said simply.

She pointed at a vinyl sign flapping from the stoplight. She hadn't noticed it earlier. "I'd forgotten that Whiskey Creek is one of the towns that host Victorian Days. Look, it starts this weekend."

"We can go, if you want."

"Be seen in public?"

"Why not? It'll shore up what you told the *Gold Country Gazette.* Show Derrick that you're really *not* sitting in some farmhouse alone and feeling hurt by what he's done."

"I've told him as much. I finally texted him back, fired him and requested that he leave me alone. I haven't put out any feelers for a new manager yet, but I'm not ready for that. I'll do it in January, when I'm further along with the songs I'm writing. Then maybe I can send a few samples and get someone based on the quality of my work, despite the downward spiral of my career."

"Sounds like a smart plan. How'd Derrick take the news?"

"He wasn't happy. Said I was an ungrateful bitch."

"That should win you back."

"Yeah, definitely not. But since he's already angry, do you think I should make it worse by allowing people to get pictures of us that they could easily post on the internet?"

"I don't see why you should closet yourself away and miss Christmas just because he's angry. He's the one who cheated, not you."

And, if she had her guess, he was seeing *more* of Crystal instead of less. "I wish I knew why I wasn't enough."

"Don't talk like that. You didn't deserve what he did. There's something wrong with *him,* not you."

But it was hard not to feel that she must've fallen short in some way. "I suppose everyone who's ever been cheated on feels inadequate."

"You need to shake that off. And you need to go to Victorian Days."

"Seeing or hearing about us being together might also provoke Noelle," she warned. "Have you considered that?"

"There's no reason to consider it. I won't let what Noelle may or may not do dictate my actions."

"So you're issuing a challenge?"

She saw a flash of white teeth as he smiled. "Are you up for it?"

"Why not?" she replied. The longer she was away from Nashville, the better she felt. She was afraid that had a lot more to do with Kyle than she cared to admit, but she didn't want to miss the fun of the holidays. She felt a spark, a lessening of the worry and doubt she'd been carrying around for the past few months, and wanted to fan that small spark into a raging fire of confidence, not allow Derrick or Noelle or anyone else to smother it before it could really catch hold.

"Great. I'll be able to show you the inside of Little Mary's. Eve always sells the best cookies during Victorian Days. And there'll be people roasting chestnuts and selling hot cider and handmade gifts."

"My parents brought me and my sisters when we were young." She could've driven herself once she got older, if she'd stuck around long enough. But she'd been too eager to get to Nashville — and since then she'd cared about little beyond how well her records were selling. So it was ironic that the promise of a small-town Christmas celebration could entice her despite her fear of stirring up gossip on various websites and on social media. None of those outside concerns seemed to matter in this idyllic town. She even began to question why she'd been in such a hurry to get out of Gold Country when she was young. Could she honestly say she'd found something better?

No. She'd enjoyed the fame, mostly because there was joy in knowing other people liked her work. The money had been a blessing, too. But what she'd achieved had come at a high cost in other areas. She seemed to have lost her way at some point and begun writing and performing only to please others instead of making sure it fulfilled her at the same time . . .

"There's the ice cream parlor," Kyle said. "Would you like a cone?"

"No." She put a hand to her stomach. "I can't eat another bite. I won't fit into my dress if I do."

"I don't see that as a problem, since you'd look even better out of it." He spoke as if he was teasing, as if what he'd said was merely a joke. But that kind of joke didn't fall under the heading of appropriate things to say to a friend. She doubted his mind would ever have gone in that direction, if not for their hug last night. Although it didn't make much sense, since she was still in love with someone else, she'd wanted to get her hands on Kyle, to touch him. So she'd used a quick good-night embrace as the excuse — and then she'd regretted it. That hug had changed something between them.

"Maybe we'd better go home," she said, suddenly feigning even more interest in the Christmas lights hanging from almost every building. "We both have work tomorrow."

Once they got back, he kept his distance. She could tell he was embarrassed by the comment he'd made in the truck. He was probably wondering where that had come from, just as she'd been wondering why that innocuous hug had felt anything but innocuous. They spoke politely, almost formally, and stepped around each other as if they were afraid they might spontaneously combust if they touched.

So she tried to put an end to the awkwardness with another good-night hug — a proper *friend* hug this time that wouldn't feel nearly as sexual as last night's. If they planned to live together for the next three months, they had to force their relationship back inside the boundaries where it was meant to reside.

For the first second, the contact was everything she'd intended. She felt him release her, heard him say goodnight. Perfunctory. Matter-of-fact. So she wasn't sure why she hugged him again, or whether she turned her head or he turned his, but a second later, their mouths came together —

warm and wet and questing. And what happened next wasn't about friendship at all.

# 20

When the truth of what was happening finally hit Kyle's brain, he froze. He was about to pull away. He knew better than to kiss Lourdes. They were plastered against each other so tightly she had to be able to feel his erection. But then . . . This wasn't entirely his doing. He was pretty sure *she* was kissing *him,* and that changed things. He wouldn't want to be rude, he told himself, wouldn't want to reject her after what she'd been through.

That wasn't much of an excuse for breaking his own rules, but the need he felt to protect her from anything negative, even his own rejection, was working against him . . .

He circled her waist with his hands, bringing her up higher, so he could kiss her more deeply. Part of him hoped such an aggressive action would startle her, that she'd back away and take the onus off him. But she didn't. If anything, she seemed to like the intensity of what he'd done. She groaned as if she was enjoying every second — and he knew then that he was in trouble. He hoped she wasn't expecting *him* to put a stop to this.

Soon, all kinds of warning bells were going off in his head. This was exactly what he'd decided he wouldn't do! For someone like him, she was *way* out of reach — a shooting star, streaking across the sky. If he tried to catch her, he'd get dragged along for a short time before being dropped painfully back to Earth.

But right now he felt even one night with her might be worth the coming crash. Three long years since he'd been with a woman made him want to lay her down and settle himself between her thighs . . .

He'd break this off in a minute, he promised himself. But it was a halfhearted promise at best, and one he didn't keep. He went on kissing her, doing all he could to make sure she lost her mind the way he was losing his.

Her hair fell over his hands. "We can't do this," he murmured as he rubbed his face in those silky waves. "We're just friends."

"*And* you think I'm too young."

"You *are* too young." Nine years was a lot. He would've been twenty-five when she was only sixteen. That was nearly a decade. But it didn't stop him from continuing to kiss her.

"I'm old enough," she murmured. "Besides, it's been a long time since you were with someone. So . . . I'm willing to help you out."

He slid his lips down her neck. "That's kind of you."

"*I* might as well be the one to end your sexual drought. Someone needs to. And what can it hurt — as long as we both know not to expect anything after it's over?"

"Right. We both understand," he breathed as he licked her soft skin.

"People have casual sex all the time." She sounded breathless as she reached up under his shirt.

"I'm sure they do. And casual is casual."

"Do you have birth control?"

"I've got a few condoms in the bedroom." He moved his hands lower, to the curve of her hips and around to the swell of her behind. It seemed as if he'd wanted to touch her ass for ages . . .

"That's good." Her voice rose as he used his tongue to caress her breasts where they disappeared into her dress.

"Good?" He didn't know if she was talking about the condoms or what he was doing to her, but he didn't really care. Letting go of what little restraint he had left was beginning to sound safe. They had an understanding. They also had some privacy. Where else could someone like Lourdes Bennett go for this type of encounter? She hadn't had sex for over a month, probably missed it. Kyle remembered how badly *he'd* missed the physical aspects of a close relationship after Olivia had moved away. Being that active and then having it all come to a halt was hard.

At least Lourdes could trust him not to give her some disease. Or hurt her. Or share intimate details when it was over . . .

"I'll take care of you," he promised.

"I know you will. The way you kiss . . . It makes me tingle all over. I swear, if every man could kiss like you . . ."

She never finished that statement, but what she'd said was enough. Hearing such praise made his own excitement skyrocket. Lord knew this type of thing didn't happen to him every day, not in a place like Whiskey Creek. He'd be a fool to miss out.

Once he'd slid her dress up over her hips, he fingered the silky scrap of fabric that was her underwear, then pressed her lower body more tightly against his.

"Sometimes friends make the best lovers,"

she said.

He wondered if she had any experience with that. Because *he* didn't. He liked the encounter so far, though. "Feels good to me."

"Great. Then we'll just . . . get rid of these clothes." Her hands were shaking, and he wasn't feeling any steadier. "I have to admit I've wondered what you'd look like," she said as she pulled off his shirt.

"You have?"

She kissed his chest. "Haven't you wondered about me?"

"Only every night." He caught her hand as she unfastened the buttons on his jeans. "But are you sure this is going to be okay? There'll be no regret in the morning?"

"No, of course not," she replied, and that was enough for him. As far as he was concerned, they'd reached the point of no return. He realized now that he'd wanted her from the first moment he'd laid eyes on her, and he was so charged up at finally being able to touch her in this way that he could no longer form coherent thoughts, let alone come up with an argument that might make him choose a different course.

"God, I'm glad the furnace at the farmhouse didn't work," he said and brought her down the hall to his room.

■ ■ ■ ■

Lourdes hadn't slept with anyone except Derrick for . . . years. Before him, she'd been too focused on her career to get involved with anyone. And she'd never been the type to take the risks associated with random hookups. There'd been her high school boyfriend. Then the guy she'd lived with when she first moved to Nashville. They'd had a rocky on-again, off-again relationship that had stemmed mostly from physical attraction, since they'd had nothing else in common. After she broke up with him and moved out, she'd gone long stretches without a love interest.

She was probably looking at another one of those long stretches now — once she returned to Nashville — so she figured she might as well enjoy herself in Whiskey Creek. Kyle wasn't the kind of man a woman ran into every day. She didn't agree with Noelle's methods of trying to keep him, but she could see why his ex was sorry about losing him. Not only was he easy on the eyes, he was solid in every other way — and there was no question that he knew how to arouse a woman.

Just before they reached his bedroom, she

pulled him back to her for another kiss — and pressed her face into his warm neck as he unzipped her dress. These days she was constantly plagued by agonizing worries. Everything had such high stakes and dire consequences. But for right now, for this minute, Kyle seemed capable of holding all of that at bay. He made her feel something both powerful and positive, and she wasn't about to deny herself what she most needed. After what Derrick had done, why should she?

She watched Kyle's face, noting his anticipation as he tugged her the rest of the way to his room and finished removing her dress. Maybe he was *just* a friend, but with him, she felt more desirable than she'd ever felt before. He didn't offer her the outlandish praise or the promises that Derrick had in the beginning. Kyle said nothing. It was the way he touched her that seemed so meaningful.

Goose bumps broke out on her arms as he took the time to look at what he'd revealed. She still had on her bra and panties, but he smiled as though he liked what he saw. In any case, he didn't take off the rest of her clothes. He kissed her until she was so ready for him to go further she was about to take them off herself — and yet she stiffened when his hand finally slipped inside her panties.

"What's wrong?" he asked, raising his head in concern.

Nothing was wrong. That was the problem. This was almost *too* right. What if, in the process of slamming the door on her relationship with Derrick, she ran headlong into a love that could be even more consuming — and ravaging? One that might have the power to make her want to stay in a place like Whiskey Creek?

That was a frightening thought. She'd sworn she'd escape Small Town, USA, that she'd make a career in music, and she had. Why would she ever allow herself to be tempted back? To follow in her mother's footsteps, after all?

And yet . . . this wasn't feeling nearly as mechanical and strictly physical as she'd anticipated. There was a tenderness that could easily be misconstrued . . .

She should voice her concerns. She didn't want either of them to get hurt — and what had seemed unlikely a few minutes earlier suddenly didn't seem so unlikely at all. This was more of an epic event than it should be. But when he murmured that everything was going to be okay, and his mouth came down on hers, coaxing her to relax by giving her a kiss so achingly sweet that she couldn't help arching into him, she swallowed her fears. And the next thing she knew, they were rolling around in his bed, completely naked as they kissed and touched and tasted.

Part of her wanted to stop, but she *couldn't.* She was reveling in the pleasure he seemed to provide so naturally, so intuitively. But it ended far sooner than she expected. He'd just begun to push inside her when someone banged on the front door, yelling in a voice filled with panic, "Kyle, get out here! *Now!*"

"What is it?" Although Kyle wasn't happy about it, he'd left Lourdes in his bed and yanked on his jeans so he could let his neighbor in. Warren Rodman rented one of his houses just down the road — the one Kyle had yet to renovate — and he worked at the solar plant. But he was quite a bit older, nearly sixty-five, and recently divorced. He didn't usually bother Kyle after hours, especially *this* late. It was nearly eleven. And he was such a mellow guy. It took a lot to get him so anxious.

"There's a fire at the plant," he said. "I could smell the smoke when I stepped out on the back porch to have a cigarette, so I drove over there, and . . . sure enough."

Stunned, Kyle blinked at him. Maybe he was still a little dazed from what had been going on before Warren arrived, because it sounded as if he'd said there was a fire at the plant. *His* plant.

Before he could interpret those words and form an appropriate response, Lourdes came hurrying out, wearing a pair of his boxers and one of his T-shirts — what was at hand in his room and easier to put on than her dress. "Have you called 911?" she asked Warren.

"I have. The fire department's on the way, but —" he turned back to Kyle "— I thought there might be a few things in there you'd like to try to save."

The reality finally cut through the testosterone-induced fog that'd momentarily put him out of touch with the regular world. He could even smell the smoke, drifting toward him on a brisk wind. "Hell, yes, there's stuff I want to save," he said and ran to grab his keys from the kitchen counter.

Lourdes must've realized he was going to rush out dressed the way he was, despite the cold, the rough ground and everything else, because she stopped him and hurried back down the hall to get him some shoes.

"How bad is it?" Kyle asked Warren.

Warren rubbed his neck. "I have no idea, boss. I didn't go very close. I saw an odd glow against the sky and knew immediately what it was. So I called 911. Then I came over here."

When Lourdes returned a few seconds later, she carried a sweatshirt as well as his boots. "Nothing in the plant is worth your life," she said, squeezing his arm. "Don't get hurt."

He wasn't even sure he responded before he shoved his bare feet into his boots and dashed out, still trying to get that sweatshirt over his head. He'd put so much time and effort into his business, had finally built it into what he'd always imagined it could be. This didn't seem possible. A fire could set him back months, *years,* if it destroyed the whole plant.

He floored the accelerator on his truck, but the three- or four-minute drive seemed to take hours. He wished it would start snowing again. The precipitation might help save the plant. But the wind was all that remained of the mild storm they'd had earlier — and wind was definitely not what he needed.

When he slammed on his brakes in the parking lot and jumped out, he saw more than the "odd glow" Warren had reported.

Flames leaped from the window near Morgan's desk. And the stench made him sick. He'd been trying not to panic, since *fire* could mean a lot of things. There were small fires that were easy to put out and didn't do much damage.

And then there were blazes like this one . . .

"Son of a bitch!" he yelled and ran around to the back, where he felt the door to check for heat before opening it. Fortunately, the entire plant hadn't been engulfed — not yet. His machinery and inventory were worth a few million dollars. The fire department might be able to save it — *if* they arrived soon. But the volunteer force was spread over several neighboring towns, not just Whiskey Creek. It could take some time for the bulk of the firefighters to get here.

Kyle grabbed the fire extinguisher inside the door and held it in front of him. But the smoke and the heat drove him back before he could reach the flames. The blaze had broken out in the offices. Kyle had no idea why or how, but he couldn't focus on the reasons, anyway. He needed to get the computers. Morgan was supposed to back them up regularly, but he had no idea how diligent she'd been. Missing files, purchase orders and contracts would cripple him when it came to filling his most recent orders.

It was getting difficult to see and even harder to breathe. He ducked low, closer to the ground, hoping he might be able to reach the front. He was going to lose all his office furniture and equipment, and the paperwork that floated between his desk and Morgan's. But if he could just salvage the computers, and the fire department put the fire out before the flames got to the back end, he could recover from this sooner rather than later.

The closer he got to his own office, however, the more certain he became that it was too late. That portion of the plant was already destroyed.

The deafening growl of the fire reminded him of a year ago, when he and his friends had purposely set one of his houses ablaze (one that needed to be torn down, anyway). That had been controlled and yet it had shown Kyle how quickly fire could consume a building.

If not for Warren raising the alarm tonight, he would've lost everything.

He could *still* lose everything . . .

A large crack reverberated over the roar of the flames. Then Kyle heard shattering glass — a window blowing out — and part of the roof fell in. A burning chunk of debris landed only a few feet away from him.

He had to give up, he realized. He couldn't save the computers or anything else. As much as his business meant to him, it wasn't worth his life.

He was making his way back when he heard someone call his name.

"Coming!" he yelled. Then he started coughing and couldn't seem to stop. He'd breathed in too much smoke, searing his lungs.

He covered his mouth, but minutes later two firemen in full regalia came charging in, grabbed hold of him and half dragged him out into the night.

"I'm fine!" he insisted between coughs and gasps. "I was just trying to get a few things. Let me go so you can put out the damn fire!"

They released him only when he was clear of the building and told him to stay put. Then they hurried over to join several other men who were training fire hoses on the blaze.

"Shit." How could this have happened? Maybe he shouldn't be feeling so grateful to Warren. Maybe Warren had been lying to him about where he'd been smoking that cigarette. Could he have accidentally started the fire?

Kyle suspected that was the most likely explanation. He and Warren — and Lourdes, of course — were the only people on the property this late at night.

But then he caught a glimpse of something that made his skin prickle and had him surging to his feet. *Was that who he thought it was?*

There was a pole light near the building, so it wasn't completely dark around the property, even this far from town. But with all the headlights from the various vehicles pulling in, the haze created by the smoke and the frenetic activity of the firemen running to and fro in front of him, he couldn't be sure.

But a car that looked like Noelle's Honda turned in at the drive, then backed up and quickly took off.

# 21

Lourdes had put on some jeans and a sweater. She knew the firefighters didn't need another person getting in the way during an emergency like this, but she was so worried about Kyle — whether he was safe and how he was coping with this tragedy — that she borrowed his heavy coat and walked over to the plant. She'd never been there before, but it wasn't difficult to find with all the vehicles barreling down the road toward it.

By the time she arrived, the place was swarming with activity. Although the sirens had been silenced, lights still swirled on the fire trucks as well as a few police cars. Men rushed around to get a better footing or a more advantageous position. And she could hear one firefighter yelling at several others through a loudspeaker. "Take it higher, Pete. Right there at the top. That's it."

She frowned as she surveyed the damage.

The front of the building had lost its roof, part of one wall and both windows. With the jagged and charred edges remaining, that section of the plant looked like the gaping maw of a monster, ready to take a bite out of any unwary passerby. The flames that danced behind the opening served as its devilish eyes. But at least there were plenty of firemen.

Knowing that Kyle had hurried over on his own before anyone else could get there made her anxious. This was a much bigger fire than she'd expected. But the first man she asked told her the building had been cleared of people and pointed her toward a solitary figure who stood off to one side, hands jammed in his pockets as he watched the water from the firefighters' hoses damage what the fire itself hadn't already burned beyond recognition.

"Are you okay?" she asked when she reached him.

He combed his fingers through his hair but continued to stare at his burning plant. "Yeah."

She wasn't convinced. "The good thing is no one was hurt," she said, trying to make him feel better. "That's what's most important. If this had broken out during the day when all your employees were inside, who knows —"

"Broken out?" He bit off each word as if he could barely speak for the stiffness of his jaw. "It didn't start on its own."

"It could have. I've heard of —"

"No. That isn't what happened."

Lourdes felt her jaw drop. "You're saying someone set this on purpose? That it was . . . *arson?*"

His eyes narrowed. "I wouldn't be surprised. The timing's suspicious, what with the threats Noelle's been making. And I'm pretty sure I saw her here earlier."

Lourdes looked more carefully at all the people who'd gathered. Some were probably friends or family of the firefighters. Others had very likely followed the trucks. Certain people did that sort of thing. But the firefighters definitely had an audience — much to the displeasure of the three police officers who were trying to keep them from getting too close to the burning plant.

"Surely Noelle wouldn't go *this* far," she said. "You told me yourself that she'd be unlikely to do anything *seriously* harmful. And destroying your plant — that's serious."

He heaved a sigh. "Maybe it was an accident. Warren could've been smoking over here instead of at his place. He could've tossed a butt where he shouldn't have. But that Honda I saw . . ."

"It was Noelle's car?" Lourdes asked. "Noelle drives a Honda?"

"Yes."

"When did you notice it?"

"Right after the first wave of firefighters arrived."

"Are you sure it wasn't another one of the men, coming to help? Or that Noelle wasn't dropping someone off?"

"I'm positive. She didn't stop long enough to let anyone out. Besides, that car's old and distinctive. I don't think I'd confuse it. She pulled in, circled around the parking lot and then got the hell out. The sight of her gave me the creeps — made me feel like she was coming back to survey what she'd done. As if she was excited about it."

It was hard to believe someone would go that far, but Lourdes knew it happened occasionally. "Are there any security cameras that might tell you what happened?"

"No, there's never been any need for that sort of thing. I've never even considered it."

"Still, if this *is* arson, they should be able to tell once they get the fire out, and things cool off."

He didn't respond. He just kept staring at the plant as though seeing it go up in smoke

371

was so terrible he couldn't look away.

"You have insurance, don't you?"

"I do, of course, but this will be a serious disruption to my business. And who knows whether the insurance company will step up the way they should. Insurance companies are notorious for doing everything possible to reject a claim or make some exception or other."

She wished she could offer him more consolation. "I'm sorry, Kyle. I feel awful about this."

"It's cold out. You should go home," he said.

"You're worried about *me* being cold? I'm the one who's wearing a coat — your coat. Here, you take it. That sweatshirt can't be doing much to protect you from this wind."

He waved her off. "Keep it. I can't feel anything."

She folded her arms to protect her hands from the biting wind. "If it's her, if it *is* Noelle, she'll be in real trouble. Maliciously setting a fire is a felony, isn't it?"

"I don't know about anywhere else, but it is in California. If she's convicted, she'll go to prison." He shook his head. "She's so used to getting away with all the shit she does. People around here have been putting up with her bad behavior for years. Her family's been doing it her whole life. But maybe she's finally gone too far."

It took the firefighters more than two hours to put out the fire and make sure everything was properly soaked. Kyle was numb by the time it was over. He sent a text to Morgan. He knew she turned off her cell at night and wouldn't get his message until morning, but he didn't want to call the house and wake her. Morning would be soon enough for her to receive the bad news. She could try to get word to the rest of his employees then, at least as many as she could catch, so they wouldn't drive in to the plant for nothing.

With a final, heartbroken glance at what he used to be so proud of, he and Lourdes got in his truck to return to the house. He'd tried to convince her to go back ahead of him. There wasn't any need for her to be out so late in such cold weather. But she hadn't been willing to leave him. She'd said friends didn't leave friends in the middle of a crisis.

He was glad she'd clarified their relationship — since the line between *friends* and something more had blurred beyond distinction right before Warren showed up.

On the one hand, the timing of that interruption couldn't have been worse, Kyle thought. Neither he nor Lourdes had obtained the physical satisfaction they'd been seeking. He was so upset by what had happened to the plant that a heavy dose of sexual frustration on top of it made him even more bad-tempered.

But it was possible that Warren had knocked at just the right time, since the interruption gave them a chance to step back and reconsider what they were doing. Kyle couldn't imagine that having sex with Lourdes would make her life any less complicated — or his any easier when she left.

He needed to get into a good fistfight, he decided. He'd never been the type to throw punches, not unless he had no choice, but he needed *some* sort of outlet . . .

"Are you planning to tell the police about your suspicions, or wait and see what they say about how the fire originated?" Lourdes asked.

He slowed as he turned onto the road, leaving the remains of his plant behind. Chief Bennett had been there, along with two other Whiskey Creek policemen, but they'd been busy helping the firemen, then putting up barrier tape so no one would get too close or enter the building until it could be deemed safe. When he'd spoken to

Bennett, Kyle hadn't mentioned the Honda he'd seen. He figured there'd be time for that later. Bennett had said he'd call Kyle in the morning, so Kyle knew he'd have an opportunity to express his concerns before too long. "I'm not sure. If they plan on doing a thorough investigation, I might wait."

"Your insurance company will probably insist on a thorough investigation, even if you don't. Anyway, in the meantime, if you don't speak up, are you going to let Noelle know you saw her?"

Kyle didn't get the chance to answer that question. He'd just parked in his driveway when another pair of headlights glinted off his rearview mirror. Someone had pulled in behind him.

"Who is it?" Lourdes twisted around to look, but because of the glare, she probably couldn't see more than the front grille of his stepbrother's Chevy Tahoe.

"Brandon." He assumed his stepbrother was alone — until he got out and saw that Olivia had come, too.

"Kyle, I can't believe it, man." Brandon slammed his car door and closed the distance between them with his usual purposeful stride. "What the hell happened?"

Kyle spread out his hands. "Wish I knew. How'd you hear?"

"Our neighbor's part of the volunteer force," Olivia explained as she joined them. "When he got home and saw that our lights were still on, he knocked. He figured we'd want to know."

"It could've waited until tomorrow. You two certainly didn't need to come out so late."

"Yes, we did," Brandon said. "You should've called me right away."

"Why? So you could watch the plant burn like I did? I couldn't save a damn thing from my office or Morgan's. The computers, the files, the furniture — hell, even some of the walls are gone. I didn't get there in time. But, by the grace of God and some great volunteers, the fire was extinguished before it destroyed my equipment and inventory."

Olivia had no makeup on — proof that she and Brandon had been going to bed. She could've let Brandon come alone, but she hadn't. She seemed truly concerned. "Do you have any idea what caused it?" she asked.

Kyle felt the weight of Lourdes's gaze. She was wondering if he'd accuse Noelle. It was difficult not to. To his mind, there was no chance that fire had started on its own — or because of Warren smoking. He'd pretty well dismissed that possibility. Seeing Noelle pull into the parking lot at that particular moment had been too coincidental. "No," he said. "Not yet."

Singling out his house key, he gestured for them to follow him to the porch. He had too much adrenaline flowing through him to feel the cold, but Lourdes's nose and cheeks were pink. She'd been standing outside too long already. "Let's go in. I, for one, could use a drink."

"I'll take one, too," Brandon said.

While Kyle unlocked the door, Brandon spoke to Lourdes. "I bet you weren't expecting so much excitement when you came out here."

"No. There've been *a lot* of things I didn't expect."

Kyle guessed Brandon wanted to question that statement. He wondered what she was referring to himself. Moving in with a stranger? Hearing Derrick admit his affair?

Or was it the fact that they'd stripped off all their clothes and nearly made love a couple of hours ago?

Briefly, the vision of Lourdes's breasts flashed in Kyle's mind — along with the memory of their taste and feel. He wanted to tell Brandon and Olivia to go home so he could drag her back into his room, wanted to forget everything that had just happened by losing himself in her. Only then did he think he might be able to sleep.

But he pushed that thought aside. What he'd been feeling when they were together before the fire had nothing to do with friendship. He wanted a *real* relationship, which meant that making love to her now was the last thing he should do. His plant had been severely damaged; he didn't need to give himself any more reason to be angry or disappointed.

"What do you have to drink?" Brandon asked. "I hope it's stronger than wine."

"I've got some whiskey somewhere." Kyle focused on Olivia and Lourdes. "You two planning to join us?"

"I can't," Olivia said.

"No, thanks." Lourdes shook her head. "After breathing in all those nasty fumes, my stomach's upset."

Kyle handed a shot to Brandon. Then he gave Lourdes and Olivia each a glass of water and dropped onto the sofa. "What a night," he murmured, and that started them talking about the fire again — how he'd found out about it, whether there'd been any chemicals left too close to other chemicals or Warren had been lying about where he'd been standing with his cigarettes, who'd locked up earlier and what Kyle's next steps would be. He paid a lot for hazard insurance, but he'd never expected to need it. He supposed he'd call his agent in the morning, and his agent would explain what to do next.

"This won't hurt you too much financially, will it?" Olivia asked. "I mean . . . you know Riley will drop everything to help you rebuild as soon as possible."

"Riley has a wedding coming up," Kyle pointed out.

She took a sip of her water. "I'm handling most of that, and it's the slow season for construction. I bet he'll jump right in. And if he can't, I'm sure your clients will understand. It's not as if you had any control over this. It was just an unfortunate occurrence. Could've happened to anyone."

Kyle wasn't feeling nearly as optimistic that he'd be able to throw himself on the mercy of his clients and expect any special consideration. There'd probably be a few who could wait, but . . . "I sell primarily to large commercial users, Olivia," he said. "They don't give a shit whether I've had some bad luck. They want their solar system to go in when it's scheduled to go in. And if they can't get the panels from me, they'll get them from someone else. I'll try to counteract that with some discounting to get them to hold out, but it'll hurt my bottom line, even if the insurance covers the other losses."

She grimaced. "But you've worked so hard. How long will it take to get the plant up and running again?"

"I have no idea." He stared at the liquid in his glass. "They wouldn't let me go in, even after the fire was out. Everything was too hot. And they were afraid more of the roof would collapse." He wasn't sure he could've tolerated the fumes, anyway. The firemen claimed they were toxic and, judging by the terrible stench, it was easy to believe. "It'll take time just to determine the extent of the damage — let alone go through the process of getting everything fixed or replaced."

"Could it have been faulty wiring?" Brandon asked.

Kyle's curiosity about what they might be able to tell him suddenly overcame his desire to keep his suspicions to himself. "You don't happen to know where Noelle was tonight, do you?"

The room stilled. Even Lourdes's eyes flew to his face. But if Noelle had a believable alibi, he'd rather learn about it now. The thought that she might have sabotaged his success out of petty jealousy, resentment or revenge infuriated him.

"Why would you ask that?" Olivia said.

He attempted a careless shrug. "No reason. Just wondered if . . . if she managed to get her job back at Sexy Sadie's, or if she came over to hang out with you or you met her for a drink —"

"Noelle's been spouting off, saying some stupid things. I told you that before," Olivia said. "But she would never purposely set your plant on fire, if that's where you're going with this. Why would she take the risk? What if someone was in the building? What if *you* were there, working late like you so often do?"

"I'm sure she could see that my truck was parked here. And all the lights were off at the plant, except for that one pole light outside."

"She's done some really dumb things, some thoughtless and selfish things. But she'd never go that far." Olivia looked at Brandon for confirmation, but he surprised Kyle by frowning at her apologetically, as if he wanted to agree with her for the sake of support but couldn't do it for the sake of honesty.

"I wouldn't put it past her," Kyle said, hoping to draw any fire Brandon's lack of support might cause. He didn't want to get his brother into an argument with Olivia just because Brandon saw Noelle the way he did.

Fortunately, it worked.

"You think it *was* her!" Olivia set her glass aside and rose to her feet.

Lourdes shifted as if she was tempted to say something but didn't.

"No," Kyle said. "Never mind." Damn it. He should've kept his mouth shut. He couldn't trust himself at the moment; he was too angry. "I'm sure she didn't do it."

"Now you're just telling me what I want to hear," Olivia said. "Well, *you* may think it was her, but I don't."

"Have you heard from her tonight?" Brandon asked his wife.

Olivia gaped at him. "Brandon, stop! Not you, too."

He lifted his hands. "Kyle's my brother, babe. And she's the only one who's got a grudge against him. It makes sense to tie down her whereabouts. If she really has nothing to hide, you don't have anything to worry about."

Brandon's words must've seemed reasonable, because Olivia's shoulders slumped. "Have they even established that it was set on purpose?"

"Not yet," Kyle said. Which was why he

should've waited. One minute he told himself to hold off; the next he was dying to hunt Noelle down.

He needed that fight he was spoiling for. Sitting here drinking was far too innocuous, especially since he couldn't keep from looking at Lourdes — and wanting her in spite of everything.

"Then why are you even asking about her?" Olivia demanded.

"Because he saw her there," Lourdes replied as if she couldn't resist speaking up. "Tonight."

The blood drained from Olivia's face, and her eyes were riveted on him. *"Noelle* was there? *When?"*

Kyle finished his drink. "After the fire broke out."

"A lot of people probably showed up after the fire broke out," she said. "Stanley, our neighbor, told us he'd never been to a fire that had so many people running around."

"I'm not arguing with that," Kyle said. "We don't have too many emergencies in Whiskey Creek, so they attract plenty of attention."

"But Stan was referring to firefighters," Brandon said. "Noelle's not a volunteer, so . . . what? She came to watch?"

"I'm not sure what she came to do," Kyle

admitted and repeated what he'd seen and how quickly she'd driven off.

Olivia bit her lip. "So you're not positive it was her car. You said yourself that it was difficult to see. That there was a lot of movement and chaos and smoke."

Kyle exchanged a look with Brandon. "That's true."

"Fine." The narrowing of her eyes suggested she wasn't happy that Brandon was taking his side. "I'll call her. Right now. And I'll ask where she was tonight."

"It's late," Kyle said. "Let's see what the police find. I only brought her up because I was hoping you could tell me she was with you all evening." Besides, at this point he just wanted them to go home before the negative emotions charging through him busted out in some way.

But Olivia wouldn't listen. She hesitated briefly, then reached into her pocket for her cell phone.

They all watched as she held the phone to her ear and moved toward the fireplace. "Hey, there you are. I thought maybe you'd gone to bed, but you're usually such a night owl."

Noelle had obviously answered; Kyle felt his pulse gallop even faster.

"I was just calling to see if you'd heard

about Kyle's plant," Olivia said. "No?" She sent them a glance that suggested this gave her hope. "There was a fire there tonight . . . It was bad — just about burned down . . . What? They have no idea . . . Of course it'll set him back . . . Don't say that. You might be mad at him right now, but he's been really good to you . . . Our neighbor told us. He's a volunteer . . . Because we were just finishing a movie . . . I feel so bad for Kyle. He's devastated —"

Kyle gritted his teeth. If Noelle had set the fire, he didn't want her to know how badly it'd hurt him, that she'd hit her intended target with a direct bull's-eye. He wished Olivia would hang up. He'd heard enough.

"Anyone would be," Olivia went on. "Of course he has insurance, but it's not that simple. It'll cover some of the losses, sure. But insurance doesn't always take care of everything. And what about the orders he'll lose while the plant's down? The clients who can't wait for him to deliver their solar panels will have to go somewhere else . . ."

It was difficult for Kyle not to snatch the phone away and accuse Noelle of lying. Even if she hadn't set it, he knew she'd seen it.

"What'd she say?" Brandon asked when

Olivia finally finished her call.

"She seemed genuinely surprised," Olivia replied.

"That's bullshit!" Suddenly too agitated to sit, Kyle stood. "She knew about the fire before you told her. I *saw* her there. Why would she pretend otherwise?"

"Maybe you only thought you saw her there," Olivia said.

Brandon got up and put his arm around his wife. "I'm sorry, honey. I know you don't want to think she could do something this terrible, not when you two are finally getting along. But she's not a normal person. She doesn't care how her actions affect others, takes no responsibility for what she does. I could honestly imagine her torching Kyle's plant."

Olivia gave him a pleading look. "Don't assume she's guilty until we have proof, okay? Kyle was distraught when he thought he saw her. He could've been wrong. I'm telling you, she was very convincing on the phone."

Kyle pinched the bridge of his nose, trying to keep his irritation at bay a little longer. "Because she's a good liar. She's always been a good liar."

"It could've been someone else you saw," Olivia insisted.

"It could've been." Kyle put his glass aside. "But it wasn't."

# 22

By the time Brandon and Olivia left, Lourdes was exhausted, but she couldn't relax. Kyle was too keyed up. She could sense his agitation, could almost feel the air crackle with his pent-up energy — and all the things they weren't saying only made it worse. She wanted to blame his dark mood on the fire, but she could tell he had more on his mind. He scowled whenever he looked at her, as if she'd suddenly become his enemy instead of Noelle.

"Do you think we should talk about . . . what happened . . . before?" she asked.

"You mean when I had you naked beneath me? No." His jaw remained hard as he reclaimed the glass he'd pushed aside a few minutes earlier and, every once in a while, a muscle twitched in his cheek.

She cleared her throat. "I know it must've been confusing, since . . . since it felt like there was a little more going on than either of us expected."

"A *little* more?" His gaze locked onto hers like a heat-seeking missile. "Do you moan like that when you have sex with your other *friends*?" He shook his head. "God, the way you looked at me, the way you welcomed my finger inside you —"

"Stop!" Embarrassed, she smoothed down her sweater. "I thought *you'd* be the one to understand how casual worked. You couldn't have been in love with that woman who tattooed your name on her arm after only a few dates, and yet you slept with her. I've never slept with anyone I wasn't in a committed relationship with. I was just trying to . . . to establish an understanding between us, to make it possible for us to have what we both wanted."

"Yeah, well, after all that talk about how it didn't mean anything, you surprised me."

"You surprised me, too!" But what more could they have done to protect themselves? It wasn't *her* fault their lovemaking hadn't gone according to plan, wasn't *her* fault that the moment he touched her, everything they'd said at the door had fallen away as if it was the words and not the actions that had no meaning. There'd been no emotional distance between them at all, which had spooked her as much as it had spooked him.

"Forget I brought it up," she said. "I thought . . . I thought we could clear the air, but you're obviously not ready."

"I can't imagine why," he muttered sarcastically.

"What do you want me to do?" she asked.

"Nothing. I don't want anything from you. Go to bed."

She didn't leave. She felt too bad about everything.

After waiting for several seconds, she tried to get him talking about something else. "It was nice of Brandon and Olivia to come by."

He made a sound of agreement, but that was it. Then he got up to pour himself another drink — only this time he carried the bottle back to the couch with him.

"It's getting late," she said.

He had no response to that, either — except to toss back what was in his glass and to pour another shot. She got up and walked over.

His eyebrows rose when she grabbed the bottle, which he hadn't yet put down.

"Are you sure you want to go on drinking?" she asked. "Facing the damage at the plant tomorrow won't be hard enough?"

She thought he might jerk the bottle out of her hand. He had that right. It wasn't her place to tell him what to do. But she was only trying to take care of him, and he seemed to understand, because after a few seconds, he cursed under his breath but allowed her to move the bottle out of reach.

"Come on. Let's get you to bed." She pulled him to his feet and led him to his room, where he fell back on the mattress, fully dressed.

After removing his boots, she was about to cover him up, but the way he was staring at her held her in place. "What?" she said.

"So are you going to let me fuck you or not?" he asked.

Her breath caught. "You think talking like that's going to take the meaning out of it?"

His eyes glittered with hurt and anger. "I can show you how it works when it doesn't mean anything," he said, pulling her on top of him.

When she didn't refuse, didn't attempt to get up, he unzipped her jeans. "Tell me silence means yes."

She closed her eyes. She should refuse, but it was the last thing she wanted to do. If she left his room right now, she knew she'd probably just come back in five minutes — or less — and by then he might have passed out. "Yes," she murmured.

He quickly dispensed with their clothes,

but instead of kissing her and holding her as he'd done before, instead of engaging his tongue and his hands and his voice, he put on a condom and turned her onto her stomach.

He didn't want to feel any tenderness, she realized. He was searching only for physical release — and she wasn't opposed to letting him have it. She wanted to feel him inside her as much as he wanted to be there, even if it had to be like this.

But everything moved too fast for *her* to feel satisfied. The feral intensity was exciting, unlike anything she'd ever experienced before — except that when he finished, she felt a strange sort of disappointment.

Since he was done with her, she started to get up. She'd known what he was going through tonight — how upset he was and how much alcohol he'd had. She figured she had no right to be surprised or offended, since he'd delivered exactly what he'd promised. *She* was the one who'd agreed to settle for whatever he was willing to give, which was why it startled her when he slipped an arm around her waist, lifted her back onto the mattress and pinned her down.

He stared at her, wearing a fathomless expression on his face. She thought she saw some regret there and was hoping he'd soften — kiss her and caress her as he'd done before.

But he didn't. He held her hands above her head as he suckled her breasts. Then he ran his lips down her stomach, kissing and biting her.

Lourdes gasped as he raised her legs over his shoulders and held them there. He wouldn't let her move, wouldn't let her withdraw from him. He'd taken control. But she didn't want to escape him . . .

She writhed on his bed, her hands clutching the bedding as his mouth brought her to a quick and powerful climax.

Although Lourdes had seen plenty of animalistic, rip-your-clothes-off sex depicted in the movies, she'd never experienced it firsthand. Not until tonight. She had to admit there was a certain eroticism to it. Still, she preferred the gentleness with which Kyle had touched her before the fire. But he'd been out to make a point, and she couldn't deny he'd done a good job of it.

When she tried to return to her own bed, once again he caught her by the waist, and this time he pulled her back against him.

She told herself she'd stay until he fell asleep and then she'd go back to her own room. Given the temporary nature of their relationship, she didn't think it was wise to cuddle up with him. That would only defeat the purpose of making love so forcefully and fast and devoid of any endearments.

But she was tired, too. And the warmth of his body provided such a comfortable place to sleep that she soon felt too languid to move. It wasn't until early the next morning, when there seemed to be several people banging on the front door and ringing the bell at the same time, that she opened her eyes and realized she was still in his bed.

Roused by the noise, he got up and grabbed some clothes. Then he took one look at her and scowled as if he wasn't too happy to see her.

She tugged the blankets up and scowled right back at him. "Don't worry. I'm not going to run out and tattoo your name on my arm or anything. You made sure I couldn't mistake 'fucking' for 'making love.' "

He pushed a hand through his hair. It was sticking up on one side, and yet he still managed to look sexy. "Yeah, well, I guess I'm sort of an all-or-nothing person."

"I didn't ask you to show me what *nothing* was like," she said. "I was just putting you to bed. What happened after that was your idea."

"I know. And I'm afraid it wasn't a very good one."

"You'd been drinking. Should I have refused?"

"Not because I'd been drinking. I'm not blaming that. Or you."

"But you're not happy about last night."

"How could I be? I was an asshole."

"People do weird things when they don't want to get hurt. But just so you know . . . I don't want to get hurt, either." He'd been vulnerable when they were together before the fire, feeling more than he should. They both had. So she didn't find it such a shock that after the fire he'd try to get what he wanted while also trying to erect the barriers he felt would keep him safe. "Anyway, as far as 'fucking' goes, that wasn't bad."

He shot her a glance but said nothing, just got dressed.

"Okay, fine," she said. "Maybe I should make things easier on both of us. Would you like me to move to the farmhouse today?"

Without bothering to put on the shirt in his hand, he swung around to face her. "No, I wouldn't. After what someone did to my plant, I don't want you by yourself *anywhere*. Do you understand?"

"Meaning you think Noelle might try to hurt me . . ."

"Meaning you don't go anywhere without me until we figure out what's going on."

"Kyle!" someone called — a female voice Lourdes didn't recognize.

"Who's that?" she asked.

He yanked on his shirt and checked his watch. "It's Eve. I get together with my friends every Friday morning at the coffee shop. I'm guessing that when I didn't show up today, they decided to come here. Brandon and Olivia must've told them about the fire."

Someone banged on the door. "Hello? Open up! Baxter's in town, man!" This was a male voice . . .

"Coming!" Kyle yelled as he buttoned his jeans.

Lourdes drew the blankets even higher. "Have you mentioned a Baxter to me?"

"I doubt it. He's one of my best friends, but he's been living in San Francisco." His voice softened slightly as he paused at the door. "You don't have to come out if you don't want to," he said, then stalked down the hall.

A moment later, the noise of quite a few people filling the house rose to Lourdes's ears. Jeez, how many friends did Kyle have?

She told herself she'd stay out of sight, as he'd suggested. She wasn't that pleased with him this morning, no matter what excuse he had to be out of sorts. What he was feeling for her couldn't be any more complicated than what she was feeling for him. But she heard several people ask about her. Then a baby cried and she could tell it was a very new baby.

Callie had obviously come with her infant son . . .

Scooting down in the bed, Lourdes pulled the covers over her head to block out the sound. She didn't want to think about babies. Chances were, her life wouldn't include them. Especially now. There were too many things she had to put right in her career. But when four or five people lamented that they wouldn't get to meet her, she felt selfish and guilty for avoiding them.

Planning to slip into the bathroom to clean up before presenting herself, she got out of bed and put on the jeans and sweater she'd been wearing when she went to the fire last night. But her makeup and hair products weren't in the master suite, and there was a man coming down the hallway, probably on his way to the bathroom, who saw her the instant she emerged from Kyle's room.

He grinned. "You must be Lourdes."

Kyle was surprised when Lourdes appeared. He hadn't expected her to brave the crowd, especially since she hadn't had a chance to shower or change. He could tell she was more than a little self-conscious and could understand why, seeing that she'd just come from his bed. Not only was her hair tangled, she was wearing the same clothes she'd had on last night. And when Brandon nudged him, Kyle knew his brother had noticed.

"It's getting serious between you two, huh?" Brandon whispered.

Kyle didn't have a chance to respond. She'd walked out with Noah, who said, "Look who I found."

"Lourdes!" Eve exclaimed. "You really *are* in town. I was beginning to wonder if Kyle was having delusions of grandeur."

She chuckled at Eve's joke. "I'm sorry I haven't been friendlier. I've been . . . busy. But if you'll just give me a minute to wash my face and brush my teeth, I'll be right out."

When she ducked into the bathroom, all of his friends turned to gape at him. "Wow, this is for real, dude!" Riley murmured. "You're with *Lourdes Bennett.*"

"That was Lourdes Bennett?" Baxter said.

"*The* Lourdes Bennett?"

Brandon looked confused. "We told you at Black Gold that Kyle's been seeing her."

"I figured *Kyle* would call me with the news." He folded his arms. "And I haven't heard from him."

"It's not serious," Kyle said. "She's going back to Nashville as soon as she finishes writing her new album."

"But it was the fact that you two are together that set Noelle off?" Cheyenne asked.

Olivia immediately took umbrage. "Whoa, we don't know that Noelle started the fire at the plant."

Cheyenne reared back, shock on her face. "Is that even a possibility? I was referring to the fight she got into the other night at Sexy Sadie's. Yesterday I heard Genevieve Salter telling the checker at Nature's Way all about how Noelle attacked her."

Olivia turned beet red. "Oh. No. Never mind."

They all looked to Kyle to explain. But he didn't want to accuse Olivia's sister without some sort of proof, other than having spotted her at the fire. She drove past his house all the time. Now that he had a fresh perspective and a cooler head, he could agree that she might just have been doing

399

more of her stalking bullshit. In the light of day, it sounded like a stretch that she — or anyone else he knew — would *purposely* set fire to his plant. "We don't know what happened," he said. "Not yet."

Lourdes came out of the bathroom before they could press him for details. She hadn't bothered to shower or put on any makeup, but she'd twisted her hair into a messy bun. Kyle thought she looked breathtaking, as always, and wanted to kick himself for the way he'd treated her last night. Clearly, she understood how difficult the situation was for him; if she'd been offended by his behavior, maybe she would've given him the breathing room he needed to overcome what he was feeling.

Kyle cleared his throat to alert them that she was ready and began the introductions. But all his friends had spouses, except Baxter, which meant he was probably presenting her with more names than she'd ever be able to remember. "This is Dylan and Cheyenne and their boy, Kellan," he said. "And this is Baxter, our friend who just moved home from San Francisco." She knew Brandon and Olivia, but Noah and Addy, Callie and Levi, Sophia and Ted — whose hot tub they'd secretly used — Eve and Lincoln and their two-month-old and

Phoenix and Riley were also there.

Lourdes was polite to everyone, but she seemed to be most taken with Callie's newborn, since Eve's was asleep in his carrier. "Congratulations on the birth of your beautiful son," she said to Callie.

"Thank you." Callie gave her a proud smile. "Would you like to hold him?"

Lourdes's eyes widened. "Um, actually, that might not be the best thing. I mean, he's so tiny and . . . and fragile."

"There's nothing to worry about," Callie said. "Just hold him in the crook of your elbow, like this."

Although Lourdes allowed Callie to put the sleeping child in her arms, she gazed down at Aiden as if he terrified her. Kyle was planning to rescue her by taking the baby, but she seemed to grow more comfortable as the minutes ticked by. After they talked about her music and her career and Angel's Camp, where she grew up, she faded into the background. Kyle saw her sit on the couch, put the baby on her lap and stare at him as if she'd never seen such a miracle — as if she was thoroughly . . . *enchanted.*

The sight didn't do much to help him, however. He'd convinced himself that he was going to embrace his bachelorhood, but spending another five years alone didn't sound quite so exciting right now. Maybe it'd be easier if he lived in a big city, where there were more things to do. But he'd been raised in a small town, where daily life was all about friends and family — and he wanted to have a family, too.

He had always thought he'd be married — and be a father — by the time he turned thirty, and here he was approaching forty.

After they discussed the fact that he wouldn't really know how the fire got started until after they'd done an investigation, and Riley had assured him that he'd shuffle his schedule around to rebuild whenever Kyle needed him, they talked to Baxter about his move and how his father was doing. He'd given up a lucrative job as a stockbroker in San Francisco to do some day trading on the internet. He wanted to be able to spend some time with his father, who'd been diagnosed with prostate cancer last summer. Mr. North wasn't responding well to treatment, which was a concern. But so was the fact that Baxter and his father didn't get along. Mr. North had never accepted Baxter's lifestyle. After Baxter came out of the closet, his father refused to speak to him for quite some time.

"But day trading is risky, isn't it?" Ted

asked him. "I have a writer friend who decided to try his hand at that, and he lost a fortune in a very short time."

"There's a high level of risk involved," Baxter agreed. "But what else am I going to do in Whiskey Creek?"

"You seemed to be doing so well in San Francisco," Riley lamented.

"And who the heck are you going to meet way out here?" Eve asked.

"This isn't about me," Baxter said. "I don't think my dad's going to make it."

Noah slapped him on the back. "Don't talk like that. Of course he's going to make it."

Kyle couldn't help watching Baxter a little more carefully whenever he interacted with Noah. They'd been the closest of friends growing up. It wasn't until a few years ago that Noah learned Baxter had been secretly in love with him for years. That piece of information only emerged when Baxter revealed his sexuality, and Noah's reaction didn't exactly make what he felt any easier.

"If the worst happens, I'd rather be prepared," Baxter said.

"It's wonderful of you." Callie slipped her arm through his. "I remember how well you nursed me through my liver problems. But will you enjoy *living with your folks*? Has your father changed enough so you can feel good about yourself?"

Baxter shrugged. "I guess we'll see. I should be able to tolerate a few months, anyway."

Kyle was afraid Mr. North *hadn't* changed. Baxter had made comments now and then suggesting that his father still had a problem with Baxter's sexuality, but Kyle was happy to have his friend back. And at least Baxter wouldn't be talking about children all the time, like his other friends — since he hadn't yet found a partner.

"Kyle, have you figured out what you're going to say at the wedding?" Phoenix asked.

"I've spent a lot of time thinking about it." He was trying to come up with something he could offer if she pressed him for details, but Lourdes interrupted before she could.

"Have you all had breakfast, or can Kyle and I make you some eggs, toast and fruit?"

"You don't have to cook for us," Sophia said. "We just came from the coffee shop."

"You must've left almost as soon as you got there," Kyle said. "Let us make you breakfast."

They exchanged glances. "If you're sure," Addy said.

Lourdes handed Callie's baby back to her. "I might've blown it with my last album, but I can cook eggs," she joked, and by the time they had breakfast on the table, she was laughing and talking with his friends as if she'd grown up with them, too.

"She's sweet," Cheyenne whispered as she hugged Kyle goodbye. "Surprisingly down-to-earth."

Ted clasped him next. "You did well."

Kyle felt like a fraud. He'd never lied to his friends before. But he couldn't claim that he and Lourdes weren't really involved when they knew she'd come out of his room this morning.

"Good luck with the insurance company," Noah said. "What happened to the plant sucks, but you'll pull it back together." He glanced pointedly at Lourdes. "At least things are looking up in other areas."

"Yeah," he said drily and was grateful when his phone rang, so he could justify simply waving to the others and stepping away from the crowded doorway to answer.

It was the chief of police who'd called Kyle. They'd spoken briefly, then Kyle had thrown on a coat and some boots and left just after his friends. He'd said he had to meet Chief Bennett and a fire investigator over at the plant.

Lourdes picked up her guitar and strummed a few chords as she imagined what the plant might look like without the cover of darkness. Would the damage be even worse than Kyle feared?

She hoped not. She also hoped that the investigation would determine how it had started. If Noelle was involved, she deserved to be punished. It'd been heartbreaking to watch Kyle see so much of his plant go up in smoke.

But that wasn't the only thing on Lourdes's mind. She couldn't stop thinking about what had happened after they went to bed last night. She'd been engaged to Derrick for almost a year, had dated him for *three.* Shouldn't she have wanted to be in *his* arms and not Kyle's? Because at no point had she even thought of Derrick.

"What's going on with me?" she whispered into the empty living room. Most of the things that'd seemed so important to her in Nashville felt far less important to her here — the fame, the fortune, the record sales. But never in a million years would she have expected to rebound from losing the "love of her life" so quickly. Why didn't she miss Derrick?

She could only guess that she'd gone

through so much in the preceding months that she'd gotten over him a little at a time — more with each argument. Maybe, amid all that anger and hurt pride, and the conviction of her commitment to him, which she'd never questioned, she simply hadn't noticed that he didn't mean as much to her as she'd come to believe.

If that was the case, Crystal had done her a huge favor, no question about it. Lourdes still had to figure out how to put her career back together now that she no longer had a manager, but at least she hadn't married a man who didn't deserve her trust. She was free and capable of moving on . . .

But to what? Could she have it all — a career and a husband and family? Or would she, like her mother, be forced to choose?

## 23

As Kyle walked through the burned-out shell of what used to be his office, he found it hard not to get mad all over again. Fortunately, his inventory was safe and so was his machinery. Only the office portion of the plant would need to be rebuilt. But as busy as they'd been lately, that was going to cause enough problems.

An hour ago, when he'd pulled in, he'd come upon several of his employees, who'd shown up, expecting to work as usual. The barrier tape Chief Bennett had put up had kept everyone out of the building, but finding the plant in its current state had shocked his workers. They were more than a little curious as to what could've started the fire. However, Chief Bennett and the fire inspector he'd brought over — a bespectacled, balding man by the name of Ronald Lee — told him not to say anything about seeing Noelle at the plant last night. So Kyle had told his employees that he didn't know what had happened, which was the truth, and sent them home for the day with instructions not to return to work until they received further word. Even if the factory portion of the plant could be made operational fairly soon, Bennett and Lee had indicated that it would take a couple of days to assess the safety of the building, investigate the cause of the fire and gather any evidence that could be found. Then Riley would have to remove what had been damaged, rebuild the necessary support posts and load-bearing walls, and clean up the mess.

With Christmas only ten days away, Kyle felt he was looking at mid-January. Luckily, he'd already promised his staff of fourteen a whole week off for the holidays, which was something he'd planned for all year. That would ease the effects of the shutdown for them. But paying his employees for other weeks they couldn't work would stretch his resources.

Despite having received the text Kyle had sent her last night, and knowing it wouldn't be possible to work, Morgan had come to the plant, too. She'd shown up a bit later than the others, since she'd been trying to catch as many as she could to save them from driving in for nothing. But she hadn't been able to stay away, had told him she had to see it for herself.

He frowned at his melted and charred computer. It wouldn't turn on, which came as no surprise. Morgan's was the same, making him all the more grateful that she'd backed up both computers yesterday. She'd assured him of that before he'd sent her on her way, as he had the others. She'd also agreed they could limp along by running the business from home until the offices were rebuilt, and before she drove off, she took his company credit card to buy them new computers.

"Mr. Houseman?"

Kyle was crouched in front of his desk, trying to pry open the drawers. At the sound of the fire inspector's voice, he stood. Chief Bennett had been with Lee as they'd carefully canvassed the grounds, as well as the building itself, going from the least to the most damaged areas. But Whiskey Creek's police chief had taken a call and stepped outside to get something from his squad car just before Kyle had gone in to see if he could recover anything of value from his office. "Yes?"

"It was an incendiary fire. No question."

"That means arson?"

Lee nodded. He came across as a strictly "by the book" guy, someone without much in the way of social skills. Kyle couldn't say he liked him, but Lee seemed to know a hell of a lot about fires. So Kyle didn't care that he wasn't very personable.

"According to the burn pattern, the point of origin isn't far from the front door."

Kyle had suspected arson and yet he was still shocked. How dared Noelle go that far . . . "But the plant was locked. You heard me confirm that with my assistant when she arrived this morning. So either someone had a key, which is unlikely, since my assistant's the only person who's got one besides me, or they broke in."

"They broke in. Smashed a window," he said without any hint of doubt. "There's a rock not far from the front door, and it's much bigger than the smaller pebbles that are everywhere else. I think the culprit drove in, took that rock from the perimeter of the property and used it to shatter the window next to the door. Then he poured alcohol inside on the carpet, and —"

"Alcohol?" Kyle interrupted. "How do you know it was alcohol?"

"Ignitable liquids with high vapor pressure will flash and scorch while those with higher boiling components tend to wick, melt and burn. What I'm seeing is definitely the former." He slid his glasses higher on his nose. "Besides, there's a broken Jack Daniel's bottle in the parking lot. Unless your employees typically bring alcohol to work, it stands to reason that whoever set the fire was running for his car and accidentally dropped it. When it shattered, he had to leave it behind. So we'll collect the pieces and hope to get at least a partial print. I doubt he was wearing gloves or he wouldn't have been so intent on taking it with him."

He — or *she*? If they managed to get a print, Kyle would have something more than his sighting of that Honda to prove Noelle was behind this . . .

"I haven't found a lighter," Lee was saying, "so I'm assuming whoever it was dropped in a match — or a whole book of matches."

"From Sexy Sadie's, perhaps?" Kyle asked drily.

"Excuse me?"

"That's the local bar."

"Right. Where your ex worked before she was fired. I remember you said that. If it was a book of matches, they were completely destroyed, so I won't be able to prove where they came from. Of course, I'm not finished looking yet, but so far, I've found no remnant."

Kyle was being facetious, anyway. Lee seemed to pick up on everything — except the subtle nuances of meaning that hinged on tone of voice and body language. "So it was quick and easy," he said. So easy that even someone who'd never done anything like this before, someone like Noelle, for instance, could've started the fire.

Lee made some notes on his clipboard. "Doesn't get much easier. No one was here. It was dark. There's no security — not that I'd expect it out here. And there are no close neighbors. Like I said, easy."

All of which made it more of a miracle that Warren had smelled the smoke. If he hadn't stepped outside to have that cigarette precisely when he did, the whole place would probably have burned. But that reminded Kyle that he'd briefly wondered about the possibility of Warren smoking too close to the building. He highly doubted that was the case, but he did feel he should at least raise the question. "Are you sure it couldn't have been started by a random cigarette butt?" Kyle asked.

"It wasn't started by a *random* anything," Lee replied. "Do you know anyone, besides your ex, who'd have anything to gain by setting this place on fire, Mr. Houseman?"

Kyle rubbed his temples. When he'd told them about Noelle, Chief Bennett had frowned as if he could believe it; he knew Noelle. Lee had merely scribbled down her name and address on his notepad. But she was the only one who had it in for him. "No."

"So just this . . . Noelle."

"Yes."

"I see. You and your ex have been divorced for five years and have no children, is that correct?"

"It is."

"And you've been paying her spousal maintenance every month."

"I'm ahead, and I can prove it." He'd already said that, too, and Lee didn't strike him as the type who'd need key information repeated.

"So wouldn't she worry about your ability to pay her if something happened to the plant?"

"You'd have to know her to understand."

"Yet she's never done anything like this before."

Kyle felt his muscles tense — with exhaustion, disappointment, frustration *and* irritation. "I told you. She gets obsessive every once in a while. In the past, she's been

414

distracted by other potential relationships. But when they don't work out, she tries to get me back. It's a cycle."

"Has she ever done anything violent before?"

He thought of all the times she'd tried to hit him, but he'd never reported those instances, so he knew they'd sound flimsy and unbelievable if he mentioned them now. "She attacked a coworker this past week."

"You said that, and I'll look into it. In the meantime, is there anyone else who might have a grudge against you?"

"I told you. No."

"No disgruntled employees or clients?"

"None disgruntled enough to commit arson!"

He glanced up from his clipboard. "Do you carry hazard insurance, Mr. Houseman?"

Kyle wished Chief Bennett would return. He didn't like what this guy seemed to be implying. "Of course. Don't most businesses carry hazard insurance?"

"Just checking." He made another note. Then he turned to go but Kyle stopped him.

"Wait a second. If anyone set the fire, it was my ex-wife. I have no reason to burn down my own business, if that's what you're thinking. This isn't insurance fraud."

"Insurance fraud is probably ninety percent of these cases," he said.

Coming from anyone else, that would be an accusation. From this dude . . . Kyle couldn't tell for sure. Still, he was offended by the mere suggestion. "That must make your job easier, but I'm afraid you're going to have to work a little harder on this one."

His eyebrows slid up as if he was shocked by Kyle's response.

"Check my finances," Kyle said. "You'll see that I'm not in trouble, that I'd have no reason to destroy what I've worked so hard to create."

"I *will* check. I have to. It's my job," he said and went back to work.

Kyle would've slammed his door, if he still had one. "Unbelievable," he muttered. Now *he* was under as much suspicion as Noelle?

Lourdes hadn't intended to tell her family about her breakup with Derrick until after Christmas. But once the gossip rags had published what they did, she had no choice. So she assured her mother and sisters that she was handling the end of her engagement without any problem and that she'd find another manager in the New Year.

She was still having trouble convincing her mother that Kyle was just a friend, however. Not only had her mother read what had been reported, she'd heard the concern in Lourdes's voice as she talked about the fire — and jumped to the obvious conclusion. Or what she saw as the obvious conclusion . . .

"If you won't come home for Christmas, there must be *something* in Whiskey Creek that's keeping you," her mother insisted.

Lourdes was beginning to regret interrupting her precious work time to accept this call. She wouldn't have done it had she not been struggling to concentrate — thanks to the anxiety she felt while waiting to hear what the police chief and fire inspector had to say. "I've finally made some headway on my new album, Mom. That's why I don't want to come home right now."

"But if you were only trying to throw off the media by making those statements, why aren't you moving back into the farmhouse now that the furnace is fixed? There must be a reason."

"I told you, I'm comfortable here at Kyle's, so comfortable that I'm starting to work again. The music is what matters. That's what I came here for. I don't want to mess up a good thing."

"Then you don't particularly like him?"

Lourdes blocked out the vision of being

417

in Kyle's bed last night. She'd spent far too much time thinking about that as it was. "Okay, yes. I like him. A lot," she admitted. "But I'm not the kind of woman he's looking for."

"*Any* man would be lucky to have you," her mother said.

Setting her guitar to one side, Lourdes got up for a drink of water. "I'd hardly call you an objective judge, Mom."

"It's true!"

"Kyle believes in me and supports me in what I want to do with my career, but he's not interested in becoming personally involved. He envisions a different sort of life for himself, like Daddy did. He's satisfied with staying where he was born. He wants a simpler life, and you know how frenetic it can get with me traveling and promoting all the time. Being gone so often, always pushing toward some big goal, especially one as elusive as making it in showbiz, is hard on relationships." Which was one of the reasons she'd thought she and Derrick were perfect for each other, why she'd never questioned it — at least at first.

"You could work through that," her mother said.

"Didn't you hear what I said?"

"I heard you say you care about him."

"I do, but we're not well suited. After seeing the concessions you made for Daddy, I don't want to go down that road."

"Oh, stop! My life hasn't been so bad. I have no regrets."

Lourdes rolled her eyes. "Yes, you do. We've talked about this before. Your voice is even better than mine. You could've been a star."

"I wish he'd been more flexible, more open to letting me pursue my own goals. But I've had a good life. If I hadn't married him, I wouldn't have you and the twins, and you girls mean everything to me."

Lourdes wondered if she'd one day regret choosing such a demanding career. *Maybe not,* she told herself. She could still have a husband and family at some point. Just . . . later, after she'd recovered from the missteps she'd taken in the past couple of years. "It's hard to miss children I don't have, Mom. I don't want to get stuck in Whiskey Creek or anywhere else I might feel I had to stop singing. If I marry someone who doesn't understand my passion for what I do, I'd only wind up feeling guilty for leaving him whenever I was away. You know, for concerts or recording or promo. I don't want to live like that." In other words, she and Kyle knew they had different goals. Why

419

set themselves up for failure?

"But I thought you'd be *destroyed* over Derrick and yet you . . . you seem fine."

She was certainly doing better than she'd expected. The disappointment was there. So was the hurt and anger at being let down by someone she cared about. But the sharp, immobilizing pain she'd experienced for the past several months was gone. Kyle had somehow anesthetized her against that. "I still love Derrick, just not in the same way. I think the past six months killed what romantic love I had for him."

"And now you've found someone else. Good men don't grow on trees, honey. So if Kyle's special, you might want to think twice, that's all," her mother said.

"Thanks for the advice, Mom. You've made your point. Can we talk about something else?"

"Of course." Her mother filled her in on the latest with Mindy and Lindy, who shared everything — including an apartment and a job serving tables at the same high-end restaurant in downtown Nashville. Renate wanted them to get serious about their lives, to show more ambition now that they both had degrees. But they were still young and having fun. Lourdes had long ago recognized that they didn't possess the same kind of drive she did. She'd worked so hard for what she'd achieved — and despite all that effort, it seemed as though she'd turn out to be nothing more than a footnote in the country music industry.

She'd just finished talking to her mother when another call came in, this one from Derrick. She didn't answer it, but she opened the photo album on her phone and swiped through it. She had so many pictures of him — in Paris, in various American cities when they were on tour, at Lake Powell on the houseboat they'd rented last summer. As she stared at their laughing faces, she remembered how much fun they'd had together. She should be suffering more than she was now that they were no longer a couple. She'd suffered before. So where had all the heartbreak and desperation of the past several months gone?

She didn't know. Or at least she couldn't come up with an answer that made sense. The only one that did echoed what her mother had hinted at a few minutes earlier — that what she felt for Kyle had changed everything.

Although he'd called around noon, to tell her the fire was arson, Kyle was gone for most of the day. When Lourdes finally saw him, he seemed to be in another sour mood. But they'd told his friends that they'd be going to Victorian Days, and he acted as if he was still planning on it.

Lourdes knew *she* could always cancel, but she felt it might be wise to let people see her out and about. Maybe that would lend support to what she'd told Ed at the *Gold Country Gazette* and stave off any gossip as to why she was staying out of sight. Maintaining appearances and pretending that all was well could make the furor over her breakup with Derrick seem inflated — maybe even passé — and that would spell death for the story in the celebrity gossip blogs.

The way Kyle's eyes ran over her when she walked out of her bedroom told her he liked how she looked, but he didn't say the words. Since they'd made love, he'd been vigilant about keeping his distance. If she happened to stand too close, he'd step away. Or if she was in the kitchen, and he had to slip past her to get something he needed, he'd either ask her to hand it to him or wait until she was gone so he could reach it without coming into direct contact with her.

"Are you sure you're up for this?" she asked as he held the door so she could precede him to the truck.

"Up for what?"

"Being out together."

"Why wouldn't I be?"

She hesitated before continuing down the walkway. "Because your plant nearly burned down last night and you're so angry about it you can barely speak."

"Staying home won't bring the plant back. That's something I'm going to have to work through, whether I like it or not."

And going out might keep them out of bed. She knew neither of them would be thinking about much else if they stayed home. "So you still want to go."

"I'd rather you didn't miss it. You need to get out."

She breathed deeply, enjoying the clean feel of the winter air. "Are we going to start with Eve's B and B?"

"Yeah. We're all meeting there. She has to stay and sell cookies. The proceeds go to a charity for children. Most of my other friends participate in raising money, too. Callie usually donates whatever she makes off the photography appointments she books during Victorian Days — although, because of the new baby, she's probably not doing it this year. Noah and Addy are auctioning off a bike at their bike store, that sort of thing. We'll hang out with whoever's available. Then we can check out whatever else we want."

"Sounds good," she said, and it was. Lourdes loved Little Mary's B&B, which was lavishly decorated with boughs of holly and wreaths and the best Christmas tree she'd ever seen. The smell of cinnamon and vanilla permeated the entire place, and the cookies Eve served were beautifully decorated *and* delicious. Eventually, when Eve needed to feed her baby, Lourdes took over at the register. That was fun and, as word got out, Lourdes was soon autographing receipts.

"This will be the most we've ever raised," Eve told her, marveling at the length of the line when she returned.

At that point, Lourdes was glad she'd come. Not only was she enjoying herself, she was doing a good deed — something else that felt nice.

"Where's the baby?"

"Lincoln took him in the back so he can get some sleep."

Lourdes could feel Kyle watching her as he lounged against one wall, talking to various friends and other people. She got the impression he was making sure no one got too close or treated her rudely, which made her feel special to him, even if he was hardly speaking to her.

Before long, she and Eve decided to put up a sign that said she'd take photographs of Lourdes posing with customers using their own cell phones for twenty dollars, money that would also be contributed to the charity.

Kyle allowed that to go on for some time. Then he must've felt her job was done, because he came by to rescue her. "We're going to walk around for a bit, before everything closes down," he told Eve. "I want Lourdes to see the rest of the festival."

"Of course," Eve said. "She's done enough here." Eve turned to her. "Thank you. You made Little Mary's the hit of the whole celebration!"

Eve leaned over to give her a hug, but when she started to pull away, Lourdes held her tightly for a moment longer so she wouldn't be just the recipient of the hug but the giver, as well. "Thank *you*. I had a wonderful time." Lord knew she'd needed to get her mind off her own troubles . . .

Eve's smile grew even warmer. "Anytime."

"I really like Eve," Lourdes said as she and Kyle walked down the street. "Actually, I like all your friends."

Kyle grunted.

"You're so grumpy tonight."

"Grumpy?" he repeated.

"Yes. What's wrong with you?"

He stopped and gazed down at her for so long she thought he might kiss her. Then he shook his head, took her hand and continued walking.

"Are you going to explain yourself?"

"It doesn't matter."

"*What* doesn't matter?"

He stopped again, only this time he whirled on her as though he was angry. Instinctively, she backed up a step, but he just moved toward her, coming so close she could smell his aftershave. "What I'm feeling doesn't matter."

"Of course it does!"

"Fine. You want to hear it? I'm pissed at Noelle for setting the damn fire. I'm pissed at the fire inspector for suggesting it might be me. But mostly I'm pissed at myself, because I can't get you off my mind. My plant's been nearly destroyed, and yet I've spent most of my day trying to stay focused instead of thinking about the way you felt last night. I can almost *taste* you as if it just happened. Even worse, I didn't get enough, didn't take you the way I *really* wanted to."

They were at Victorian Days; this was the last thing she'd expected Kyle to say. She glanced around. Fortunately, no one seemed to realize they'd left the B and B. She could hear a teenage girl telling her mother that she'd gotten a picture with Lourdes Bennett. But with everyone bundled up for the cold and moving in clumps, no one appeared to notice that she was now standing in their midst. "How do you want me?" she asked, throat dry, heart pounding.

There was a challenging glint in his eyes as he stepped closer. "Where I can watch as I make you tremble. See the look on your face when —"

That was as far as he got before she grabbed him by the shirtfront and pulled him behind the closest building. "Then what are you waiting for?" she asked and dragged his mouth to hers.

# 24

Kyle had expected what he'd said to intimidate Lourdes. She'd just come out of a painful breakup, should've run for cover when confronted with such a frank admission. That was what he'd been aiming for. He needed a way to win the war he was fighting against himself, and he'd thought if he revealed he wanted sex *with* meaning, she'd retreat to protect herself from anything too intense.

But she didn't. Instead of rebuffing him, she'd tugged him into the dark alley behind Callie's photography studio. And now she had his shirt up, her mouth on his chest and her hands a bit lower, in much more sensitive territory, although he still had his pants on. He should take her home, he told himself. If they were going to make love again, they shouldn't do it here. She deserved better. But the longer he put off stopping, the harder it became to even consider it.

So much could happen on the drive home; for instance, sanity could return. And he definitely didn't want that. Not yet.

"Lourdes, someone could see us." He did feel obligated to warn her. Obviously, she wasn't thinking straight, either. She had a lot more to lose than he did if compromising pictures appeared on the internet. But who would be in the alley? The celebration was in the center of town. And the same desperation he felt seemed to hold her in its same grip.

Although it was too dark to see clearly, he was fairly sure she smiled up at him as she unbuttoned his pants. Then she knelt down and put her mouth on him, and the intense pleasure that brought destroyed the rest of his common sense. His knees nearly buckled, and he had to lean against the building for support. But before he could lose control, he brought her to her feet. He didn't want to come that way; he wanted to be inside her when they were face-to-face. So he made quick work of helping her remove the thick black tights she wore beneath her skirt, and then he found the condom in his wallet.

As he lifted her up against the building,

he could hear his fellow townspeople singing carols around the big Christmas tree in
the park a block over, but he didn't care.
He had to have her now, right in the middle
of Victorian Days, because nothing else in
the world seemed to matter.

Maybe it *had* to be like this with her, he
decided. Otherwise they'd overthink it,
second-guess what they were doing. When
it was over, Kyle was breathing too hard to
speak, but he wasn't willing to release her
too soon. He continued to hold her up
against that building, feeling his heart
pound as he buried his face in her neck and
struggled to catch his breath.

She didn't seem any more eager to separate. She kept her hands in his hair and her
head resting against his as if these few
seconds were as important as everything
that had happened before.

When he finally set her on the ground and
they hurried to dress and straighten their
clothes, he also tried to help fix her hair.
The way it fell about her face made her look
thoroughly ravished and he didn't want that
to give them away.

He was afraid she might say something,
might want to "talk." But he wasn't interested in trying to figure out what the hell
was going on. What was the point? It

wouldn't change the facts. He didn't put her anywhere near the "you've really fucked up your life now" class of mistakes that Noelle fell into, but he knew he was asking for more disappointment and pain. When it came to Lourdes, he just couldn't seem to stop himself.

Fortunately, Lourdes said nothing. She simply stared up at him as he did his best to take care of the small things she wouldn't be able to see without a mirror. "There you go," he whispered. "You look great. Fine. No one will notice."

She allowed him to take her hand. He was about to guide her to the edge of the celebration, where he hoped they could slip into the crowd, but a bitter voice he knew all too well broke the silence.

"Well, that was entertaining."

Lourdes felt her stomach drop. Kyle's hand tightened on hers, and he turned to confront his ex-wife. *"What are you doing here?"* he demanded.

"Certainly not what you've been doing," she countered.

Lourdes cringed. She had never had sex in public before — couldn't believe she'd been caught the first time. Did Noelle have pictures?

She doubted it. Fortunately, there wouldn't have been enough light.

"You've been following me again," Kyle said.

"Because I need to talk to you."

"No, you don't. We have nothing to say to each other."

"Yes, we do! I was your wife. Can't you at least give me . . . give me a few minutes?"

*"For what?"* he growled.

Lourdes could feel Kyle's anger. She knew Noelle had to feel it, too. It seemed to take her off guard, was probably something she'd never seen before. With the fire, he'd finally lost all patience.

Noelle's eyes darted in her direction, even though she addressed Kyle. "You have to quit telling the police that I'm the one who set fire to your plant, Kyle. It's not true."

"*Don't* try to tell me you didn't do it," he said. "I *saw* you there."

"Because I heard the sirens and . . . and I wasn't far away. So I drove over to see what all the excitement was about. But I was just as shocked as everyone else when I saw those flames."

"Which is why you left in such a hurry? Because it came as such a surprise? Funny, but everyone else who came by actually stuck around to watch."

"I was afraid you'd see me! I didn't want you to know I'd been driving past your place again."

"Of course! You just happened to be driving by right at that moment."

When she stepped out from the shadow of the building, the moon's weak rays revealed the fear in her eyes. "I'm there a lot. You know that. But I'm telling you I didn't do it! I . . . I could never do something like that to you. You're . . ." She took a deep breath and seemed to switch tactics. "You're just trying to get rid of me once and for all, so you sent the police over to get my fingerprints, hoping I'd end up in prison."

"I admit that no one'll be happier to see you there than I will," he said.

"Kyle!" she cried.

The way Noelle said his name, with a gasp, told Lourdes that comment had hurt.

"Leave me alone," he said and began pulling Lourdes along with him as if Noelle didn't matter, as if he'd leave her right where she was, calling after him.

But Noelle didn't stay put. She followed them and began talking even more loudly. "You have to listen to me! You have to call them off! *Please?*"

Lourdes tugged on Kyle's hand to get him

to stop walking before they reached the crowds. She didn't want this to become a public spectacle, with Noelle screeching at the top of her lungs that she'd just watched them having sex in the alley.

When Kyle came to a halt, so did Noelle. She seemed to understand that she was dealing with a much more determined man than he'd ever been before. She'd pushed him too far. "Lourdes, go to Eve's," Kyle said. "I'll come for you there. I don't want you involved in this anymore."

"I won't leave," she said. She didn't trust Noelle, was afraid Noelle might claim he'd hit her or even raped her. Lourdes wouldn't put anything past someone who might have committed arson, and Noelle seemed so desperate tonight.

"I'm tired of your lies," he said. "I'm tired of everything about you. What you look like. What you say. How you think. All your so-called emergencies. What does it take to get rid of you? For you to realize I've never loved you and never will?"

When she rocked back, he cursed under his breath as if he hadn't meant to be quite that cruel. No doubt those words had come from the depth of his frustration — and been helped along by all the other extreme emotions he'd felt in the past twenty-four hours. "Look, I have no desire to be as hateful as I'm being right now. I'm sorry. I just . . . I need you to leave me alone, okay? The police will investigate. If your fingerprints match the ones that were left at the scene, they'll arrest you. If they don't . . . then maybe it *was* someone else."

"But I've been to the plant. I've touched things. Remember when A.J. and I came to get the water heater? Even if my fingerprints are there, that doesn't mean I set the fire," she insisted, her voice much smaller than before.

"No one else has anything against me, Noelle," he said. "Only *you* have ever made my life miserable."

Lourdes guessed that Noelle was about to cry, although she couldn't tell for sure. "It . . . it had to be Genevieve," she said. "She did it knowing you'd think it was me and *I'd* get the blame. That's her way of taking revenge for when . . . for when I gave her that bloody nose at the bar."

"Now it's Genevieve who's to blame?" Kyle scoffed. "Will you just stop? No more lies! No more anything. And God help you if you ever do anything to Lourdes. If you so much as breathe a *word* about what you witnessed here tonight, I'll tell everyone what you did to our baby — while accepting all their sympathy for your supposed 'miscarriage.' "

If she'd been about to say anything else, that shut her up. It was tough to tell in the meager light, but Lourdes was pretty sure she'd gone pale.

Putting his arm around Lourdes, he led her through the crowds. She'd expected him to use more caution when they walked back onto the main drag. But he was beyond caution. He marched her to his truck. Then he drove them both home.

When they reached the house, Kyle poured himself a drink. He offered Lourdes one, too, which she refused.

"You don't think Noelle could've been telling the truth about that Genevieve person, do you?" she asked. She hadn't said anything on the way home, hadn't even mentioned what they'd done in the alley, and of that, he was glad.

Kyle pulled his gaze away from the whiskey in his glass. "No, but I'm sure the police will check into the possibility."

"It'll be interesting to see whose prints, if any, show up on that broken bottle."

"Didn't you hear Noelle?" he said. "She's trying to cover for that by saying she's been at the plant quite a few times."

"So she could've dropped that bottle before?"

"I believe that's what she's trying to suggest."

"You really don't think it could be Genevieve?"

"Genevieve's not nearly as likely as Noelle."

"Do you know Genevieve well enough to call and ask what she was doing that night?"

"No. I've only met her once or twice. She hasn't been living here that long." He might call her anyway, though. Noelle had acted more vulnerable tonight than ever before. But she was such a great actress. She could've been faking it all.

Lourdes moved her purse over to the counter. "You said something to Noelle . . . about the miscarriage."

He took the final swallow of his drink. As he put down his empty glass, he was tempted to pour himself another but decided against it. "You mean the abortion?"

"Yes. Why do you think she did it? She didn't want the baby?"

"I guess not. It was just another thing to be used for whatever she could get out of it. The pregnancy had already got her what she'd initially wanted. She proved that she could 'steal' her sister's boyfriend. That

Olivia had nothing on her." He shrugged in a sad way. "The baby had served its purpose."

She sat down next to him at the table. "But she didn't tell you? Didn't include you in the decision?"

"No. She claimed it was a miscarriage and did everything she could to make me feel sorry for her. She even hinted that it was my fault, because we'd argued beforehand."

"Did you ever check her story? Try to find proof?"

"I made some calls, but all that stuff is private. No one at any of the clinics I tried would divulge whether she'd been in, despite the fact that we were married and I was the father." He rubbed his face as he remembered. "And I didn't search too hard. Part of me wanted to believe her, even if it meant being deceived. If she'd done what I suspected, I knew I'd only hate her more."

"So you were still trying to make your marriage work."

"For a while. As far as I'm concerned, marriage is about commitment as much as love. We didn't have love, so I was trying to make up for it with determination. I knew she was her own worst enemy, and I thought I could help her. That she'd somehow be better or different if I could make her happy and secure. With time, I hoped I could learn to love her."

Lourdes crossed her legs. "Even though you suspected her of ending the pregnancy that was the reason for your marriage? That's not much to build on."

"Turns out, it was impossible. I could hardly stand to touch her after that. Bottom line, my intentions were good, but —" he poured himself that second drink, after all "— I just ended up causing us both more pain."

"And you feel guilty about it."

"That's why I've put up with her for so long. I tried to make her happy, but I couldn't force my heart." And now he wanted Lourdes, as if life with a country music star was any more realistic for him.

Kyle cursed to himself. He'd even seen it coming and couldn't sidestep it.

"You told me you don't have anything you could say about marriage at Riley and Phoenix's wedding. But with the way you feel about commitment, it sounds to me as if you do."

"They're in a completely different situation."

"They are. They have the benefit of love. But marriage still takes commitment."

He eyed her. "What are you doing? Trying

439

to get out of writing my speech for the wedding?"

"Just trying to guide your thoughts." She pulled her laptop over. "Why don't we open a document and get that started?"

"Not tonight." Kyle was exhausted. He had no energy for writing speeches — and yet he could easily have taken Lourdes into his room and spent hours with her. They'd only had a couple of hit-and-runs, nothing like the kind of night he would love to spend with her.

He was trying to convince himself to go to bed alone when her phone buzzed.

"Is that Derrick?" he asked.

She checked. "Yes," she said with a sigh. "He's been calling more than ever lately."

This was a text. "What's he saying?"

" 'I have something I need to tell you. Please call me,' " she read aloud.

Kyle finished his second drink. "Are you going to?"

"No." She put her phone down.

"But you *are* going back. To Nashville. You'd never consider staying . . ." He held his breath as he waited for her answer. He had no right to ask so much of her, but he couldn't let her leave without telling her that he was over Olivia. That he loved *her* and that he could offer her everything he had and could ever be.

She looked troubled when she faced him, and he knew, even before she answered, that it wouldn't be enough. "I've never met anyone like you, Kyle. I could . . . I could fall in love with you. Maybe I already have. From the beginning, there was . . . something about you. But we want different things out of life. You've made it clear that you'd never want to leave Whiskey Creek. And I can't stay."

"You could travel for work. When you needed to." Kyle had never dreamed he'd make that concession so quickly. But other couples conquered various challenges. It might not be his *ideal* future, wasn't what he'd sought or planned, but he hadn't expected to fall in love with a professional singer.

Another text came in before she could answer.

Since he could see the words, Kyle read it at the same time Lourdes did. "Come on, Lourdes," Derrick had written. "This is a hit song. You can't miss it."

"Looks like it's work-related," Kyle said.

When she glanced up, he could tell she was excited by the message and tempted to respond. He couldn't blame her. She wanted to rebuild her career, and Derrick could of-

441

fer her the help he couldn't. "Go ahead and call him," he said and went to bed to give her the privacy to do so.

# 25

Derrick had found the perfect song. He could've given it to Crystal, but he was reserving it for her. He'd even played it for her. He'd had to call in a lot of favors, and pay a pretty penny to the songwriter, who owed him a favor, or he probably would've lost it to Miranda Lambert, since she'd also shown interest. But he was confident it was right for her, and Lourdes had to agree.

She'd never been able to fault his taste in songs, or his business acumen. He'd helped her build what she'd created so far, and it would be so much easier to continue with his support. Although she'd planned to find a new manager in January, she was now thinking about hiring Derrick again. He was a known entity, someone with plenty of experience and knowledge about the biz.

There was no telling if she'd get someone half as good if she switched . . .

Giving her this song was his way of keeping her in the fold, she realized. But she wasn't entirely opposed to staying, despite what he'd done.

When her phone rang again, she looked at it in surprise. She'd just finished talking to Derrick — she was still holding her phone — so what was he calling about now? He needed to give her time to think . . .

But this call wasn't from Derrick; it was from Crystal.

Lourdes curled the fingers of her free hand into her palm. Did she care to talk to "the other woman"? What on earth could Crystal have to say to her?

In the end, curiosity overcame her reluctance. Hoping she wouldn't live to regret it, she slid the answer button to the right. "Hello?"

"Lourdes? Thanks for taking my call. I . . . I wasn't sure if it would only make matters worse, but I felt like I needed to say something."

Lourdes sank onto the edge of her bed. "I can't imagine what we'd have to discuss."

"Well, I bet we can both agree that I owe you an apology. I'm really, *really* sorry. And I just have to say it's been awful watching Derrick go through this, when I know I'm partially to blame. I can't explain exactly what happened that night, but —"

"You're saying it was just one night?" Had Derrick been telling her the truth about that?

"Yes, it was. I swear. We'd had a bit too much to drink. We were excited about the sales of my latest album. We were making plans, and then it got late and . . . and before we knew it . . . things went too far. I wanted Derrick to tell you right away, but he was so afraid of losing you that he made me swear I'd keep my mouth shut."

"I saw the picture that was posted on the internet where you two were making out over lunch, Crystal."

"We weren't making out! We were talking — about *you* and what we were going to do to right our wrong and how terrible we both felt."

"So you're not seeing him now."

"No. Absolutely not. Our relationship is strictly professional. I asked him not to drop me. I'm just getting started in my career, and I really need his guidance. But I'm not after him in any other way, and . . . I felt . . . if there's anything I can do to make things right between you two, I needed to do it."

Lourdes rubbed her right temple. She told herself she shouldn't buy into this, that it was another of Derrick's attempts to convince her to overlook his latest indiscretion, and he'd only cheat on her again. But Crystal sounded so sincere. "I've hardly heard from him since he confessed the truth."

"Because he's been searching, night and day, to find you the perfect song. He told me it might be the one thing that'll bring you back to Nashville long enough to give him a chance to prove himself."

"He could've come here."

"He said that wouldn't help your career."

But it might've helped *her*. Didn't he care about that? How could he miss the fact that love and security were more important than anything to her?

Actually, somehow that didn't surprise Lourdes. He'd done that kind of thing a lot, which was why so much of their relationship revolved around her career.

"Anyway, in case you still won't answer his calls, I think he's found that special song. It's called 'Crossroads,' and he had me listen to it this morning. I loved it so much, I'm green with envy that he's reserving it for you. But I understand why." She paused, then added, "You need to call him. Trust me. It'll be your next big hit."

Lourdes thought of the night Kyle had phoned Derrick, pretending to be someone from *Country Weekly* magazine, and Crystal

446

had obviously been with him. "I don't know if I can believe you," she said.

"Why not?" she asked. "I have no reason to lie. How would it help *me* if you came back? Or if you reunited with Derrick? The gossip rags will make me look like someone who couldn't hang on to the man she tried to steal. That won't be flattering, but even though I wasn't actually trying to steal him, I deserve that for what I did, so I'm willing to take the bad press. The only reason I'm doing this is to try to make things right."

Suddenly, everything seemed to be turning around. Keeping Derrick as her manager and recording a song as great as "Crossroads" could put her back on top. She also liked what she'd written so far and had begun to feel she'd have some great material of her own to follow up the new song.

"Thank you," she told Crystal. "I appreciate that you've made what had to be a difficult call." She took a deep breath. "I also respect it," she admitted. "It's not often you run into that kind of thing these days." Especially in the entertainment industry . . .

"Thank you for allowing me to apologize. I don't want to destroy anyone's life or career or anything else. My motto is 'Do no harm.' "

After she disconnected, Lourdes sprang to

her feet and began to pace. Her hopes and dreams had been revived! She'd been offered a second chance!

Then why did she feel so depressed at the thought of leaving Whiskey Creek? Sure, she cared about Kyle, but he was really in love with Olivia. He'd made no secret of that. He'd let her know, from the very beginning, that he'd never get over his stepbrother's wife.

She should buy a ticket and head home as soon as possible. And she shouldn't worry about anything else.

Except she knew in her heart that Kyle's feelings for Olivia had changed — and so had her feelings for Derrick.

Kyle took a shower, then dropped onto his bed and stared up at the ceiling. He could no longer hear the hum of Lourdes's voice, so she was off the phone. He thought she might come to him. Lord knew he wanted her to. But as the minutes ticked away, he guessed she wouldn't. She was going back to Nashville. Whatever song Derrick had sent her had tempted her beyond her ability to refuse.

It was almost one when his phone indicated a text message. He was half-asleep by then and didn't want to wake up enough to check it. But after the fire and what had happened with Noelle tonight, he didn't dare ignore it.

"What have you done now?" he grumbled, but the text wasn't from her. It was from Brandon.

Tell me you did not have sex with Lourdes in the alley behind Callie's studio tonight.

"Damn Noelle," he muttered and wrote his brother back.

No.

Liar. Noelle's over here sobbing to Olivia about it. I can hear her.

Noelle needs to keep her mouth shut.

She says you hate her and want to see her go to prison.

As harsh as that accusation was, Kyle didn't have it in him to deny it.

Does that surprise you?

Not especially. But I'm almost convinced she didn't set the fire.

449

Don't listen to her. No one's a better liar.

Agreed. Still. She's sounding sort of believable.

She had both motive and opportunity. And she has no alibi.

You don't think it could've been Genevieve, like she claims?

Genevieve wasn't the one whose car pulled in and then took off like a bat out of hell.

Good point. So let's talk about Lourdes. Things are heating up with her, huh?

As Kyle stared at those words, it felt as if he had a thousand pounds of sand crushing his chest.

No. Not really. She's had something come up — an opportunity of some kind. I'm pretty sure she'll be going back to Nashville early.

When? Not before the wedding, I hope. Riley and Phoenix were hoping she'd sing one song — the one for the first dance.

I doubt she'll be here to do that.

Too bad. Are you at least bringing her to the rehearsal dinner tomorrow night?

If she wants to come, he wrote back. He was just leaning over to set his phone on the nightstand when he heard a soft knock. "Come in."

The door opened and Lourdes stepped inside. "I . . . um . . . I hate to have to tell you this, but . . . I'll be leaving on Tuesday," she said.

It didn't matter that he'd expected as much — Kyle's stomach muscles tensed. "You're going back to Derrick."

"I'm going back to Nashville, *not* Derrick," she clarified.

At least the fact that she wouldn't be around long hadn't come out of nowhere. He'd known it from the start, even if this was a lot sooner than they'd planned. "That's what I figured. Derrick can give you what you want."

"In a professional sense, yes." She came closer to the bed. "I'm sorry."

"We knew this would happen eventually." So why hadn't he done a better job of protecting his stupid heart? "Thanks for telling me."

"That's it?" she said. "That's all you're going to say?"

He sighed deeply. "What else can I say, Lourdes?"

She peeled off her T-shirt and stood there, nibbling nervously at her bottom lip as she stared down at him, wearing only her panties. "There's still three days before I go. Do you want them?"

As his gaze settled on her breasts, Kyle told himself not to be a fool. He already cared far too much about her. At the rate he'd been falling, three more days — especially the kind of days she seemed to be offering — would bury him so deep it might take as long to get over her as it had Olivia.

But three days was still *three whole days.* So he threw back the covers and invited her into his bed. If he was going to crash and burn, he might as well make it one hell of a conflagration.

The way Kyle made love this time was completely different. He was in no hurry, for one thing. And he was so gentle it almost brought tears to Lourdes's eyes. She was astonished by how much he seemed to feel — and what *she* could feel for a man she'd known for such a short while. The poignancy of those emotions amplified the pleasure of every kiss, every touch, every embrace.

It wasn't long before she was convinced that she'd made a serious miscalculation in coming to his bed. What they'd shared before had affected her deeply enough. She'd never experienced that kind of raw, powerful sensuality, had certainly never allowed anything like that to drive her to the point of risking a public display. But she trusted Kyle in a way she'd never trusted any other man. And following that experience in the alley with this slow, sensual act just added an exclamation point to her infatuation with him. It had all happened so quickly — and yet it was going to be so difficult to leave. Even with the promise of that fabulous song Derrick had found for her.

As Kyle kissed her forehead, she had a feeling this trip to Whiskey Creek would soon seem more like a dream than a memory. She'd come here feeling like a bird with a broken wing, and Kyle had taken her in and carefully tended her until she could fly again. Just connecting with him had somehow made her whole.

Their eyes met as he rolled her onto her back and put on a condom. As strange as the thought was, since they'd already been together twice, this felt like the first time they'd ever made love.

He watched her face as he pushed inside her and didn't look away when he began to thrust. He held himself above her and moved slowly, methodically, drawing out the pleasure for as long as possible. She noticed how the intensity of his gaze sharpened when her breathing grew labored, and she arched toward him, saw his nostrils flare as she gasped right before crying out in release. Then the barest hint of a smile curved his lips and he closed his eyes to concentrate on his own pleasure, until his climax followed hers.

She could tell by the way he pulled her to him afterward and hooked his arm protectively around her that he was feeling a great deal. But she was glad he didn't voice those emotions. She knew it would only make it harder to leave.

Maybe he knew the same thing.

They showered together the following morning — and wound up making love beneath the spray. To Kyle, it felt like a honeymoon, or what a honeymoon *should* be like. Now that he and Lourdes had given themselves permission to enjoy their final days together, before she went back to resume her regular life, they couldn't keep their hands off each other. There was no more holding back. All inhibitions were gone. All pretenses, too. They just wanted to be together, refused to waste a minute on any other part of life — like eating or sleeping or including friends and family.

After the shower they went back to bed, where they made love yet again.

"You recover quickly," she teased.

"Because you're making me squeeze a lifetime into three days. But the party's over now. I've exhausted my supply of condoms." He dropped onto the bed beside her. "A guy who hasn't had sex for three years doesn't usually get this lucky all of a sudden. I wasn't prepared."

She laughed as she leaned over to kiss his shoulder. "There's a store in town, isn't there?"

"There is. If only I was willing to leave you long enough to drive over."

She ran her fingers along his jaw as she gazed down at him. "We can't stay inside the whole time I'm here. We have to leave at some point. You have that rehearsal dinner tonight."

"True." He closed his eyes for a moment, enjoying the gentle movements of her fingers. Then he opened them again. "Are you coming with me?"

"Am I invited?"

"Of course. Riley and Phoenix were planning to ask you to sing at the reception while they danced. Brandon texted me about it last night."

"Did you tell them I'd be gone?" She seemed disappointed that she couldn't do it.

He nodded. Only when the subject of her leaving came up was there any strain between them. But he knew, now that Derrick had devised a surefire way to put her back on top, she wouldn't be happy in Whiskey Creek even if he managed to convince her to stay. And, to him, that would be worse than letting her go.

Lowering her hand, she glanced away as if she felt guilty for being the one who would eventually tear them apart. "Sure, I'll come to the rehearsal."

Kyle did what he could to banish their inevitable parting from his mind. "Good. Then I won't have to handcuff you to the bed while I'm gone."

She laughed. "That was my alternative?"

"Sounds reasonable to me. If you weren't going with me, the only way I'd be able to tolerate being away from you would be to know you were home waiting for me, naked in my bed."

"I'm pretty sure that would just encourage you to leave early."

He kissed her neck, breathing in the scent of the soap they'd used in the shower as he did so. "Or maybe I wouldn't make it over there at all."

"I can't say I'd blame you. After three years of celibacy, you're making up for lost time."

"What's happening here has nothing to do with that," he said.

"And how do you know?"

He smoothed her hair off her face. She was being playful, but what he had to say was completely serious. "Because I'm in love with you, Lourdes."

She sobered instantly. "We just met, Kyle."

He shook his head. "Doesn't matter."

"What about Olivia?"

"I think I got over her the second you stepped out of your rental car at the farmhouse. Until then . . . I just hadn't met the right woman."

"You don't love her anymore?"

"I love her the way I should — as a sister-in-law." How he could so easily give Lourdes what Noelle had always wanted, he couldn't fathom. But there it was.

Her expression was troubled as she stared up at him. "Kyle, I . . . I had no idea this

457

would go so fast."

He tucked the covers around them. "Neither one of us saw it coming."

"Will you hate me when I'm gone?"

"For breaking my heart?" He frowned. "Maybe for a while," he teased.

## 26

Lourdes loved Kyle's friends. They welcomed her warmly and seemed so natural and comfortable around her — even joked with her as much as they joked among themselves.

Of course, they were probably ecstatic that Kyle was finally showing interest in someone besides Olivia. Lourdes could see them nudging each other when he wasn't looking. No one was saying anything about him — or her — out loud, but she could tell they were all excited that he seemed to be moving on.

They loved him . . .

Which meant she was about to break every heart in the room.

But she had no choice. She had to go back to Nashville. What else could she do? Her career was there.

She knew, as soon as she returned, Derrick would start pushing her to forgive him for Crystal so they could go ahead and get married, as they'd originally planned. But his indiscretion with Crystal wasn't the biggest obstacle standing in their way. She no longer loved Derrick enough to marry him.

The conflict she felt made her stomach churn. She didn't want to end her relationship with Kyle. But what choice did she have? She knew what her career demanded; she also knew it wasn't what would make him the happiest. How could she even focus on him in the next six to twelve months?

While the others noshed on chips and salsa, shrimp and dip, cucumber sandwiches and other appetizers, she declined all offers of food and sipped at the water she'd requested instead of the champagne everyone else was drinking. She certainly didn't feel like celebrating, she thought as she watched Kyle laughing with his stepbrother across the room. She and Kyle had mentioned that she'd be returning to Nashville to record a very special song, but they hadn't added that she wouldn't be coming back. These were *their* three days, before everything changed, and they weren't about to ruin or waste them by taking others into their confidence.

"Are you bored yet?" Baxter asked, stopping by the refreshment table for another glass of champagne.

"No, I'm fine," Lourdes said with a laugh.

"Too bad you won't be here for the wedding," he said. Then Riley called him over and he left Lourdes alone, enabling her to study Kyle some more.

He was handsome, the kind of handsome she'd close her eyes and dream about when she was back home. She couldn't keep from staring at him tonight, or acknowledging that he looked even better in the nude . . .

Kyle glanced over, caught her watching him and smiled.

How was it that instead of living with the heartbreak of losing Derrick, she was feeling that rare but giddy sensation of falling in love?

"Your face brightens every time you look at him."

Lourdes turned to see Olivia and felt the heat of a blush. Of all people to notice how Kyle affected her . . .

Or maybe it was logical that Olivia would be more aware of what was going on with Kyle than the rest of the group. She'd probably been keeping a pulse on that since they split up. She'd have to, in order to maintain the careful balance necessary for them all to get along.

"There's no one else quite like him,"

Lourdes admitted.

Olivia's lips curved in a conspirator's smile. "Trust me. You're speaking to a convert. I may not be in love with him in that way anymore, but I'm a big fan of Kyle's." She popped a chip into her mouth. "So you're over Derrick, then? That's all in the past?"

Lourdes detected a hint of concern. They were happy for Kyle, but they also wanted to be sure she wasn't playing him. "For the most part. We'll still work together. At least we'll try."

Olivia smiled. "I hope that turns out well for you."

"Thanks." In an effort to shore up her decision, Lourdes told herself she could get over Kyle as easily as she had Derrick. Her first Nashville boyfriend had once told her she wasn't deep enough to fall in love for real. Maybe he was right — and, if that was the case, she was doing Kyle a big favor.

It was better for both of them that she was going back to Nashville, getting back to work. She *knew* she loved music, *knew* she wanted to be involved in that. All the rest was . . . less clear.

"It's different when the right person comes along," Olivia said.

Was that what had happened with Brandon? He'd come along and Olivia had somehow known? How? And was Kyle, not Derrick, the right man for Lourdes? Or was there someone else, someone she'd meet later?

"How do you know when you've found the right person?" she asked.

Olivia didn't have an opportunity to answer before Kyle approached. "We're done," he said. "You ready to go?"

With a nod, Lourdes said goodbye to Olivia and everyone else and walked out of the reception center under Kyle's arm. He asked if she wanted to see a movie or go ice-skating in Sacramento, where there was an outdoor rink set up for the holidays. But she told him she'd rather go to the store.

"For . . ."

"What do you think?"

He nodded as he figured it out. "Ah, right. How could I have forgotten? That'll be our first stop."

As it was, he barely had the chance to buy the condoms, drive home and turn off the engine before she started kissing him. She felt strangely possessive of him. It had to be the dwindling time and all the things they had to face in the next two days that brought such urgency to the way she touched him.

He didn't complain when she straddled

him before he could open his door. "Do I have something you want?" he joked.

"I want this," she said and undid his pants.

His hands slid up her shirt. "It's cold out here. Wouldn't you rather go inside?"

"No. I have to be closer to you. Now."

The horn went off a second later, but even that didn't stop them. "Don't worry, Warren went to see his kids this weekend," Kyle whispered, his voice hoarse.

She bit Kyle's lip just hard enough to make it plain that she wouldn't *let* him stop.

Somehow he managed to get them out from behind the steering wheel, silencing the horn, which was quite a feat, since they were both half-clad. Then he laid her down on the bench seat and shoved her legs apart, taking her as hard and fast as he had in the alley.

She braced herself against the dashboard and the seat as she surrendered to the satisfaction of being with him. At the same time, she told herself she'd be fine without this, without *him.*

Because it was Nashville that held everything she'd ever wanted.

Kyle watched Lourdes as she studied the computer screen. It was early, but they'd gotten plenty of sleep. They'd been in his bed since they'd come home from the rehearsal dinner last night, talking, laughing, massaging each other, play wrestling, sleeping or making love. They'd probably *still* be there, if hunger hadn't driven them out.

While they were in the kitchen, he coaxed her into sitting down and helping him write his remarks for the wedding. He had to get it done before she left; he felt it would be much better with her input. He'd searched the internet for sample ceremonies, and he'd found some decent ones, but he wanted Riley and Phoenix's ceremony to have more of a personal touch.

"Why don't we start by having you tell me what's special or unique about them," Lourdes said.

"There's a lot. Phoenix and Riley were together for a short time in high school. She wasn't the usual type of girl. He was into sports and dated cheerleaders or one of the girls in student government, so she was a . . . departure for him and not someone his folks thought he should be with. She came from a sad, dysfunctional home, dressed all in black and wasn't exactly a stellar student. Not that she isn't smart." He took a sip of the coffee sitting beside him. "Anyway, his folks said they wouldn't pay for college if he insisted on 'ruining his life' with 'that girl,' and when he finally folded under the pressure and broke up with her, Phoenix took the news really hard. She was pregnant, not that anyone knew it at the time, and scared to death. And she was madly in love with him, so she was heartbroken, too."

"At the rehearsal tonight, I overheard someone say that she spent a long time in prison. What for?"

He slid his cup and saucer away from his elbow. "I'm getting to that. Just before we graduated from high school, someone ran down Lori Mansfield, the girl Riley was dating after Phoenix."

"You mean with a car?"

He nodded. "Phoenix looked like the obvious culprit. Everyone knew how jealous she was of Lori. There was even some evidence to suggest it *was* her — enough to get a conviction. It wasn't until last year that the truth came out."

The color drained from Lourdes's face. "Don't tell me she was innocent."

"She was. They took her baby away from her when she had him — gave him to Riley, who raised him — and she hardly heard from Riley and Jacob during all those years."

"That's heartbreaking!" Lourdes said.

"It is. And yet, as soon as she got out, she came back to Whiskey Creek, because she wanted to get to know her son. And long story short, she and Riley wound up finding each other again and realizing that they were still in love. Their story is not only unusual, it's —" he searched for the right word "— inspiring, I guess. This isn't just *any* marriage. This is Phoenix getting what she always deserved."

"So maybe you could talk about the kind of love that endures."

"And forgiveness," he said. "If she wasn't able to forgive, this wouldn't be happening."

"How old's her son?"

"Jake's a senior."

"She's waited a long time."

He took another sip of his coffee. "See what I mean? Why I feel she needs someone who has more experience than a jaded divorced guy to help commemorate this occasion?"

Lourdes propped her chin on her fist as she considered what he'd told her. "Why don't you start out talking about how some things, some of the most beautiful things in life, are hard-won but transcend everything else?"

"Love conquers all."

"Yes."

He hesitated for a second. "I like that approach, but we have to be careful not to make it too mushy. I don't want tears in my eyes or anything. I'd never live it down."

She laughed as she reached over to kiss him. "We can't reveal that, deep down, you're a big softy?"

"Problem is, you don't have to go that deep to figure it out."

Still smiling, she was about to say something to tease him — he could tell by the glint in her eyes — but his phone rattled on the counter. He'd silenced the ringer.

He got up to grab it. He'd been waiting to hear from Chief Bennett about the fingerprints on that broken bottle and didn't want to miss him.

Sure enough. The call was from the police station.

He showed Lourdes his display and then answered. "Tell me you found some prints on that bottle, Chief," he said once they'd exchanged hellos.

"Yes. That's the good news. There are plenty of prints."

"Do we know who they belong to?"

"We do."

Kyle felt his breath catch. "So what's the bad news?"

"They aren't as conclusive as we'd hoped. They belong to both Genevieve Salter *and* your ex-wife."

*"What?"* Kyle leaned on the counter as he tried to digest what he'd just heard. "Does Genevieve have an alibi?"

"She says she was home, at her mother's house, asleep."

"And is her mother backing her up?"

"Her mother claims she heard Genevieve come in that night, but she has no idea what time. She was in bed herself and didn't completely wake up."

"So it must've been late."

"Not necessarily. Marilee went to bed at nine, right after she got Genevieve's son to sleep."

"Was Genevieve working at Sexy Sadie's that night?"

"She was, but business was so slow, they let her leave at ten instead of keeping her on until two."

"Then it could've been her." He wasn't sure how he felt about that. As far as he was concerned, she had even less reason to set fire to his plant than Noelle did.

"There's nothing so far that rules her out."

Cursing under his breath, Kyle returned to the table and sat down. "So what's next?"

"Genevieve says she's willing to take a lie

detector test. She admits she hates Noelle, but not enough to set fire to someone else's business."

"That makes sense to me."

"Even if she made Noelle look like the guilty party?"

"She could do other things, more direct things, to get back at Noelle."

"She swears she'd never do either, and she has no record."

That didn't account for much. Noelle didn't have a record, either, but she would've had one if he'd ever reported her behavior. "Are you planning to have someone administer the test?"

"I'm considering hiring an expert, yeah."

"Will Noelle take it, too?"

"No. Unfortunately, she refused. Said there's no guarantee it would be right, so she doesn't see the point."

Or, more likely, she already knew she'd fail . . .

Kyle remembered Noelle's panic in the alley, after she'd followed him and Lourdes. She'd sounded pretty convincing . . .

But then he thought of the moment he'd spotted her car the night of the fire, and the hair stood up on the back of his neck. If she wasn't responsible, she would've stopped and rushed over to ask what had happened.

Plenty of other people had been drawn by the sirens. At the very least, she would've spoken to the firefighters. She was so obsessed with him that a fire at his plant would've been irresistible for her, even if she didn't want him to know she was in the area. She would've figured she could lie her way out of that as she did everything else. Instead, she'd bolted and then she'd acted as if she didn't know about the fire when Olivia called her later.

"It's not Genevieve," he said decisively.

"How do you know?" Chief Bennett asked.

"I know my ex-wife."

"I can't arrest her on your gut instinct, Kyle."

"You think it's her, too."

"I do," he admitted. "Poor Genevieve was in tears when I questioned her, *genuine* tears. Noelle seemed almost . . . gleeful. Made my cop's intuition go crazy. But I need proof, and there just isn't any."

Damn it! Not only would Lourdes soon be gone, Kyle was going to be left with the cleanup and construction at the plant, knowing that the person who'd been responsible could do it again. And because she was a woman, he couldn't confront her in the same way he would if he was dealing with another man.

"What is it?" Lourdes murmured.

Apparently, she'd noticed from his expression that he had an idea. "I'm going to pay Noelle a visit."

"Don't do anything stupid," Chief Bennett warned, overhearing him. "Leave it to me. I'll get to the bottom of it eventually."

Kyle wanted to believe that, but he had no faith. Noelle was too clever, too good a liar. She'd turned deception into an art she'd spent a lifetime perfecting, and she made it work for her. She'd gotten away with almost everything she'd ever done by twisting, evading or shading the truth.

But he was going to use what he knew about his ex-wife and her methods to beat her at her own game.

She wasn't getting away with this.

## 27

Noelle smiled when she saw Kyle pull up in front of her house. Here he was — at last. And what perfect timing! She'd just gotten home from the boutique where she worked thirty hours a week, so she still had on her nice clothes. He would see her in the formfitting black pencil skirt and sheer top, with her lacy bra showing underneath. She'd bought the outfit with him in mind. He liked classy, understated women. This fit that bill, and yet she looked sexy at the same time. A tourist driving through town had nearly crashed into the hardware store when he saw her emerging from the shop tonight. Size 36DD boobs had a way of catching a guy's attention, especially in the blouse *she* was wearing.

Kyle would notice, too.

After checking her hair and makeup, she went to the door, where she hesitated so she wouldn't appear too eager. Only when he knocked for the second time did she answer — once she'd arranged her expression into one of polite confusion.

"Kyle! What are you doing here?"

"Do you have a minute?" he asked.

Although she widened her eyes as if his desire to come inside surprised her, it didn't. She'd guessed she'd hear from him. For a while there, he thought he'd gained the upper hand by threatening to withhold her spousal maintenance, but she'd punished him for that. Now she just needed to get him back in her bed, to remind him that there'd been some positives in their relationship, too. "I suppose so," she said. "Now that I'm only working one job, it's not like I have to rush off to Sexy Sadie's."

He didn't comment on her job situation, even though she felt he owed her an apology. If not for the way he'd been treating her, she would never have caused trouble for herself there.

"Come on in." Instead of leading the way, she stood back so he'd have to brush past her — and made sure his arm came in contact with her breasts.

"Did you ever get a new water heater?" he asked as she shut the door before following him into the living room.

"Not yet. My folks are having a friend

install one on Monday. I've been showering at Olivia's."

"So you saw your sister this morning?"

"I did. Briefly."

"Did she tell you that Lourdes is going back to Nashville?"

"No, but wasn't Lourdes always planning to go back?" She gave him a patronizing smile to emphasize her point. "She's a country music star, Kyle. It's not as if she'd ever stay *here.*"

A muscle moved in his jaw, but his voice remained more pleasant than she'd expected. "I mean she's going back much earlier than we thought," he clarified.

"For good?"

"Looks like it."

Even better. Lourdes had created a huge problem. It was comforting to know she'd soon be out of the way. Then maybe Kyle would quit wishing for something he wasn't going to get and settle for a woman who *did* want him — like her. "I bet you're broken up about that."

"I wish she'd stay. But as long as I'm wishing, I also wish my plant hadn't been damaged by that fire."

She perched on the chair closest to him and leaned forward to allow him an unrestricted view of her best assets. Lourdes had an okay figure, but as far as Noelle was concerned, she could use a little more on top, especially for Kyle, who appreciated that sort of thing. "I had nothing to do with that," she said.

"Are you sure?" he asked.

She smiled sweetly. "Positive."

"Did Chief Bennett tell you that your fingerprints were found on the broken bottle recovered from my parking lot?"

"He did. He stopped by the shop earlier. But he said Genevieve's fingerprints were also found on that bottle. And, like I mentioned to him, Genevieve's are the ones that are out of place, not mine. I've been to your plant many times. I was in that very parking lot *twice* the night A.J. and I picked up that old water heater, remember?"

"You've reminded me of that before. And I do remember, since I was there, too. But nothing fell out of the truck. That bottle wasn't on the ground when you drove off."

"So? Maybe I've been to the plant since then, to see what you were up to. It's not unusual that something of mine would be left behind, including a bottle Genevieve and I must've shared. We drank together a lot. I've never denied that."

"But you *are* denying that you set the fire at the plant."

476

Feigning what she hoped was a pretty scowl, she said, "*Of course* I deny it. It wasn't *me,* Kyle. I've told you that."

"Then why won't you take a polygraph test?"

She gestured as if the very thought was ridiculous. "I've read about those. They're not reliable. I don't see any point in wasting my time."

"Even if it would reassure me?"

Could she possibly pass a lie detector test? If so, that would be the best route to go, but just in case, it wouldn't be wise to take the chance. "Stop trying to talk me into it. You're hoping I'll fail so you can convince everyone *I'm* the guilty party. You know, I don't really trust you anymore."

"You don't trust *me.*" He laughed softly. "That's rich."

"You've been really difficult lately," she complained.

"Is that why you set fire to my plant? To strike back at me? Bring me in line?"

She folded her arms, fully aware of how that pushed her breasts higher and made them strain against the sheer fabric of her blouse. "I'm sorry you're so convinced I'd do such a thing, but . . . it doesn't really matter what *you* believe. Chief Bennett told me he wasn't going to arrest me. He can't.

He doesn't have any evidence."

Kyle leaned close enough that she could smell his scent. It was a scent she remembered well, a scent she craved. She was tempted to put her hand on his arm but held off, hoping there'd be an opportunity to touch him later. "What is it about me?" he murmured.

This took her off guard. "Excuse me?"

"What did I ever do to deserve so much of your attention?"

She wished she knew. She told herself all the time that he *didn't* deserve her. What other woman would hang on for so long, knowing he was in love with her sister? "We're meant to be together, Kyle. Like Phoenix and Riley. Phoenix has always loved him, but for years he believed she killed Lori Mansfield, and he didn't want anything to do with her. Now he knows that isn't true. You think terrible things about me, too, but just like Phoenix, I'm not as bad as you've made me out to be."

He sat back and regarded her coolly. "Are you saying you *didn't* abort our baby?"

She forced herself to maintain eye contact with him even though she wanted to look away. "No! I would *never* do that! We fought sometimes, and I . . . I acted immature and demanding. But I loved you. I *still* love you.

And you'd love me, too, if you could see how much I've changed!"

Throwing his head back, he laughed out loud.

She usually didn't have trouble convincing people of anything she said when she was trying this hard . . . "What?" she asked, feeling out of sorts.

"You've *changed*?"

"I have!"

"You just set fire to my plant!"

He was different these days, more adamant and determined, and it made her uneasy. Somehow, she had to get through to him once and for all. "No, I didn't!"

"Yes, you did, so stop lying. I'm here to tell you that you'll never get another dime out of me, Noelle. The check I gave you on the first of December? That'll be your last."

The dark anger she'd felt when she had the abortion — the desire to hurt him — swelled inside her, making it hard to talk without raising her voice. "Kyle, don't start this again. I'm getting mad."

Seemingly unconcerned, he shrugged. "I don't care how mad you get. I mean it."

She stood up. "You might be able to hold out for a few months, but you'll have to pay me eventually. We've talked about this before. I can *force* the issue."

He came to his feet, too. "No, you can't. If I have to spend every penny I have on lawyers and litigation, I will."

"You say that because you're assuming I can't afford to fight back. You're wrong. I've got my parents in my corner now. They won't let you do this to me. We'll get our own lawyers."

"If that's the direction they want to go, fine. We can all drain our accounts. But when it's over, even if you win, I *still* won't pay."

*"What?"* He'd been stubborn at times — like when she'd wanted to buy a new house or car and he didn't think it was practical. Still, he'd never gotten *this* stingy. "Olivia will hate you if you treat me like that."

"I hope not, but that's the chance I'll have to take."

She got the feeling he didn't care about Olivia anymore, either, which was another difference she noticed in him. "Then you'll go to jail!"

"So be it," he said flatly. "I've finally realized that the only way I'll ever be rid of you is to accept whatever losses I have to in order to make it happen. And I've reached that point. I don't care about the consequences. You will have no more hold over me. Do you understand?"

Curling her hands into fists, she stepped closer, got right in his face. "You son of a bitch!"

He *tsked* as if she was the most pathetic person he'd ever seen. "You shouldn't have set fire to my plant, Noelle."

When she tried to strike him, he caught her wrist, which just made her angrier. "Let go of me!" she cried.

"Don't ever lift your hand to me again," he said.

He'd always been a sucker for tears, so she started to blink and sniff. "Things could've been different, for *both* of us, if only you'd allowed it."

He remained unmoved. "You can stop the show, Noelle. I don't love you, I never have and I never will," he said and let her go.

"You're a bastard!" she screamed. "I'm *glad* I did it. Here I've been feeling bad that I let my temper take over, but now I'm mad I didn't burn your damn plant to the ground! Next time, I'll make sure you're in it!"

His eyes narrowed. She didn't think she'd ever seen him look so dangerous. "Did you just threaten my *life*?"

"You heard me," she growled. "You'd better pay me my spousal maintenance, or you're going to lose a lot more than your plant."

He stepped back. "And if I call Chief Bennett and tell him what you said?"

"I'll deny it. It'll be my word against yours — an ex-husband who's trying to get out of paying his alimony."

The smile that curved his lips seemed so incongruous with his anger of a moment before — and with what she'd said — that a sick feeling entered the pit of her stomach.

"There's one small problem with that plan," he said.

She'd made a mistake. She wished she could take back the past few minutes, but something told her it was too late to even try. "And that is . . . ?"

"I'm not the only one you admitted it to." He lifted up his shirt to show her that he had a small microphone taped to his chest.

"You . . . You're wearing a wire? You set me up?" She gripped her throat because she suddenly felt as if she couldn't breathe. She'd never dreamed backwoods Whiskey Creek would be so high-tech. She'd thought that was something that happened in movies or maybe in big cities like Chicago and LA.

"I figured it was time for a little honesty," he said, and the next thing she knew, Chief

Bennett was in the living room, handcuffing her.

As soon as Kyle returned, Lourdes put down her guitar. She'd decided to try to make some progress on her album, to help keep her mind off her imminent departure from Whiskey Creek, and surprised herself by making furious progress on the song she'd been writing for him. Somehow it was all flowing and coming together fast. But she didn't want him to hear it yet. First, she'd finish it, and maybe even record it, so it would sound its best.

Besides, she was anxious to hear what had happened with Noelle.

"How'd it go?" she asked. "I've been texting you, but I haven't heard back."

"I forgot to charge my phone last night," he replied. "It ran out of battery about the time Noelle got arrested."

Lourdes jumped to her feet. "Arrested? *She's going to jail?*"

"Yes. My idea worked. All I had to do was rile her up, make her mad enough to lose control, and . . . she admitted it." He hesitated. "Actually, it was more like she threw it in my face, thinking there wouldn't be anything I could do about it."

"And Chief Bennett heard?"

"Every word."

"I wish you'd let *me* go."

"I doubt she would've done it if you were there. And after today, I'm even more convinced she's not right in the head. I've said that for years, but I didn't mean it the way I do now. I don't want you anywhere near her. Ever. For all we know, she'd get it into her head that you were behind my decision to trick her, or that I'd want her if I didn't care for you, or . . . whatever. The way she twists things, there's no telling what she might do with the most harmless detail."

Taking his hand, she drew him over to the couch. "Have you told Olivia and Brandon?"

"No. My phone's dead, remember? After Chief Bennett put her in his squad car, I came straight home. But I'm sure they've heard. Noelle's probably called her parents by now, and her parents have called Brandon and Olivia."

Lourdes tried to imagine what it would be like to hear that one of her sisters had set fire to someone's business — and couldn't. "I feel sorry for them. Bad enough finding out she's guilty of arson, but doing what she did to someone else they know and love? They're definitely going to have mixed emotions."

"Brandon won't. He pegged Noelle for a sociopath from the start. He won't feel bad to see her get what she deserves. But Olivia? She's always felt guilty for being popular and well liked when her sister wasn't. That's why she's cut Noelle so much slack and tried to get along with her."

"Do you think this is the end of it? That Noelle will leave you alone from now on?"

He ran a hand over his face. "Who can say? While I was there, she mentioned how long Phoenix has loved Riley — that Phoenix hung on through all those years in prison — which makes me a little nervous."

Lourdes smiled ruefully. "I can see why, especially since she won't have to spend as long behind bars as Phoenix did, will she?"

"No. Chief Bennett said it could be two to six, depending on the judge. But he's guessing it'll be at the lower end of that range, because no one got hurt."

"That means she'll be back one day."

"Whoa!" He held up a hand. "Let's not talk about her coming back. Let's enjoy the fact that she'll be gone for a good, long while."

"Okay." She snuggled up to him, content just to feel the warmth of his body, to hear the sound of his heart beating so steadily beneath her ear.

They sat like that, in silence, for several minutes. Then he said, "We're down to one more day."

Closing her eyes, she wrapped her arms around his waist. "Let's not talk about that, either."

When Lourdes woke up the next morning, Kyle was gone. Assuming he must've had to deal with something connected to the fire or Noelle's arrest, she clasped her arms around his pillow and relived the tender moments they'd shared during the night.

She'd never been like this, she realized. Never been so head over heels. Given her situation, it didn't make a lot of sense that she could fall so deeply in love. She'd come to Whiskey Creek firmly believing she was in love with someone else. And yet there was no denying how she felt. She could only hope she'd be so busy in Nashville that her enthusiasm for her work would take some of the sting out of leaving Kyle behind.

Throwing back the blankets, she sat up and searched for her phone. Derrick had texted her several times yesterday. He'd tried to call, too, but she hadn't answered. That could wait until tomorrow, when she hit Nashville, or later in the week. But her mother had also called, to confirm the time

486

she'd be arriving.

Lourdes spoke to Renate for a few minutes, then propped herself against the headboard as she went through the other texts and emails she'd ignored.

There were a few business items from Derrick. He'd spoken to her old label. They were interested in a demo of the new song. That was encouraging. She never should've left Boondock Records to chase the dream of becoming even bigger by switching to pop. Had Taylor Swift not made it look so easy, she probably wouldn't have.

Anyway, Derrick was putting out a few other feelers and had generated some interest.

Crystal had texted her, too.

I'm so glad you're coming home. Is there any chance we could have lunch?

Lourdes didn't like that Derrick had communicated her plans to the woman he'd cheated with, didn't care for the fact that they were still in close contact. She wasn't jealous; it just made her feel odd that they were all carrying on as if nothing had happened. But she supposed lunch with Crystal would be smart from a professional standpoint. It would go a long way toward letting people know they weren't feuding over Derrick, as some might expect.

Sure. I'll give you a call when I'm settled, she wrote back, then climbed out of bed to wash her face and brush her teeth and hair.

When she was done with that, she picked up her guitar. Kyle's song was turning out to be even prettier than the one Derrick had purchased for her, and she was eager to finish it.

She worked on it for another hour, until she heard Kyle's key in the lock. Then she set it aside to meet him at the door.

"Where have you been?" she asked.

He grinned at her. She could tell he hadn't taken time to shower this morning. He'd thrown on his clothes and a ball cap and left, but she liked him a little scruffy. "I had to pick something up."

"What?"

He looked slightly embarrassed. "Maybe we should eat first."

She studied the sack in his hand. It had the Black Gold Coffee emblem. "You bought breakfast?"

"An array of muffins."

"That sounds delicious but . . . are you trying to make me fat so I won't look good onstage?" she teased.

"Would it make you stay?" he asked.

When their eyes met, she knew he was far more serious than he'd sounded. "Kyle, I *can't* stay."

"Even if I give you this?" He reached into the muffin sack and pulled out a small velvet box, which he handed her.

So much for waiting until after breakfast. Apparently, he *couldn't* wait. But Lourdes was afraid to take it. She could guess what was inside. "Kyle . . ."

He shoved his hands in his pockets. "I had to do something. I had to at least try."

Hoping she was jumping to the wrong conclusion, that it was just a keepsake necklace or a pair of earrings to remember him by, she opened the lid — and stared down at the very engagement ring she would've chosen for herself.

"Eve told me you posted the ring you wanted on Twitter. She sent me pictures of rings similar to the one you liked. They were all yellow gold, so I went with that."

She could hardly breathe. "I do prefer yellow," she said. "I'm tired of almost all jewelry being set in white these days."

"And she said you liked the princess-cut diamond."

"You got *exactly* what I would've chosen." And judging by the size of the diamond, he hadn't been concerned about the price.

"But?" he prompted.

She lifted her gaze. "You know what stands between us."

"We could make it work." He cupped his hands around hers, which held the ring. "So what if our lives aren't as compatible as *we* are. That might not be what we would've chosen, but . . . it doesn't change the way I feel. I don't want to let you go. Will you marry me, Lourdes?"

She felt tears burn her eyes. "You don't understand."

"I *do* understand. All the traveling won't be easy. You'll be split between here and there, and I'll hate having you gone so much. But I can't let you leave me — not without telling you that I'd give everything I have, everything I am, to make you happy. I'll support your music. Whatever you want to accomplish." He rested his forehead against hers. "No one else could love you more," he whispered.

Tears welled up and slid down her cheeks.

"Say yes," he coaxed. "Your career is important. So is mine. But what we feel for each other is important, too. This kind of thing . . . it doesn't happen every day."

"Kyle, I need more time," she said. "This is . . . This is too fast."

"I understand. But I had to tell you before

490

you left. You should know what's waiting for you here — if you want it."

Struggling to swallow around the lump in her throat, she nodded.

"Would you like to try it on?" he asked, indicating the ring.

A tear dripped from her chin. Of course she'd like to try it on, but she couldn't. She was afraid it would break her heart when she had to take it off.

He wiped her tears, then put the ring down and raised her chin. "It's okay. It's too soon. And it's a big decision for you. You don't have to answer now."

She moved her thumbs over the razor stubble on his jaw. "Don't let anything ruin this day," she murmured.

"I won't," he said and carried her into the bedroom.

# 28

She was gone. Kyle had hoped Lourdes would give him an answer to his proposal before she left. He wanted something to cling to. But she hadn't. To his knowledge, she'd never even tried on the ring. She'd never mentioned it again, either. And the most telling sign, at least in his view, was the fact that when she drove off, she immediately turned around, got out of her car, hugged him fiercely and whispered that she'd never forget him.

There'd be no danger of that, if she was coming back.

"Are you okay?" Morgan asked.

She'd brought over his new office computer and was helping him recover his files, but Kyle's heart wasn't in his work today. He kept glancing over at the kitchen drawer where he'd put the velvet box that held the ring. He'd bought it from Hammond & Sons Fine Jewelry, the only high-end jewelry place in town. Yesterday, after he'd roused Eve to get her advice, he'd had to call George Hammond at home and drag him from his bed to open the shop early, but George had been nice about it. Kyle knew him well enough that he could also take the ring back, and he figured he should do that before George assumed the twenty grand Kyle had paid was going to remain in his pocket. Kyle had spent more than he'd ever dreamed he would on any piece of jewelry, but if Lourdes had accepted it, he wouldn't have cared about the price.

"I'm talking to you." Morgan snapped her fingers in front of his face.

Kyle blinked and shifted his gaze. "What'd you say?"

"I asked if you were okay."

"I'm fine. You've asked me that twice since you got here."

"Because you're not yourself."

"Let's stick to business."

"Fine," she said. "There's plenty of that to talk about. The insurance adjuster called. He wants to come out and take a look at the building tomorrow morning. What time should I tell him?"

"The earlier, the better." Fortunately, Riley had rearranged his schedule as promised, so he'd be able to do the work right away.

He was already writing up a bid to keep the insurance adjuster honest in his estimation of the losses.

"I'll shoot for eight, but he's coming from Sacramento. I'm guessing it'll be nine or ten."

"Whatever time you set up, let Riley know about it, too. I'd like to have him there, if possible."

"I have no doubt he'll be there. Your friends would do anything for you."

"Yeah," he said, but he realized he'd said it a bit too absently when she nudged him.

"I would, too. So will you cheer up? You make me feel like crying, and I never cry."

He forced a smile. "I don't need to cheer up. I'm not sad."

She rolled her eyes. "You're kidding, right? You're so devastated I almost feel I should check your house for sleeping pills or anything else you could —"

"Stop it!"

She grinned at him. "Think of the bright side. Maybe Lourdes is gone, but so is Noelle. She's going to be punished for what she did."

Punishing Noelle wouldn't restore his plant. But he was happy that she couldn't harass him anymore. In that respect, the next few months were going to be heaven . . . "She almost got away with it."

"It was a close call. How'd Olivia and Brandon take the news?"

"Brandon wasn't surprised. Olivia felt bad, but she doesn't blame me. Noelle got herself in trouble."

"And tried to frame Genevieve for it! That's evil!"

"Needless to say, Genevieve's also happy the truth has come out."

He fielded several calls from clients who'd heard about the fire and were checking on the status of their order. Then Morgan said, "Are you all set for Riley's wedding?"

"For the most part." He needed to put the finishing touches on the speech that Lourdes had helped him write. And the bachelor party was this Friday, only two days before Christmas. All his friends were excited, but he was having trouble feeling much enthusiasm for anything.

Lourdes was grateful her mother was the one who picked her up from the airport and that Renate hadn't allowed Derrick to talk her into letting him go instead. Apparently, he'd tried. Her mother had a big bouquet of exotic and expensive flowers she said were from him, but Lourdes wasn't in a hurry to read the card.

Although she and Derrick needed some time alone to talk, she wasn't ready for that quite yet. She hadn't given him any indication that she planned to reconcile, but it was natural, she supposed, for him to think there'd be a chance. She'd been gone only three weeks. A person's life generally didn't change that drastically in such a short time.

"I'm so glad you decided to spend the holidays with us," her mother said, her smile too bright as she persevered in ignoring Lourdes's dour mood.

Lourdes nodded. It was good to see Renate. They'd always gotten along well. But she'd left the love of her life behind in Whiskey Creek, and she couldn't get the song she'd written for Kyle out of her head. She'd drafted the rest of the lyrics while she was on the plane and couldn't wait to finish it. She kept humming those last few bars so she wouldn't forget them. No matter what happened from here on, she'd dedicate it to him.

"So . . . how'd it go in California?"

She turned to stare out the window, already missing the quaint little town. "Fine."

"Did you see anyone we know?"

"You mean from Angel's Camp? I didn't get down that way. I wasn't there long enough."

"Will you go back after Christmas to finish the album?"

Lourdes felt a crushing sense of loss. She'd wrestled with herself the entire plane ride. She was worried she was making a terrible mistake, closing the door on what she and Kyle had started. But she knew how hard it would be to maintain a long-distance relationship, how different that was from what Kyle wanted to achieve — and how susceptible she'd be to trying to keep him happy if he wasn't, just as her mother had her father. "No." She cleared her throat. "Probably not. I'll finish it here."

They drove in silence for the next ten minutes. Then her mother shot her a cautious glance. "Will you be getting back together with Derrick?"

"Absolutely not."

Renate lowered the volume on the radio. "He seems to expect you to."

She studied the gray sky overhead. "We'll have to figure out how to deal with the past."

"Meaning you're going to try to continue working together."

"I hope we can."

"And what about Kyle?"

"What about him?"

"Will you still have a relationship with him?"

"No."

"Because . . ."

"Because one of us would get hurt."

"You're not hurt now?"

"We haven't known each other that long, and it's easier to move on sooner rather than later."

"You're *that* sure it wouldn't work out."

"I wouldn't be doing this if I wasn't."

"Okay. I'm happy as long as you're happy."

Lourdes managed a smile so her mother wouldn't know she felt like crying and, thankfully, Renate talked about other, more cheerful things. They had several cousins coming for Christmas dinner. Lourdes's groundskeeper had done a beautiful job draping her trees and shrubs with Christmas lights. Mindy had an interview at the school district where she wanted to teach, so she might finally be moving on with her life.

As soon as Renate pulled into her drive, Lourdes thanked her mother for the ride and hurried to get her luggage. She was afraid Renate would want to come in. They hadn't seen each other for several weeks. But her mother obviously realized she needed some privacy; after a brief hug, Renate murmured that she should call if she needed anything and climbed back behind the wheel.

Lourdes rushed inside. She'd thought she'd find solace in the familiar, in *her* house, bought with *her* money, from *her* singing. But the house just felt . . . empty.

The following day Lourdes rubbed damp palms against her jeans. She was meeting Derrick for breakfast. She'd refused to see him last night. She'd needed time to adjust to being home, to determine how she wanted to proceed. But she couldn't put him off indefinitely. They had far too much to discuss.

When he'd asked if he could pick her up, she'd insisted on driving into town on her own — to their favorite crepe place. They came here quite often. So did Taylor Swift, Keith Urban and his wife and many famous people. Some of the other patrons stared but rarely did anyone try to approach or take pictures. She appreciated their restraint and the fact that the owners of The Crepe Café tried to protect her from intrusion — by keeping an eye out for it and, if necessary, asking the offending party to leave. Lourdes especially appreciated knowing they'd look out for her today, when she was so nervous. She would've gone to Derrick's house, or had him come to hers, except that she'd wanted to be on neutral ground, somewhere open and public, where she could walk away if she needed to.

She sat with a cup of tea, alternately eyeing the door and the clock. He'd texted her that he'd received a business call and was running a few minutes late, but she'd expected him to be here by now.

She was just getting her phone out to call him when she spotted his BMW pulling into the lot. He wasn't as handsome as Kyle, didn't have the same rugged sort of appeal. He was thickening around the middle, had a weak chin, which he compensated for with a full beard, and some gray in his hair. But he was always well-groomed and well dressed. And he was a genius about music.

She watched while he parked and made his way toward the entrance, then stood to greet him.

"You look gorgeous!" he said but hesitated, as if he wasn't sure whether or not to touch her. In the end, she leaned toward him for a brief embrace, which only confirmed what she already knew. She wasn't going to marry him. Those feelings were gone.

"You look good, too," she said. "Are you all set for Christmas?"

"No. Haven't done any shopping. And it's right around the corner."

"The packages in the picture I saw online were all Crystal's?"

He reddened at the reminder but nodded. "I met her for lunch, to . . . to discuss everything, like I said."

"I remember."

"So are you excited about the song I found?"

" 'Crossroads'?"

"If we decide to keep that title."

"I'm thrilled about it. But —" she slid the salt and pepper cellars closer together "— you may not want to give it to me after we've had a chance to talk."

Raising a hand to stall her, he focused on the waitress who was coming to take their order.

When they were alone again, he removed his coat and scooted his chair closer. "Before you make any decisions, I have a few things I'd like to make clear." His gaze locked with hers, and he continued more stridently, "I believe in you and your talent, and I am thoroughly convinced that, on a professional level, we can recover from the past six months. On a personal level, I want you to know that I love you and I'm sorry for what I did. Sincerely."

She took another sip of her tea, more uncomfortable than reassured. "It's okay. I forgive you."

His voice took on fresh hope. "You do?"

"I do, but —" she cradled her cup so she wouldn't wring her hands "— that doesn't mean we'll be able to get back together, Derrick. I'm afraid what we had is over. My feelings have changed."

He gaped at her for several seconds before recovering enough to respond. "It's too soon to decide that. Let's give it some time. Can we give it some time?"

She shook her head. "That would be pointless."

He stared at the floor. "Is it that man you were with in Whiskey Creek — Kyle Houseman?" he asked when he looked up. "Is *he* the reason?"

"He's part of it," she said. "What happened between Kyle and me was . . ." She shook her head as she searched for the words to describe their attraction, their feelings for each other.

"It was unlike anything I've experienced."

"Meaning with me."

"With anyone."

"I see." He sat back as the waitress brought him his coffee. Then he lowered his voice. "Were you communicating with him before you went out there, like I read in all those blogs and . . . and articles? Is that why you chose Whiskey Creek?"

She felt her jaw drop. "No, I only said that to save face."

"I'm not sure I can believe you, seeing that so much has changed."

"Are you kidding?" she said "*You* were supposed to go to Whiskey Creek with me, remember? You're the one who decided to stay here."

"But you were *living* with him."

"By accident. If you'd been with me, that never would've happened. When there was no heat at the farmhouse, we would've gone to a B and B."

"I only stayed here because I had too much business to leave, Lourdes. Otherwise, I would've come."

"I'm not complaining," she said. "I'm merely letting you know that I didn't *plan* what happened. It was just . . . one of those things."

He sighed and raked his fingers through his dark hair as if there were so many emotions going through him, he didn't know whether to hit something, yell or . . . maybe even cry. "When you came home so quickly, I thought . . . I thought I still had a chance. Or was it the promise of 'Crossroads'? Is that the only reason you're here? For the song?"

He'd offered her that song as an enticement, so it hardly seemed fair that he was angry with her for being enticed. "For the song — and my career."

He'd just taken a sip of his coffee. But at this, he set his cup down. "You're serious. It's over."

"Yes. I'm afraid so."

"After three weeks."

She nodded.

He took his phone off the table and put it in his pocket. Then he stood up as if he'd learned everything he needed to know.

"You're leaving?" she said.

"What else am I supposed to do?" He grabbed his coat. "You just told me you're in love with someone else."

"We haven't talked about our professional interests."

"What professional interests? You fired me, remember?"

"I've reconsidered. I'd be interested in having you continue as my manager."

"Yeah, well . . . that won't work for me. It'd be too hard."

"You've still got Crystal," she pointed out. "Even though I begged you to let her go."

"So you *are* holding that against me. You

say you've forgiven me but you're still angry about one stupid indiscretion for which I've apologized again and again?"

She had a lot to say about that *stupid indiscretion.* Easy to be glib about it when he wasn't the injured party. But she doubted he'd understand that. She decided to focus on what mattered now, anyway. "I'm *not* angry, just trying to make you aware of the contradiction."

"It's different with Crystal. I don't love her. It won't break my heart to record with her and tour with her, all the time wanting to touch her while knowing she doesn't want me back."

"So we're parting ways *completely?*" Lourdes had been afraid of this; it was the reason she'd been so nervous. She knew losing Derrick would be detrimental to her career.

He shrugged. "I don't know. Give me a chance to try to figure this out."

That was probably wise. "Okay." She nodded. "Let's talk again after Christmas."

"I've never seen you so . . . dispassionate," he said.

She was dispassionate about *him.* Kyle and her career still meant everything to her, but she wasn't sure she could have both, and having to make a choice was agonizing.

"I'm sorry, Derrick."

"What you felt for me died that easily?"

"I think it's been going on for a while — since we started having so much trouble."

"So it goes back to Crystal?"

"I guess she brought out the worst in both of us."

"Are you going back to him, or is he coming here?" The way he asked that told her he wouldn't be happy to have Kyle in town.

She clasped her hands together under the table. "I haven't decided yet. Probably neither."

Once again dropping his coat on the chair, he returned to his seat. "Why?"

"We want different things out of life. We're going in different directions." She still believed they might be smarter to make a clean break while they had the chance — to preserve the memories they'd created, rather than trying for more, failing and ruining *everything.*

"Then I'll continue to work with you," Derrick said. "As long as there's hope for us, I'll keep working."

"You're saying you'll dump me as a client if I go back to Kyle?"

"Rebuilding your career isn't going to be easy. I'm doing it because I love you, but if I can't have you, and this becomes strictly a business decision . . . I'd see it differently."

"So no song — no 'Crossroads.' "

"I feel like a jerk saying this, but . . . no 'Crossroads.' We're in this together, or we're not in it at all. There's no cherry-picking, Lourdes, taking only what you want from me and leaving the rest."

She nodded. In a way, that made her angry. He should be doing whatever he could to further *all* his clients' careers. But he'd worked hard for her in the past, and she'd moved to pop against his advice, which was a setback for him, too. Also, she knew Crystal could release that song as easily as she could, and there'd be less work involved in negotiating the contract and the support necessary to overcome a failed album, since Crystal didn't have a failed album.

"You're forcing me to choose between Kyle and my career?"

He offered no apologies. "Do you need time to think it over? Or do you know what you want?"

She wanted what every musician wanted. She wanted to be on top, in demand, out with a new album every year that was more popular than the one before. Music was her life, and after everything she'd been through in the past twelve months, she was terrified she wouldn't be able to earn a living without Derrick. He had the experience, knew all the right people. He could navigate the industry better than anyone. She wasn't even certain she could get another manager, not while she was in her current situation. It was Derrick's romantic interest that made him willing to keep trying with her.

"I can't promise anything."

"All I'm asking is that you keep an open mind and give me a chance to prove my love."

She drew a deep breath. What would it matter, if she and Kyle didn't really have a chance, anyway? "Then let's record the song."

# 29

Christmas dawned bleak and cold, with snow flurries and an overcast sky. Kyle supposed most people would appreciate a white Christmas, but the weather did little to cheer him up. He drove over to Morgan's house, as well as the homes of his other employees, to deliver their Christmas bonuses. Then he returned to his empty house, sat by the tree and listened to all of Lourdes's albums — even the pop songs.

Riley had already started work on the plant and was hurrying to get the bulk of it done before the wedding. He said the subcontractors could finish the rest once he left on his honeymoon, so Kyle would be able to move back into his office the day after New Year's and restart production. That was good news. Kyle tried to encourage himself by being grateful for that and anticipating how much better things would be when he could get to work in earnest.

But no matter what he tried to tell himself, there was no remedy for the gaping hole Lourdes had left in his life.

"Stop it! You only knew her for three weeks," he grumbled. "You're being ridiculous."

Still, ridiculous or not, she was all he could think about. He picked up his phone and stared at it. He was dying to call her, to hear how she was doing and what was happening with the songs she was writing for her next album. He was even curious about what was going on with Derrick.

But he didn't want to intrude on her life. He of all people understood how miserable it was when an old flame tried to hang on. He'd told Lourdes he loved her. He'd offered her a ring, a ring he hadn't returned, which was pretty pathetic and further proof of his complete devotion.

"She knows what she's walking away from," he muttered. And he couldn't blame her for leaving. She was so talented. She deserved to soar as high as she could in the music world. Nothing he had to give her could compete with fame and fortune, and it didn't help that he'd known this all along.

He was about to allow himself to text her, just a simple "Merry Christmas," when Brandon called.

With a sigh of relief, he answered his cell.

"Hey, where are you?" Brandon asked.

Kyle stiffened in surprise. Christmas dinner wasn't for three more hours. "I'm at home. Where are you?"

"In the car, driving over to play football at the high school. It'll be a cold, muddy mess, but I can't think of anything that'll be more fun. Didn't you get my message?"

Kyle remembered seeing something come in; he'd been using his GPS to find the homes he had to visit to deliver those Christmas bonuses and had forgotten to go back to it. "Sorry. Missed it. I was busy."

"No problem. Some of my old school friends are in town for the holidays and they put this game together. Ted and Noah and the others won't be there, but I'd love it if you'd come."

Kyle frowned at the Christmas tree he'd chopped down for Lourdes. He wasn't doing much of anything except torturing himself, so why not? "I'm on my way."

As soon as he disconnected, Kyle went back to the screen where he'd written "Merry Christmas," but before he could hit Send, he realized that the greatest gift he could give Lourdes, since she'd chosen a different path for her life, was to let her go.

So he deleted it.

■ ■ ■ ■

Lourdes was sitting on the couch at her mother's house, smelling the wonderful aromas coming from the kitchen while strumming the song she'd written for Kyle. The melody of "Refuge" went through her mind all the time, which made it even more impossible to forget him.

"Oh, who am I kidding?" she muttered under her breath. She couldn't have forgotten him, anyway.

With a sigh, she put her guitar on the floor so that she could lie down. She'd been so tired since she'd come home, had almost no energy . . .

She'd barely closed her eyes when her sisters came out of the bathroom, still arguing about which one had purchased a certain eye shadow, something Lourdes had been trying to tune out.

"Lourdes, you can't go to sleep," Mindy said as soon as she spotted her curled up on her side. "The cousins will be here any minute. They flew all the way from Florida to see you, and you haven't even changed."

She lifted her heavy eyelids. "They're coming to see *all* of us."

Lindy rested her hands on her hips. "Let's

be honest. I'm sure they're more interested in you. You're famous! *Everyone's* more interested in you."

Too bad Lourdes wasn't more interested in them. Although she'd thought she'd be eager to spend Christmas getting re-acquainted with Jesse and Lisa, and meeting their husbands, she didn't seem interested in anything these days, even her music. Yesterday Derrick had tried to get her into the studio to record "Crossroads," but she'd told him she wasn't feeling that great and put him off until after Christmas.

"What's wrong?" Her mother, overhearing the exchange, appeared at the entrance to the living room.

Lourdes shook her head. "Nothing."

Renate finished drying her hands, tossed the dish towel on the counter and crossed over to her. "Honey, you haven't been yourself since you got home."

"Of course I have," she said.

"No. You're so quiet and lethargic," Mindy said. "Are you sick?"

"You've hardly said two words since you showed up this morning," Lindy complained. "You just keep strumming your guitar and playing the same tune."

"I'm not sick. I'm resting. Or I was *trying* to rest . . ."

That hint did little to get them to leave her alone. "Are you not sleeping well?" her mother asked.

As a matter of fact, she *hadn't* been sleeping well. She hadn't been eating well, either. But she couldn't admit that or she'd have her mother coming by to check on her even more often than she already did. "Everything's fine. I'm happy I haven't lost my manager and that Derrick's going to help me rebuild my career. I'm glad Crystal and I can still be friends — well, professionally polite to each other. Despite what she and my former fiancé did, she and I are having lunch next week. And Derrick has found me a great song to record that we both think will go platinum. Things are looking up."

"Then why are you acting so down?" Lindy asked.

"I'm adjusting to being back, that's all."

"It's that man you met while you were in Whiskey Creek, isn't it?" her mother said. "Kyle."

Lourdes didn't answer. She rubbed her temples as if she had a headache, but the source of her pain wasn't anything that specific.

"Why don't you call him?" Mindy asked. "Talk to him? See how he's doing?"

Lourdes dropped her hands. "Because I

514

don't want to string out our breakup. Don't want to make it any harder than it has to be."

"It's Christmas," Lindy said. "I'm sure he'd love to hear from you."

Maybe she *would* call Kyle, if she could trust herself not to tell him how much she missed him and how badly she longed to be with him. That would only raise his hopes, hopes she'd most likely dash all over again because she couldn't walk away from Nashville.

"It's better this way," she insisted.

"It's better to be miserable?" Lindy said.

"Sometimes you have to make sacrifices for what you want."

Her mother's chin puckered as she frowned. "I'm not convinced you really know what you want."

"If I choose Kyle, I'll be kissing my career goodbye," Lourdes said. "That's not an option."

"They don't *have* to be mutually exclusive," her mother said, bending over to smooth the hair off her forehead.

Lourdes pushed herself into a sitting position. "Yes, they do. Derrick will drop me. He said he would. And then there'll be no 'Crossroads,' and probably no deal with my old label. Derrick got them Crystal. They want to keep him happy, so he'll bring them more young talent."

"That's your fear talking," her mother scoffed.

*"What?"* Lourdes said.

"You don't need anyone else's songs," she replied. "And I'm willing to bet you don't need Derrick or your old label, either. There are other people out there who make good music and might be interested in a talented artist like you."

"And if there aren't?"

She took Lourdes's hand. "Maybe being a big star isn't the only life that will make you happy. Maybe the joy isn't in the end result — in the success. Maybe it's in living, loving — and trying."

"But it's such a risk," she murmured. "Especially since I don't know Kyle all that well."

"You'll never get to know him any better if you don't give yourself the chance," she said and got up to finish the cooking.

Kyle was as nervous about Riley's wedding as Riley probably was. He'd memorized what he planned to say and fully believed what he'd written. But therein lay the problem. It was a lot easier to joke around with his friends and hide his more serious feelings behind the laughs and the ribbing. He wasn't looking forward to standing in front of half the town and revealing his more sober thoughts on love and marriage. After everything he'd been through — and everyone *knowing* what he'd been through — he felt too exposed.

"You're going to do great," Eve murmured, giving him a brief hug as she hurried past, dressed in her teal bridesmaid's gown. (He knew better than to call it green; he'd been educated on the difference while they were decorating and setting up.)

Lincoln, Eve's husband, was holding their baby, but used his free hand to slug him in the arm, backing up what she'd just said — that he'd do fine. Kyle smiled as if he wasn't worried. But the second they walked away, he glanced at his watch. *It'll be over soon,* he told himself.

Ten minutes before the ceremony was supposed to start, Olivia asked him to take his place. She was in full-blown wedding-planner mode; he could tell by the intensity of her focus.

"You all set?" she asked.

He nodded, and she hurried off to see that everything else went according to plan.

The friends and family who'd shown up early watched him expectantly, making him eager for the people in Riley's line to come and join him at the front so his audience would have something else to look at. He was starting to perspire and wished he could loosen his tie. Although it was a cold, crisp day outside — the storm that had rolled in on Christmas Day was gone — the heat inside seemed overwhelming. He straightened his shoulders, trying to cope with his discomfort as more people straggled in, chatting excitedly among themselves.

Kyle recognized Riley's parents, who'd given Phoenix such a hard time when they were in high school. Even the parents of the girl Phoenix had been convicted of murdering had come, along with their living daughter. Only their son, Buddy, wasn't with them. Kyle guessed he wouldn't be coming; he'd been too unkind to Phoenix when he'd thought she was guilty.

A lot of people were there. But Kyle noted that Phoenix's mother wasn't in the audience. He'd just decided Lizzie must've refused to come, when Phoenix's older brothers, whom Kyle had met an hour earlier, helped her through the door and down the aisle. She was so obese she couldn't fit in a wheelchair, so she had little choice except to walk. She inched down the aisle on swollen and purple ankles, but she was wearing a dress and her hair had been done. She also had a corsage pinned to her chest.

"I don't need to sit in front," she said to the people who were trying to lead her. Riley bent his head closer to hers and must've encouraged her to sit in her "place of honor" because she screwed up her mouth, stared down at the rose-petal-strewn walkway in front of her and allowed him and the others to half support, half drag her bulk onto the bench that had been positioned for her on the front row.

"God, it's hot in here!" She spoke so loudly almost everyone could hear. Then she wiped her upper lip, turned to glare at those who were staring at her and pulled a fan from her purse.

Kyle regretted paying such close attention to her entrance when Lizzie's rheumy eyes shifted his way — and narrowed.

"What are *you* looking at?" she snapped.

"Ignore her," Riley whispered as he came to stand by Kyle. "She's just self-conscious."

Phoenix's oldest brother hurried out, and not too long after, the music sounded. It was starting . . .

Jacob appeared first and came to stand by Riley. Then the groomsmen walked in with the bridesmaids and finally Phoenix walked in on the arm of her oldest brother.

As she came toward them, gorgeous in a mermaid-style gown, Kyle tried to overcome his nerves. He really didn't want to screw this up for her. She'd been through so much . . .

Her brother's tattoo "shirt" extended well above his collar. He had his ears pierced and his hair bleached and spiked on top — and looked even more ill at ease than Kyle felt. It was obvious that he'd lived a hard life and wasn't accustomed to wearing a suit. Kyle would've bet fifty bucks this was his first time.

But Riley didn't seem to notice anything except his bride.

"Isn't she beautiful?" he whispered as he watched Phoenix, and somehow that put Kyle more at ease. This wedding was meant to be. Maybe it was the perfect moment for some serious reflection on love and commitment, even if it did have to come from him.

Unfortunately, when Phoenix's brother handed her to Riley and the two turned to face him, that comforting feeling fled and, inexplicably, Kyle choked up. There was no explanation for his emotion, except that he cared so much about both Phoenix and Riley. He figured caring was okay; he just couldn't break down in front of everyone he knew.

He cleared his throat, trying to gain control. But that didn't seem to solve the problem. He had to do it two or three times, until Lizzie groaned as she shifted and said, "Are you going to get on with it?"

Fortunately, that broke the spell. Several people snickered. Then Kyle was able to laugh, too, and proceeded to tell Phoenix and Riley, and everyone else, what the Beatles had already said so well — *love is all you need.*

## 30

It had been great to marry Riley and Phoenix and to witness their happiness. It'd also been great to visit with Gail, since he didn't get to see her very often. Kyle always enjoyed hanging out with his friends, but he'd had enough socializing tonight. He was ready to go home, except that he didn't feel free to leave. The reception wasn't over. They'd eaten and taken pictures and had the toasts and special dances, but the live band was going to be there until eleven, which was more than an hour away, and the bride and groom hadn't yet left for their honeymoon. He stood by the champagne table, his tie loosened as he leaned against the wall, watching his friends dance with their brides or hold their babies. Only Baxter stood near him.

"A lot's changed in the past five or six years," Baxter mused.

"Yeah. But for the most part, everyone's

happy," Kyle responded. "That's what's important."

Baxter selected his own glass of champagne. "Are *you* happy?"

Kyle shrugged. "I'm doing better now that the plant is almost repaired."

"That's not what I was talking about."

"I know." He sipped from his glass. "How's your father?"

"I'm worried about him or I wouldn't have moved home. I love it here, love being with all of you. But I wouldn't have come back if it wasn't for my father."

"I guessed as much," Kyle said. "I'm sorry. It's shitty timing, shitty luck. I hope he pulls through."

"He's just ornery enough to do it."

They continued to observe the revelry until Kyle had finished his champagne. "Do you think they'd notice if we left?" he asked as he put down his glass.

Baxter checked his watch. "It's too early," he said. Then Callie came over and drew him away. She'd met someone who had a question about a particular stock, and she thought Baxter might be able to answer it. That provided Kyle with the perfect opportunity to slide over to the exit. He'd done his part. The fact that they'd all helped decorate had saved Riley some money, but the cleanup would be handled by Riley's parents, some of their church friends and the staff here at the venue.

Kyle had just stepped outside, finished removing his tie, which he stuffed in his pocket, and taken a deep breath when a different song started. A woman was singing this one, which was odd, since he didn't remember seeing a woman in the band. It made him curious but not curious enough to go back. He started toward his car and would've kept going, except that a second later, he recognized the voice.

Lourdes had never been so nervous about a performance. It wasn't just that she was crashing a wedding. By coming back to Whiskey Creek, she was putting her whole future, her entire career, on the line — as well as her heart. After achieving success, losing it and wanting it back so badly, trusting her instincts had been especially difficult. She'd walked away from her best chance at success when she got on the plane to come here. But she knew she wouldn't be happy, even if she returned to the top of the charts. Not if she had to live without Kyle.

Besides, showing up and taking the stage didn't really count as *crashing,* since she would've been invited to sing if she'd stayed.

She'd seen Maroon 5 crash weddings on YouTube to sing their song "Sugar," and everyone loved it. So she hoped this would go over just as well. She couldn't think of a better way to debut the song she'd written for Kyle.

"All the things I never knew . . . until I met you," she sang as she began the first chorus.

Everyone had stopped talking. They'd even stopped dancing. She recognized many of their stunned faces as they turned toward the stage, including Phoenix's and Riley's. Noah and Addy, Ted and Sophia, Brandon and Olivia. They were all there, and the rest of Kyle's friends, too.

But she couldn't find Kyle.

"Oh, my God, it's Lourdes Bennett!" she heard someone exclaim. Then her name went through the crowd like a ripple, and even those around the perimeter who hadn't yet realized what was happening started paying attention.

Lourdes caught the sound of Kyle's name, too. She could tell everyone was searching for him. So where was he? Why wasn't he here?

She was beginning to worry that he'd already left, when the crowd parted and she saw him standing in the center of the floor with his collar loosened, looking casual and yet elegant at the same time.

She experienced a moment of terror, wondering if she'd made a mistake doing this in public — *doing this at all.* When she'd told Derrick she was returning to Whiskey Creek, he'd severed their business relationship and given "Crossroads" to Crystal, which Lourdes had expected. Now she was entirely on her own and would have to start over, not much ahead of so many other artists who were trying to gain the ear and the confidence of the right people. But whether she made a comeback or not, she hoped to have Kyle as her husband and life partner.

If getting back on the country music charts didn't work out, she could always do weddings, she told herself and couldn't help smiling at the lengths she was willing to go for the man who was walking slowly toward her.

"I never knew love . . . until I knew you," she finished.

The room was completely silent as the final notes of the song died away. Everyone was too intrigued by the drama playing out before them to clap.

Shaky and a bit breathless, she set her guitar aside and stepped back up to the microphone. "I'd like to wish Phoenix and Riley a long and happy life together. I hope they aren't put off by this little surprise."

"No way!" Riley called as everyone applauded.

She grinned at him. "That song is called 'Refuge.' This is the first time I've ever sung it in public, but it seemed appropriate to do it here, since I wrote it in Whiskey Creek." Her gaze landed on Kyle. "And the man I wrote it for is a good friend of yours."

Several people whistled as she gestured for Kyle to join her onstage.

"What are you doing?" he murmured as he reached her, his soft lips curved in that half smile she found so sexy.

"For anyone who couldn't hear, he'd like to know what I'm doing," she said into the mic. "And to tell the truth, I'm not sure. I've never gambled on love the way I'm doing now. You see, I know Kyle doesn't really want a music artist for a wife, especially one who's as involved in her career as I am. But, in spite of that, he asked me to marry him before I left. And I didn't answer. I was too afraid to say yes and didn't want to say no. So . . . I've come back to see if he'll ask me again."

She thought he might ham it up for the audience. She'd put him on the spot, after all, had probably embarrassed him. But he seemed too caught up in the moment to care about who might be watching. He never took his eyes off her.

"I don't mind that you're a performer," he said, speaking into the mic himself. "What's important to you is important to me. So I'll support you in that, and I'll do everything I can to make sure you don't regret coming back to Whiskey Creek — if you'll marry me."

"I'm not too young?" she teased.

"I don't know . . . Nine years is nine years."

Everyone started to boo.

"Sounds like I'm outvoted," he teased back. "No matter what age you are, you're just right for me."

"Then I have your answer. It's yes," she said, and he pulled her into his arms to kiss her.

"Tell me you still have my ring," she murmured amid all the noise and congratulations people were shouting at them. "I *love* that ring."

"I took it back," he said.

She pulled away. "*You did?* I've only been gone a week!"

He chuckled at her disappointment. "It's

at home, waiting for you," he told her and
kissed her again.

# EPILOGUE

*Four weeks later . . .*

"So we're planning *another* wedding?"

Kyle moved his chair to one side to give Baxter room to join them. Since Baxter had arrived at Black Gold Coffee a little late, the tables they'd pushed together were already about as crowded as they could get. But now that he was living in town again, the whole gang could be present for coffee on Friday mornings, and this was one Friday when they were. Even Eve's husband, Lincoln, who rarely showed his face in Whiskey Creek because of his unusual past, had made the drive from Placerville with her and was sitting at the table with his coffee.

"You weren't expecting it after what happened at *my* wedding?" Phoenix asked, laughing at his surprise.

Baxter's eyebrows went up. "Last I heard it was a ways off."

When Lourdes's hand tightened on Kyle's, he felt the same rush of happiness he'd experienced every day since she'd come back to him. She'd been in Nashville quite a bit — more than he'd consider ideal — but she'd spent all her weekends with him, and he'd gone with her on the last trip. He hoped they could make enough compromises; he knew he was going to give it everything he had. "It is," he conceded. "It'll be next winter, on December 1."

"We're just handing out the initial assignments," Lourdes explained.

Baxter looked from him to Lourdes. "Do I get one?"

Lourdes grinned at Kyle. "Olivia will be the planner," he said.

"Of course," Callie responded. "We couldn't have a wedding without Olivia as planner."

"And Brandon will be my best man."

*"Of course,"* Noah chimed in.

"The rest of you? You'll all be in my line —"

Before anyone could say "of course," Lourdes broke in. "Except the women. You'll be in mine."

"*All* of us?" Addy asked in surprise.

"All of you, along with my sisters and mother."

Dylan whistled. "That's going to be a long line."

Lourdes winked at him. "Fortunately, there's no limit."

"Sounds great to me," Riley said. "We'll be there, ready to help with anything you need."

"I'm glad to hear that." Kyle shifted his focus to the man who'd been the latest groom. "Especially from *you*."

Riley's eyes widened. "What? Don't tell me —"

Kyle clapped him on the back. "Yep! *You're* going to be performing the vows, buddy."

Riley shook his head. "I asked for that, didn't I?"

"You'll do great," Lourdes said, giving his arm an affectionate squeeze.

Kyle was delighted by how quickly she'd become one of the gang, how easily she fit in.

"Just don't choke up the way Kyle did," Noah said with a laugh.

"Here we go again," Kyle groaned.

"I still can't believe I missed that part," Lourdes said.

"I'm glad you did," Kyle grumbled. "I wish everyone had missed it."

"I thought it was wonderful," Phoenix

said, but she would say something like that. Phoenix had more empathy in her little finger than most people had in their whole bodies.

Kyle rubbed his chin. "I knew the second it happened I'd never live it down. So I hope you *do* choke up," he told Riley. "I hope you cry like a baby."

Riley motioned for everyone who'd jumped in to quiet down. "You're going to be a tough act to follow," he said. "But I'll do my best. Maybe by then I'll feel more experienced at this whole marriage thing." Leaning over, he dropped a kiss on Phoenix's lips, and Noah threw a balled-up napkin at them.

"Enough! My God, no one's seen wedded bliss until they've seen you two."

Callie nudged him. "I hope you're kidding, because it wasn't too long ago that you were acting the same way about Addy."

"I *still* act that way about Addy," he said, putting his arm around his wife.

"So have you decided what you're going to do with your house in Tennessee?" Eve asked Lourdes.

"Sell it," she said. "Since I'll be living with Kyle here in Whiskey Creek, it makes sense."

"Then where will you stay when you go back to do things like you're doing next week?" Ted asked. "When you meet with those prospective managers and Broken Bow Records to demo 'Refuge'?"

"My mother's talking about returning to Angel's Camp," Lourdes said. "She misses it. Or maybe she'll come here, since it's close. But I can always stay with my sisters. They love Nashville and plan on being there for a while."

Cheyenne broke off a piece of muffin for her one-year-old. "So you're going to be able to juggle it all?"

Lourdes leaned a little closer to Kyle. "I think so," she said.

He took her hand, with his engagement ring on it, and kissed her fingers. "Everything's going to be fine. You guys just be ready for the wedding. We'll handle the rest."